STICKS & STONES

STICKS & STONES

Norm Thabit

iUniverse, Inc.
New York Lincoln Shanghai

Sticks & Stones

iUniverse, Inc.

For information address:
iUniverse, Inc.
2021 Pine Lake Road, Suite 100
Lincoln, NE 68512
www.iuniverse.com

ISBN: 0-595-28931-2

Printed in the United States of America

CHAPTER 1

❀

She loved to watch his face. So much expression. Wonder. Joy. The only time he wasn't wide-eyed was when he was contemplating something new. His mouth would set, the brows would crinkle over faraway eyes. When understanding struck, the wide came back to the eyes, and the smile was always broad. Always. Even if the topic wasn't joyful, or fun, or even pleasant. She had asked him about it, cycles ago. He was still adolescent then, the answer typically exceeded his age.

"How can you be so happy about something so horrid?" she had asked. The topic on this night had been a stew of potion that would do foul things, and smelled it.

He just broadened his smile, and said, "I'll never use this on anyone, and now no one can use it on me." He paused, and added, "Knowledge is sweet."

"But the smell!" She was getting shrill from frustration.

"The flowers on my walk in the morning will just smell sweeter for tonight's memory," he replied, ignoring her distress.

He really talked like that. All the time. Enough to make anyone crazy. This from a teenager.

Well, she wasn't frustrated with him any more. They had been together for seventeen cycles now, and she had given in to his constant barrage of joy, now passing her time watching his face. Etching it into her memory, for he was leaving this Valley. And though it was to be a short journey, she was afraid. She had thrown everything she could think of at him, as had the select few she brought for his instruction. They had taught him all their tricks, except that lately he had been teaching them. But there was one terror left to him, and she couldn't prepare him for this one. People.

He would be eighteen soon, and he had to go to the Mating. He was amused.

"I don't need or want a Mate," he said. "You've told me I don't have to take one, so why go? I'll just stay here. I'm perfectly happy here."

"You're always perfectly happy," she replied, "but you are going just the same. You don't want a Mate now, but if you don't Register now, finding one later will be almost impossible." She didn't think he would find one anyway, but for his sake, she couldn't *not* have him go, in spite of the risk.

"Okay." Just like him not to argue if the reply made sense.

The woman's name was Arima. She was a witch, though she didn't think of herself that way. To her mind, she was a teacher and a Grader. Arima was one hundred and twenty cycles old. Old by human standards, but not for her craft. She was tall for a woman, with a slender build and slender face. She had let her hair go white, not caring for the artificial looks of cosmetic Healing. She wore the traditional tunic of a Master, with a round White badge sewn onto the bodice below her left shoulder. On that badge was the number Ten, with the additional markings for Master and her Grader status.

His name was Steef. At eighteen, he had grown about as much as he would. Half a span shorter than her, he would have been slender as well, if not for the muscles developed from cycles spent climbing through mountains and caves. His dark brown eyes looked darker still against wheat colored brows and hair. He wore simpler garments, which were clean and in good repair, but had no adornments of style or wealth. His badge was also White, and bore a Five with no other markings. He was unsure about the badge.

He was just a few sevendays past his first birthday when his parents had brought him to her tent for his Grading. Parents were required to have all children Graded between their first and second birthdays, and Arima was assigned the Territory of plush mountains and valleys where Steef's family worked their land. She held two Gradings each cycle, this one at the harvest Festival, and another at the planting Festival. For an entire sevenday, the people would come down to the tents set up on the flatland. Vendors and craftsmen would sell their goods to the simple folk, who would party for a while and then disappear with their purchases back into the hills.

The small family had appeared at threequarterday on the last day of Festival. All music had stopped, thankfully. As the ranking White here, she was supposed to sit in on at least a few of her own Guild's musical offerings, but she never did. She enjoyed listening, but hated to play. Most of all, she had lost her taste for Guild activity. The only noise filtering in to her tent now was related to packing and leaving. She hadn't seen any children for two days, since most parents came to her early on in any Festival, even before they visited the other tents and vendors. But then, most parents were excited about having their children Graded. Steef's parents were terrified.

She was in her tent, doing some packing herself, putting away badges and stones, when two of her Buzzbies 'Pop!'d in. They started circling inside the tent frantically, buzzing too fast to keep up.

"Pill, would one of you please tell me?" she asked calmly. Both of them stopped buzzing and 'Pop!'d to a hover directly in front of her face.

"*zzzzzzzzzz*"

"You know I can't understand you there. Now deliver your message properly, or leave. I'm busy." She was still calm. That wouldn't last.

The Buzzbies pivoted to face each other, then one of them landed on her left shoulder and walked quickly to the bottom of her ear.

"*There is a child outside,*" buzzed the small, quick voice.

"That is not real news," Arima replied, "Though it is rather late in the Festival."

"*This is no ordinary child.*"

"I get a lot of 'not ordinary' children," she sighed, "Can you be more specific? No, I'll just go see myself."

"*Get your eyelenses. Now.*"

Well, that was intriguing. She picked up her lenses and went to the tent entrance. Pausing, she put the lenses on before opening.

What she saw were two slender young adults, both of them fair-skinned with blond hair and brown eyes. Both were Green Two's, their respective staffs no more than sticks, really. The Father was holding a blanketed bundle of Power. Arima felt it almost like a blow. The Mother had been crying. A lot. The Father was shaking and looked grim.

"Bright day, children. Please come in," Arima spoke in soft tones for their sake, while shielding her eyes. She was glad to have an excuse to turn away, and almost sprinted to her trunk where she retrieved a stronger set of lenses, the ones she used at Guild meetings. Turning back, she brought a bench for the couple and gestured for them to sit. After another pause, she took up her staff, just in case.

"*We warned you.*"

"No you didn't. Not really. We'll talk later," replied the now flustered witch. "About your sense of humor. Again."

"'Scuse me, Mum," spoke the Father. His voice shook too, "Were you sayin' somethin'?"

"Just to myself," she responded. Bringing her tone back under control, she asked, "Please tell me what you fear? You will come to no harm here."

The slender Mother had been looking for a chance to explode, and it began almost as a screech, which became an intelligible wail, "My babe's go' no Power! He's gonna be a 'Nert, an'...now it'll be 'fishul!"

Arima understood instantly. Parents could often see their child's Power at birth, when it was raw, even if they didn't have the Sight to see Power in general. These people had expected to see their baby's Power, and hadn't. They were sure that the child had no Power, and would be assigned to a future of common labor. Inert people had little hope in this world. She resolved to be comforting.

"There are times when parents can't see their baby's Power," she replied soothingly, "And I definitely feel Power here." This was true. It was giving her a headache. "Would you please unwrap the child?" She had assumed that it was a Cloaking blanket, for she hadn't Seen any Color, and with this much strength, she should have.

The Father pulled the flaps open to reveal a boy child. "He's called Steef. He jus' passed his firs' birthday."

Arima's life changed at that beat. The blanket hadn't been Cloaking anything. It was just a blanket. She couldn't See the child's Power Color because there was...*no Color*. He Pulsed...with waves of...Clear Power. She rocked back, her breath catching in her mouth. Her hands started shaking, and she had to fight the impulse...to run. It was then that the child turned his small head, and caught her eye. A tiny hand reached in her direction, companied with a laugh. A gurgling, happy laugh that washed through Arima like a Healing. Her shakes stopped. Her fears were gone, in spite of reason.

She turned back to the couple and spoke, holding their gaze seriously, "You need have no fear of Steef being inert," she assured them, with a hard swallow, "His Power is strong! You couldn't See it..." she hesitated and drew a breath. She couldn't believe she was saying this, "Because...it has...no Color!"

They had imagined many different answers, but that wasn't any of them. The Father sounded almost angry through his fear, "Don' play with us, Mum! He's gotta have *some* color! Red, Green, Bl...Black even! There's only seven of 'em, and Clear isn' any!" He was getting louder.

The old witch didn't reply right away, giving everyone a pause for calming. *Maybe some tea* she thought, turning to the fire and the pot that rested on it. She poured a cup for each of them, and offered. They hesitated.

"I oath that it will not harm you. It is only tea," again as soothingly as she could muster. That wasn't entirely true, but she had made the tea for herself earlier, with only a bit of relaxant. They could all do with some. And she'd only oathed that it wouldn't harm them. She sat then, hoping that the casual gesture might relax them further.

"Let me explain," she went on. "It is true that there are only seven forms of Power found in people. White, Black, Red, Yellow, Blue, Green, or Brown. Those of us that can channel Power are blessed with only one. But there are legends from the past…that sometimes…a Clear would occur. A person that can channel any of the Colors of Power. Some of us in the White Guild have believed in those legends…some haven't. And in you walk…with a Clear. A strong Clear. We must take him for strength testing." Arima marveled at how calmly she was saying these things. What had the child done to her?

There was no sound in the tent for several beats. This had been a lot for the young couple to take in after an already long, stress-filled day. They looked at the witch. Looked at each other. At the babe. They relaxed a bit. Their baby wasn't Inert after all.

Then the Father had a new thought, and with it, new tension. "Strength testing!?" he cried, "Can' you tell us his strength? In't that what you do!?"

Arima smiled for the first time since they'd arrived, "Yes Sir, that is…*exactly*…what I do. I am a fully certified Master White, qualified to Grade any Color, any strength. But no one in my lifetime has seen a Clear, and no one I know of would know *how* to Grade this child's strength." She took a beat for that to sink in, and went on, "But there is a way."

The Father blinked, eyes getting wider, "Your pardon, Mum. Meant no disrespec'. Bu' we been savin' all we can jus' for this Gradin', an'…an' we can' 'ford…," his air failed him. The mouth was still working, but nothing was coming out. His wife took his arm and they both just shook together.

Arima rose again from her chair. She was a White, after all. Among other things, a Healer. She stepped up to the two of them, put her staff into the dirt floor between them, gathered just of a bit of Power, and pushed it gently through her staff. The stone at the top of her staff Pulsed briefly with a small White light. They didn't see it of course, but the effect was immediate. Straightening themselves on the bench, they began wiping tears from each other's faces.

The Healer knelt before them, then. "This is nothing but good news for you...and your child. He is not Inert. He has great Power. Unique, special Power. And there will be no fee of any kind. Not for anything done here...or later. I *may* invite some other Masters for his training, and I oath you, they will not charge either, I will see to that. There really is only one problem for you to deal with. If word gets out about Steef and his gift, people will come just to see him. His life will be much like this Festival, only all cycle 'round. It's not a proper upbringing." Pausing, she lowered her voice, "We must consider how to keep these matters to ourselves." One finger went to her lips, which she bent into a knowing smile.

Finally, the Mother spoke again, this time her voice was soft with relief and fatigue, "Wha' should we do?"

Still smiling, Arima reached and took the young woman's hand. "We must make a brief journey...to another Valley...some distance away. Can you gather your things quickly...and quietly?" she asked. This last thought had a bit more urgency. The hope of secrecy was building inside her.

The Father spoke again, with a nod, "Yes Mum. All our travel belongin's is packed outside." He took a breath. "Please, Mum. Where would we be goin'?"

The old woman straightened once more, with creaking knees that needed a Healing they would not get now. Walking slowly to her piles of cases, she opened one, and dug into it. From somewhere near its bottom came an old blanket that had once been expensive and fine. Turning to the Mother, Arima said, "If you would, please put this around your Son. It will Cloak his power from prying eyes." *And mine.* To the Father, she answered, "As I said, the boy needs a proper Grading. For that...we must go to the Cats."

Before either of the parents could digest those words, they witnessed the first of what they later just called 'wonders'. Arima turned her head slightly, and spoke into the air, "Pill, would you please inform Masters Lexter and Bone that we will require private transport tomorrow at first light? Thank you."

"They won't like the short notice," came a voice from under her hair.

"No they won't," she replied. "Remind them if they complain...politely mind you...that I have come to their families on short notice myself when a Healing was needed." She quickly added, "And don't tell them where we're going."

"They'll want to know how long the journey will be."

"Fair enough," she sighed, "Tell them they can be back by dark."

There was a 'Pop!' from Arima's left shoulder that sounded louder than it was, the tent was so quiet. Both of her visitors jumped slightly on the bench.

Turning her head to the Buzzbie under her right ear, she said. "Pill, I need you to go to Master Seafer. You will find him at…"

"*We know where he is. Why Seafer? There's a perfectly good Green Master here at the Festival.*"

Arima knew that Master Zellin was near. She didn't trust him, but she didn't want to say that. Besides, she wasn't looking for a Green, especially. She was looking for Seafer, who happened to be a Green. But she didn't like lying, especially to a Buzzbie. "Seafer has something we will need," she replied patiently. "He *is* old and stubborn, though. Older than me. Surely more stubborn. He will not want to listen. Tell him exactly this: 'Arima says she has found what you have been waiting for.' Repeat that until he stops yelling. I want him to meet us at the Valley of the Cats. And tell him to bring his treasure. *All* of it. Insist on it. That will get his attention."

Another 'Pop!' from her right shoulder and the young couple, whose mouths were now hanging open, jumped again. Followed by a third 'Pop!' from her left shoulder as another Buzzbie arrived. She was about to speak to it when she noticed their faces, and caught the laugh that wanted to come.

"They are Buzzbies," she smiled brightly. "Pill, would you show yourself please?"

The left-side Buzzbie crawled out from under her hair and moved onto her shoulder, just as a fourth 'Pop!' announced the arrival of a new right-side Buzzbie.

"Give them a closer look," she said. "Their child is going to give you something to talk about for tens of cycles."

Unfolding its wings, the Buzzbie lifted off her shoulder, buzzing across the space between them. Hovering just before the bewildered couple, it stopped at their eyelevel. They saw what looked like an oversized bee, perhaps double their baby's fist. To them, it *was* a bee…just bigger.

Arima had seen that look before, and went into what the Buzzbies called her 'teacher' mood. "Don't ever call them bees. It really makes them mad. They are every bit as intelligent as we are."

"*Smarter,*" came a voice from her right.

She frowned slightly. "Hush Pill. Anyway, they ride under my hair on both sides. They have such small voices that they have to speak directly into my ears for me to understand. About the only thing they're good for besides wise-cracks, is carrying messages."

The Mother found her voice again, and asked, "Wha' was the poppin' we heard?"

"Well, they don't *just* fly. They really don't even *like* to fly. But somehow they can 'Pop!' themselves instantly to anywhere they want to go. They refuse to explain to anyone how they do it. I personally think they don't know themselves…"

"*Ha!*"

"…You get used to the popping after a while."

"They mus' be really fas' if they're back already."

This time she did laugh. Just a light chuckle. "Oh no! These two are not the ones that just left! Every time one leaves, another takes its place."

The young man had to get into the conversation, "Please Mum, bu' you called 'em all by the same name?"

"I call them Pill", she gave with a nod, "It's their family name. Only the Creator himself could ever tell them apart."

The hovering Buzzbie must have tired of the conversation. It suddenly Pop!'ed back under her hair, delighting her guests.

"Well, you mus' be Powerful for true," breathed the Mother, "To command such magical beasties."

Arima smiled again, softly. "Not really. They hang on to most everyone of Master strength. Truth is, they're just plain nosey. I couldn't get rid of them if I tried. A Black could…maybe…if any Black could ever hit one."

"*As if anyone would try.*"

"Pill," continued Arima, "Go to the LaborMaster. Tell him I will need three warm bodies to get my things to the Landing Field before dawn." And again to the couple, "Have you had lastmeal? I expect not, though you won't admit it. Well, I have some tubers and a bit of meat. Let's prepare it, shall we?" This last to the young woman. Arima's calm was wearing off, and nerves were making her chatty. "You'll stay here tonight, of course. Tell me your names, and we'll get acquainted."

There was still no sun when Arima arrived at the Landing Field. Her choice to go early had been wiser than she had given thought to, for few people were about. A busier time, and her entourage might have caught unwanted attention. Three laborers with their pack beasts laden with her cases, and two young adults clinging to a baby and their pitiful few bundles. Awaiting them at one corner of the field were two sleepy, grumpy Masters in their boat.

The boat was the second 'wonder' for the young couple. From the ground, it looked like a huge bowl, with a pole sticking straight up above it at one edge. The bottom of the bowl/boat was sitting in a deep hole in the ground. They could make out many such boats, in holes all over the large field. The party climbed a ramp to an edge halfway around from the pole, and stepped in. The bowl/boat was five staffs across. Its top-edge was protruding two staffs above ground, with another staff's measure of depth below ground. There was a seating bench below the rim, all around the boat, interrupted only by a passway through to the bottom. The laborers carried Arima's trunks past two wide eyed parents through this passage and deposited them at the bottom of the boat.

"'Rima!" cried the shorter of the two Masters, and he didn't sound happy, "Why in the name of the Creator are we up so early, and where are we going, and why all the mystery?" His tunic had a Brown patch that said Ten.

Arima winced at his volume, "Bone, if you know how early it is, then you should know not to shout and wake people," she whispered fiercely. "And we'll discuss our trip in a few beats." This last was given with a small glance at the laborers, who were waiting to be paid. Tending to that, she patted them on their way and waited until they were well out of earshot.

"Masters Lexter and Bone, let me introduce to you Stem, and his Mate, Maleef. Children, Master Lexter here," she pointed to the tall slender one, who wore a Blue Ten, "Is our Steerman. Master Bone is our Lifter." She had left Steef out of the conversation. "Masters, these young people and I will be traveling to the Valley of the Cats. We would like to leave as soon as possible, please." Arima gave her sweetest voice, hoping she was appearing calmer than she felt. She made her way to a bench in the back of the boat, and sat down. Stem and Maleef followed slowly, for they were looking at everything around them.

"They must not get out of their valley much."

"This is probably their first time," replied Arima, "And before we're done, they'll never want to leave home again."

"Who's 'we'?"

"You'll see."

As they sat down next to her, she could see they were full of questions. She loved questions, so she got them started. "What do you want to ask first?" she asked cheerfully.

"Well, Mum," replied Stem, "Now tha' you mention it, I always though' Browns was miners an' worked in dirt. So wha' is a Lifter?"

What a wonderful question! It would take some time, and distract them while they got under way. She noticed that Lexter had unfurled his sail and

Bone had already clamped his staff into its saddle. The Brown now had both hands around its shaft, and they would be Lifting any beat. Arima deliberately locked the young couple's eyes before she spoke.

"These two Masters are a perfect partnership," she began. "Master Bone is a full Brown. And you're right, Stem. Some Browns are Miners. But a Master Brown can project their Power onto anything that comes from the ground. Dirt, stone, or metals. This boat is made of a combination of those things. Bone here can make it lighter and lighter until it rises up off the ground." She felt the boat Lift slightly to prove her point, so she leaned in a bit to hold their attention. "Now here's the tricky part. Bone can Lift it, but he can't make it go anywhere. Without a Steerman, we'd just go straight up, and straight down. So he partnered up with Master Lexter there. Full Blue. He can control the weather…"

"Yes Mum," Maleef interrupted, "We ha' to hire a Blue sometimes to bring us rain for our crops," she said.

She's getting into it. Good. "That's right, Maleef," Arima nodded, "What strength was this Blue?" Arima knew that they were already above the trees, but she couldn't allow her eyes to wander.

"Her number, you mean, Mum? Why, she wore a Seven."

"Well, Master Lexter over there is a Ten. All Masters have to be Tens. And even then, they study for cycles and cycles before they get a Masters rating. Lexter does more than bring rain." Arima was gesturing now, but carefully. She didn't want a sweep of her hand to make them look out. "He can call the wind. Call it and Steer it. Once Bone gets us high enough, Lexter's wind will Steer us to our destination." *Oops,* that was the wrong thing to say.

Stem alerted. "Wha' do you mean 'high enough'?" he asked. But Maleef was already looking up and out. Arima braced herself for Maleef, for she was holding the baby. What they saw was the top of a mountain passing under the boat. The tents of the festival were specks and getting smaller.

They took it pretty well. Stem just went pale and silent. Maleef squeaked once, and fainted. Arima caught her, careful not to actually touch the baby, and lowered her to the bench. Putting her hand on the young woman's forehead, she probed slightly and found nothing of concern. Just a faint. She would wake soon. Arima let her rest. Turning to Stem, she found him taking breath in large gulps, and actually getting some color back in his lips. She rose and made her way to the front of the boat.

"'Rima, why would you be goin' to the Cats?" inquired Bone. Lexter didn't even turn around. He rarely spoke at all. She liked that about him. Bone hadn't stopped, though, "You haven't been there in cycles. Somethin' special about these two?" He jerked a thumb towards the back of the boat.

"No," her face giving no emotion, "There's nothing special about them." Well, it was true. It was the baby that was special. "But the Festival is almost over, and it has been a while since I checked my Grading." This was her first outright lie, and she was glad it was Bone. A good Red would have seen right through her.

"Well them Cats might not be too glad to see you any more," he went on, "Hope they fed last night."

Me too she thought. What she said was, "How long, Lexter?"

He turned slightly to give her a thin smile. Turning back to his mast, his voice was gentle with contentment, "Just before quarterday, Arima. I'm enjoying a bit of natural tail wind."

Enjoying is the right word for it. The man just loved to fly his boat, and the masts of these things were surely the largest staffs anyone could have without being showy. Expensive, too. That would explain why most of them had relatively small stones in them. She looked to the top, but she could never see the stone that had to be there. *Oh well.* "Thank you Lexter. And you, Bone. While we're here, do either of you need any attention?"

"Not while I'm Steering, Arima," answered Lexter, without turning this time. "Perhaps when we land."

But she could count on Bone. "Well, my creaky-bone's come back in my hands an' knees, 'Rima. An' Lexter don't need me for a while." He grinned. She'd never met a Brown that didn't have joint problems. Too much of their youth spent playing in rocks.

"Go lay down, Bone," she smiled, "I'll be right there." As he stepped away, she got closer to Lexter, and spoke quietly, "Is it back, my friend?"

Still watching his Steering, Lexter nodded slightly.

"We'll tend to it as soon as we're down. You should really come see me more often." He just smiled again. "Meantime, keep us in the light, would you? Wouldn't want to fuse one of Bone's knees."

That did it. The smile cracked into a chuckle, "I don't think he'd notice the difference, Arima. But I'll give you your light."

She patted his shoulder and turned to Bone. He was also a Master in receiving Healings, and already lying on the bench, his thick frame lying as straight as he could get it. Big silly grin, he enjoyed his Healings as much as Lexter enjoyed flying. She stepped over and knelt at his legs. Putting her hand on each of his knees in turn, she could feel some swelling and fluid in each. She laid the stone of her staff directly on the first knee, and then paused. She concentrated on the sunlight hitting her back, gathering the heat, storing the heat, letting the Power fill her until…she pushed…and the stone Pulsed White. The knee relaxed. The fluid drained. The swelling was gone. She repeated the process for the other knee.

"Scoot down here Bone," she commanded, "And we'll do your hands." He was forty cycles younger. He could do the scooting. There was no one here to help *her* knees. Soon he could make fists with both hands again. "Now turn over, I want to check your back." Sure enough, it was knotted up. "Bone, you really should try to lose some weight," she scolded as she Pulsed. "It would help your back. Now help me up."

The rest of the journey passed quietly. Stem and Maleef huddled together, with a near death-grip on the baby. Soon enough, Arima began to recognize the familiar shape of ridges that was the northern edge of the Valley. In the far distance rose the peak of high mountains that shielded the southern side. She had been here often in her youth, though not much any more. She thought back, and with a shock realized *it's been eleven cycles!* She wondered if she would know any of the Cats at all. *That could be really sticky.*

As the boat glided over the first ridge, she saw two of the great beasts lift themselves off of rocks and turn down a path into the Valley. She took it as a hopeful sign that they still watched for human visitors. She could tell from the condition of the Valley that it was still being occasionally tended. The Valley itself was just under sixty leagues long, and twelve leagues at its widest point. Actually almost a longish bowl that ran mostly north and south. A small river meandered generally through the center in a winding path. While the bottom of the Valley was mostly flat, the sides leading up to the ridges were steep. That shape was why the Cats had relocated here to begin with. They could get in and out, but the herds of feed beasts that roamed the flatland were trapped. She saw a small group of cattle off to the east, and some sheep down in the center of the flatland, near the Landing Field. The Field itself was huge, having once been used constantly. Nearly a hundred landing bowls still dug into the plain, but it was apparent from the grass in them that they didn't get used now. Only a couple of them looked as if they'd been used at all, and it was toward one of these that the boat steered, as it began descending.

Arima gave her head a bit of a shake to clear out some memories, and spoke quietly, "Pill, please go see where the ClanCat is, so I'll know how much time we have." Pop!

"Pill, please go see what Master Seafer's progress is. I really want him here for the Grading." *So he'll believe me.* Pop!

Two more Buzzbies Pop!'ed in. Lexter brought the boat to a stop directly over a landing bowl, and Bone set it down gently. They had arrived at the Valley of the Cats.

"Bone, now that you're feeling better," Arima spoke with more energy and confidence than she felt, "Why don't you and Stem see to the trunks while I have a word with Lexter."

Pop! "*The ClanCat is an eighthday southwest of here. Already heading this way.*" Pop! They didn't like to crowd each other. Usually two Buzzbies at a time.

She and Lexter climbed over the edge of the boat and stepped lightly onto the ground. "They shouldn't have quit digging the bowls this deep, Lexter," Arima mused. "I've never liked those wooden ramps."

Lexter's laugh sounded almost like a cough. Probably out of practice. "Guess it gives the carpenters something to do, 'Rima."

They walked far enough away to be out of earshot, then Arima gestured for Lexter to sit. She knelt beside him and set the point of her staff in the dirt between his knees, where it sank down on its own deep enough to stand upright. Then she put her hands on either side of his head and closed her eyes. Slowly, she moved her hands down to his shoulders. "Lift your arms." Her hands went into his armpits and continued their journey down his sides to the waist. If she was going a little faster than usual, it was only because she already knew what she would find.

"Well, it's been worse," she spoke almost to herself. Lexter had organ-moss. Nasty stuff, it would grow on the linings of a person's organs and eat into them, disrupting their function. Left to itself, it was always fatal. Most Power people suffered with it. Some a lot. Some a little. Browns seldom had much, while every Blue she'd ever met was full of it. She had a theory that it had something to do with the Sun, since Blues worked in sunlight constantly, while Browns sometimes didn't see it for a cycle. She didn't share her theory with anyone. No one had listened to her for twenty cycles, anyway.

"All right, my friend," she said briskly, "You know how this works." She rose and grasped her staff, while Lexter stretched out. Hers was the only profession where someone else would touch one's staff while it was working. She tuned it for his body rhythm, and then tuned it for the Power she was getting from the ground. "I'll be back." She left him there, holding her staff between his knees, and headed back towards the boat.

Pop! *"Seafer is eleven leagues away. They are making good progress. The Steerman is young and apparently likes a lot of wind."* Pop!

Bone came huffing up to met her halfway. "Moss again, 'Rima?" he asked softly. She didn't know he *could* speak softly.

"Yes, Bone, but not as bad as before. We seem to be keeping up with it."

"Well!" he boomed. That was the Bone she knew. "If you're determined to stay, we'll be goin'!" He nodded up the Valley. Turning, she could see a few Cats in the distance, loping their way.

"We are staying, Bone. We'll give Lexter a few hundred beats, then you can go. "We'll be needing you back, though, when the Festival traffic is over. We will probably be ready for transport in three or four days. Can you come get us then?"

"Sure 'Rima." He grinned and winked, "That is, if we can find you."

❈   ❈   ❈

Lexter and Bone were still in sight, when a second boat appeared over the ridgeline. She could just make out the people in each boat waving at each other. *Probably wondering why these crazy old Masters were acting REALLY crazy.*

The three of them were sitting on her trunks. It was hard not to look. More of the big Cats were appearing at various spots from the trees around the Valley. Finally, Stem couldn't take it any more.

"Please, Mum," he was trying to keep his voice strong, but it broke into squeaks here and there, "Wha' *exac'ly* are we doin' here?"

Arima was too occupied with the approaching Cats to realize how tired she was. She'd had a full Festival, the shock of her life yesterday, a short night, and a stressful journey. She watched as the first Cats arrived and stopped, starting to form a circle around them. They left a wide enough area for the approaching boat to land, as it was about to. Later, it would occur to her to ask pardon of the poor young people.

"We are going to witness one of the true marvels of our world," she mused. "Or we're going to be Cat food."

CHAPTER 2

❀

The boat carrying Seafer had an interesting view as it landed. They saw Cats coming from everywhere, and the circle that was forming. Inside that circle was a landing spot, a pile of trunks, one old woman sitting and watching the Cats, and two young adults lying in the grass, unmoving. On closer inspection, they would have seen something stirring on top of the woman, but they were giving close attention to landing the boat.

As the Masters hurriedly unloaded his small collection of trunks and added it to the pile with Arima's, Seafer came hobbling up. Seafer was a good ten cycles older than Arima, and looked it. He had once been average height, but was bent now with a bad back that he refused to get Healed. He had dark skin, and hair that had once been black and curly, was now white and wispy. He used his tall staff as much for a walking stick as a tool now. And his temper was not improved with age.

"'Rima," he gruffed, "Was it really necessary to send so *many* Buzzbies? Blamed aggravating having them Pop!'ing all over the orchard! My bees won't be coming back for a sevenday! And it's…"

"Seafer," she had to stop him or he'd go all day, "I only sent one."

"Well, I got hundreds, maybe a thousand." His face was as red as it ever got. Probably been that way all morning.

"Pill," she queried, "What is he talking about?"

"It is a most unusual child."

She didn't like it when their answers made *no* sense, but she knew better than to waste beats arguing with a Buzzbie.

"Well, old friend," coming back to the Green Master, "We are here for a unique Grading. This could be the chance you've hoped for with your little project." She hoped it might settle him some to put his mind on something new. Nope.

"Like I haven't seen Gradings before! Why I..." He was interrupted by a rising growl, causing Arima to hold up her hand. They both turned.

While Seafer had been venting, more Cats had arrived and the boat had left. They were now completely surrounded by Cats. Dozens of them had completed the circle and were standing ribcage to ribcage. Judging by the rising mood, the ClanCat was close, so she took her staff to rouse Stem and Maleef. They needed to witness this. The Pulse she gave them had enough Power to ensure that they didn't pass out again. It was almost painful to be near the baby, but she checked him anyway. He was smiling, sitting there on Maleef's belly, pointing at the Cats and waving his arms.

As she straightened, the circle of Cats opened at one end, and a large male padded through. They all started growling again, even louder, but the circle closed back and otherwise, they didn't move much. She walked toward the ClanCat, recognizing his splash at once. He was one of the older cubs of the last ClanCat she'd known. *Good, maybe he'll remember me.*

They both stopped when they reached a space apart of about three staffs. All growling stopped and the quiet sounded strange with its suddenness. Arima slowly clasped her staff in both hands, held it in front of herself and bowed. "Your majesty, it is good to see you again. I hope your Father Rested well." She paused for his reply. Looking up into his eyes, she knew if he said anything at all, they would be all right. His other option was a midday meal. He watched her unblinking for fifty or so beats, then issued a low growl, almost a moan.

This set off a reaction in the circle, not all of it sounding like approval. The ClanCat turned and spat an angry growl back at them that had immediate effect.

And they still have discipline. Good again.

She spoke again, "Majesty, we come to honor you and your Clan. We come to beg for a Grading." She stopped there, knowing that would get a new reaction from the circle. It did. *They are great beasts, but they sure are stuffy!*

"Majesty!" she shouted, "Will you speak with me?" He had to know she would ask. Probably been chewing on it the entire time he journeyed here. But he made her wait anyway, she assumed for appearance' sake. She hoped. Finally, his answer. The ClanCat turned his head, and tilted it up slightly, exposing his neck to her. He made no other move. Relief flooded through her, and she realized with a start that she had feared his rejection more than being a meal. Slowly, she stepped to him.

He had grown, of course, since last they met. Her eyes now came only to his chin. He was almost two staffs long. *I'll bet he weighs as much as twelve grown men.* Dark orange in color, as they all were, with his own distinctive white splash on the front left shoulder. His horns were more than triple the length she remembered. A full three spans, at least, they started just inside his ears pointing up, and slightly forward. Perfectly straight, they had the shape of a piece of bread dough that was rolled thick, then twisted into a spiral until it came to a point.

She loved these Cats. Everything about them. Well, maybe not their appetites.

When she was close enough, Arima took care to hold her staff away from him with one hand, while reaching up with her other, placing it on his neck.

"It has been long, Healer. Why have you stayed away?"

"Majesty," she said, "There are many more people now than when I was here last. But not many more new Healers. My beats are not my own. I regret the days missed here." That was true.

"So many more two-legs, and still they do not need us, do they? I remember when they needed us more."

"They need you now, oh King," she replied sincerely, "They just no longer know it. They have grown stupid. I hope you also remember that I fought to keep your place with my people."

"I do remember. My sire remembered your courage often. That is why we welcomed you. What is the Grading you speak of? Do you not now do that yourselves?"

"Yes we do, Majesty, but this child is not like other children. He is strong in the Power, and his Color is beyond my Sight. Will the Clan Grade him for us?"

Beat...Beat...Beat.

"It would be good for the young males to learn the Grading. It will be done."

"Not too young, Majesty," Arima replied quickly, "This child is very strong. I wouldn't want any of your Clan to die in the attempt."

"We shall see. We are still a strong Clan." She felt his mirth in the reply.

No point in waiting she thought. Without releasing her touch on the Clan-Cat, Arima called over her shoulder to Maleef, "Bring Steef out here, child." Of course, Maleef's legs weren't working well just then, so after a pause, she added, "Seafer, would you help Maleef with the baby, please?"

"Don't know what all the fuss is about," he grumbled, "Come now, child...it's just a Grading." With one hand on his staff, he took her elbow with the other and they began hobbling out together. The slow pace didn't seem to bother Maleef, and Stem, who was probably a brave enough Mate on normal occasions, was content to remain right where he was.

While this was happening, the ClanCat had called to the Clan. To everyone else, it sounded like more growling, which didn't improve anyone's moods, but Arima was still in contact, *"After so long a wait, once more we are needed! Meevverr, Timmerr, Aannerr. Step out and prepare to offer your horns."*

At once, three males emerged from the circle, which closed in behind them again, so that the remaining Cats were still touching. The young males approached. If size alone were a gauge, then they were of different ages, for the smallest was no larger than Maleef, while the largest was just a hair above Arima's head. They padded to the center of the circle and stopped…right in front of a terribly shaking Maleef. Then they knelt…and finally stretched out full length on the ground, keeping a space apart, careful not to touch each other. They waited. Seafer started to walk Maleef to the smallest of the three.

"Wait!" called out Arima. "Your Majesty, pardon me for saying so, but this one…" she tilted her head towards the smallest male, "…would be at risk from this child! This is our first Grading in so long. Let us not Rest so fine a youngster from this."

The ClanCat responded instantly, *"Meevverr, there is no shame in being young. Take your place."* The young Cat was less than eager to listen. He got up slowly and stared directly at Steef for a beat, causing Maleef's shakes to increase. Pawing the ground once…twice…he returned to the circle.

Seafer edged Maleef right up to the paws of the second Cat. "Now child," he said softly, "Put the babe on the ground at its paws." Maleef wasn't too sure about this, but Seafer repeated himself and actually started to bend over with her. "That's right…now sit him up…facing the Cat…good…now, let's us just back away slowly, shall we?"

This was actually Arima's first good look at the boy, since she'd been avoiding him as much as possible. Here with the Cats, however, the child couldn't possibly do her any damage, so she looked closely. She saw a smallish child with a good bone structure. Golden hair, pale skin. And he was smiling! Laughing even, while looking up at what must be to him a mountain of Cat. Back in the days when this ritual was common, many babies had to be coaxed through their fear. Few actually enjoyed it.

The Cat had waited until the adults were a few steps away. He swayed his head a bit, to get the child's attention, then he bent at the neck to bring his head down. Down came the horns, as well. They were nowhere near the size of the ClanCat's, which of course was the point. But they were big enough to get

Steef's attention. Two pretty toys to play with. As children will do, he reached up with both hands and grabbed the horns.

The Cat's body, which was already on the ground, just slumped. His head rolled to one side, which pulled the horns out of Steef's hands. Steef thought this was part of the game and started clapping.

"Well, Healer, I think you just spared Meevverr's life. His pride will survive the blow. This is indeed a Powerful child. Aannerr, step out and take your place. Putting you to sleep will serve no purpose."

The remaining Cat rose with less reluctance and went back to the circle.

"Letterr," rumbled the ClanCat. A male came forward that was measurably larger than the one that had just left. He laid himself near the now-sleeping Timmerr. At Seafer's instruction, a slightly less terrified Maleef picked up Steef and set him in front of the newcomer. This suited Steef, who liked this game. In only a few beats, there were two sleeping Cats.

It wasn't long before there were five sleeping Cats, the last one being enormous.

The ClanCat and Arima were still standing together, both of them slightly in shock.

"Healer," said the ClanCat, and she could feel the sigh in him, *"You remember more Gradings than I. Can you recall any that reached to the ClanCat himself?"*

Arima answered with a slightly shaking voice, "No, my King." Then she added, "Majesty, could I ask that you tell your Clan not to eat us before you wake? Your pardon, but it may come up."

"I will, but there is no need. A ClanCat cannot be put down. And my Clan would not harm a child such as this, in any event." He turned toward Steef, breaking their contact, and growling his instructions as he strode the few steps.

Arima was sitting on one of her trunks, giving instructions to a Buzzbie, "I don't care how important they think it is, you must *not* let this be known outside of the Pill hive! And no Masters that I don't approve in advance. They'll come and take this child." *Or worse.*

But this was no ordinary Buzzbie. It was one of the twenty or thirty Boss males that ruled the hive, and they liked explanations. Thorough explanations. *"We don't much like Hive-wide rules coming from a human, Arima. Even you. The other Masters should know."*

"Pill," she replied slowly. She was trying to keep her temper. "There's been trouble brewing for cycles, and no one knows that better than a Buzzbie. You must also know there are Masters who serve themselves more than serving others. They would turn this child into a weapon to be used for those purposes. Let's see if we can prevent that, shall we?"

"All right, Arima. Speaking for the Hive, we agree to your silence. For now. But I have one question for you that you may have trouble answering. What kind of weapon will YOU make of him?" And Pop! he was gone.

That's a good question. She didn't have an answer.

※   ※   ※

Stem had brought the trunks over to where the six Cats were still sleeping, and erected Arima's own two small tents over them as much as they would cover. She had kept Steef in the middle of the pile of trunks as much as possible. It certainly helped her headaches. There were Cats pacing around the area at all times, though she knew they were taking turns. At around dusk, the ClanCat finally opened his eyes, and slowly lifted his head. She had been stroking his fur, careful to avoid the horns, and so heard his first words.

"How long?" he asked.

She tactfully turned her head and began studying Steef closely. "Just over a day," she said gently. This had to be touchy for him.

He didn't speak for a long while. His next words were that of a true ClanCat.

"This is serious," he said without a hint of concern for his own embarrassment, *"Timmerr is at grave risk."*

Privately, she thought Letterr might be also. The other three should rouse soon enough. If the Cats slept too long, they would starve to death in their sleep. This was new for her, too. She had seen HornCats put to sleep before, but never Cats so large, and the smaller they were, the longer they slept. She really didn't know when, or even *if*, the smaller two would wake.

"Your Majesty," she said, turning to look at him again, "Could some of your nursing females possibly try feeding them? They might take the milk in their sleep." It was a slim chance, but she could think of nothing else. She had sent an urgent call for a Yellow to come help, but he might not get here soon. And besides, who ever heard of Healing a HornCat, anyway? She didn't know if it was possible.

"That might work. We will try." He rose slowly, getting his legs. *"And when we are alone, I am still Rivverr. We were friends once."*

He had surprised her. She felt sudden tears filling her eyes. At last she said, almost in a whisper, "Thank you for pardoning me."

"*There is nothing to pardon. You were one. They were many. There is no dishonor in losing a battle fought well. But you should not stay away so long again. The young cubs should learn of your kind by meetings, and not stories from old Cats...We must not forget.*"

"Rivverr," she smiled slightly, and looked as if she would blush at the name, "If I have any say in the matter, I won't be leaving for a very long time. But that can wait. First, you must see to Timmerr and Letterr. Later, we will talk again." With that, the ClanCat left.

❧   ❧   ❧

She had been forming a plan while He slept, the inaction after the Grading giving her time to think. When Stem and Maleef had brought the child into her tent, she had instinctively come running to the Cats, where she had always felt the most secure her whole life, until things changed. She now also had time to explain things to the young parents, and they needed to understand, at least in part. She refused to imagine what would happen if any of the Guilds learned about this child, as they surely would if the family left this Valley. But how could they stay?

She didn't say any of this to them at first. She didn't realize it completely herself, at first. Fortunately, there were other conversations to have anyway. Once they had gotten used to the idea that they weren't to be eaten, Stem and Maleef wanted to know why six sleeping Cats were so important. It was a sign of the changes to her world that she even had to explain.

"You are both Green Two's, so you understand about what the Power is..." she had given this as a statement, but it was really a question. Grade Two's of anything rarely got any training at all.

Stem answered for both of them, "Well, Mum, no' really. All we really know is tha' when we plant things, being Greens, why those things jus' seem to grow better than the 'Nerts' stuff does." He added, "And our sticks help o' course. We use em a special lot at plantin'. An' sometimes when Maleef pushes really hard, she can for hones' true see some Green sparks come outta hers. I'm 'fraid I can't make tha' claim myself," he admitted honestly.

Maleef jumped in, perhaps covering her Mate's awkward beats, "Tha's why we Mated up in the firs' place, Mum. We being so weak in the Power, we jus' figured two Greens together might make a life better'n two Greens apart. An' then little Steef came along, an' we couldn't see his Color, an' we got scared. We figured we was jus' so weak, we killed his chance. But he's jus' such a sweet baby, an' a joy to have with us. In fac', we get a lotta visitors 'cause…"

Arima interrupted her, to get back to the point. "Why don't the two of you take your staffs and let me See your Power?" she asked. "It might help me understand better where Steef has gotten his gift." She doubted it, but it sounded good.

They excitedly held their staffs up in front of themselves with both hands, and pushed. Indeed, there was a distinct Green glow at the tip of Maleef's staff. Stem's staff showed nothing, however. Arima did See a bit of Green where his hands met the staff, so she asked, "Stem, could I see your staff for a beat? I'll be very careful with it."

He was shocked, "Yes Mum! O' course! I'm honored, Mum. You bein' a Master an' all, an' takin' a interes' in us." He thrust his arm out, offering his staff.

Arima held the small stick in one hand. It really was little more than a stick. No carving at all, just polished smooth. She smiled at the sliver of greenstone at the tip. Most of the untrained thought that they should buy gems of their own Power Color, as if it would help. The stone was not shaped or cut at all. Just a chip, really.

Slowly…cautiously…she pushed a tiny…tiny…bit of Power into it. If she burned up this poor man's staff, they would both be mortified. She needn't have worried. The wood was just dead. Completely inert. And someone had probably sold it to Stem for more than he could afford. Just another failure of the Green Guild to watch over thieves masquerading as craftsmen.

"Stem," she handed it back to him with a sigh, "May I suggest that you get another staff before your next planting? I don't think this one is serving you well." She thought about if for a beat, and added, "In fact, I'll go with you to the carvers, and we'll see that you get a proper one."

Stem got completely flustered at her offer. For the second time since they'd met, his lips moved, but nothing came out.

She continued, "Now children, I'm going to take a beat to explain this Grading. It's important that you understand, for Steef's sake. Please just be patient with me."

"Tha's all right, Mum," replied Maleef cheerily. "We both like learnin' new things."

Arima would remember those words, over and over, for the next seventeen cycles. She began, "As you know, there are really two different kinds of people in our world…those with Power, and those with no Power. We sometimes call them Inerts, which isn't a particularly kind thing to say. We are either born with it, or not. What you may not know, is that *we*…really don't have any Power at all. Stem, have you ever needed to water your crops, and dug a ditch in the ground to carry water from a stream to your field?"

He nodded, completely wrapped up in her words.

"Well, we are like that ditch. The ditch doesn't make the water, it just carries it and delivers it. Our Power comes from the world around us. It's everywhere. If you jump up in the air, there is a Power that pulls you back down. Our Sun beats down on us with Power every bright day. There are other sources of Power as well. Some of us are born to catch that Power, and deliver it up again. But as it passes through us, it changes. When it comes out again, it has a Color that some of us can actually See. And each of the Colors does different things. There are seven, as you know, and we all only get one. At least until Steef came along."

"Your pardon, Mum," whispered Maleef, looking around, "Bu' where do these Cats figure into this?"

Arima smiled. "Patience, child. We'll get there. Now Stem, that watering ditch, if you dig it deep and wide, what's going to happen?"

"Well, Mum, I 'spect I'll get a lot o' water."

"That's right. And if you dig it shallow and small?"

"Not enough water t'do any good, Mum."

"Right again. Now, when it comes to Power, some of us are like that big ditch, and some aren't. There are actually several different sizes of ditches, but over time, we've learned that it's best to divide them into ten ratings, with One being the shallowest ditch we can measure, and Ten being a ditch that almost matches the stream itself."

Arima watched as the concept soaked in. Their eyes got a little wider, and both of them glanced at the badge on her tunic that clearly said 'Ten'. *Good, maybe they can get how serious this is.* Then they both looked at each other, and the 'Two's that they wore. A slight slumping occurred then, as they glimmerred more clearly what their place was. *I had hoped to avoid that* Arima thought with an inward sigh.

She went on. "Now the Grading. There are a few of us…always Whites…who have the Sight…to view other people's Power. We can See how brightly it glows, and what Color it is. Not all White's have this Sight, but the ones that do…are trained as Graders. We have learned that it's best to Grade people when they are young, as their Power is still raw. As people get older, they can learn to cover it…we call it Cloaking…and they can't be Graded at all, if they don't want to."

"But, for hundreds of cycles, we used to Grade a different way. We used a method that couldn't be Cloaked. One where mistakes couldn't be made by the Graders." *Or sold.*

"We used the Cats."

"HornCats are not like any other beast in our world. The Power that we people have…they absorb. Like a dry soak-rag on a spill, they just soak it up. And the bigger the Cat, the more Power they can take. Especially through the horns. Back when we always Graded here, a Grader like myself would often arrive with ten, fifteen, maybe twenty children. Our only task back then was to help decide how large or small of a Cat to start with. If the Cat goes to sleep, the child's Power has overwhelmed it, and we need a bigger Cat. If the child goes to sleep, he or she has been drained. The Grader will wake the child, and let it recharge while they Grade someone else."

"After a while, sometimes several days, by changing the sizes of the Cats, we can determine *exactly* the Power level of a child."

There was silence around the little camp for several beats while they took this in.

"Your pardon again, Mum," whispered Maleef, still concerned about the Cats. "Does it hurt the beasties?"

"No," Arima chuckled. "If there is one thing any Cat loves, it's a good sleep."

But Stem hadn't spoken. He looked around at the sleeping Cats. *Good, he's getting it.*

Finally, it came out. "Master Arima…".

Strange he should address me that way now.

He went on, "Ma…Ma…Master Arima. They're *all* sleeping. All them Cats. Steef in't sleeping, b…b…but *all* the Cats *are*. Shouldn't Steef be sleeping? Do we need some bigger Cats?"

Arima put her hands on her knees and pushed herself up. She gestured for them to follow, and walked over to the smallest Cat, where she knelt and stroked his side. "Now this fine young fellow is called Timmerr," she said lovingly. "He would be a match for any Five and possibly even a weak Six. It is actually rare to start children on a Cat so large, but even so, I was concerned for Timmerr. As I told you, Steef's Power is strong."

She stepped to the next Cat. "This is Letterr. He could easily handle an Eight. A Nine would probably be close to a tie." She stood and walked to the center of the row of Cats. Pointing to the third Cat, she let out a breath, and shakily said, "Now I've been Grading for over seventy cycles. Over two thousand children in all. Some cycles, we wouldn't have a Ten at all…" her voice got a bit faint, and her eyes were off watching memories. After a few beats of silence, she came back, "Certainly not Master class, anyway. I've personally Graded one hundred and twenty-six Tens. Still have a record of all their names. Fifty-nine went on to make Master."

Still holding a finger pointing to the third Cat, she turned to them and said, "*None* of them would have gotten past *him*."

Seafer had come up and joined them while she was speaking. He said nothing, waiting for Arima to complete her Grading by informing the parents of the results. The four of them stood for a while looking from one Cat to another. Stem and Maleef kept drifting their gaze toward the three larger Cats that Arima hadn't mentioned. Finally, they were all looking at the huge Clan-Cat resting peacefully at the end of the row, and Stem asked The Question, "So jus' how much Power does our boy have?"

Arima had clasped her hands to her chin, contemplating what to tell them. There was no good answer. "I…just…don't…know," she breathed. To them she said, "What we *do* know is that Steef has great Power, certainly higher than any Master now living. His future is bright. In fact, with the proper training, there is actually no office, or profession, or craft he couldn't Master." *But we're out of big Cats.*

Seafer respectfully waited a few beats for the parents to respond. When they said nothing, he jumped in with his own question, "Arima, what Color is the child?" he asked excitedly. He had visions of training the boy if he was a Green.

"Why…regrets, Seafer," she replied. "It slipped my mind in the all the excitement. The child has *no* Color. He's as Clear as he is strong."

"'Rima, this is no occasion for jesting!" Seafer almost-barked, "And these children have enough shock to deal with, without you teasing them like that…no one is Clear…it's not possible!"

"It's never happened, you mean. It's not possible to drop a ClanCat, either. Is it?" she asked pointedly, turning back to look at the Cat and make her point.

Beat. Beat. Beat.

"Hee hee. Well, you've got me there…you know, 'Rima…when word gets out about him…why there is going to be some ruckus!…"

Good, he's getting it, too, she thought. *Let's see if he can talk himself through it.*

"...why, every Guild would want him...and not just 'cause of his strength...why some of them would want to experiment with him...try some of that Color mixing...like they're always going on about..."

At the word 'experiment' both Stem and Maleef jerked around to listen closer.

"...and the duels!...why every young hotblood Ten...in *every* Guild...would want to duel him...to test themselves!...why, when word gets out about him...you know, 'Rima...that boy would be better off never going to *any* Guild!...never liked my Guild anyhow...and sure don't like it now...don't owe them a thing, anyway..."

He's getting there! And the children are hearing all of it. They've heard too much from me anyway. She was enjoying the way his voice rose and fell in his excitement.

Seafer was still going. "...why we ought to just send the poor boy back with these nice children here...and let him grow up on his own...well, no, we can't do that either...he's *got* to have training...or he might blow something up...or blow himself up...well *we* could train him...couldn't we 'Rima?...that's the answer...yep...we *will* train him...I can just take that retirement the Guild's been pushin' on me...and so could you!..."

This is better than I could have hoped. I wonder when he breathes?

"...but where?...not my orchards...that's certain...people would see that somethin' was goin' on......"

Seafer stopped. He hadn't been looking at her, just pacing as best he could and waving the free arm that didn't have hold of his staff. He looked at her now, "That baby can't leave this Valley, 'Rima...no one ever comes here any more...probably the only private spot there is..."

"...and *we've* got to stay here, too!"

CHAPTER 3

Arima's smile had been growing, while Stem and Maleef had been swiveling their heads in unison between the two Masters, as they tried to follow the conversation.

Seafer's eyes narrowed as he finally caught sight of her smile. Bending at the waist just a little further, he pointed a finger at her, "You already knew that, didn't you!? I hate it when you're ahead of me!...but you know that, too, don't you?...you do it by purpose!"

Arima looked kindly on her old friend and replied, "I just think it's best to let you come to your own conclusions, Seafer. But since you hate catching up, let me give you my next thoughts." She motioned them all back to the trunks, hoping a more relaxed conference would ease the tensions they all felt. She began, addressing Seafer directly, "I agree that this Valley would be the safest place for the child. But you and I have two concerns before we set up a permanent shelter here. One," and she held up a finger, "Steef is not our baby. Stem and Maleef have to decide for themselves what future they want him to have." This wasn't just fluff for their ears. She meant it, though the young couple would probably follow her lead. If she felt compelled to force the issue, she could bring in a Red to persuade them professionally. Neither of those choices appealed to her though, no matter how important this might be. A second finger went up, "Two...this isn't our Valley. It belongs to the HornCats, and they might not want the company."

Both of the Masters halted their conversation, and pointedly turned to the bewildered young parents, who were trying their best to keep up. They, in turn, looked at each other.

Finally, Stem spoke for them, "Beggin' your pardon, Mum, but if we under-stan' wha' you're askin', you wan' us to come live here?…if'n that is, them Cats are agreeable to it?"

Arima and Seafer both nodded together.

"An' you…both o' you…think tha' would be better for our Steef than gettin' his schoolin' in the village, like normal?"

Seafer exploded before she could stop him, "Of course it would! You think any o' those villages have Masters just sitting around waiting to train on babies!? Why, that boy would get…"

Arima cut him off. "Seafer, you'll scare them. Or worse, offend them. It's still their baby." Turning back to Stem, she looked him in the eye, and spoke clearly, "Stem, I've never been a Mother, and have no right in any case to tell you two what would be *best* for your child. But I *am* experienced in Guild pol-itics, and what passes for training and the life of a gifted student in our world today. I think I can safely say what would be *worst* for your child, and that would be the life that Seafer described earlier. He may have the style of a charg-ing bull, but he's right." Taking Maleef's hand, Arima gentled her voice, "So if you and Maleef decide against our counsel, and you take Steef home, I would beg you to raise him completely to yourselves, on your land. I can help you there, and see to it that his Grading attracts no notice." *Why not? Everyone else is cheating!*

"And this old man," she poked Seafer lightly in the shoulder with a bony fin-ger, "Has spent too many cycles alone in his orchards to know gentle speech, but he is right about one *other* thing. There is nowhere else in our Territory where Steef would have the kind of tutoring that he could get from us."

"Meant no offense, children," muttered Seafer. He stood and gave them a bow. The formal kind, with his staff grasped in both hands before him. They were shocked. Grade Two's never received bows. Not even from Ones. Here was a Master, paying them respect! Arima didn't comment, but thought…*He realizes that this child is the final answer to his research, and they can take all that away. A little humility won't kill him.*

"Why don't the two of you stretch your legs in a little walk?" she asked. "The Cats won't bother you, and I need to discuss some things with Seafer. It will give you some beats to talk over your decision."

After they had left, Arima turned to Seafer and said, "Let's assume for now that they agree…and that the Cats agree…and we get this wild idea started. You and I must make some choices right now that we will have to live with for many cycles."

"Who we gonna get, you mean," he replied with a twinkle. "I'm not completely thick, you know. I suppose you'll want at least one Master from each Color?"

"Almost right…almost right," her voice trailed off as her head turned and she focused on the mountain peak in the distance. It would be beautiful when the sun set. "No *more* than one Master from each…and I would love to know if you can think of a Black or Red you can trust?" Actually, there *was* one Black that Arima thought might be trusted, but *she* would never be allowed to come.

"I take your point, Arima," said Seafer. "The plain truth is, I've been in my orchards so long, I don't know much of anyone, any more. Except this. I know the Brown we're gonna want. I mean, we've kinda gotta get Mokam for Brown." He looked embarrassed.

"I assume you'll explain why," she asked. She didn't know a 'Mokam'.

"Well, he's been working with me on my project," Seafer replied, his eyes taking on even more light, "Off and on for the past six or seven cycles. It really won't work without his help, and the sooner we get it started, the better."

Arima had thought of something else while Seafer spoke. Instead of answering Seafer, she spoke to her Buzzbies, "Pill, does your family serve Mokam?" she asked.

"No, the Paals work with Mokam. Why?"

She shook her head slightly at Seafer and said, "Paals". Then she added, "Seafer, are you still carrying Pills?" He nodded and she let out a breath.

"It occurs to me," she said to no one and everyone, "That if we are going to keep this a secret, it would help to limit it to one Buzzbie family."

"We don't work that way, Arima. You know we share information with some of the other families."

"I understand Pill. But we are going to need a new arrangement for some very special circumstances. Would you please fetch me a Boss Pill? Thank you." Pop! To Seafer, she said, "Let's assume that we get Mokam for Brown. Let's also assume that we are going to wait a while on a Black and a Red. We still need to choose a Yellow and a Blue. There's no real hurry on a Blue…the child won't need weather training for some time…but we need a Yellow right away to tend that littlest Cat. He'll die if we don't." *I will not allow that!*

Seafer would have laughed at the 'littlest Cat' remark, if this weren't so serious. That Cat was at least as heavy as he was. Still, Arima loved these beasts, and she was his friend. He patted her lightly on the forearm for a beat, while they each said nothing. Then he said, "Why you know, there has to be a Yellow assigned to this Valley! *Someone* is tending those herds for the Cats. We can send for *them*." He felt very pleased with himself. For a beat.

Arima shook her head again, "If you looked at the Landing Field, you saw that no one is coming here often, which means that they only come when they have to. Which means it's a youngster who doesn't *remember!*" She spat out the 'remember' like it was an oath. "And," she went on, "they wouldn't send a Master for these herds, anyway. A Six or Seven could easily handle the duty. But we need a Master. We need a Master for the Cat right now, and we will need a Master later for the child." She remembered Andor, the Master Yellow who was tending the Valley when Arima was just a young woman learning her craft. Her apprenticeship as a Grader had brought her here often, and it was Andor who had taught her to love the Cats. But Andor was old then, and gone now. She also remembered he had no apprentices of his own. No other Yellows to tend the Cats.

Pop! *"You sent for a Boss?"*

"Why, so I did, Pill. Thank you for coming so quickly." She wasn't trying to be funny, Boss Pills had busy days. "Have you been keeping up with what is happening here?"

"Of course."

"Then you already know how impor…wait, Pill, have the Pills told any other families, yet?"

"No. The story isn't finished."

That surprised her. She couldn't help it, she burst out with a barking laugh. When she caught her breath, she went on, "Regrets, Pill. No offense meant. But I don't think this story will be ending for a while."

"That is occurring to us. We haven't decided what to tell. Or when."

"Out of curiosity, Pill. How did you know this child was so unusual? You can't See Power."

"No, we can't. But we could FEEL his. Waves of it."

That was new. Made sense, though. Those same waves were giving her headaches. "Well, I have two requests for you, and they are important."

"Important to whom?"

She forced herself to stay calm. *Regular breaths* she told herself. And, she had to admit it was a fair question. "It could be that this will be important to everyone before it's over. But for now, it's important to Seafer and myself, and we ask that you consider making it important to Pills."

"Spoken well. Give me your requests."

"We ask that you…actually all of the Pills…keep the story of this child and his Grading to yourselves."

"For how long?"

"Indefinitely."

"That is asking a lot."

"And I'm not finished. We would also ask that you take over service of Mokam from the Paals."

"Trading with Paals is only a small formality, but while Mokam isn't far, it's actually not our territory. And Pills dislike mines."

Seafer was apparently getting an account from his own Pills, for he spoke up, "We've *got* to have him, Arima. It's not an option."

"Will he come, Seafer?" she asked.

Seafer nodded. "When he hears what it's for, he'll come. Don't know for how long, but he'll come."

She went back to the Buzzbie, "It would seem, Pill, that that solves the problem of Mokam. He'll be *here*, and there are no mines here."

"We'll contact the Paals immediately." Pop! her other Buzzbie left, while the Boss remained. *"This other matter is more than I can agree to without a full Hivemeet. We will inform you when it is decided."* Pop!

But Arima had had another thought, "Wait Pill!" she cried. She was temporarily out of Buzzbies, but Seafer wasn't, and she heard one leave him. Beats later, the Boss was back.

"Yes?"

Did he actually sound testy? *Oh well* she thought. "Seafer and I are hoping to bring a Master of every Color here for the child's training, and we want to be careful about who we invite. Trouble is, most of the Masters that we know well, are our own Colors. Seems to me that the Pills would know most of the Masters, at least better than we do. We would ask that you make some suggestions…and we're in a hurry for a Yellow to save the youngest Cat." Without knowing it, she had said exactly the right thing. His tone changed from annoyance to pride.

"A Master asking for advice? No, TWO Masters asking for advice! I assume you would also want them to be Masters that work with Pills?"

"Exclusively," she replied. She thought he would like that. "And hopefully, they would not be too very happy with their Guilds."

"We respect the Cats too, Arima. I will answer your Yellow question now, and we will consider the others later. We trust Zimth and Antee, and both are currently within two days of here."

"What are their crafts, Pill?" She had heard both names, but really didn't know either of them.

"Zimth is a Herder. She is young, but a strong Master. Headstrong, too. No love for her Guild, but she does love horses. Antee is a BeastHealer. In his sixties. Doesn't like the new experiments the Yellow Guild is doing. Even on insects, which we like, of course. His Power is not equal to Zimth's, but he did pass the Master tests."

"What do you think, Seafer?" Arima asked politely.

The old Master had been listening intently. In fact, while this had been going on, his staff had sunk a full span into the ground. He noticed this with a start, and jerked it back out. "Pill," he asked, "Do either of these people have Mates?"

"No."

"Then I would choose the BeastHealer, 'Rima. More useful now. And prob'ly more useful later."

Arima had wanted to jump at that too, for Timmerr's sake. It was a sign of how important this was to her, that she would even consider risking a Cat on this choice, if she had to. "I agree with you, old friend, but for a different reason. Antee is old enough to remember a real Grading."

"Be warned, Arima, Antee is very intelligent. He will not be easily fooled."

"Pill, would you please send my respectful greets to Master Antee? Ask him if he can spare the beats to tend a sick Cat. Please do not tell him about the child. Seafer and I will decide on that after he arrives. Convey our urgency, and that I will bear his expense."

"One of us will bring our other answers when we have them." Pop!

There was a good bit of Pop!'ing going on for a while. Seafer had to convince Mokam that this wasn't a jest, and…'yes, bring all of our preparations. Yes, *all* of it'. Meanwhile, Arima was struggling with an overscheduled Beast-Healer, who, come to find out, had three apprentices. *We forgot to ask that* she scolded to herself. *What else did we forget?*

Mokam had never really expected that Seafer would actually follow through on his wild idea, but he didn't really mind. He knew it would be expensive, but he had more wealth than he needed. In fact, since he rarely left his mines, he needed very little. Actually, he was already retired, but the young Brown Master appointed to oversee the mining had asked him to stay on, which suited

Mokam well. He had to admit, Tilko was a better Digger than he had ever been. In turn, Tilko had willingly admitted that Mokam was a better Searcher. It impressed Mokam that Tilko would take such a humble attitude, in spite of his youth.

The two Masters would go at least once every sevenday to the ends of the shafts, alone. Tilko would carry mapping supplies, Mokam only his staff. Once there, Mokam would lay his staff against the endwall, and press his body to it. Spreading his hands against the stone, he would send a Pulse through the next section of uncut mountain. Eyes closed, he would recite to Tilko where the precious stones were to be found. Tilko would record the effort, and dig *exactly* where he was told. Dig with a skill and trust that Mokam enjoyed watching. They weren't really friends, but they still enjoyed and appreciated the mutual craftsmanship of the other. And in the process, they had both also accumulated their own small fortunes, each being rewarded by their Guild with a small portion of each dig.

Now Seafer wanted to bite into that fortune. It wasn't wealth that Seafer was looking for, but wealth *was* measured in Dust, and Seafer needed the Dust for its own sake. *Oh well.* Like most Browns, Mokam kept his own Dust. He didn't deposit it in the Vault in Town. He had never developed a taste for little numbers scribbled on parch. So carrying the actual physical Dust to Seafer wouldn't attract attention, because no one would know. Besides, what those Vault people passed out as Grade One was a jest. A not-too-funny jest. His Dust though, was as pure as a skilled Master could make it. And Seafer wanted *all* of it. Well, what Seafer thought was *all*, and what really *was* all, weren't the same *all*. Besides, Mokam was curious, in an abstract way, if Seafer's idea would actually work. So he was going.

More disturbing to him than the Dust, was the switch of Buzzbies. He had lived and worked his entire Master's life with Paals. He liked them. Respectful, they were. Respectful enough to speak up so a half-deaf Brown could hear. These Pills had better do the same, or he wouldn't put up with it. Didn't have to last long, anyway. He'd get Seafer fixed up, and come back to his mines and his Paals. He had no intention of staying longer than he had to with the Cats.

It wasn't that he was afraid of the Cats, like some of the younger lower Grade Browns who worked his mines. Why, he himself had been Graded by the Cats, though he didn't remember it. His children had also been Graded that way, but not his grands. No, not afraid. But there were no beasts in his mines, and he wasn't a beast person. *What was Seafer doing in the Valley, anyway? Oh well, guess he has to plant the thing somewhere.*

So, the morning after hearing from Seafer, he found himself walking alone to the Landing Field near his mine. Behind him floated only two trunks, which he pulled along with a tether. One of the trunks carried the few personal things he expected to need, the other was full to the brim with Dust. He carried his staff, of course. He had left his small personal cave sealed behind a wall of hardstone, and Locked. It would take a Brown stronger than himself to break that Lock, and there weren't many of those. He hadn't waited long at the Field when the boat came floating into view and landed. He boarded and they left.

The trip would take all day. The boat handlers had thoughtfully brought along food for midday. He made some courteous chat with the Lifter, which protocol required. But Miners and Lifters didn't mix much. He could never understand how a perfectly good Brown could stand all this sunlight! Flying just didn't give him the thrill they obviously enjoyed. He finally sat himself in the back of the boat and passed the beats in his own thoughts.

Antee, Master of Yellow, was a busy man. There were always more beasts to Heal than beats in a day, and his apprentices often couldn't help. Yellow Guild didn't require him to apprentice anyone below Ten, but they never said 'no' if he was willing, and he was always willing. So, instead of one Master's apprentice at a time, he often had several lower Grade Yellows following him around. The drawback was, they sometimes *couldn't* Heal the injuries or diseases that were brought in. So his beats were full.

Antee didn't know if he should laugh or cry. He knew Arima by reputation only, and her reputation was not highly thought of. He remembered the furious battles she had fought with her Guild over the Cats and the Gradings. She'd had little support, for no one outside of the White Guild really cared how they ran their craft. His own Guild had stayed out of it, which he had thought strange at the time. They were BeastMasters, after all, and this fight concerned the noblest beast in their world. His opinion was not shared by all Yellows. Many of them didn't like the idea of a beast that absorbed Power. Couldn't Heal one. Couldn't breed them. Couldn't control them. They won't be missed. So the Yellows officially stayed out, and Arima lost her fight with the White Guild.

He had heard they sent her to a fringe Territory, away from the Valley and away from her Cats. It didn't surprise him though, that she was back there. Two things *did* surprise him. She obviously thought he could Heal a Cat, which was foolish. And why had she sent specifically for *him*. They didn't know each other, and he certainly wasn't closest. So he asked Pill.

"*Because we told her to.*"

"*You* did!?" he started.

"*Yes.*"

He went right past surprise into shock. Several more questions came to mind, but the one he asked was, "Okay, why did *you* pick me?"

"*We trust you.*"

Several cycles later, after he'd had time to consider what he'd been trusted with, Antee would decide that that was the single best compliment of his life. Right now though, from his view, this conversation had turned strange. "Trust me with what?" he asked.

Pill didn't answer. At all. And *that* was strange enough that he decided right then to go. He couldn't spare any extra beats, and his three apprentices couldn't really carry it, but he *had* to see what could get Pill to shut up. Foolish, wasteful trip. Can't Heal a Cat. But it would be good to see the great beasts again, just the same.

It wasn't a short trip, and Arima had made it clear that she thought haste was needed, so he quickly packed a few garments and spoke to the apprentices. As a last thought, he grabbed up a few potions and powders and stuffed them into a carrybag. With that, he went to meet the boat that Arima was sending.

CHAPTER 4

That first day back in the Valley had been a full one. First, the Grading. Then all of their conversations. Finally, the messages. Pleadings really, between them and Mokam and Antee. Yet Arima rested fitfully that first night in the Valley. She still had six sleeping Cats in her thoughts. Stem and Maleef had not come to a decision yet, or at least not indicated one. Would the Cats welcome them? And the Buzzbies would *not* leave her alone, wanting to argue with her long after dark, until she finally barked at them, and they *all* left.

She woke slowly the next morning, to the aroma of beanbrew. Looking around, she found Maleef sitting and feeding her Son next to a small fire. An old dented pot sat in the fire, issuing fumes that drew her out of her pad. Arima's mood was softened by the gentle smile Maleef gave her.

"Brigh' day, Mum," greeted the young Mother. "Las' o' the brew is yours. Men are up an' gone."

"Oh, *really*?" she said, "and where did they…"

Pop! "*What's more, we don't think the Guilds should be left out!.*"

Count on Pill to do the work of a pot of beanbrew.

"Pill!" she snapped, "I am not awake. I am not in the mood. And I am speaking to Maleef! You don't have to leave, but you *do* have to *shut up!*" The Buzzbie stayed, but did go silent.

Someone had thoughtfully moved a trunk near the fire. She plunked down on it and poured some brew into the only cup she saw. While she blew on it to cool, she absently held up the pot and looked at it. Arima was not wealthy by Master standards, but the thought came unbidden *this I would have discarded long ago.*

Steef must have finished, for Maleef pulled him away and covered herself. Putting him to her shoulder, she began a gentle rocking. Still with the soft smile, she said, "It still brews jus' fine, Mum." There was no trace of embarrassment in her voice.

"Yes, it does," replied Arima, taking a sip to prove her point.

"Me an' my Mate, we aren' 'fraid to work, Mum. An' our babe's never been hungry, an' he never will be while we be a'breathin'. She stated this as a fact, not a defiance.

"He surely does seem to be a happy child," agreed the Healer, wanting to get the conversation away from their poverty.

"Oh, yes'm," brightened Maleef, "Actu'lly, he's kinda unnat'ral happy."

Arima flinched a bit inside. "What do you mean, 'unnatural'?" she asked slowly, not wanting any more surprises. Too late.

"Well Mum, you see, he never cries," Maleef was too cheerful talking about her Son to catch Arima's apprehension.

"That does sound happy enough," Arima agreed, with premature relief. "Why do you call that 'unnatural'?"

"Beggin' pardon, Mum, bu' you don' un'erstan'," Maleef went o. "Steef *never* cries. He has *never* cried. No' once. No' even when he was birthed, an' the Healer popped his bottom." And then the Motherhood in her just gushed out. Not noticing Arima's widening eyes, Maleef kept on. "I tried to tell you yesterday, 'bout how all our kinfolk an' neighbors like to visit. They preten' to be lookin' in on Stem an' me, bu' they're really jus' wantin' to see Steef here, 'cause he's always so happy, an' they always get happy 'round him, an' they're always smilin' when they leave. But me an' Stem, we don' mind, 'cause they always bring a li'l somethin' to eat with 'em. An' 'sides, it's a neighborly way o' life." By now her eyes were sparkling, and her voice had the energy of a glad Mother.

Arima's mind was racing. *Is the boy an Empath, too? No, Empaths absorb emotion, not project it. Whoever heard of someone projecting emotion? Why,* she chuckled to herself, *the same people that have heard of a Clear! The same people that have seen a Power drop a ClanCat. No one.* To Maleef, she asked, "If Steef never cries, how do you know when he's hungry? Or…soiled? Or just wanting attention?"

Maleef 's brow took on a thoughtful crinkle as she answered, "Well Mum, when we figured out tha' Steef wasn' gonna let us know 'bout them things, we just took to checkin' him regular like. An' sometimes, like when he's soiled, he gets this funny look on his face, like he's tryin' to figure ou' wha' it is botherin' him. Then it gets fixed, an' he's back to grinnin.'" Maleef then gave a grin herself, indicating to Arima where Steef might have found his.

Arima couldn't help herself, her amazement overcoming her tact, "All that constant checking of the child! How do you do it!?"

She got a peaceful, happy version of the Mother's Answer, "Well Mum, we jus' do wha' we gotta do," said Maleef with a shrug. "'Sides, he's jus' such a *sweet* baby! It don' seem like all tha' much."

Beanbrew forgotten, Arima stared at the woman for a beat. This...girl...really, and her Mate had a life of hard work that Arima could not imagine. For the sake of their child, they had endured two...*was it really just two?*...days of what must be to them some amazing challenges. Here she sat, giving the last of her brew and calmly taking complete joy in her child. *I like this woman* she admitted. She laid a hand on the girl's shoulder and surprised herself by saying, "Maleef, I oath you...Steef will never go hungry while I'm breathing, either."

Steef took that beat to burp, and both women laughed. Maleef must have felt a bit more secure, for she asked, "Beg pardon, Mum, bu' seems to us you been kinda 'voidin' Steef, an' we thought maybe, uh, you din't *like* babes?" Her eyes had lowered a bit. She wasn't as bold as she thought. But the question was asked.

Arima laughed again. A gentle laugh this time. "No child, I like children just fine." *At least, I think I do.* "But Grading Whites are especially sensitive to the Power other people put out, and Steef's has been giving me headaches. That's why I've been keeping him near the Cats. They help lessen the blow."

The young Mother looked relieved, and appeared to come to a decision. "Well, Mum, I can' really speak for my Mate, bu' we're prob'ly gonna 'cept your offer to help with Steef...'pendin' o' course on wha' the beasties say."

Before Arima could reply, Pill spoke. *"Are you ready to continue our conversation?"*

"Pill, I really have no other compromise to offer. Seafer and I will gladly consult with you about the major issues with this child. But without secrecy, there is no point starting anything here in the Valley. Why don't you send me your usual two family members while you Bosses decide whether or not you're joining in on our project?"

"Fair enough." Pop!...Pop! Pop!

✤   ✤   ✤

One thing Arima hadn't anticipated was the waiting. She and Maleef took an inventory of their foodstuffs, and decided what they might need for the next few days. Pill was sent with orders to the nearest merchant village. This entire chore took them only to quarterday, when the waiting and fretting came back. And Arima was reminded of something else she had overlooked. They would need regular boats to bring them supplies. *This is going to be complicated.* Without thinking, she moved a trunk herself over to where the ClanCat was sleeping, sat down, and began stroking him. Maleef brought her some food just past midday, sitting on the ground at a respectful distance, and the two women passed the beats in friendly silence. Steef spent his time crawling after Cats, who would wait until he got close, then lumber up from the ground, pad a few staffs distance, and stretch back out again. Arima couldn't tell if they were annoyed or enjoying it, but Steef was laughing non-stop.

Her anxiety got pushed back with activity later that day, when the Boss Pill arrived with their decision, and the ClanCat awoke. The entire Clan got active then, with orders being growled, and many of the Cats voicing their opinions in general. Maleef got apprehensive, running over to pick up a bewildered Steef, and came back to stand near Arima. The Healer patted her hand for assurance.

Stem and Seafer arrived next, with Stem half carrying the old Master, who was as irritable as Arima had ever seen him. "Don't know which is worse," he was growling as well, "Putting up with old, slow bones, or wasting a whole day! If Stem here hadn't been along, I'd probably be out there forever."

"What were you doing, Seafer?" Arima asked. She was too stressed to think of chuckling at him.

"Why, lookin' for a likely spot to plant, of course." He seemed surprised that she didn't know.

That's a little premature she thought, but she let it lie. Fortunately, their conversation was cut short.

Pop! *"Mokam's coming."*

Pill was right. Looking up, she could see a boat floating into view. *It's too late for them to go back. They'll have to stay here tonight. Wonder what they'll think of all these sleeping Cats.*

Seafer's mood improved immediately. Grabbing Stem's arm, he practically dragged the tired young man towards the Landing Field. Calling over his shoulder, he said, "They'll be wanting paying, 'Rima! You got any Dust?" He didn't stop or even slow down.

Arima sighed. *He's spent so many cycles in those orchards of his, he's got nothing put back. Well, I started this. I guess I get to pay for it.* She didn't hurry right out there, however. They weren't going anywhere soon.

The ClanCat returned with several nursing females. Special attention was given to Timmerr, but Letterr was also tended to, while the ClanCat stood near and watched. Neither Cat took the milk. The ClanCat issued a soft rumble and the females withdrew. He then padded over to Arima, who stood to receive him.

"*They have gone back to their cubs. Others will come in an eighthnight to try again.*" Looking over at the landed boat, he asked, "*Do you require another Grading?*"

"No, Majesty. They are here for another purpose. Can you give me a few beats to speak of it?" She forced herself to speak slowly and calmly, not wanting to convey to him her urgency. When she had fully explained what they wanted to do, he surprised her again.

"*You would make a village here with us?*"

"Well, there won't really be enough of us to call it a village, but yes, we are asking to live here."

"*And YOU would be staying here with the child?*"

"Yes, Majesty. I would be staying. I might leave occasionally for errands, but they would be very short trips, and not for Healing anyone. This would be my home as well, if you agree." She had a fear that her presence might defeat the whole thing.

"*If YOU are staying, the other two-legs may stay also. We will eat only four-legs. You should never have left.*" He must have embarrassed himself, for he broke contact, and padded away, leaving an open-mouthed Arima blushing like a young girl.

Pill buzzed, "*Close your mouth, Arima, before I start picking between your teeth for pollen. What did HE say, anyway?*"

Her stress just ran off of her. She felt like she was standing under a gentle waterspill and getting clean for the first time in twenty cycles. And she determined right then that she would be living here, regardless of the others, for the rest of her life. She was home.

She actually giggled, and said, "Why, Pill, He just told me they were thinking of adding Buzzbies to their diet! Such a delightful thought."

"You need to sharpen your jesting, Arima, you're out of practice. I have instructions to report the Clan's decision as soon as it's made."

"Well go then, you oversized bee! He said YES!" Pop!

Arima needn't have worried about concealing things from the boat crew that brought Mokam, as they wouldn't come out of their boat. *They're young, and don't understand.* She was feeling frisky now, and had a thought of asking one of the Cats to jump up into the boat and sniff them. *Calm yourself girl. You might need them to come back sometime.* Seafer and Mokam were conferring in the field halfway between the boat and their little camp. Seafer looked up and motioned for her to join them.

When she got to them, Seafer jumped right in, his excited voice giving no sign of the day's long efforts, "'Rima...we need to do some scouting for our spot tomorrow...can we afford to hire this boat for the morning?" There was the beginnings of a wild look in his eyes. *He knows he's running out of cycles, if this doesn't work. I hate it, but I've got to bring him back to ground.* He had given no introductions.

"Yes, Seafer," she started, then paused a beat, "Now that you ask, the Clan-Cat said yes, and I believe Stem and Maleef might agree as well."

The Green Master rocked back as if she'd slapped him. Then, bowing his head a bit, he said in a quieter voice, "Pardon 'Rima...got 'head of myself again, didn't I?...I'd tell you it won't happen again...but we all know that's not true."

Mokam gave a laugh and slapped his friend on the back. Arima just smiled and walked over to the boat. She paid them for their trouble, and asked if they would stay an extra halfday tomorrow. They resisted until she told them they would not be waiting on the ground, but taking Seafer and Mokam around the Valley. They named a price, and she paid them again. Out of courtesy, she invited them to their fire, knowing they would refuse. They did.

While the others slept, Arima joined the ClanCat that night in a vigil over the five sleeping Cats. In the dark of midnight, the next Cat awoke groggily. Based on that timetable, she and the ClanCat both knew that the next three Cats should wake in time. They also knew that Timmerr, being measurably smaller than Letterr, would not. The youngest Cat was still not taking milk from the females.

She was standing next to the ClanCat with her left arm around his right front leg, a spot she would become accustomed to. "I've sent for a Master Yellow, Majesty." She was trying to sound hopeful. "A BeastHealer, specifically. He will be here soon after the Sun."

"Be at peace, Healer. We know the risk. We are the Clan. We do not turn from such things. We will moan greatly for Timmerr at his Resting."

"He will *not* die! Not if *I* can help it!" she said fiercely.

"You did warn me. The choice was mine."

"Thank you, Majesty, but it's not pardon I'm looking for. I'd rather just save Timmerr." With that, she went to her pad and got what little sleep she could.

❧   ❧   ❧

Pop! *"Antee is coming."*

She hated waking up to an arriving Buzzbie in her ear. She suspected they knew that, and did it by purpose. She rose to find everyone already up except Seafer. *Yesterday was too much for him* she thought. Another of the Cats had also just wakened. She was amused to see the boat Mokam had come in was floating several staffs above the ground, with a fixline thrown down to hold them in place. They didn't mind waiting, they'd been paid. They just weren't going to wait on the ground. She left Seafer to his rest and walked right past the brew on the fire to meet Antee's boat.

She didn't know him, of course, but his Yellow badge was identification enough. She gave a formal bow. "Thank you Master, for coming so quickly," she spoke as graciously as she could. "We are in great need here." She liked the look of him. His eyes were already looking keenly to the Cats, and she saw none of the loathing for them that had become so familiar to her.

He returned her bow, which startled her a bit. "You must be Arima. I should tell you, I hold little hope for being a help here. These fine beasts are outside of my Power."

Fine beasts! She marked herself to actually thank Pill later. Antee had been *their* choice, after all. As the two of them turned from the boat, she noted with surprise that the Steerman was stepping out, as well. What was especially unusual was the young woman's age. Arima judged that she couldn't yet have seen her thirtieth cycle, yet here she came. *A youngster that's not afraid of the Cats! Here comes a story I wish I had the beats for!* She was impressed enough that in spite of her haste, she waited for the young Blue to join them. And she also gave Arima a bow!

"Bright day to you, Master," said the woman, "With your permission, I would like to witness this."

Arima was so pleased, she actually glowed her stone in the return bow, something she hadn't done for, well, she couldn't remember, "Bright day to you, young Master, and you are welcome for my part. Though this is not my Valley, I believe his Majesty won't mind." This day had started so well. If only now Antee could help Timmerr! "My name is Arima," she added as they turned back towards the Cats. She noted that the boat's Lifter did not leave his boat.

"Yes Master, thank you," replied the flyer, "And my name is Cassa. Master Antee has spent most of yesterday instructing me that much of what I was taught about the Cats, and…about you…your pardon…might have been a bit wide of the truth. I decided to see for myself."

"Told you that you'd like Antee."

"And you were right, Pill," Arima said, smiling. "I won't say that often, so enjoy it."

As they approached the sleeping Cats, Antee sank his staff into the ground a good two staff distance from the closest. Without saying anything, he walked to the largest of them, and placed his hands on the chest, being careful to stay clear of the horns. A crowd of Cats began to form, and the ClanCat also arrived. Everyone waited quietly as the BeastMaster went to each sleeping Cat in turn. Turning from Timmerr, he looked a bit weak, and walked back to Arima slowly, wiping his forehead.

"Didn't want to risk my staff, on the chance I might actually try to use it," he said wearily. "But they still drained me a bit." His brow crunched up, as he turned to Arima to say, "Arima, I don't feel anything wrong with them. They appear to just be sleeping." Arima could see it strike him. He pointed a finger at her, and cried, "You held a Grading, didn't you!?" He didn't sound accusing, just stating a fact. Then something else occurred to him, and turning back to the Cats, took several beats to look at the largest one still left. Antee then gave her a shrewd squint of his eye, and asked, "How *long* have they been asleep, Arima?"

She couldn't avoid answering, not if Antee could help Timmerr. "At midday, it will be two full days," she said with a sigh. Pill had been right about this, as well. This man was not stupid. *Let's see if he can be discrete.*

Antee's eyes opened wide, then glancing at Cassa, he visibly relaxed.

Yes, it looks like he can she thought.

But Antee was speaking again, "You're worried about the youngest one starving, eh?" She nodded. "And you called me to wake him, right?" She nodded again. And then he started laughing! He was *laughing*! But despite her puzzlement, she did catch that it seemed to be a kindly laugh.

"You furhead," he went on, but he still sounded kindly. Wiping a tear from one eye, he said, "Ooohhh…hmmm…well, you really didn't need me at all, you know! But I understand…I really do. They *are* beasts, so naturally you thought 'Yellow'. And you must have been torn with worry. I know you love them. Just slipped your mind, is all."

She couldn't stand it. Taking his arm, she said, "So tell me!"

"Arima, they're *just* asleep! Deep sleep, yes, but *only* asleep! You're a Healer…don't you carry some stinkstick for fainters?" He looked down to his carrybag, and started digging through it, so he didn't notice her begin to shake. Cassa *did* notice, and stepped up to help steady her. Arima's knees were a little weak, and tears were already rolling down her cheeks.

Cassa helped her to one of the trunks, as Antee walked back to Timmerr. Taking two small sticks from his bag, he broke them under the Cat's nose. Timmerr immediately started breathing faster, and his paws began to twitch slightly. Antee repeated the process for the other two Cats, the largest of which roused completely, with a growl that didn't sound welcoming. But the ClanCat had been watching the entire time, and growled him down, which probably saved Antee's hands.

The commotion finally woke Seafer, who clambered from his pad with all the swiftness he could muster. Clearing his eyes, he looked into the sky and exclaimed, "We've wasted a good quarterday!…'Rima, why didn't you wake me…what are you crying for…oh, good, the Cats are waking up!…where's Mokam…who're you…must be the Steerman bringin' Antee…is that Antee over there?…I'm Seafer, bright day…enough o' that…where's Mokam…there you are…we're wastin' light, let's go…'Rima, you all right?" He suddenly stopped next to her.

She was taking deep gulps of air, while a helpless Cassa stood over her. She just nodded.

Antee, meanwhile, who was normally comfortable around beasts of any kind, had stepped quickly over to them as well.

The crew of the first boat had seen the stir of the Cats, as had Cassa's Lifter. All of them were shouting that they were ready to leave…*now!*…which got Seafer stirred up again.

Arima finally recovered enough to look and see that Timmerr was waking a bit. That crisis over, she turned to the next. Seafer really did need a scouting trip, and a boat to go with it. Besides, she'd already paid for it. She motioned to everyone and the group of Masters trod back to the boats. The crew of the first boat wanted to give her Dust back. Right now! And was Mokam staying or going with them? The Lifter on Cassa's boat was screaming at her to get back aboard, they were leaving too. He didn't even mention Antee. The solution for all of this came from a surprising source.

"If I can make out what they're screaming," Cassa coolly observed, "Someone was wanting a daytrip around this Valley?" She turned to Arima, but Seafer answered.

"Yep. Me and Mokam. We're gonna do some scoutin'," he said. "Take a half a day, at least…which we just barely got now…since nobody woke me up."

Ignoring him, Cassa half shouted at the first boat crew, "You boys already been paid for the work, and now you want to leave? That's against GuildLaw, you know! Tell you what we'll do, you give *us* the Dust, and we'll make the daytrip for you. Save you from a penalty." In a half-voice to the Masters on the ground, she said, "It wouldn't matter. As long as the Guild gets their permit fees, they don't care what we do, short of crashing into each other."

That's when her own Lifter started shouting. *He* wasn't going on a daytrip *anywhere* in this Valley. They were going home and find themselves a proper fare.

Everyone suddenly stopped. Partners don't disagree in public. Especially Steermen and Lifters. Their work involved public safety. And in front of other Colors!

Cassa walked the remaining couple of staffs to the edge of her boat, but she still spoke loud enough for them to hear, "This boat's going on a daytrip around this Valley! End of discussion," she said. Her hands were on her hips, her back was arched, and she stared at the man unblinking.

But the Brown in her boat was unmoved, "No boat of mine's gonna stay here another beat!"

Cassa's face broke into a wicked smile, "But this isn't *your* boat. It's *my* boat. And we're staying," she said firmly.

"No, Cassa, *you're* staying. *I'm* going." With that, he jumped out of the boat, and sprinted to where the other boat was floating. They lowered briefly, helped him on with a clap on the back, and departed.

Cassa turned and came back to their little group, who uncomfortably didn't know what to say. She broke the tension with a serene look on her face, "I go through a lot of Lifters." She shrugged. "And it looks like you lost your Dust, Master."

Seafer took that as a sign that *his* problem was now back to priority, "I admire your spirit, Miss…but now we've got a boat with half a crew…and I, uh…*we* still need to look around…and soon." He looked as if he would explode, and his dark face got as red as it could. Arima reached out and put her hand on his cheek, checking…no, his pressure was acceptable.

Seafer hardly noticed Arima, for Cassa gave a grin, and cheerfully said, "Got a Master Brown right there," pointing at Mokam, "If I heard right, you're Mokam. Bright day, Master! My name is Cassa. Would you care to Lift my boat for us?"

"Him!" exclaimed Seafer, "He's a Miner…Miner's don't Lift boats…Mokam you ever Lifted a'fore?…get us all crashed…well what else is there?…Mokam, *say* something!"

Everyone was smiling or outright grinning. Even Antee, who had no idea what Seafer was raving about, and Arima, whose eyes were still puffy.

Mokam got a gleam in his eyes, and motioned towards the boat.

"Wait just a beat," interrupted Arima. "Has it occurred to you old thick-heads that you have no idea where to look, and this is a *big* Valley?" She was getting another idea. She liked this Blue.

Seafer sure didn't want to wait, "What 'Rima!? What?" He was almost dancing.

"Calm yourself, old friend. We just might save you some beats, or even days, in the end," she said kindly. "Let's tell the ClanCat what you're looking for, and he can tell you where in this Valley your spot exists." *If it does.*

Seafer didn't like it, but since it made too much sense to be argued with, he nodded.

Fortunately, the ClanCat was still watching over Timmerr, who was almost ready to stand. The odd assortment of Masters trooped behind Arima to where he stood. Arima waited until he noticed her, then approached and took his leg. She spoke quietly, and directly in his ear.

"Rivverr, my friends need instruction about where in your Valley they might find what they seek," she said.

"Tell me what they seek, and I will tell you if it is here."

"I don't really know. It is for the Green Master, and he knows best what he needs. He should tell you himself."

"No."

"No?" She knew it was a delicate subject, but his answer had come quickly and firmly.

"No two-leg has ever touched me for speech except you. I am not inclined to change that."

She was touched, but this time her surprise was for a different reason, "Not even during the Gradings? No one touched you then?"

"That was long ago. I was almost still a cub myself. They spoke to my sire. Only my horns were touched."

"Will it change our bond for them to touch you?" She wasn't quite ready to give up just yet.

"We are friends. That does not change."

"Will you be diminished in the eyes of the Clan?"

"No. There is much four-legged food. They will not challenge me over speech."

"Then I would respectfully remind you of your own words. Eleven cycles ago, I lost a battle because I fought alone. Now, here are four Masters, all of different Colors, who have come to your Valley on their own. It would help in the next battle if I did not fight alone." *If there ever is a next battle.*

"How would speech change that?"

"How can they love you as I do, if they don't know you?"

He said nothing for several beats, and she waited calmly. Even if he agreed, there was no guarantee it would affect anyone's decision, anyway. But it wouldn't hurt. Finally, he spoke.

"The FoodMaster journeyed two days to help Timmerr. The Clan is gladly in his debt. I will repay this debt. The others I must trust you about. It will be done once only."

"I understand."

Arima stepped away from him then and motioned to the other Masters. Gathering them in close, she whispered, "You need to understand two things. No one but a White Grader has ever spoken to *any* Cat, and after this, no one will again…aaaannnnnd…you can tell anyone you want that this happened, because no one will *ever* believe you." She looked around at each of them in turn, catching their eyes. They understood.

As Stem and Maleef watched, Arima directed two of them to each side of the great Cat, then returned to her spot at his neck. Following her lead, they all reached out trembling hands and touched him.

She said, "Masters! Meet His Majesty, the ClanCat! Wisest and strongest of the wisest and strongest of beasts! Please give a proper greeting."

All of them responded in turn, though Cassa's 'bright day, your Majesty' sounded a bit squeaky.

"The Clan welcomes you to our Valley. It is good to be honored once more. The Healer tells me you seek direction?"

At that, Arima nodded to Seafer, who strangely spoke slow and cautiously as he described what he was looking for. Arima noticed that Antee's stone was glowing, and Cassa's eyes shone almost as brightly. The ClanCat directed them to three likely spots.

"The ground with the waterspill is close to many of our caves, including my own. It would please me for you to choose it, if it suits you."

Arima was amused to see that Seafer could no longer speak. *That doesn't happen often* she thought. Mokam spoke for him, booming out, "Thank you, Majesty! We will look there first!"

"I am glad the Healer persuaded me of this. You all have good spirits, and it has been long since I felt the different Powers, though I do not miss the other two. The little SkyMaster is especially strong and bright. She cheers me."

Arima felt a small jolt of jealousy. She didn't want him to like this too much. She reminded herself to act her age. When all conversations and courtesies were complete, she thanked him, and they all took their leave.

Seafer immediately headed for the boat, so with sighs all around, Mokam and Cassa followed. As soon as Cassa had a grip on her mast, Mokam shoved his staff into the Lifter's hole, and the boat shot straight up into the air. All of the people on the ground gasped as one, catching the attention of the Cats who were still there. Man and beast together tilted heads back to watch the unusual ascent.

The boat quickly became a speck in the sky, it had moved so fast. It stopped, and just as suddenly...began plunging back down again! Heads all around tilted back down to follow the impending crash, but at a height of about a hundred staffs, the boat began to slow, until it came to a stop hovering just above the ground.

They could see Cassa clinging to her mast with a grip that would choke a Cat. She was as pale as a person could get. They couldn't see Seafer, but they heard him gasping for air, apparently in the bottom of the boat.

Good thing he didn't eat this morning Arima thought, in true Healer fashion. *This will kill him yet.*

And there was Mokam, standing with one hand gripping his staff, and one hand on his belly, bent over laughing with a full wind.

"HOAR, HOAR, HOAR...Miner can't Lift a boat...HOAR, HOAR, HOAR...Liftin' before I had hair on my chest...HOAR, HOAR, HOAR!"

Cassa spun around and knuckled him in the shoulder, and the boat began to Lift at a gentler pace. Those on the ground felt the wind pick up a bit from Cassa's Blue. The sail filled, and soon the boat had disappeared in the direction given.

Arima and Antee stood together and watched the boat depart. Without turning, Antee spoke, "So...the legend has come to life, eh Arima?"

She didn't know how he meant that, exactly, so she replied innocently, "What do you mean, Antee? Oh, and I want to thank you..."

"You've got a Clear, haven't you? I assume that young couple over there with the child? Did you presume to run it all the way up to the ClanCat?"

"Well, that was *His* choice, really, not mi...what?!"

"Told you to be careful."

This was already going a too fast. She glanced, to see a smiling Antee looking at Stem and Maleef. He asked, "May I see the child?"

"I...I...don't...see...why not...how...?

He started walking towards the small camp, with her following lamely behind.

"You were a little too eager to share the ClanCat, Arima. That ritual has been guarded by you Graders for as long as the Yellow Guild has been keeping records. We always wondered why, you know, with some of us, I suspect, a little jealous. Amazing experience...," he glanced over at the few Cats that remained, "...anyway, you didn't just share it, you *talked Him into it*! And two of us at least, total strangers. All Master class. All different Colors. You *had* to have a motive other than simple directions."

"We did warn you."

Antee stopped abruptly, causing Arima to bump into him, "I heard you buzz, Pill! Don't get too smug! Your odd behavior with Arima's greets is what first set me wondering." He started walking again. "And I've noticed that the warnings you like to gloat over are always the ones that make the least sense."

"Uh, pardon, Arima."

"Finally, we have some very sleepy Cats. I've only been to a few Gradings since my Mastering, but that biggest one...that's a Ten sized Cat, or I'm a rodent! And you tell me he's been asleep for two days!" They had arrived at Stem and Maleef, as Antee rolled his eyes skyward. "Which means he dropped hard and fast. Which means...you kept going with bigger and bigger Cats. Did the ClanCat drop?"

There was no point...now...in *not* telling him, "Asleep for over a day."

Antee whistled.

"Bright day, children. My name is Master Antee, though I prefer you just call me Antee." Turning to Maleef, he went on, "Young missy, could I possibly have a peek at your child?"

Maleef half bowed, half curtsied to his courtesy. Reaching for the corner of the Cloaking blanket that was still wrapped around the boy, she pulled it back to reveal his blond curls and smiling face. Steef, for his part, saw a new and friendly face looking back at him. He did what all friendly children do, holding up his arms to Antee.

Arima felt the same wash of joy blast through her that she had first experienced in her tent. Antee didn't feel the wave, he only knew this was a happy child that wanted to be held. He reached for Steef.

Fighting a feeling of giddiness, Arima called out, "Antee, wait!" Too late. Steef climbed right into Antee's free arm.

But Antee was still holding his staff in the other. The same staff he had glowed his stone in only a few hundred beats earlier. The same staff that he had not yet drained. The staff that was fully charged. Arima would long wonder if that really mattered anyway.

Antee and Steef were enjoying each other, no one noticing her call. His stone immediately began to vibrate, which quickly became a shrill hum. Suddenly, with a loud CRACK!, it split into several pieces, which couldn't go anywhere, being held in place by the wood.

Arima gasped. Everyone turned to look at Antee's now-ruined staff. Instantly, Maleef started crying, and Stem started his pardons.

"Oh, Master! Oh, Master! Oh, Master! I'll work i' off, Master! Swear to th' Creator, Master! Wha'ever i' takes!"

Arima doubted it. She knew that these two humble children couldn't earn in a lifetime the cost of a Master grade staff. And truth was, it wasn't their fault.

Antee must have agreed with her. When he saw the splintered stone, his eyes flew open, but he looked back at Steef with a pleased smile, and suddenly burst out laughing. "You know, ahhh, hmmm," he said between laughs, "I've had this old staff for too long, anyway! Never have liked it much. Good excuse to get a better one." He drove the shaft into the ground, and put his free arm around Maleef. "You know, it's almost midday, and I'm starting to get hungry! Young man, if you would ask your Mate here to fix us some midmeal, why, we'll just call the deal struck!"

Pop! *"Seafer says the second spot is as good as the first. They're going to look at the last one, he says, to be thorough."* Pop!

"Thank you, Pill." They were relaxing with full bellies, stretched out on the ground and propped against the trunks. Maleef was a good cook. There were only a few Cats left, and she'd had to request those. Only females at that. The males wanted to keep their horns away from those little hands.

After a long pleasant quiet, Antee asked, "You're not going to register the boy, are you?"

She just shook her head slightly.

He laid his head back and closed his eyes. Lowering his voice to almost a whisper, "They'll have your staff, you know."

She looked at her staff stuck in the ground next to his. It was truly beautiful. Antee's looked plain next to it. Ornately carved out of blackwood, with two cupped hands at the top facing each other, holding a large, pure redstone. It was exactly one staff tall, and not all staffs actually measured a full staff, even Master grade. It had taken her a while to get used to the weight.

"Not this one, they won't," she replied. They could have her old one, the registered one. It was stored in one of her trunks.

Antee smiled, "Oh, ho! An unregistered staff! And a fine one, at that. That must have drained your Dustpile."

It hadn't. It had been a gift from a grateful Father whose only daughter had nearly died of the fever. The man had been a Vaulter, and could afford excesses, for she had to admit, Antee was probably right about its cost. But that had been long ago, and no living person now knew she had an unregistered staff. Except of course, Antee.

I've got to watch every word! she thought. What she said was, "I suppose they'll take yours, too. Of course, that is presently not much of a loss."

Eyes still closed, he grinned broadly, "They won't, you know. *I'm* not the one who's supposed to register high-Powered children. Still, someone would probably take a disliking to me keeping this a secret."

"Does that mean you *will* keep this secret?"

"Yep."

"*Told you…*"

"Shut up, Pill. Antee…thank you."

Antee was quiet for several beats. Finally, he said, "I think I probably owe you that, at least, Arima."

"Oh? And why would that be?"

"I didn't stand with you at your last fight, and I…we…all of the Yellows…*should* have. Your were right, back then. And I knew it. And today just proved it."

"He is impressive, isn't He?"

Again, Antee was quiet for some time. When he did speak again, the subject had shifted, "We have three crazy Masters roaming around this Valley. Do you know them well?"

Now it was Arima's turn to smile, "I've known Seafer my entire grown life. Since the day I Registered for Mating, in fact. He asked that first day if I would Mate to him. I refused." Seafer had been honest about it. He'd had his Mastery for a few cycles, and was already working his orchards. Being a clumsy man, he kept falling out of his trees and breaking himself. Said he 'figured it'd be better to have a Healer around, than hafta lay there a day 'til someone found me'. They'd been lifelong friends ever since. Neither of them had ever Mated with anyone else, either. "I don't know Mokam at all. Seafer invited him. And Cassa arrived with you."

"Did you know that Mokam is one of the wealthiest Browns in the Territories?"

"No, but it doesn't surprise me. It's the Dust that Seafer is after…no, no," she had caught the look on his face, "…he cares nothing about wealth. No, just Dust."

"So what are they doing? Can you tell me?" he asked politely enough, and he *would* need to know. Maybe.

"Seafer needs to find the right spot for a planting," she answered.

"And he's planting…what?"

"An acorn. Well, several acorns, probably. He's going to grow a tree." *He hopes.*

"All this fuss over a tree? What's the Dust for?"

"Why," she answered brightly, "That's what he's going to plant it in!"

❦   ❦   ❦

Pop! *"The supply boat is coming. They heard from the boat that left this morning, and they say they won't land near the Cats."* Pop!

Arima rose slowly, stretching. Looking up she saw an eighthday had passed. *Decent nap, and I needed it.* The Pop!'ing had roused the others, as well.

"Stem," she asked, "Would you mind helping the supply boat unload? They don't want to get close, and they'll probably want to hurry. They've already been paid." *Or they would have turned around before now* she didn't add.

"Thankye, Mum," he was eager to reply, "Gladta, Mum."

Still stinging over the staff, no doubt she sighed.

❦   ❦   ❦

They were standing in the same spot from which they had watched Cassa's boat depart, and now they were watching it approach. From the Buzzbies, they had learned that Seafer and Mokam had both settled on the first spot, the one near the ClanCat's cave, to do the planting.

"So, Arima," began Antee, "Do you have any idea just how strong the boy is?"

He couldn't see the shake of her head, so she replied, "No way I know of to calculate it. We ran out of big Cats." She continued a small shake of her head.

"Maybe we could just get a whole Guild full of Masters to duel with him at once," chuckled Antee.

"That would have to wait until he's old enough to understand how to duel," she said. "And besides, I'm not much of believer in dueling."

"That's not what I've heard about you."

"Sometimes people just need to talk about something," she sighed, "And I was just a child, then." Teens, actually. Trying to make herself known in the White Guild. She'd done that, all right. More than once.

"Well, without Cats or dueling, it's going to be difficult to learn how much Power he's got."

"We may never know."

The boat was coming to a rest. They started making their way to it.

"Got any ideas about how to train a Clear?" he asked cheerfully.

"No…you?"

"None at all."

❦   ❦   ❦

"'Rima, we've got to go at first light!" Seafer was almost dancing, he was so excited. In fact, he *was* actually bouncing up and down a bit. She was pumping food and water into him while he raved, but she couldn't get him to sit. He hadn't eaten all day.

"*Chew* your food, Seafer. Here, take some more water. When you've finished that meat, I've had some whitefruit brought in. The ones you like…no, leave your staff. You can crisp the others tomorrow. One soft one won't kill you." He was so picky about his fruit. She often wondered if that had been what sent him into the orchards to begin with. She glanced at Antee, who took her signal and started making his way around behind Seafer.

Seafer finished off the meat without looking at it. He was talking as fast as he could to anyone and everyone, only interrupted when she shoved something else in his hand or mouth. After she watched him down a small jug of water, she held her hand up right in his face.

"Enough," she said gently. Everyone was smiling at him, but only Antee knew what was coming. "You have had enough. Enough work, enough surprises, enough of everything for a man your age. You need a real rest," she concluded. It was then that he finally noticed that she was the only one at the camp actually holding a staff.

"No...'Rima...wait..."

"Good night," she said sweetly, as her stone Pulsed.

Antee caught him before he could fall, and they stretched him out on his pad. She went to work on him, Healing his swollen joints and overworked muscles, checking his pump and pressure. When she was done, she said, "You don't have to whisper. If I don't wake him myself, he'll sleep for two days. I'll check him in the morning, 'cause the Creator knows, he'd never give me pardon for making him sleep any longer than needful, while there's something to plant." Everyone around the fire laughed, and went back to their own meals.

"So," she went on, "While my staff is charged, does anyone else need anything?"

CHAPTER 5

They were all in the boat, floating down the Valley to the south. She was enjoying the trip, having never actually seen much of the place. *As often as I've been here, you'd think I would've looked around a bit.* But there had always been work to do. Except for the steep rock walls hemming it in, the Valley looked much like most she'd seen. Trees. Grass. Occasional herds of livestock. And waterspills. Lots of them. Small and large, all feeding into the small river that ran the length of the Valley floor.

It was just past midday. Seafer was pouting a bit, but she figured he'd liven up when they arrived at their destination, and planted his acorns. He was as rested and recovered as she could get him, and still have him speak to her. They had loaded everything into the boat that would fit, for the spot they were floating to would be their new permanent home. Not much had been left behind, and one more trip would retrieve that. The important things were Seafer's little wooden box, and Mokam's good sized one, and both of those had been packed in first.

She felt the boat begin to descend, and looking in that direction, her face lit up. *Seafer knows his craft, at least.* She was looking at a towering stone face at least a hundred staffs tall. It looked like the Creator himself had taken a spoon and scooped out a mouthful of rock, for there was a cove of stone wider than it was tall, facing out into the open Valley. The stone walls leaned back away from the cove at an angle, with a waterspill coming from almost the center top that fell, struck stone, fell again, striking and falling until over the cycles it had carved out pools in the stone at varying heights. The cove faced east...*he'll catch the morning sun*...in a stretch of the Valley that was narrower than most. She could plainly see the opposite cliff walls, just over a league away.

The boat came to rest hovering just above the ground at the entrance of the cove. Cassa wouldn't take it in, fearing what her wind might do in the surrounding rock walls. They lowered a steprope, and Stem climbed down first, followed by Mokam. Seafer was anxious to go, but Arima made him wait. Stem and Mokam walked a short distance away, and Stem began clearing stones at Mokam's instruction. When the old Miner was satisfied, they both stepped back. Mokam sank his staff, and as they watched, the ground caved in, forming a perfect bowl for the boat to settle into. Cassa slid the boat over to the hole, and Mokam had to slowly climb back aboard to lower it.

Finally…finally, Seafer could clamber off and head to his precious planting. He carried his little box, and as the rest of them followed, they noticed Mokam's box floating behind him on his tether. Upon reaching the center of the cove, Seafer gave a new surprise. He handed the little box to Maleef!

"Child…if you would…hold this close to the babe at all times…no, don't worry…it won't hurt him at all…Mokam…let's get to work."

Mokam set his box down, and came over to Seafer, "What do you have in mind?" he asked.

Seafer's hands were waving, and once or twice Mokam had to dodge his staff, "Well…first we need t' know how far down the soil goes…before it hits bedrock…I'm gonna want either soil…or loose gravel…for twenty staffs in every direction…for the root system."

Mokam's eyes widened. "Twenty staffs!" he exclaimed, "*Twenty* staffs? For the roots? I don't know much about trees, old friend, but even *I* know that would be *some* tree! Are you sure?"

Seafer just smiled and nodded.

They'd all heard the conversation, of course. Cassa was the first to ask what they all were thinking, "Master Seafer, how big is this tree going to get?"

Seafer never took his eyes off of Mokam, who was laying his staff on the ground, "That's really going to be up to the babe, Master Cassa," was his cryptic answer.

Meanwhile, Mokam had stretched himself on the ground, covering his staff. With his hands laid flat on the dirt, he charged his staff, and Pulsed. After only a couple of beats, he apparently got his answering Pulse, for he turned his head and spoke to Seafer, "Bedrock at nine staffs across the entire cove. Seafer, you *sure* you want twenty?"

Seafer nodded, with a satisfied smile on his face.

"All right, then," said the stone Master. He sat back up to look at the other Masters seriously. "I'm giving a discharge warning," he declared. There was a chorus of Pop!'ing as all of the Pills left at once. Waiting until all four of them had acknowledged, he continued, "Everyone needs to move back out of the cove. There's going be some shaking going on." He chuckled a bit. Arima and Seafer began draining their staffs as they turned.

But Stem didn't move. "Your pardon, Master," he actually started wringing his hands, "But shou' you be a'doin' this ou' here by yourself? Maybe I shou' stay wi' you jus' in case." He glanced at his Mate and child, and Arima realized that this honest little man was getting worried about all the fuss going on over his boy. It also occurred to her that it had probably begun with Antee's staff. She was going to say something to comfort him, when Mokam took care of that for her.

"HOAR, HOAR, HOAR...thankee, Son...HOAR, HOAR...thankee for true...HOAR...know you mean well...HUHmmm...but no little rock's gonna do me any hurt. You can be a help, though, if you've a mind to. Just you carry my little box there with you. Can't Lift it, or my discharge might set it off. Wouldn't want that, would we? That's good. Now, you go on with the rest."

The little group withdrew while Mokam waited, Stem waddling under the weight of the box. As they reached the boat, Arima turned around to See that Mokam was indeed fully charged. He had spread himself back on the ground, and a Brown glow had spread out from him that was several staffs high. The others couldn't see it, of course, so as she watched it build, she turned to Maleef and said, "You're in for a treat, child. It's not often you get to see a full Master discharge. And I can't recall ever witnessing a Brown one."

Mokam was apparently satisfied with his charge, for as she watched, the Brown glow just went WUMP straight into the ground. The air went CRACK! and that was followed by a deep underground rumble. As they watched, a ripple spread through the ground. Centered from Mokam, it looked just like a stone had fallen into a still pond. The ripple stopped exactly as it reached the edge of the Cove.

As one, all four of the watching Masters intoned, "What is Mastery but a gift? How good is a gift unshared? We witness a sharing." Stem and Maleef took turns staring at each of them, but none of them spoke further.

After a few beats, Mokam stood up, grinning broadly. He started towards them. They all began to step back towards the cove, when Seafer stopped them.

"My turn," he said with his hand up. He repeated Mokam's solemn caution, "Discharge warning." He met Mokam halfway, where they slapped shoulders. Seafer reached the center of the cove as Mokam arrived at the boat and said, "I needed that!" They all congratulated him on a clean discharge.

Meanwhile, Seafer was sinking his staff halfway into the ground. Standing completely upright for the first time since they'd arrived...*I didn't know he still could straighten up!*...he held the stone to his belly, and began to glow Green. Arima watched as Seafer's charge built. When she judged he was about ready, she said for their benefit, "Here it comes."

Again, the WUMP. Again, the CRACK! Only this time there was no rumble, nor any ripple. The ground in the cove seemed to be dancing and...stirring. This only lasted for a few beats, but when it settled, new fresh grass began springing up at once, and every growing thing already in the cove looked brighter and healthier.

Again, four Masters gave their intonation.

Both Stem and Maleef were looking bewildered, so Arima gave them a brief explanation, "Masters don't often give full discharges, children. There's rarely a need for that much Power, and it must be done with care."

Maleef looked down at Steef as she asked, "Ha' you ever done one, Mum?"

Arima didn't tell her that it was considered bad manners to ask. The girl might never ask anything again. The resultant laughter from the other Masters would only add to Maleef's discomfort. She decided to answer truthfully. "Not counting duels...," and she shot a glare at Antee, "...the need has arisen twice. Both times were village-wide epidemics."

Antee decided to help her over her awkward spot, and jumped in, "Well, you know, I've had to discharge several times, actually. Stampedes, mostly." Then, he added, "Not recently, though."

"Four for me," threw in Mokam, who didn't really know why they were discussing this, but was not to be left out, "Not counting today. Seems some stonehead Sevens just can't dig anything without tapping into a melted rock-spout."

They would come to learn that Cassa could be counted on to blast through any delicate matter. "You know why it's bad form to ask that don't you?" she blurted, oblivious to the reaction from Maleef. "It's because some of us with Tens on our chest aren't really Tens at all, and just can't *do* a discharge! If we don't bring it up, no one ever has to admit they can't. Ought to be a crime, wearing a Ten when you're not! And not to be left out, I've only had to do it once, thank you, but I was *required* to perform a discharge to get my Mastery. At least the Blue Guild still maintains *some* standards!"

Arima patted Maleef's shoulder, quietly telling her it was all right.

Antee wasn't quite done with Cassa, "Out of curiosity, what does a Blue have to discharge *on*?"

Her jaw set as she said, "They fly us out to sea, and we have to kill a swirl-fury storm. No less than a Grade Two. I happened to get a Four."

"I would think you'd have more Master apprentices than you do swirlfuries."

"Not if the GuildMaster is sitting out there, stirring them up." She looked really mad, and Antee wondered why until she added, "He sent me that Four by purpose. He didn't like me much, and he wanted me to fail. I fixed him, though." Her brows came down over hardened eyes. "I turned that storm around and sent it back to him. Put Locks on it so he couldn't touch it. Then, just before his boat dumped him, I killed the storm." Even the slow smile crossing her face couldn't get the eyes to move. "Don't know what made him maddest, that I sent the storm back, or that he couldn't break my Locks! But the Guild Council had to admit that I had performed a discharge. Ha! Did I ever!"

Antee had taken a step back to give her room. He noticed that there were dark clouds racing across the sky in their direction, and concluded that he wouldn't *ever* goad her again. In an effort to make peace, he said, "That must have been something to see. I wish I'd been there."

Looking up, she saw the clouds, too. Taking the few steps to her boat, she reached from the ground, lightly touching the very bottom of her mast/staff. The clouds began to break up. "No, you don't," she said, "Trust me."

They were standing in the middle of the cove, all of them grouped around a hole. Mokam had opened the hole to Seafer's instructions.

"Now," said a beaming Seafer, "We need the Dust." Mokam stepped over to where Stem had set his box down, and Lifting it high enough to reach easily, he opened it. Everyone looked in, and there was a general intake of breath. The box didn't just have Dust in it, it was *full* of Dust! The only space not filled with Dust was taken up by a handfull of perfectly round, clear stones. Mostly pea-sized, a few were twice that large, and two of them were the size of eggs. Once open, the entire contents of the box began to Pulse with raw Power. Mokam reached in and picked out the stones, putting them in his tunic pocket.

"That's real, for true, grade one Crystal Dust...isn't it?" Cassa blurted out. Even Seafer seemed to be impressed, and he had known what was coming.

"Actually, you'd have to cut it, then cut it again at least...to get it down to grade one," replied Mokam, as he pushed the floating box to center it over the hole.

"You mean, grade one isn't pure Dust?" Cassa was watching the box, as they all were, while she spoke to Mokam. "They're cutting it down, and giving off that's it's pure, why isn't that...OH MY BENDING STAFF!" Her eyes flew open, and her hands clasped to her ears.

Mokam had turned the box over and dumped all of the Dust into the hole.

Seafer was hopping again. He fairly bolted to Maleef's side, where he gently removed his own small box from her grasp. Holding it fast to himself with both arms, the Green addressed the group, "I must ask all of you to drain yourselves and your staffs...can't have *any* Power hitting the box when it's opened." He looked at each of them, including Stem and Maleef, who brightened with the flattery.

That was thoughtful of him thought Arima.

"Hee, hee, hee," he cackled gleefully. "I'll just wager..." breaking the seal, he peered inside, "...I knew it! I just knew it!...they've sprouted!" Thrusting the box out, he exclaimed for anyone, "Look, they've sprouted!"

They all looked, of course. Inside the small box were five acorns, all of which had a single green sprout sticking out. Seafer shook a bit as everyone looked, and as soon as they had all peeked, he threw himself to the ground, and gently placed each of the five acorns into the hole, sprout-side up. Jerking back up, he began to feverishly push the dirt back in. Meanwhile, Mokam set his own box down, and looked as if he were going to help Seafer close the hole.

"No, Mokam!" exclaimed Seafer, "No Power!...just dirt." With that, Stem, Mokam, and Antee bent over and pushed dirt until the hole was filled. That done, Seafer just flopped over onto his back, and laid there muttering, "Seventy cycles...seventy cycles...seventy cycles."

Cassa was standing straddle over the now-filled hole with her arms crossed, and had her jaw set again. "Someone is going to explain what I just saw," she defiantly declared. It wasn't a question. "We are in the middle of a wilderness...no one around but Cats...and one Master just dumped enough wealth to run all of GuildTown for an entire cycle...into a hole in the ground...so that another Master could put five little acorns there! Someone is going to explain what I just saw!" she repeated.

Still lying on his back, Seafer broke his litany long enough to say, "It's 'cause of the babe, o' course! Seventy cycles!" He was not going to be much further help.

Arima looked at Antee, who returned the question in her eyes with a 'why not' shrug. She started to speak...

"No! Arima! No!"

The Buzzbies had returned, as soon as the wumping! and cracking! had stopped. They had remained silent throughout the planting, watching quietly while Masters did crazy things, which seemed to be what they lived for. Now all of the Buzzbies on Arima, Antee, Mokam, and Seafer began to buzz excitedly.

"Pill, what is your problem?" asked each of them, almost together. All of the Pills hushed, except Arima's.

"You can't include Cassa! We won't work with her! We refuse!

Arima just stopped, "Ah...um...uh" One hand sort of waved at Cassa, another at Pill.

Arms still crossed, an almost wicked smile flitted across Cassa's face, "Having a little trouble with your Buzzbies, Arima?" she asked quietly, "I've had that problem myself, once or twice."

"She can't keep a Buzzbie, Arima! All of the families have tried her! No one stayed!

And for the first time in her memory, her other Buzzbie was speaking over the first.

"She doesn't listen! And she flies too fast! And look at her hair!

Apparently, four Masters got that last message, for all of them suddenly looked at Cassa's hair. Arima hadn't noticed before, possibly because her attention had been occupied, possibly because she just hadn't thought about it. But Cassa's hair was pulled back and tied into a tail, hanging straight down her back. And Arima understood. Buzzbies liked the cover of their Master's hair. It's why so many Masters looked like they had just come out of the wilderness themselves, with long windswept, unkempt hair. It had become, over the cycles, an honorable sign of Mastery to keep your hair that way. Some of the lower Grades had copied it occasionally, never really knowing why, but they never kept it for long. Arima had assumed that Cassa had tied it back for flying, as some Steermen did. They would usually loosen it after landing. Cassa kept it that way for a reason.

Cassa's smile broke into a grin, "They're complaining about my hair, again, aren't they? That old argument is as useful as a broken staff!" Antee and Stem both flinched. "What they *really* don't like is that I don't take any sass off of them! Ever!...And never will," she concluded.

Arima was trying to absorb this impossible situation. She had to have Pill's cooperation. No way around it. She would like to have Cassa's. They certainly needed a Blue, and this one seemed as likely as any. Lexter was just too nice. He would never grasp the importance of what they were doing. Cassa had passion, which could work in their favor. Unfortunately, it was her passion that was getting in the way now. Arima made up her mind.

Holding up both hands, she said, "Please just everyone stop for a few beats. Mokam," he looked up at her, "You need to hear this, too. Let's find some shade, first, and have a quiet little talk." The little party tramped through the now-soft soil to the inside edge of the cove, where the wall shaded them. Arima slowly sank to a seated position. When they had all joined her, she began.

"There is indeed a mystery going on here, today. And it's not really Seafer's acorns, though they are part of it. Mokam, Cassa, Antee, and Seafer," she included them all, knowing that Antee would catch on, and hoping that Seafer would, "I have begun a project here that will not include any Guild activity. Anyone's Guild. Now…or ever. I could use your help with that project, but before I am willing to tell you more, you first have to agree…individually…right now…to that condition. If you cannot agree to keep this from your Guild's, then our time here is done. I thank you for what you've done, and we'll all be going home." She waited.

Mokam, who had never thought past getting Seafer's acorns planted, looked puzzled, "What mystery? Seafer, did you know about this? I thought you just wanted to plant a tree!" Seafer did not speak.

Good, he's caught on! The others don't need to know about his involvement if they aren't joining in.

Cassa broke in, "I don't know if I care a lot about your project, Arima, but my curiosity is up. I wouldn't mind finding out what's going on, if it does no harm. Are you planning any harm to the Guilds? Or…*a* Guild?"

Arima shook her head, "No, but they might do harm to me, if they find out what I'm doing." *Or you* she didn't add.

Cassa, "And after everything I've seen today, you're telling me that Mokam and Seafer are not in on this?" She looked at each of them.

Mokam shrugged, "I'm just here to help Seafer plant his tree."

Seafer, "Sure hope it works."

Mokam, "If this isn't about the tree, then what *is* it about?"

Cassa, "Seafer said something about the baby. What's a baby got to do with a tree? I just thought they were here for your Grading."

Seafer, "Oops. Pardon, Arima."

They all stopped. Antee was watching, smiling, enjoying. Arima was waiting with as blank a look as she could put her face into. There was silence.

Beat. Beat. Beat.

Cassa, "Arima, you *oath* me that this does no harm to any Guild!?"

"Cassa, yes. I oath you. I mean no harm to any Guild, including my own. Further, I oath you that nothing I will be doing will in any way hurt *any* Guild. Also, I oath you that I am deadly serious about keeping this completely secret from any Guild. Finally, I oath you that if any of the Guilds finds out what is happening here, they probably *will*...kill...anyone involved." That stopped them again, but they had a right to know. She then added, "One other thing, Cassa. If you do get involved, you will *have* to cooperate with the Pill family. They, in turn, will cooperate with you. Agreed, Pill?"

"We will if she will."

Beat. Beat. Beat.

Antee understood completely the blast of questions and misgivings everyone must be having. He broke the silence, "I'm in, Arima."

Seafer quickly followed, "I'm in too, Arima."

Cassa looked at each of them. She grinned, and said, "You know, I couldn't care less about the Blue Guild! They've never given me anything but a badge, which I earned, thank you. I just don't like the idea of being nice to a Buzzbie!" Throwing up her hands, she exclaimed, "Oh, I'm in! I'm in!"

They all turned to Mokam, who suddenly looked uncomfortable. "Well, I'm too old to care much about dying. My wife has passed, and my children grown. Brown Guild is doing strange things that I don't much agree with. But, Arima, you're asking a lot, on very little." Looking at Seafer, he asked, "Seafer, you really know what's going on here, don't you?"

Seafer nodded.

Well, so much for protecting Seafer.

"And is it worth all of this foolishness?"

Again, Seafer nodded, then added quietly, "And more."

Mokam took a breath, and said, "Good enough, old friend. Arima, I'll go along."

Arima allowed herself to breathe again. "I give regrets, but I have to ask you each to oath me on this."

Before anyone could take offense, Antee again settled it, "I oath you."

Seafer, "I oath you."

Cassa, "Why not? I oath you, Arima."

Mokam, "No such thing as half a hole, Arima. I oath you."

Without any more drama, Arima held her hand out to Stem and Maleef, who had been watching wide-eyed as five Masters were oathing themselves over their baby. "Maleef, bring out your child, pumpkin. Cassa, you guessed right, but you're still in for a shock. No, please keep him wrapped, child."

Maleef set Steef on the ground in the middle of the seated Masters. He sat looking at them and gurgling. Smiling.

Arima began explaining to them about Steef's unusual amount of Power. There was resistance at first, but Seafer chimed in that he had witnessed the Grading, and Antee confirmed that the three Cats that were still sleeping when they had arrived surely represented better than Ten strength. When he added what had happened to his staff, Mokam jerked up.

"I'll have a look at that later, if you like," offered the Brown.

Then, of course, she had to bring in the reason why *they* were all being involved. Oddly, Cassa accepted it right away, but Mokam was skeptical, "Those are just old fables, Arima. Clear can't really happen."

"Mokam," she replied patiently, "I'll gladly make you this offer. If Steef here never shows any sign of Brown power, why, your part in our little family here can be over. All but the oath of silence. If he *does* show Brown though, I'm hoping that you'll train him. Either way, it will be a while before we can know."

She went on, "The ClanCat has agreed to let us stay here indefinitely. Stem and Maleef have also agreed to stay," she nodded to them solemnly. "I will be staying here as well. I plan to leave active White service, and make this my home."

"Me too!" exclaimed Seafer, "I've got to see if my sprouts work!"

For the first time since the conversation began, Antee had a question, "Seafer, you've got my Power plugged on this one. What is so special about a tree? I'd think you would have seen enough trees in your life."

Seafer's face lit up, "I've been wantin' to tell you all day…but figured 'Rima needed to work her things out first." He started talking as much with his hands as his lips, waving around, "No one's ever seen a tree like this!…couldn't plant it without a strong child…it's a staff tree!" And then he was off, "I know, I know, you can make a staff from the wood of almost any tree…but only the hardwoods'll hold a charge without splittin'…and the softwoods pass Power so much faster than hardwoods…but they don't hold up…an' what we needed was a fast wood that wouldn't split, y' see…only there isn't any such…but there is now!…if it grows, o' course…but I'm sure it will…so I worked on joining the two together…a wood as strong as the hards, with the wide grain of the softs…supple, but tough…and I made the acorns from parts o' this an' pieces o' that…only they wouldn't grow!…wouldn't sprout!…less'n o' course I blasted 'em…they sprouted then!…but the saplings I got were tuned to me…only me…and when they grew, I got no new acorns…I think 'cause they'd been blasted…so I needed somethin' to set off the acorns to growin'…somethin' that wouldn't blast 'em…I needed a child…a *really* strong child…raw Power……never 'spected a Clear though!…hoowee!…told 'Rima to watch for me…she's a Grader, y'know…started this thing seventy cycles ago…been just *waitin'* for the last fifteen cycles…put those five acorns in that box fifteen cycles ago…never opened it since…put Locks on it that *no one* could break…and they sprouted!…right through the box and the Locks…the babe here sprouted 'em!…now I'm gonna just sit here the rest o' my days and watch it grow…and hope for acorns!" He didn't really wind down, just had to breathe. "It's gonna work! You'll see!." They didn't know if he was trying to convince them, or himself.

"Seafer, I just have to ask…" Arima said, surprising everyone. They assumed she just knew about it all. "…Why did you only bring one box of acorns? You used to have so many of those things."

Seafer seemed to lose some of his spunk as he replied, "You're right, o' course. Had twenty boxes of five to start…fifteen cycles is a long time…even for acorns…this box was the freshest of the lot…and the last…the others went dry…could o' made more, I suppose…just didn't seem it was ever gonna work out to find the right child…but all five o' these sprouted!…didn't they?…so it's all right…yep, it's gonna be fine…just fine…"

The magnitude of his effort and his long cycles of waiting subdued them all. They also understood now why he'd been so excited for the last two days. Everyone paused a few beats.

Finally, Antee said gently, "Master, won't *this* tree be tuned to Steef?"

Big grin, "Yep! It surely will! Little Steef there will have a treefull of staffs to choose from!…but the acorns!…they'll be untuned…if we get any…and they'll sprout on their own!…just needed to grow one…good…tree."

And finally Cassa got to ask, "But the Dust! All that Dust! What good does Dust do for a tree? It can't be for riching the soil?"

The old Green was still nodding. Arima wondered if he realized his head was moving. "No, little Blue missy, I riched the soil m'self. You watched me do it. In fact, that soil…well, another time…the Dust is for the tree, o' course…it's gonna suck up all that Dust and spread it through and through all the wood…y'see, little Steef here won't be *makin'* staffs from his tree!…oh, no!…hee, hee, hee, hee…he'll be pickin' 'em!"

❦   ❦   ❦

They spent the little bit of the remaining daylight making plans. Seafer had insisted that they make camp near the boat. He had one more surprise for them. That evening, when they were all making ready their pads, Seafer asked that Steef's pad be put exactly on the spot where the acorns were planted.

"You fine children can sleep there, too, o' course," he said generously to the parents, "But it's important that the new sprouts keep gettin' charged from the baby". It did give them their first small measure of privacy since walking into Arima's tent. They took their lantern and pads, and made their way off.

In the morning, Arima had intended to set up her tents until more permanent shelter could be arranged, but Mokam had a better idea. He worked half the morning away with his staff, cutting neat little caves into the rock faces inside the cove. Setting the entrances deep enough that water runoff from the cliffs couldn't get in, he also framed a clever staggered passage that would keep most of the wind out. Fashioning three in each wall, they now had nine separate accommodations. Finally, he framed a sanitary hut near the opening of the cove that straddled the runoff stream feeding into the river. He thought he was done. Seafer didn't think so.

"I need a hut over the sprouts," he announced cheerily. "With a clear top-wall to let light in, and vents to let fresh air in."

Mokam was not amused. In less than a morning, he had already put in a full day. "Whatever for, you old twighead?" he grumbled.

"They're gonna have to have shelter from the weather, o' course."

"Who's going to need shelter?"

"Well, the babe, o' course...an' his Mam an' Pap!...he's got to spend as much time as possible with the sprouts, don't he?...don't figure a small boy'd want to just stand there all day when he's awake, do you?...'course not!...so he's gotta *sleep* there, don't he?...yep!" Seafer considered the matter explained, clapped Mokam on the shoulder, and hobbled off.

Mokam stared at his friend's back for more than a few beats. Shrugging his tired frame, he finally went back to work. Picking a likely section of stoneface, he sliced off five slabs, and floated each of them over to the planting. Four of them became vertical walls. The last one stopped and hovered just above the frame. He called up what looked to an amused Arima like about half a charge, and burst it at the slab. It went completely clear. He set it in place. *Now* he was done, whether he was done or not.

Arima brought him some fresh water and fruit, which he accepted grate-
fully. "Everything you've done here, Mokam, well it's more than I would have
dreamed for. Thank you," she said sincerely. "If it's any comfort to you, I think
we're about done asking from you for a good while. Except for Lifting the
boat."

"You know, Arima, I kind of enjoyed the Lifting. Hate to admit it, but I did.
It had been a long time. I won't mind it every now and then." They had agreed
last night that Cassa's would be the only boat to visit from now on, meaning
also that she would be their supply boat. And whenever Cassa came, Mokam
would be doing her Lifting. For her regular daily work, she would find another
Brown, who, she admitted, probably wouldn't mind a break every now and
then. They had all gotten a laugh from that.

For Cassa, Mokam, and Antee were going back to their regular lives. They
wouldn't live here, at least for now. They had all agreed there was no need for
five Masters to sit here and watch a little boy grow. Steef couldn't start any
Power training before his fourth cycle, and shouldn't be needing Color-specific
training at least until six. Or so they thought, for, they all also had to agree,
their only training was in their own respective Colors, and no one knew how to
train a Clear. What if he could mix his Colors? Who could train him in Pink?
What did Orange Power do? It was an interesting conversation around the fire,
that first night of what they later came to call their 'conspiracy'. It kindled their
imagination. It would not be their last.

Mokam was still talking, around a mouthful of one of Seafer's whitefruits,
"I still want to look at Antee's staff before we leave. Might be able to help him
there."

That reminded Arima. She had oathed Stem to help him with his staff.
"Mokam," she said in her sweetest voice, "Would you happen to have a little
chip of something to make a new staff for Stem? The one he's carrying is just
dead, and I'd like to help him out if we can." She threw in the 'we'.

"Is he really just a Two, Arima?"

She nodded, with a little sigh, "Yes, I'm afraid so. Not a strong one either."

"Well, I wouldn't mind him having one of the wee little Crystals you know,
but I don't think he'd be able to get it charged. Even the smallest. Let me study
on it." He added, "Meanwhile, let's see what we can do for Antee."

Antee had had little to do that morning, so he'd contented himself with sitting in the shade at the edge of the cove, and watching the Cats that passed and
frolicked in his vicinity. That seemed to suit him, for he hadn't moved from the
spot all morning, paying little heed to the activity in the cove. He stood as they

approached. Arima noticed he was still holding his useless staff. *Habit* she thought.

When they reached him, Mokam just held out his hand towards the staff, without a word. Antee handed it over with the same conversation. Mokam examined the shattered stone closely. Finally, he put the stone of his own staff against Antee's and sent a Pulse through it into his cupped hand. His brow furrowed, and he turned the staff around to look at the crafter's mark. Frowning outright, he glanced at Antee, "How long have you had this staff?" he asked.

"Close to ten cycles," replied Antee, "Why?"

Mokam didn't answer. Instead, he asked another question, "Has it given good service? Discharges work all right?"

Truly puzzled now, Antee responded, "Well, to tell the truth, Mokam, I've never been known as a strong Master. My discharges have always fallen a bit short of some others I know."

"Now that's an honest Master."

Arima hoped Antee hadn't heard that from his own Pill, though she agreed with the sentiment.

Mokam gave Antee a warm smile, which was rare for him, "Well Arima would be better at telling you how strong your Yellow glow is, but I can tell you it's a wonder you didn't blow yourself up with this stone. It's flawed. Or *was* flawed…before it became downright cracked."

Arima suspected that Antee was a hard person to surprise, but Mokam had done it. His eyes flew open, then narrowed, "You mean, all these cycles, my *staff* has been impeding my Power? I paid a fortune for that staff!" His face was getting red. "Paid extra to get a Master certified stone! *Life* is at stake with a Master Yellow!" There was spittle flying out, now. "Why, the times I felt so inadequate! Because of my stone? And the beasts I just couldn't…quite…save!" That caught him up, and his face softened, eyes got watery. "Some of those were fine beasts," he whispered, "Fine beasts."

Looking up at them, he said, "Do you ever wish sometimes…that you were a Black? Just for a little while. Could be useful at times."

Mokam took his arm and spoke softly, too, "I can't bring back those beasties you speak of, but I can fix this staff so that it doesn't happen again. The wood appears unharmed."

Antee let his tears fall freely. After a beat, and a deep breath, he said, "Master, I don't mean to tell you your craft, but I'm pretty sure that stone is ruined." He tried to smile a bit, to soften the insult.

Mokam didn't take any insult, "HOAR, HOAR HOAR...'course it's ruined..." this was accompanied with a hard clap on the shoulder "...HOAR, HOAR, HOAR...busted to bits...HOAR, HOAR, HOAR." He gathered himself a bit. "No, no. We'll just replace it...with one of these." He drew out the Crystals that he had put in his pocket the day before, and picked one of the two large ones. "Useful little trinkets. Never leave my caves without a few of them. Never know, y'know."

The rest of the group had noticed the small ruckus, and gathered around them. With a trunk full of Dust being dumped into the ground the day before, they hadn't given much attention to the stones, but they gaped now. Antee exclaimed, "Master, that's a pure, polished Crystal!..."

"Yep, that's what it is, all right."

"...I can't accept that! And I surely can't *pay* for it! Thank you just the same."

Cassa was still impressed from the day before, "Master Mokam, my family's not exactly poor. It's how I can afford to behave pretty much any way I want. But I don't believe my Papa could buy one of those in five cycles of payments! Do y'know what that thing's *worth*?"

Mokam feigned shock, "'Course I know what it's worth...to those thieving scum Red Vaulters in town! It's why they follow me around whenever I leave my caves...because they know I've got 'em. And I do, too. Piles of 'em. And can get more! Hmmm, well. But you know what this little rock actually *cost* me? I'll show you." He spun around and pointed his staff at the nearest rock face, some five staffs away. Arima Saw a bolt of Brown erupt from the staff. The next beat they all heard the screech of groaning stone as a split appeared. Another couple of beats, and a rock flew out, which Mokam floated over and landed at their feet.

"Not actually Crystal, of course. No Crystal in this rock here. But it's a good greenstone. Just needs a bit of cleaning."

"Now!" he went on briskly, "If we've gotten that out of the way! Seafer." He handed Antee's broken staff to Seafer, "Surely a Master Green is good for something more than sticking little nuts in the ground! HOAR, HOAR, HOAR."

Without a word, Seafer held his staff to Antee's, and Pulsed. The wooden fingers that held the stone in place withdrew back into the body of the staff, and the broken pieces of stone fell into Mokam's outstretched hand. Seafer then held the lifeless stick perfectly straight while Mokam balanced the new Crystal at the Power end. One more Pulse from Seafer, and the fingers stretched back out, clasping the new rock. Together, they handed the repaired staff to a speechless Antee.

"You'll be wanting a little care with that at first, Antee," Mokam advised, "It's not a large Crystal really, but it is completely pure. It'll give more charge than you're used to."

Mokam wasn't finished, however, "And with your permission, I'm going to hang on to this mess." He held up the pieces of broken stone. "The crafter's mark on your staff tells me which Brown passed this stone, and he should know better! He *does* know better! He surely will know better when I'm done with him at the GuildHall! And I'll just take this along with me to show them. That *will* be fun!" He stopped and thought for a beat, then grinned. "Hmmm. Don't need every scrap of this, though," he added. One more little burst of his staff, and a clean, balanced chip of stone fell off the main piece.

"Seafer," the Master Brown said, with a wink to Arima, "Could you leave your little sprouts alone long enough to go find me a grade Two stick?"

CHAPTER 6

❀

The cove dwindled from view quickly, as they all waved at Seafer and Maleef on the ground. Everyone else was leaving for one reason or another. Even Arima. She had intended to stay, but Stem had to go back to arrange for some of his kin to work their land. That meant Cassa and Mokam had to make an immediate return trip anyway, so she was going back to GuildTown for a general Healing. She needed her health, and now was the time. This was a remote Valley, and Steef would be needing her for some time. Performing White Healing on yourself was dangerous, and few Masters even attempted it any more, so she needed one last trip in. It would be more courteous to make her formal leave of service in person anyway, rather than use the Buzzbies for the message.

They were going to drop Stem near his home, not at the Landing Field near the Festival meadows. The Landing Field would have left him with a three day walk, so they would swing in to his valley. There was no landing bowl there at all, he said, so he'd just climb down the steprope. *At least he's young* she sighed with some envy.

Antee would be going on with them to GuildTown, where he would catch another boat back to his own land. But he wasn't going to stay there. "We have enough time with the baby that I can finish out my apprentices' current cycle. Then I think I'll just turn that over to the Guild, and get a transfer. I've got some seniority, and the Territory that includes our little cove...," he smiled, "...well, none of my fellow Yellows likes to be assigned there. Too far from where the Dust is. Then, as Yellow Master of the Valley of the Cats, why I have to make official visits, don't I?" He looked very pleased with himself. "They'll think I've plugged my Power for true! Heh, heh. But they'll probably spend most of their time wondering how I got this stone in my staff."

Arima had to admit he had a point. Yellows never made much Dust. The farmers and herders they served didn't have much Dust to pay. He might have the first Crystall'ed staff in Yellow history. He spent most of the morning's boat ride playing with it.

Since there was a lot of flying time in front of them, they had decided to finish that last day out with transferring their remaining goods to the cove, and start off at first light. Seafer, Arima, and Maleef had set up some belongings in individual caves. Even Cassa, Antee, and Mokam spoke about bringing some things in for their own caves. Arima had also taken the time to send a message of her plans to the ClanCat, and that she would be returning for good in just a few days.

When dawn arrived, Seafer met them at the boat with a request for Cassa, "Your pardon, Blue Master, d'ya think…since you're a'leavin' and all…I was wonderin'…"

"You really need to get to the point soon, Master Green," Cassa took a stern tone with him, but her eyes were bright with jest, and her mouth twitched, "I've already called the wind, and he'll be here soon."

"Well…y'see…uh…the sprouts'll be needin' a drink, y'know…and, well…could you call up a wee bit of rain for 'em?" he finally got out. Arima couldn't remember when Seafer was *ever* shy.

"Is that all!? I was expecting something serious, you took so long. Sure! Not a trouble. The pressure's been dropping since yestermorn, anyway." She strode to her boat and, stepping in, put both hands on her mast. Arima watched a small Blue glow gather at the top, then shoot quickly off into the sky. "There you are, Master Green. A nice soaking rain for the next three nights. Now, if you people would be good enough to board, we really should be going. Master Mokam," and she gestured for her new Lifter to place his staff.

Since then, Arima had been watching Antee play with his new stone. The Yellow Master also helped Stem learn how to use a stick that actually worked. Stem, for his part, was gleeful as a child that he could get a Green glow out of it. Antee then took the time to explain to Stem how to draw in the sunlight for a charge, since the young farmer had depended all his life on the Power he got from the ground.

This experience will have the extra benefit of helping the two young people she mused. *That'll feel good. It's been too long since I was of any real service to someone.*

❦   ❦   ❦

Stem had been dropped off and they had traveled the remainder of the day in their own thoughts. There was still a bit of light left when Mokam began descending the boat. Arima looked out and saw a real Landing Field approaching, one of many interspersed around the Territories for travelers on long trips. They would be spending the night in the boat. This was a sparsely populated area, and there were no hirehuts around.

That actually seemed to serve the mood of the four Masters. Conversation around the lanterns was subdued. They would be reaching GuildTown late tomorrow, and the full import of their 'conspiracy' was sinking in. Or so Arima thought. She didn't much mind her own risk. She'd been on the fringe of her Guild for twenty cycles, and held no false hope, or even interest, in repairing the strain. But these other people had some new hard choices facing them. Cassa in particular, was quiet. As little as Arima knew the girl, quiet didn't fit her any more than her newly loosened hair.

"Are you troubled about all this, Cassa?" she asked sincerely. She didn't need to explain what 'all this' was.

Cassa started a bit, brought back to ground from wherever her thoughts had been, "Why no, Master. You mistake me, I think. I'm concerned more about where I'm going to find a Lifter. That last one…you know, I don't even remember his name!…anyway, he deserved the tonguing I gave him, the stonehead!" She jerked back, "Oh! Your pardon, Master Mokam, please…your pardon! I meant no offense to Browns in general!" She truly looked troubled.

"Pardon given, missy," replied Mokam. "In fact, that young whelp *is* a stonehead! He did one cycle of apprenticing in our mines, and his brains never matched his Power." He was scratching his stubbly chin. "You know, miss, I can think of at least six Master Browns who have left active service, and have nothing to do all day but dig holes and fill 'em back up again! I'd wager I could get a few of them to do some Lifting for you." He stopped for a small smile, "Of course, you might want to practice a bit of easytongue on 'em. They've got too many cycles on 'em, after all, and the force of you just might kill one of them…HOAR, HOAR, HOAR!"

Cassa spent the remainder of the evening bouncing from sheepish, to glum, to cheery. Arima felt for her growing pangs. *She realizes that this nice little boat isn't good for much if it's stuck on the ground.*

❦   ❦   ❦

Over the small peaks, the traffic sleds with their brightly colored flags came into view first. Once inside the ridgeline, the familiar shapes of the seven GuildHalls dominated the valley floor that was GuildTown. Located just south of center in the nine Territories, it was the largest collection of people any-where, and all activity was connected one way or another to the Guilds.

This valley also ran north and south. Smaller than the Valley of the Cats, and not as steep, it was full of huts and tents. The huts spread north, past Town proper, filling the valley and climbing partway up the northern slopes.

Immediately below them, occupying the southern tip of the valley, the larg-est Landing Field in the Territories. They were making their way there now, but had had to slow down to enter the traffic lanes. The controllers' sleds were arranged all up and down the valley, floating in place on tethers. They all had directional flags waving. Cycles ago, an attempt had been made to use Buzzbies for traffic messages, but the flags had proven easier to understand. They weren't subject to interpretation.

On the eastern side of Town was the arena where most social events were held: Festivals, sporting matches, and duels. She knew the arena well. It was a bowl in the ground, the flat center of which was exactly fifty staffs across in every direction. The sloping sides had been stepped for seating. All of it artifi-cially cut out long ago by Brown apprentices needing practice.

She could also see off to the west of town, separated by intervening fields, Nert Hollow. She had long felt guilty calling it that, even to herself. But in truth, the inhabitants of the place called it that themselves. They were Power-less people, relegated to roles of service and labor in Town. The meager amounts of Dust they earned barely kept them alive, their existence noted by the wealthy in Town only when a service didn't get done.

Arima had spent a lot of time there during her own apprentice cycles, offer-ing Healing for free to those who would accept it. Not all did. Some called it 'unnatural'. Some were openly resentful, or even hostile to anyone with a staff. She had found the large side-town remarkably clean, the rows of worn tents and old camps maintained from necessity and pride. The food offered had been simple, but tasty. And those that did receive her had always offered their best. Eventually, her Guild learned of these excursions, and made her stop. 'Can't be giving away Healing for free, can we?' she was told. 'Why, those ragtag would come to expect it'.

There was an awkward few beats when they landed, for Antee was taking his leave of them. The others would be traveling together at least once more, but he was going on in the morning to his home. Their friendship had been too brief for truly warm parting greets, and too intense for anything formal. So they settled for awkwardness, and a shoulder-clasp apiece. Mokam headed off to the Brown Hall, Cassa to her parents' hut, leaving Arima and Antee standing alone.

"Arima, whatever comes next," he began, "It bears repeating that I think you were right all along. One more full day, and you're out of it. Don't let them beat you down." Without waiting for a response, he turned and strode off.

It was dark when she arrived at the White GuilHall. She paused a beat on the steps to gaze up at the lanterned façade, and sighed. The stonework that was the three story front wall was adorned with a single stone carving. A pair of HornCat horns, stretching up directly over the entrance door and reaching the windows of the third floor. For the last twenty cycles, every visit she had made to this Hall, and her visits were becoming rare, she expected the carvings to be gone. She had come to wish they *would* remove them. It had gone past irony, and was now insulting, at least to her. She made her way inside to the third floor padcloset that had become her home some eighty-plus cycles ago. All active Masters were accorded their own permanent privacy closet until they left service, or died. This would be her last stay here. She would never have dreamed, on her first night here, that it would become a place of dread. She wouldn't miss it now.

Next morning, she made her way to the ground floor public closets. A few of the Guild people she passed gave greets…but only a few. The public halls opened to the road, of course, but there was a back hallway for Guild use, and she wended her way through until she came to the roster board, wanting to see who was on duty. She didn't know most of the names, many of them working their apprentice time under the careful eyes of their respective trainers. Spotting a name she knew and could relax with, she headed for the appropriate halls to which he was assigned. Finding a seat at their back entrances, she sat and waited. Eventually, he came out of one of them, saw her, and bowed slightly.

"Bright day, Master Arima," offered Ormis, "May I be of service?"

She had always had difficulty liking Ormis. She had been one of his many tutors, back forty…no, fifty some cycles ago. It wasn't that Ormis had offensive manners to him. Just the opposite. He was so bland, she had often thought of him as emotionally inert. And it wasn't as if Ormis' life was easy. He was a Ten that had never made Master. Never really been considered for the Mastery program, and had never questioned the Guild's decision. Enough Power to be useful, not enough to be influential. So, while she didn't enjoy him much, she respected him, for he handled his place in life gracefully. Not being a Master, he had had no voice in the turmoil that swirled around her twenty cycles ago. He would do.

She stood and returned his bow. "And a bright day to you, Ormis," she responded cordially. "I require a complete Freshening. Would you have the beats and the space?"

"I am at your disposal, Master," was his reply. "But perhaps I should get a Master for you?" It wasn't unheard-of for Masters to receive Healings from non-Masters, just rare. It often took Master strength Power to push through a Master's system and be thorough.

"You and your strength will suffice, Ormis. Unless you've forgotten how to do a Freshening?" She gave him a shrewd look.

He looked startled briefly, then nodded, "That was a jest, wasn't it Master? And a compliment, as well, I think. I thank you for both. Shall we begin?" He gestured to one of his assigned closets.

She noted upon entering, that nothing had changed in this closet since she had done her own apprenticing. Same stone walls, same dirt floor, same rack of Guild-owned staffs in varying strengths. Draining her own staff, she placed it into the rack in one of the empty slots left there for that purpose. Without a word, she stretched herself out on the dirt. Ormis took the strongest staff in the rack, and sank it into the floor at her head. Then kneeling over her, he began to run his hands down either side of her, beginning at her head, and ending at her feet. Concluding his search Pulses, he stood again, and spoke down to her.

"Nothing we wouldn't expect, Master. It appears that you haven't had a Freshening in about twelve cycles, and you are indeed due. But I really need to get a stronger staff for you. Will you excuse me?"

"You may take mine Ormis, if you like."

He gave her a quizzical look, "Master, you surprise me. You had that same staff when you trained me. You know that over the cycles, it must have picked up some of your tune. Any Healing that staff did on you would…"

"I meant, Ormis," she was firm, but not unkind. She had to stop him. She only had one day. "That you could use mine elsewhere if needed, to free up another." She smiled slightly.

"Oh...thank you, Master, but I'm sure I can find one. I won't be long." He left.

Arima spent half the morning lying on the ground, with the staff above her pumping out White Power. The light filled the closet, at least for her. For what seemed to her the thousand times thousandth time, she gave a silent intone of thanks to the Creator for gifting her with Sight. She would never quite understand how Power people could gauge their usage without Seeing their own Power, even though she had taught the principles many times over to apprentices. She could feel the Healing flow through her, Freshening her joints and muscles, and knowing it was doing the same to her organs. When she was done, she felt ten cycles younger, which of course, she was.

Well, not really she thought. She knew that a Freshening could push back aging, but you couldn't stop it completely. A ten-cycle Freshening really gave you an extra six or seven cycles, if you didn't abuse yourself by, say, falling out of trees. Like some people she knew.

The staff had stopped for only a few beats when Ormis re-entered. He helped her up, and placed the staff in the rack. Taking her own, she gave him a serious bow, "I thank you, Healer, for your gift. May you receive many such yourself," she intoned from cycles of repetition.

But Ormis didn't complete the ceremony. He looked a bit embarrassed. "Your pardon, Master," he didn't meet her gaze, "But there are new GuildLaws. There is now...a...fee."

She looked at him in surprise for several beats while he almost squirmed. Then she gave an hesitant laugh, "Ormis...did you just make a *jest*? Good for you!"

Ormis was still squirming, "I wish it *were* a jest, Master," he still didn't look up. "They require us to charge all Guild members now, regardless. A fee for the Guild, and...another...for my time." There was an awkward silence for several beats.

"I offer regrets for your discomfort, Ormis," she said gently. "I will gladly pay. But if you dislike it so much, why go along with this silliness?" She took her Dustbags off of her belt as she spoke, and opened one, retrieving her cups.

He looked up now, "They are serious about their new GuildLaws, Master. They took staffs from several who refused. I cannot help people if I have no staff...so, I collect their Dust, and I give my share to some Messengers I trust. It goes where it will help." Seeing her holding her bags, he continued, "Your pardon, Master...it's two and one, cup one, grade Two."

Taking her bag of Two, and the smallest of her three cups, she scooped two scoops into his outstretched Guild bag, and one cup into his personal bag. Each of them put their belongings away.

"Ormis, I have held out hope for you since first you apprenticed with me," she said seriously. "You have confirmed that hope today, while at the same time, taking my Dust. Be well, and may all your days be bright." With that, they parted.

She was hungry, but that would have to wait. She had skipped firstmeal, not wanting any food inside her for the Freshening. And Freshenings always left you hungry anyway, your newly charged body starting to hotly burn fuel right away. But she put that off to go back to her padcloset, and gather the few private things she had kept there over the cycles. Once she left the Hall, she wasn't coming back.

Carrying her bags, she next made her way to the official closet of the Guild, and went through the formalities of leaving active service. It was custom for Masters with assigned Territories to give warning before taking leave, but the Guild officers she met with didn't seem to mind her suddenness at all. In fact, they seemed pleased. She took that as a sign that future re-instatement might be a little difficult. This severing of their relations was permanent. She kept telling herself that it didn't matter, it didn't matter. What finally helped was a vision of their new cove, and spending time with Rivverr. She decided she could eat a bit of something.

Arima knew that most of the hostels in town were owned by Reds. She didn't trust many Reds, certainly none that operated hirehuts. You might find yourself eating old moldy food, and begging for more. So she made herself go to the Guild's own dining Hall, which was mercifully almost empty. Taking some food, which she now had to pay for, she found a table and sat alone to eat in peace. She almost made it, her small meal nearly completed when a sweet voice behind her made her stop.

"Arima! It's *sooo* good to see you! I *dooo* hope all of your days have been bright! Now, *wwhhat's* this I hear about you?"

She didn't turn around. There was no need. Putting her lapcloth to her mouth, she spit a mouthful of food back into the cloth. She wouldn't be wanting any more food. "Greets, Vinntag," Arima said, with no small resignation, "There is no guessing what you might have heard about me." *Or said yourself.*

Arima didn't bother to rise, or even move. *Let the lying begin* she thought, tiredly.

Arima's back didn't deter Vinntag. She bustled around the table so that they were facing each other. She was a short woman, more than a span shorter than Arima. Dressed in expensive tunic and trous, with embroidery from the ground up. Even her badge was embroidered, instead of attached. A White Ten, with Master's marks, Grader's marks, and now, Arima saw, Council Member's marks. All stitched onto the tunic by hand. Not Vinntag's hand, she was sure. *No, probably some desperately poor Inert. Someone with talent and no hope.*

Vinntag was carrying a staff that had to weigh at least half what she weighed herself. Arima glanced at the staff with concealed amusement. It was a full staff tall, towering over the small woman. Its stone was a pure Crystal the size of Arima's fist. *I wonder if she can charge that thing? Probably not.* Hand carving covered the top third of the wood. But it wasn't the size or expense that amused Arima. It was the inlay. Yellowmetal inlay throughout the carving. Any Pulse of Power above level Five would melt that yellowmetal instantly. Vinntag had no intention of *using* her staff, just displaying it.

"*Wwelll*, that you're *lleeaving* us of course!"

"Yes, I am leaving active service," Arima answered with little emotion. *Which is why you came looking for me. To gloat.*

"Why *deearr* Arima, you just *mmusst* reconsider! *Howwevver* will we get by without you?"

Arima knew that Vinntag didn't expect a serious answer to any of this, so she offered none. Instead, she shifted the topic. "That is a fine looking staff, Vinntag. The inlay is particularly attractive." What she was really saying was 'that's a truly expensive toy you've got there'. Both women knew it.

"Oooh, thannk you, Arima! It's Council Member quality, of course. You know, we really *mmusst* see about getting *yoouu* a new staff soon. Dear me, why you've had *tthhatt* one for as long as I can remember!"

Actually, Arima *had* had this staff for as long as she'd known Vinntag. She had brought her old staff on this journey, leaving the unregistered one back in her new cave, safe. This was the same staff she'd carried in her first cycle of Master's apprenticeship. Her parents had saved Dust for three cycles to buy it. It had no adornments, and it carried a greenstone, which was also plain, but very large. The stone had proven over many cycles to be pure and sound, handling all of her discharges without taking any hurt. And Arima had had to prove the staff's worth almost immediately upon arrival at this very GuildHall, with the woman facing her now.

Arima had been seventeen when she arrived to start her apprenticeship. Most students weren't admitted to Master's apprentice training until they were eighteen, so her age drew attention. She came from a modest family. Vinntag's family was wealthy. Vinntag was in her fourth and last cycle then, and had a reputation of being the strongest Ten of any student at the GuildHall. A reputation that Vinntag liked, and planned to maintain. Every Ten that arrived got a duel challenge from Vinntag, the beat they appeared. Some declined, and were forever branded and snickered at. Arima had never declined a challenge. She'd also never lost one. And each defeat infuriated Vinntag enough that she would immediately challenge again. The sixth, and last duel occurred at the end of that first cycle of school. Vinntag had foolishly posted this one on the public boards, so the duel had to be held in the arena, instead of on White grounds. Vinntag had arrived with a flourish, brandishing her new staff. She always did like flashy staffs. This was, of course, the sixth staff she'd carried this cycle, as the other five were now ashes. Vinntag was sure this staff would prove strong enough.

Vinntag knew better, of course. She wasn't fogheaded, just desperate. The best staff in the Territories couldn't make up for a lack of Power. That duel had left Vinntag with a day-long nap, and needing a seventh staff. It also served to establish Arima's Power status in her Guild. She'd had very few challenges for the rest of her cycles of study. All of that…done with the same worn staff that Arima now had leaning against the table. Both women knew that, too.

"Well, this one has always seemed to serve me well enough, Vinntag," Arima replied with an impartial face. Did she see just a flicker in that frozen smile Vinntag always wore? "So when did the Guild start charging its own members for Healings? And food?"

Vinntag's smile took on a look of satisfaction, "Isn't that just the *besst* idea!? We are *allso* improving our charges to the public. The extra profits will help improve the grounds, and *aalll* Whites can start enjoying a better life!" She was actually squirming with glee.

That explains the expensive new staff Arima thought. What she said was, "I'm unclear how charging our own members is going to give them a better life, Vinntag."

"Why Arima! What a positively *wwickked* thing to say! You'll see. I'm *verry* excited for the future of White Guild!" When Arima gave no reply, the small Master went on, "I understand *yoouu* made a trip back to the Valley, Arima. *Whatevvverr* for?" Vinntag's voice was as syrupy sweet as ever, but she was throwing her best Pulse. It was Vinntag that had begun, and led, the movement to abandon the Cats. She was reminding Arima that she had won the duel that mattered.

Not that Arima would ever forget. Every conversation with Vinntag was a duel in itself for Arima. The woman represented everything Arima detested in her own Guild. But Vinntag had the lure of Dust to attract support, and Arima knew from long experience that these battles were lost before they began. Only now there was something back in the Valley to give her hope. Something the older woman couldn't know or understand. Or hurt. It was time to end this final duel. She had other duties to complete today.

"Sentiment, Vinntag. I missed them." *Well, that IS one of the reasons I went.* It wasn't a complete lie.

Vinntag had to have the last word, "Well, then maybe this *rresst* will do you some good. I *dooo* hope so! Bright days to you, Arima." And it was over.

     ❦   ❦   ❦

When Arima exited the Guildhall, she stopped at the bottom of the steps, and just stood for a long beat with her back to the wall. Taking a deep breath, she turned toward the center of Town. One test left.

"Pill, is my brother at his work?" she asked quietly.

"Arima, you know we don't keep up with non-Masters."

"Well, can you find out? I should at least see him before I leave."

"Pills aren't allowed to Pop! into the Vault any more, Arima. We'll have to ask a Pool. We will, if you insist."

"No, I don't need to know that badly. Can you still go into the Vault on me?"

"Yes, but only the two of us. And we can't leave you once we're inside."

"Well, he's probably there. And if not, they'll know where he is. But all of these new rules are making for a strange and unsettling world."

"One reason we're cooperating with your project in the Valley."

"Surely you aren't counting on one little boy to repair all this?" She swept her hand at the Town, as best she could. She was carrying several bags along with her staff.

"No. We're counting on a strong and unique Master to get proper training, without agenda. If that happens, we expect to witness a lot of fun. He's a bit out-numbered to be saving the world, no matter how strong he is."

Arima was impressed, "Pill, do you realize that you just gave me an answer that made sense?"

"A mistake. We'll be more careful."

        ❧   ❧   ❧

The Vault was an imposing structure. It had been designed completely square in each direction, and was three stories tall. There had been heated debate at the time of its construction. The Red Guild wanted more floors, but since all Guild buildings were three, every other Guild had complained until the Reds had relented. They got in the final Pulse, however. There were several floors underground, formed by Browns at Red expense. No one but the Vaulters now knew just how deep it went.

As Arima entered, she Saw that the main hall was filled with Red glow. *They aren't even trying to hide it any more* she sighed to herself. She knew that several sets of eyes were watching her trundle up to a receiving table.

"I would like to meet with Vaulter Maar, please," was what she gave to the polished man she faced. Every hair was exactly aligned. No wrinkle would dare approach his tunic. He even smelled nice. He wore a Six.

"Would you care to state the nature of your concern, Madam?" he asked smoothly.

"No," she didn't give it rudely, she didn't give it kindly. She waited. He waited.

She noticed that the table quickly began to glow a brighter Red. "Don't you think it best that you mention your business with so important a Vaulter, Madam?" His voice was starting to sound positively silky, almost musical.

She brought her gaze back to his eyes. *Clever of them to bury a stone somewhere in the table, making it an operational staff.* Shrugging the carrybag off of her left shoulder, she revealed her badge. Tapping the Grader's mark below her Ten, she said, "You're wasting your Red, young man. My business is my own. You may, however, tell him his sister would like a few short beats." She started waiting some more. The young man never stopped smiling, or being polished. He also never moved or twitched from his table. In spite of that, after a couple hundred beats of them waiting at each other, a tall slender man in expensive tunic emerged from a door in the back wall. He also just waited, until Arima's gaze turned that way. Gathering her things, she marched across the floor through a wall of stares, and a few whispers of 'That's Arima!' 'That's *her!*' and so on. Her bags, her wild Master's hair, her worn tunic and staff, all in contrast to the sanitary Vault and its occupants.

"Well, this is fun," buzzed the left-side Buzzbie.

"*Antee was right,*" came from the right, "*We'd love to see them jump if your stone glowed Black right now.*"

She let the two Pills banter. It helped her focus.

Once inside Maar's workcloset, she and her brother faced each other stiffly. He with his hands clasped behind him. She didn't bother to set her bundles down, this wouldn't take long.

He broke the silence, "I see you still don't mind embarrassing me." His voice was a Vaulter's silk. She would have preferred a cold voice, but that would have been too honest for him.

"It's not like they just discovered I was your sister, Maar. If they think less of you for it, my being here won't make any difference." She gave him a beat for a reply, but there was none.

"I'm not here to bicker, Maar. I came to tell you that I have left active service. I will be making my home some distance from here. It will be a great while before we see each other again." *If at all* she didn't add.

Still he didn't reply. She couldn't help noticing that he still made a habit of glancing at her badge, covered as it was by her bundles. His gaze strayed there again and again. She had never mentioned it to him. She doubted that he knew he was doing it. But there was a White Ten on her shoulder, with Master marks, and a Red Nine on his. He'd grown up watching his older sister get the attention, the influence, the Power. His entire youth had been spent on an inner battle between the sister he once loved and enjoyed, and the ambition and attention he craved. When the ambition finally won, everyone in the family had lost.

The two of them hadn't ever actually spoken on the true cause of his resentment. Perhaps the stress of the day caused her rashness. Maybe it was her concern that she might not see him again. She took a chance, "If it had been a choice I could make Maar, I would have gladly traded badges with you, to get my brother back." Her voice was soft and hopeful.

He continued his glare at her, but his fixed features acknowledged her by a pursing of lips, "At least I made the most of the gift I *was* given," he came back with. She hadn't expected much, but that was a *bit* more honesty than she would have looked for.

Well, it's not like I should be surprised. She didn't bother to point out that he had achieved all of the status and wealth anyone could want, without a Ten badge. All that envy wasted.

"Well," she said briskly, "Let's strike our deal, then. I would ask that you be the handler of my Dustpile, in my absence. I will occasionally need to make purchases. Also, since my Pills are no longer allowed in this building, I'd like to send any of these transactions to you at your home. Is any of that objectionable?"

He gave a small shake of his head. Whatever his faults, he was scrupulously honest in all deal strikings, especially when Dust was involved. It was a large factor in his success, in a world of Vaulter Tens. And he was still her brother. He might not like it, but he'd do it.

"Thank you, Maar. Deal struck. May I ask about Linzel and the girls?"

"Linzel is well. The girls have already been Graded, 'Rima. You needn't concern yourself."

She knew that. He'd gotten Vinntag to do the Grading, of course. To Maar, it would be imperative to use the most prestigious means to anything, and Vinntag was the highest ranking Grader still active. Arima had not bothered to inquire on their Gradings, since anything Vinntag touched was subject to the amount of Dust involved. There was no point in mentioning to Maar that she'd known about the Grading. Non-Masters never really appreciated the impact of Buzzbies. "I understand Maar. I was wondering, though. I have a few extra beats today, not many, but a few. It's almost on the way. Would you mind if I stopped in to meet my nieces?"

He flinched at the 'nieces'. "It would be best if you didn't, 'Rima."

She stood silent then, regarding her brother. Finally, she said, "Then I will leave you. Thank you for your beats, Maar. May you find brighter days."

✹   ✹   ✹

One last deal to strike. She found herself standing at the head of Mercantile Row. Looking down the long line of stone buildings, the Red glow made her eyes sting. She took out her lenses, and put them on.

"Pill, if I start behaving oddly, or purchasing things I don't need, mention it please. And if it gets really bad, get word to my brother. He'll make them stop."

"How will we know when your behavior is odder than usual?"

"Well, for one thing, I would probably be acting politely to insects." With that, she ventured down the Row.

Anything made commercially in the Territories could be found for sale here. There were several staff crafters, of course. Even two small shops that would sell you a boat. They didn't keep them here, these were just the striking shops. Garments. Furniture. All of the mercantiles were owned and run by Reds.

Commerce wasn't the only thing Reds did, but Reds were the only ones doing it.

Not all Reds were dishonest. She could remember that in her lifetime, the Red Guild was more interested in scholarship than Dust. They had spent their Power on communicating knowledge. Now they were focused on persuasion, and separating the unwary from their Dust. They had started changing their motives long before the Whites. Now, few Reds could be trusted. One of the few who still could, owned a general mercantile, or at least he did. She made her way there now.

The large shop was exactly as she remembered. All of the shelves were stocked neatly, with the wares grouped sensibly so that people could shop without hindrance. She was always struck by the floor. There actually *was* a floor. Wooden one at that. Dilruk didn't need his feet on dirt to strike deals. He brokered goods and services, not Power. The floor was a reassurance to her. A new owner would probably have removed it immediately.

Amid the other customers and clerks, she didn't see him, so she waited just inside the entrance. She knew he'd see her. He saw everyone in his shop. She didn't have to wait long, "Arima, I'll be right out," came a muffled voice from one of the back closets.

He MUST be doing that with Buzzbies. She hadn't seen or heard any, but it felt better than believing he could see through walls.

The portly merchant came through a back door removing his flour-covered apron, and took a fresh one from under the counter. He put it on as he scurried to her. "Bright day to you, Master Healer! It has been too many cycles since your shadow fell on this floor. You are well?" Timing himself to finish his greets just as he stopped in front of her, almost tipping on the balance of his toes, with hands clasped together at his chest. He never carried his staff in the shop, despite his rank.

"A very bright day to you, Master Merchant," she returned with a satisfied sigh. "And yes, I am well, thank you. The rich aroma of this place would Freshen anyone."

"I know why you're here, Arima," he said with a gleam in his eye, "But you're too late. Your Dust is useless to you here now, and I'll not be peddling you a thing." He broke into a broad grin.

"Well, don't let your Guild hear you say that, Dilruk. They'd take your staff for sure."

"They can have my staff, Arima. Haven't used it in cycles, anyway. I wouldn't carry it at all, but my Mate won't let me out of the hut without it. She says it would be shocking." He reinforced his grin, "But I'm serious, Arima. I won't peddle you anything at all."

His good humor was soothing enough that she didn't mind his baiting, "All right Dilruk, *why* won't you peddle me anything?"

"Becaauusse…an extremely wealthy Master Brown was here at first light this morning. He gave me two things. A list of supplies…and *this*." Dilruk reached under his apron, and into a pocket. He drew out his hand and held up a Crystal. It was the second large Crystal that Mokam had been carrying. "This Master Brown…he had a strange laugh, by the way…told me to watch for a Master Healer named Arima. This Healer would be on the Row sometime today to buy supplies. Without fail, she should be found and prevented from spending her own Dust." Dilruk looked about as content as he could get, and he was practiced at being content, "As if I needed to watch for you. Where else would you be deal striking?"

Then his business sense got the better of him, "I've been holding this all day. You did take plenty of beats getting here. This needs to get to the Vault…with a little escort, too." He held up an arm, and snapped his fingers. One of the clerks came rushing over, as did two other people. She hadn't noticed them before, but two Seven Blacks had been standing quietly in one corner, watching everything. Handing the Crystal to his clerk, he said, "They're expecting you. Hurry now." The three of them left.

"Well Arima, I know your tastes, and unless you're planning on starting up a Healing colony, it will take you a while to spend that! Look over this list, and see if anything has been left out. We've already delivered these goods to a boat out in the Field, and I sent two more guards to watch it." He handed her the list.

Mokam had been fairly thorough. She only added some Healing powders and potions that he wouldn't have thought of anyway. A bit of bread and cheese for lastmeal tonight. And, as a last thought, a few toys for the child. Dilruk noted all of it, and nodded.

"We'll send this over right away. I think I'll just keep those guards there overnight…'til you leave in the morning. And I've got something else to show you." He spun around and raced over to his counter, with her slugging along behind. He pulled a sack out from behind the counter.

"When I heard you were coming, I sent for these," he said, opening the bag. He pulled out a round orange fruit. "Tangyfruit. First picking of the cycle. The little ones that you like. And Arima…these aren't going on the tab," this last was given with a wink. "Now unless you're just Mated to all those bags, why don't we put them on the cart, and have my boys drop them at the boat on this last trip?"

❦   ❦   ❦

Arima was standing outside the shop, absently peeling the one tangyfruit she had kept out of the sack. The rest of the fruit, her purchases, and her own bags were on their way to Cassa's boat. She was lightened in spirit and load. The first bite of fruit was sweet, and juice ran onto her chin.

She intended to spend the night on the boat. The weather was clear, if a little brisk. She could have ridden the cart there, but there was still a bit of daylight left, and Dilruk had put a bit of frisky back into her.

"Pill, you're going to occasionally need to bring messages to my brother," she pondered aloud.

"True. Your point?"

"Well, it occurs to me that you need to know where he lives."

"That's a mistake, Arima. When we need to, we can ask Peel."

"We won't stop, we'll just blow right by, like a quiet wind."

"And while we're blowing, maybe catch a look at two little girls?"

"Pill, I don't know what you're talking about."

"Arima, you don't need enemies. You do just fine on your own."

❦   ❦   ❦

They were almost within sight of the hut when Pill spoke again.

Pop! *"She knows you're coming!"*

"How? You didn't tell her."

"You're not really THAT thick, Arima…well, you're here, aren't you?…maybe you ARE that thick. She has her OWN Buzzbies, you know. Peel is with her."

Arima didn't reply. The hut was just coming into view, and Linzel was standing on the stoop, staff in hand. Arima continued down the lane until she was directly in front of the hut. Stopping, she turned to face Linzel. They were about four staffs apart.

"She can kill you from here, you know. Maar made it clear…"

Arima whispered, "From here, Pill, she could kill me anywhere in Town. Now be still, she's not killing anyone today."

Her brother had Mated well. Very well. That had been his intention, of course. He had Mated fairly late in his life, to a much younger woman. He had been waiting for exactly the right combination. Linzel was truly beautiful, and her beauty was all hers. No cosmetic Healing here. As a Grader, Arima could See when someone had traces of cosmetic Healings. They always left White smudges. Some women had smudges all over them. Some men, too. If she paid attention, a brief walk through Town was a comical trip. But Linzel was carrying only what the Creator had given her, and still bested most of the beauties in Town.

Just as important to Maar's selection was her Power. Linzel was a full Master Black. Arima had never known if Maar specifically wanted Black, but he certainly wanted a full Master. If he couldn't *be* one, then he was going to Mate one. When Linzel came along, Maar had pursued her relentlessly, lavishing gifts on her poor family. Maar had also befriended Linzel's brother Zellin, a Master Green. The two of them had similar...interests. Linzel's Father had relented, and coerced her into Mating with the much older Vaulter.

Now in her mid-forties, she had repaid Maar well. She had refused to bear him children for over twenty cycles. Only the Creator knew what had changed her mind.

Arima liked Linzel. She was also sad for the girl...woman, now...and her sterile life. It wasn't unusual for Matings to be deals struck, affairs of Dust or mutual family's benefit, but this was extreme. In turn, Linzel had always been warm to Arima, for reasons that she'd kept to herself.

And so, here they were, facing each other. They didn't have Maar's permission to speak, and unless Linzel was going to kill him soon, they really should have his permission. It *was* his family, like it or not.

When forever was just about done, Linzel raised her staff...

"We tried to tell you..."

...grasping it in both hands, she bowed low. Her stone began to glow, the Black Power fairly blazing until the woman herself was hard to see. Arima returned the bow and the glow. Should anyone have been watching, it would have been a real show, Black on White. When the greeting was over, Linzel raised one finger, and leaving her staff still glowing slightly, turned and went into the hut. She emerged with her daughters, one in each arm. She set them on the edge of the stoop, where they each held onto a separate leg of their Mother for support, looking at the strange woman in the road.

They were of slightly different heights. The smaller of the two had her Mother's red hair, and her Father's Red Power. From here, she looked to be a Six, perhaps a weak Seven. The taller girl was of slender build, with the same dark hair that Arima had once enjoyed. And she had her own Power blaze going, as well…White. She was a Ten White.

It was too much. Just…too much. Vinntag she could handle. Maar too. Those were old pains that she knew how to deal with. This was a new pain, and unfamiliar. Hands sliding down her staff, Arima slowly sank to her knees, as sobs began blasting through her like a discharge. So much to be missed.

It took her a while to recover. When she finally looked up, she saw that Linzel had been quietly weeping with her.

Despite the Freshening this morning, she felt old. Slowly pulling herself up by her staff, she met Linzel's gaze again. The younger woman made no effort to hide her own grief. In Linzel's face was the loss of a friend. Her daughters' loss of an Aunt. The professional loss that one of her daughters could've enjoyed having a Master tutor. For her part, Arima longed to tell Linzel about the Valley. About the ClanCat. *Come with me, Linzel. There's a little boy there who needs a Black Master.* She wanted to say so many……well.

Maar should be pleased. Neither of them had spoken a word. It had been the best conversation of Arima's life. With another bow, she left.

"We offer regrets, Arima. That was really hard."

"Pill, some pains are worth owning."

❁   ❁   ❁

Cassa found her the next morning, just before sunrise. She was curled up in her pad, on top of an amazing pile of crates in the bottom of the boat. There was a bit of cheese and bread next to her, uneaten. The Blue Master knelt and touched the Healer's shoulder, bringing her awake instantly.

"Your pardon, Master, but you look terrible. Are you ill? Did you have a troubling yesterday?"

Arima sat up, and surprised herself by reaching for the bread, taking a nibble, "I've had worse," she said around the food.

Sadly, that had once been true. But the Valley beckoned. It was time to wait for a little boy to grow.

CHAPTER 7

"Antreema! Antreema! Antreema! Antreema! Antreema! Antreema! Antreema! Antreema!"

Arima was in her usual place. Rivverr was stretched out asleep in the shade, and she was sitting propped against him. They were just outside the cove, under a rock outcrop that Mokam had formed a cycle ago. None of the adults much stayed in the cove for anything but sleeping any more. It had become Steef's playground, and for safety's sake, they mostly stayed out here.

They had all waited as long as they could. It was planting Quarter now, with everything turning green and growing. This coming harvest Quarter, the boy would be four. It was customary to wait until a child's fourth birthday before starting any training at all, but it couldn't wait any longer, or someone was going to be killed. Just ten days ago, after a particularly full day of charging around the cove, and climbing on the rockface of the cove, and playing in the waterspills of the cove, Steef was coming in to his Mother's call for lastmeal. The tiny body that headed her way was full up. Full of a good day's play. Full of excitement. Full of Power. Just as he reached her, something tickled his nose, and he sneezed. What came out of his nose could be cleaned. But what came out of his mouth was Black, and it blew a hole in Maleef's upper leg. Thankfully, it missed the bone, but Arima had spent the better part of two days Healing the woman, and contemplating what the wound would have done with a different aim.

For almost three cycles, all of them had come to jump whenever Steef had displayed any bodily function. Burps, belches, hiccups, coughs, even breaking wind, all held unpredictable peril. Thankfully, the occurrences were all trickle releases, and not real discharges. Some of them had even been funny. A burp might bring a small herd of beasts galloping up to stop at the edge of the cove, waiting expectantly. A day of hiccups had once left the cove covered in beautiful flowering plants. But there were the more serious incidents as well. At two, Steef was still getting his legs under him, when, after a tripping spree, he had caught himself on a rock wall, only to find the rock as soft as porridge. Both hands had sunk in up to the elbow, when suddenly the stoneface hardened back up. Steef was unhurt, but he was thoroughly stuck. They'd had to feed him and clean him, in place, for the five days it took for Cassa and Mokam to clear their duties and come fetch him out. The child had spent the entire time with a look of wonder on his face, as if contemplating why he couldn't get his hands out. He hadn't cried once.

Nor had he cried the next cycle when a windstorm almost killed him. The adults had decided that outdoor play might be safer away from the rock walls of the cove, and carried him out into the open flatland. He had spent the morning chasing flutterbyes, and having a staff-full of fun. Then one of the dainty insects landed on Steef's nose. He was thrilled, of course, and began dancing cross-eyed around in circles, with his hands waving wildly above his head. The resulting wind had knocked all the adults flat, while the boy's tiny body was picked up and flung a distance of eight staffs, where he landed in a heap. That one had taken Arima eight days to Heal, and was very close. Steef never complained, but he lost his taste for flutterbyes after that.

Steef's nature complicated the situation. The child just loved hugs. He'd hug any leg that came into view. He had left off reaching to be picked up, but would attack anyone's legs with gusto. To the Masters, it was warming and terrifying. Two of them just didn't allow it. Mokam was one, insisting on formality, requiring a bow from the boy at each meeting. "He's got to learn decorum," was his explanation to the other's surprise. Arima was the other reluctant huggee, for a much different reason. The headaches. The older Steef got, the more raw Power he radiated, and the more her head hurt if he got close. She had taught him to keep a distance of two staffs from her at all times, and though he obeyed, it was obvious he didn't understand.

So, when it was clear that Maleef would keep her leg, Arima and Seafer had sent out their Buzzbies with a call for a gathering. It was time to teach Steef to drain, if they could. Draining would solve everyone's problems. Well, not Mokam's passion for decorum, but everyone else's worries would be soothed. Arima and Seafer could have handled it alone, but by now, the other three had developed a passion for seeing the boy do well. Even Mokam couldn't argue about the Clear classification, not after the rock melting incident. So they were coming. Stem and Maleef had given Steef the duty of watching for the boat, and it had apparently come into view, causing him to call her.

'Antreema' was what Steef had gotten out his parents' efforts to teach him 'Aunt Arima'. Then there was 'UncaSeef'. 'UncaAntee' had gotten everyone snickering so much, the poor Yellow had tried to get it changed, without success. Mokam had insisted on Master Mokam, which came out 'MassMoke', and they all agreed he got what he deserved for being so stuffy. Cassa had immediately become 'Sassy', which stuck so well that she couldn't have changed it if she'd wanted to. Which she didn't.

Arima opened one of the two eyes she was resting, to see him running furiously in her direction. He always ran furiously. He wasn't *unnaturally* small, but as small as a child of his age could be and still be natural. He preferred to be naked, and they had allowed it for a while, later deciding that for his own safety, and Mokam's decorum, he should at least wear trous. So here he came in his trous, legs pounding furiously, arms flailing furiously. If you watched just the arms and legs, you got the impression he was flying, and so he thought he was. If you watched his body, with all the tiny ribs flexing, you would see that those short little legs weren't really making good speed, for all their effort. His face was pure concentration. Brows furrowed, eyes watching the ground ahead, he had already learned that uneven terrain was to be respected.

He was carrying his little stick. He never went anywhere without his stick, since the adults around him had theirs. Seafer had seen to it that the sticks Steef carried were inert. No one wanted to think about a live staff in his hands just yet.

Stopping his usual two staffs distance, he pointed, "They're coming! They're coming! Come on Antreema! They're coming!" The poor child was under strict orders from everyone not to bounce, but he wanted to. He settled for trembling. He couldn't jump either. Or tumble. Just run and tremble. He just *had* to learn to drain.

Arima had told him that this visit would include his first lesson. He didn't know what she meant really, but it sounded good, and besides, he loved all his "Unca's and his 'Sassy'.

They all gathered near the Landing site. Four adult humans, one child, and two Cats. Rivverr was there, of course. And Timmerr. The younger Cat was fully grown now. Not nearly as large as Rivverr, he was large enough. He was always present when Antee arrived, and followed the Yellow Master everywhere he went, until it was time for Antee to leave again. Then Timmerr would disappear into the hills until Antee's next visit. Timmerr never let Antee touch him for conversation, or even just affection. On those occasions when Antee tried, Timmerr would give a half growl/snarl, and back off. When Antee would give up and turn away, Timmerr would come back to follow him again. The Cat would sleep outside Antee's cave when the Master was there. When Arima had asked Rivverr about it, all he would say was that Timmerr was giving Antee the respect he deserved.

The arriving Masters stepped out of the boat, and first gave homage to Rivverr. He tolerated it, despite the fact that he was no longer ClanCat. One of his many cubs was now in that post, and Rivverr was enjoying his declining cycles with his friend. Then hugs and shoulder-slaps all around, as Steef delighted himself in a forest of legs, after first giving MassMoke his bow.

They retired to the fire and food for the remainder of the day, sharing news and stories. The lesson would wait until morning.

❧   ❧   ❧

"Now Steef," started Arima, "I want you to go to the sanitary hut, and empty yourself at both ends, if you can." If they succeeded in getting him to make the correct push, there was no point in having him soil himself.

"Okay!" He spun, and was off, pounding over to the hut and disappearing.

It was just barely light. Without strong sunlight, Steef wouldn't have as much charge to drain. It had been agreed that Arima would lead this effort, since she could detect his Power levels most accurately. She was wearing her eyelenses, which would help some with the headache. They wouldn't do much against a discharge, but that couldn't be helped. The others were giving a respectful distance, all but Rivverr, who insisted on standing with Arima.

Steef came pounding back, stopping at his usual separation. To his delight, she waved him closer. She knelt in front of him, and gently removed his stick, setting it respectfully on the ground. "Steef, you need to listen closely," she began. He nodded earnestly, never taking his eyes from hers. "We're here to see if we can get you to push your Power back into the ground. Do you know what I mean by your Power?" she asked.

He scrunched his face up for a beat, and said, "You mean my tickle, Antreema?"

She smiled, "That's right, your tickle. Right now, without the Sun out brightly, tell me where you tickle most." She had to know if they really were talking about the same thing. His answer would tell her.

He returned her smile now, "Without the sun, I always tickle most in my feet!" He looked down at his bare feet.

Relieved, Arima went on, "Right again, my little man. Our feet always tickle don't they? Well now, we're going to push that tickle right out of your feet. How far up are you tickling right now?" He put his hand to his waist. Good. His levels roughly matched everyone else's at this time of day. "Okay, now I want you to close your eyes, and think about that tickle. Concentrate on the tickle. Do you feel it?" He nodded. "That's good. Now take a deep breath and hold it." His chest filled. "That's right. Now when I tell you, I want you to push hard at that tickle, and push it right out through your feet. Just your feet. Nowhere else. Ready? Go!" She flinched. If his charge went anywhere but his feet, this could be a long day. Or a really short one.

It didn't. She felt his radiant Power go down at once. He had gotten it right. Most children did get it right the first time, but most children didn't almost blast their Mother's leg off with a sneeze, either. She reached out, and for the first time in nearly three cycles, she touched the boy. Running her hands up and down his legs, then his arms to be thorough, she checked him. He was empty. He was also starting to sway.

"Shortstick!" called out Cassa from behind her, "Breathe, Son! Take a breath!"

Arima chided herself for her single-mindedness, but stayed focused enough to watch for incoming Power with his breath. Sure enough, he filled back up to his waist.

"Very good, Steef. Very good. Now, let's try that again." She put him through the process several times. "Now this time, I want you to push exactly the same, only this time we're not going to hold our breath. Ready? Go!" It worked again. Again and again, she made him repeat it.

"You're doing just fine, pumpkin," she said warmly, "Now, can you *hold* the tickle at your feet while you breathe?" His smile disappeared, replaced by his wide-eyed 'I don't understand' look. "What's wrong?" she asked.

"I *like* my tickle, Antreema! Do I have to make it go away?"

"Steef, sweetie, your tickle won't ever go away for good. It's always there in the ground waiting for you when you need it. What we want to do is teach you how to control it, so your Mama won't get hurt again." *Should I have said that?*

"You mean my tickle is bad? My tickle is what hurt Mama?"

"It's not bad if you control it, Steef. It's only bad when it's…wild…yes, that's it. Only wild tickles are bad. Can you hold yours in the ground for just a few beats, for practice?"

His eyes unfocused, as he concentrated on his feet. She took that as a 'yes', for his Power stayed exactly at his feet until she spoke again, and interrupted him.

"Very good, Steef! Very good!" she exclaimed. "Now we are all going to take turns today, helping you practice controlling it! Give me one more push, and hold it there for me. There's something I want to do. Good, good. Can you hold it?" He nodded. "You've got to hold it for Aunt Arima, Okay?" He nodded again. She reached out, and drew him in, hugging him deeply. He squealed with delight, and she whispered, "Don't stop holding it, Okay?" She could dab her eyes later.

✤   ✤   ✤

Take turns, they did. Off and on for three days. They would put a hand on a drained Steef, somewhere on his body, and tell him to fill up to their hand. They didn't have Arima's Sight, but as Masters, they had sensitivity and training enough to feel his Power when they touched him. They were careful to keep the charge out of his arms, lest he wave them, and discharge by accident. When they were done, he could drain himself from any part of his body that was touching the ground, or fill any specific part of his body, leaving the rest empty. Stem and Maleef watched the entire process, and soon asked if the Masters could help them learn to do it. Their own training had been crude, since no Masters had been available for Twos.

"UncaAntee?"

"Yes, Steef?" As usual, Timmerr was right behind him, taking his lead from Rivverr, in spite of the risk.

"How come I get cold when I push my tickle out?"

"Well, the Power that we all get is what keeps us warm in cold weather. It's why we don't have to wear heavy clothes, and why we don't have to cover our feet, no matter how cold it gets."

"We don't cover our feet...so we can push and pull our tickles better?"

"That's right."

"And Sassy uses her tickle to fly her boat?"

"Yes, she does."

Steef loved to fly in Cassa's boat. Since he had gotten old enough to know he was flying, whenever they visited, he asked for a trip around the Valley. The first experience had been a disaster. Cassa had meant well enough, but carelessly had set Steef on the edge of her boat next to the mast. He had given the wooden pole a tight hug, which resulted in Mokam and Seafer putting a new stone into the top of it. Mokam had taken to stockpiling an assortment of Crystals in his cave, for emergencies. It hadn't taken long until Seafer needed one as well. Arima's staff had been the only truly safe one, since she'd been keeping her distance.

"So how does Sassy get her tickle way up in the boat, when she can't touch the ground?"

Antee stared at the little boy, dangling his kicking feet over the edge of the rock. *That was a good question!* "Well, you see, Steef, we have to drain our Power into the ground. There's no place else to drain. But we can fill up with Power from the sun. That's why Cassa only flies during the day."

"Okay."

Antee felt pretty good about it. His little charge had come up with a good question, and Antee had been able to give an answer that Steef could under-stand. Over the next few cycles however, all of the Masters would learn to fear the question Steef gave *after* he said 'Okay'.

"UncaAntee?"

"Yes?"

"If Sassy isn't touching the ground…and she's getting her tickle from the sun…how come she still doesn't cover her feet?"

And Antee was stuck. There was no good reason for Cassa to be barefoot. Trouble was, no Powered person *ever* covered their feet. Footcladdings were for Inerts. Now how could he explain *that* to this little boy? Most children just grew up knowing these things. But most children grew up around other chil-dren, not HornCats. He hated the only answer he could think of, "Steef, you'll just have to wait until you're older to understand."

"Okay."

Arima had Rivverr. Antee had Timmerr, sort of. Cassa had her boat. For that matter, Mokam had Cassa's boat. Stem and Maleef had Steef. And Seafer…well, he had a tree.

It wasn't really *a* tree. It was really *five* trees. It just looked like *a* tree.

That first cold Quarter had been the hardest wait of his long quest, but it had been worth it. It seemed to everyone that the sprouts had known exactly to the beat when the last freeze was done, and up they came. Right in the center of the small hut, until it had been necessary to move Steef's pad aside to give them room, they grew so fast. And they did something that even Seafer wasn't expecting. When they reached about one span in height, they began to twine around one another. By the time that first hot Quarter was done, they had almost reached the topwall of the hut, and the five sprouts looked like one tall, tapered, twisted trunk.

That was almost two cycles ago now, and things had changed a bit. The hut was gone, removed by Mokam on his first visit after the second cold Quarter. The sprouts, which is what Seafer called the tree, had started growing again, almost as if they were on a timetable. They/it had pushed the top slab completely off the walls, so Mokam took everything down, and the small family had moved into one of the caves.

The tree stopped growing.

They knew, because Seafer insisted on measuring it each day, and each day it was always at least a bit taller. Until the move into a cave. Then it just...stopped. And Steef started having trouble sleeping. On the fourth morning, Stem and Maleef had wakened to find their Son had found his way in the night to the base of the tree. There he was, curled up between two roots, deep asleep.

And the tree started growing again.

From then on, Steef spent every night with his tree, only now he didn't sleep next to it, he slept in it. He had watched Seafer climb it every day, and by the time he was three, he was following the old Master up. The spiral trunk gave good foot holds for tiny feet. Maleef had been alarmed that first morning when she couldn't see him, until he answered her call from inside the branches. On the morning of the draining lesson, Seafer's measurement was six staffs, four spans tall, and five staffs wide.

All of those branches grew straight out from the trunk, level with the ground, at even heights. They would all curl slightly up at the tips, and from a distance, the general shape of the tree tapered gently to the top, where the spiral point stuck out. Since nothing about this tree was normal, everyone sort of accepted that it had odd leaves. If you could call them leaves. Seafer had said he'd mixed things up a bit, and the leaves showed it best. They weren't broad and sectioned like most hardwoods. They weren't needles like most softwoods. They looked like Seafer had taken a softwood needle in its middle with both hands, and stretched it into a flat, broad cone. As if that weren't odd enough, they only grew *up* off the limbs. Never down, never sideways, only up. Steef would comment a few cycles later that he gave up using a pad for sleeping altogether. The leaves were more comfortable.

But easily the strangest thing of all about Seafer's tree involved the Cats, and the dirt. Seafer had an eager explanation for the dirt, and would tell anyone and everyone as often as they liked, which wasn't often. Arima got to hear it first, within a sevenday of her return from GuildTown, "Y'see 'Rima, this is gonna be a hungry tree…'cause it's gonna grow a lot…and o'course trees gotta eat just like everythin' else…so I kinda had to come up with a way to feed it…a lot…an' then it occurred to me that since trees feed from the dirt…I needed dirt that would feed a hungry tree…that was part o' all that stirrin' you saw…so this dirt'll stay fallow and stirred for all time…and it soaks, 'Rima!…soaks up anythin' that gets on it…except o' course livin' things…though I don't know…if you laid there long enough…anyway, that's why the dirt around the cove is so soft to walk on all the time…except o' course right around the trunk…had to give it somethin' solid to hold to…an', oh!, around the inner walls o' the cove, o' course, where we have to walk…so anyway, it'll just soak up anything that hits it…even rocks over time…but the softer somethin' is…the faster it'll soak…and all of it'll feed the tree!" He had told that so often now, he could probably do it asleep. In fact, he usually talked of his dirt with his eyes closed, and head tilted back.

As a result of this marvelous dirt, the cove stayed neat and tidy, all by itself, day and night, cold or hot. They just had to be careful what they set down, and where, and for how long.

So the dirt in the cove soaked up anything that touched it. And it fed the tree. And apparently one night shortly after Seafer's discharge had stirred this wondrous dirt, one of the Cats discovered just how well that dirt absorbed things. Ironically, this discovery occurred in the most natural way possible, for such an unnatural dirt, and unnatural result. Whichever Cat it was must have been pleased, for the next night there were twenty Cats feeding the tree. Then fifty. Then over a hundred. Every night after true dark, they would show up. Sometimes singly, sometimes an entire tribe. And feed the tree. The funny part was, no matter how often they came, they always seemed surprised by the results. They couldn't turn around fast enough, watching their efforts disappear into the ground.

No matter how many Cats came, and it was always a lot, each new morning would bring a perfectly neat cove with soft, stirred dirt, and no sign that a Cat had been there. It was a well-fed tree.

Mokam also put the soaking dirt to his own test. Twice each cycle, he would bring at least one box of Dust, and he and Seafer would spread the Dust around the tree in a circle. It usually took a couple of days for the Dust to get completely absorbed, but it eventually disappeared.

So they all thought they were beyond surprise from this tree and its dirt. They were wrong. It was the fourth morning from their arrival, after three days of draining lessons. They were all wakened by Maleef screaming. She was always first up, starting a fresh fire, fresh brew, and beginning the meal. Not today. She was standing in front of her cave, looking at the tree...and screaming. Or looking at where the tree probably was, for it was impossible to see. The air around it was crackling, and a swirling cloud of Power in every Color pretty much obscured the tree itself.

The Masters all came running, as best they could this early, and approached the center of the cove cautiously. They were met by a pounding Steef, who popped out of the cloud running earnestly towards his Mother. "Mama! Mama! Mama! What's matter Mama?" he cried as he ran. Stopping abruptly in front of her, he stood with both hands twisting his little stick frantically.

Maleef, in turn, swallowed her Son up in her arms, and spun round and round as tears of relief sprung from her. Stem had come up, and wrapping his arms around them both, they just held close.

Meanwhile, five bewildered Masters were still creeping towards the cloud that once was a tree. Antee was the first to reach a hand out, but as his hand got close, sparks and crackles made him jump back again. As one, they all turned, and stared openmouthed at Steef.

"This is the kind of story we live for. If we live long enough to tell it, we'll tell it for as long as we tell."

None of the Masters acknowledged hearing any of their Pills.

After they were calmed somewhat, Stem and Maleef carried their also bewildered Son to where the Masters stood. Antee spoke for all of them, "Steef, can you tell us if you did this?" he kept his voice calm, as Steef's eyes were still wide from the screams.

"Did I do wrong, UncaAntee?"

"No, sweet boy, you didn't do anything wrong. But we sure would like to know what you did?"

"I climbed up at sleeptime, like Mama told me. Only when I got up there, I 'membered Antreema said I should push out my tickle 'cept my feet, 'cause I'd sleep...uh..."

"Cooler," Arima chimed in.

"...uh-huh, that...but *you* told me, UncaAntee, that I hafta be on ground. But I was already up...so I pushed anyways, just to see...an' my tickle went out fast!…even outta my feet!…and Antreema was right, it felt gooder…so I went to sleep. Did I do wrong?" He was still wringing his stick.

"Hush, now, pumpkin," cooed a wet-eyed Maleef, "You din't do anythin' wrong. You did jus' fine. Hush now."

They were brought back to reality by the sound of Seafer hitting the ground. He just…sat…straight down. At least it was soft dirt. He started alternately holding his hands skyward, then clapping them at the cloud/tree. *He* now had tears on *his* face. They gaped at him, then the cloud, then Steef, then back to Seafer. He seemed to be either giggling or sobbing. They discovered it was both.

Arima knelt over him and asked, "Seafer, are you all right? Is this…thing… hurting you?"

With a final fling of his hands straight up, he crowed, "Don't y' see, "'Rima!? Everyone, don't y' see? He's *charged his staff!*" The words hung in the air, punctuated by the crackling of the cloud.

The four Masters jerked around, looking at the cloud with a different eye. Cassa had just enough beats to say, "You mean the *whole* tree is char…" before all four of them joined Seafer on the ground.

❧   ❧   ❧

They were all sitting in Cassa's boat. It was threequarterday, and they'd been out there all day, watching. All of them, including Steef. Especially Steef. They didn't want him near the tree until the charge dissipated. One of his hiccuping spells could level the cove, or worse.

Every so often, one of them would say 'It's *got* to go down soon', or something similar. The Cats were fascinated as well. Every Cat within a half-day walk was sitting around the boat, barely moving. Watching.

To make conversation, Arima gestured to the Cats, and said, "They can't see the Colors you know. They don't see Color at all. Apparently they *can* see the cloud in general."

Cassa asked, "If they don't see Color, how do tell us apart?"

"They tell me that each Power has a different flavor when it hits their horns," Arima replied with a shrug.

Antee joined in, "What do they say about our little dilemma over there?" He nodded towards Steef.

Arima chuckled. "Rivverr calls him 'the little MixMaster.'"

Even Stem and Maleef smiled at that. They hadn't smiled much all day.

Antee wasn't done, "If they don't see Color, what *do* they call each of us?"

She gave him a sly grin with that one, "You're a…FoodMaster."

Antee got it at once, "Because to them, everything I work on is…"

"Food," she finished for him, nodding. "Cassa's a SkyMaster. Seafer would be a GrassMaster, only that doesn't really fit, does it? I think we'd all have to agree he is truly a TreeMaster." She nodded to him, he smiled dazedly. "Mokam is a StoneMaster." She stopped.

"And you would be…" nudged Cassa.

"Healer. Just Healer. It's all I've ever been called," she said, wistfully.

Antee judged from her tone that it would be best to move on, "So what do they call Reds and Blacks?"

"Liars and Killers."

☙   ☙   ☙

Just before dark, Cassa called out, "It's going down! I definitely see the top of the tree!" She did have the eyes of a flyer, after all.

"I think we still should sleep here tonight," said Mokam. He'd been pretty quiet all day.

Arima agreed. She went over to Steef to tell him, "Pumpkin, we're going to have to stay here tonight. You can sleep in your tree again tomorrow night."

"Okay." He'd been playing quietly all day, mostly with his little stick, mimicking every motion he'd seen them make with their staffs.

They were all watching the conversation, and Steef's stick twirling, when Antee spoke up, "Early or not, I think we'd best start him on *some* staff training. He needs to learn to drain his wood, too. Otherwise, none of us will ever sleep well again." To which they all agreed.

They guessed/hoped the tree would be drained by morning. Meanwhile, for the first time in over two cycles, it didn't get fed that night.

☙   ☙   ☙

Next morning found them all out in the flatland in front of the cove, about a hundred staffs past the boat. They had drawn sticks to choose who would teach him to fill and drain a staff. Arima had been left out of this process, the reasoning being they might need a Healer in a hurry. As Cassa and Steef walked another fifty staffs from the group, her body began shaking like one of her sails in a cross-wind. She was carrying a tiny branch that Seafer had gone and plucked from the now-dormant tree. Even this little piece of the tree was twined like the trunk. As they walked, for curiosity's sake, she sent a small Pulse into the wood, but it felt dead to her. Bewildered, she wondered if perhaps Seafer had chosen a piece too young to be useful.

"Pill, you might want to watch from one of the other Masters," she said absently. Pop! Pop! *They didn't argue with me that time* she mused.

Steef was striding happily next to her, taking huge steps to keep up, and grinning non-stop. He didn't know what was coming, he just assumed it would be great. He loved his Sassy. Cassa wanted to just keep on walking, but lacked a good excuse. She finally stopped, and her little charge looked up brightly. She knelt.

"All right, Shortstick!" she said more brightly than she felt, "Hand over that twig you're carrying." He stuck his arm straight out, and she relieved him of his toy, tossing it over her shoulder. "Now listen close, Shortstick…" he nodded "…In a beat or two, I'm going to hand you this new stick. It's not like the one you've been carrying. This one works…" *at least it's supposed to* "…so we're going to have to be reealllyy careful."

His eyes widened, and his head bobbed up and down furiously.

"Let's start by draining yourself down to your feet…got it?…good." She handed him the small twig. "Hold it in both hands. Now bring your, uh, 'tickle' slowly up, and move it out to your hands. Just enough to fill your hands only, all right?" She touched one of his wrists, and yep, a charge passed through. She released him "All right. Here's the careful part. Slowly, very slowly, push that tickle out of your hands into the stick."

Tongue sticking out, he watched the stick intently as he pushed. Then he grinned, "Sassy! The tickle's gone! Is it in the stick?"

"Hold really still, Shortstick, while I check." She couldn't stop her hand from trembling, though she tried. Her fingers lightly touched the stick. It was still dead. Forcing a smile, she said, "That's just fine, kiddo! Bright work!" She moved her hand back to his wrist. "Now pull the tickle back, slowly…that's right." To her surprise, she felt the charge come back into his forearms. Her face took on a puzzled furrowing. "Pull the tickle all the way back, and drain it into the ground, all right?" He nodded.

She turned to the group, and shouted, "Pill!"

Pop! Pop!

"Tell Seafer that I can feel his charge move out and in, but the wood is still just dead." Pop! Pop!

She could see them conferring, then…

Pop! *"Seafer says you won't be able to feel the wood charge, because it's completely tuned to the boy."*

"Well that's just fine! Now how in the Creator's name am I supposed to know if he's actually charging and draining?"

Pop! Pop! *"Seafer says to get the boy to make a small Pulse."*

"You're jesting!"

"That's a plausible assumption, but no, no one is jesting."

She took a deep breath. "Well, why not! I had no particular plans for the next ten cycles anyway!"

Pop! Pop!

"Shortstick," she squeaked, "let's do that again! Just a tiny tickle...tiny, tiny, tiny." The little tongue came out again, and he nodded. "Okay then!" She scooted on her knees until she was behind him, and pulled his little body against her own. "Now tilt the wide end of the stick away from us...that's good. Now slowly push that tickle right out the end of the stick." Her curiosity for the event helped her keep her eyes open, so she saw...she could actually *see* it...a bubble...like a soap bubble...only Red...push its way out the end of the little stick. When it reached about the size of her thumbnail, it separated, and started to float...

BANG!

She opened her eyes to find herself lying flat on her back, with Steef sitting on her chest, bent over almost nose-to-nose. "Sassy, you Okay? Sassy, you Okay? Sassy, you Okay?"

She was more than Okay, she felt great! She loved her boat, she loved her flying, she loved this field, she loved Steef, she loved everything! Even Buzzbies. Grabbing his head in both hands, she gave him a big kiss on the forehead, "I'm good, Shortstick! Are you all right?" There was something she needed him to do...oh, yes..."Climb off now, kiddo, and drain yourself completely."

The rest of the day was spent showing him how to drain his stick. He learned to drain it through his body, and he learned to plant the point into the ground, and drain it there. They hoped he would understand the final instructions. Mokam gave them to him, almost sternly.

"Steef, you must never charge up your tree again, unless we tell you."

"Okay."

"You must never discharge your stick, unless we tell you."

"Okay."

"You'll be playing with the old stick. You must never use the new one, unless we tell you."

"Okay."

"Antee, has it not occurred to you that the boy sleeps in a tree full of live sticks, and can get one anytime he wants?"

"And if you have a better idea to keep him safe, Pill, we'd all like to hear it."

❦   ❦   ❦

"So is it now safe to be near the little MixMaster?"

It was almost dark, and Arima was back in her favorite spot, propped against Rivverr under the outcrop.

"I'm not sure it will *ever* be safe, but it might be safer than it was." *As long as we remind him constantly to drain.* She sighed.

"Then I must go. I will return before it gets dark again." He abruptly clambered to his feet, causing her to flop back.

"Oh! All...all right." She watched him pad off.

She didn't have much time to ponder Rivverr the next day. They all pestered Steef all day to stay drained. The spunky child maintained his light spirits throughout their nagging, but he did seem to have lost interest in playing with his old stick. He still carried it, he just didn't play with it much.

She was helping Maleef get lastmeal started when Rivverr reappeared. He padded into the cove with a bit of a tired gait. Suddenly, from the cove's edge, darted a young male HornCat. Tail held high and straight, he ran and jumped on Rivverr's side, fell back, and started a barrage of attacks from every angle. Rivverr just ignored him, and came up to Arima. The younger Cat sat down a staff behind the great male, his tail swishing back and forth.

Arima looked at the young Cat, wondering what this was about. He had a unique chest splash, white of course, but shaped almost like a leaf from a hardwood tree. His horns weren't over half a span. She judged his age at about two cycles. He probably weighed about twice what Arima did.

"This is my cub. I sired him with my oldest female. She was too old, I think. She bore only the one cub. He does not behave as he should. He prefers play to duty. None of the other cubs tolerate him. He will be companion to the MixMaster. He is under severe instructions not to hurt the little one." With that, Rivverr turned his massive head, and let out a roar. The cub cringed, and backed up another staff. *"Perhaps the MixMaster's Power will keep him calm."*

She wanted to refuse. Orders or no, accidents happen, and this little cub made ten or twelve of Steef. But how could she refuse Rivverr? And she knew that if the cub didn't fit in with the Clan, he'd be turned out into the hills, where he was likely to starve. She could at least see what happened when they met.

"Pill, where is the whirlwind?"

"Cassa has him at the boat. She's teaching him about flying."

"Would you ask her to bring him here, please?" Pop!

They appeared soon, and made their way towards the group. When Steef caught sight of the cub, he squealed and started pounding fast as he could. The cub rose and shot straight for him. When they met, both stopped, leaving a space. The cub then lowered his head and began to circle Steef, sniffing. Steef's face was pure wonder and joy. He held remarkably still. When the cub finished its circle, it hesitated for a beat. Then, lifting the front of its body, put both front paws on Steef's shoulders, knocking him flat on his back. The adults heard the cub give a low growl, causing them all concern.

"I am Kivverr! Play with me…or I will eat you!"

CHAPTER 8

❁

There were only three things that could separate Kivverr from Steef: Kivverr's feedings, of course; the sanitary hut; and Cassa's boat. They didn't find out about the boat for a while. At all other times, wherever Steef went, Kivverr went, including sleeping in the tree. Steef had only spent one day being disappointed with his little inert stick, and thereafter, he hardly noticed the stick at all, though he insisted on carrying one at all times.

The next half cycle was a most tranquil time for everyone in the cove. The four permanent adults took turns every eighthday shouting "Steef, drain yourself!" and life became fairly uneventful. They also reminded Steef every night to drain before climbing up to sleep, just in case. Whether their diligence, or his young experience, made the difference, the tree stayed quiet as well.

It was a bit too early yet to start real training, but there were empty beats to fill, so Arima and Seafer began teaching Steef his letters and numbers. The lessons also included Stem and Maleef, as they were eager to sit in. In fact, the young couple had spent a lot of time from the start with the Masters, learning everything they could think of to ask. Being Greens, naturally they were especially drawn to Seafer. The old Master had difficulty at first, warming to the idea. He had never apprenticed anyone, and certainly not Twos. He didn't really know how. But Stem and Maleef were young, and had strong backs, and there were crops to grow each cycle. And, truly, the sprouts didn't need watching much. He'd done his job almost too well.

The adults also passed some of their time with their music. It was awkward at first, since Colors never played with other Colors. It just wasn't done. So, the three Greens would always get out their flutes, and have a thoroughly rough time slogging through the few tunes that they all knew, while Arima would watch and listen and feel like an audience. She hadn't played much since child-hood, not since her Mother finally stopped insisting. There were a few times during her stays at Guildhall when a public White concert was required. Then she would get out her small stringbox and bow, and go through the motions.

But from the first in the cove, she was an audience of one, not counting the baby and the Cats, when about every other night for two Quarters, there was a Green flute concert. So one night, she had dragged out her little four-string, tightened it up, and to their shock, joined in. They didn't actually say anything, and soon enough, no one thought much about it. In fact, they thought so little about it, that they played together on one of the nights that the three other Masters were visiting. At least they started to. They were actually pretty eager to show the others the two tunes that practice had made recognizable. Well, they would have played, but they were interrupted before the second note sounded. Mokam was first.

"Stop right there!" he shouted.

"You can't be serious!" was Cassa's almost simultaneous outburst.

Antee just laughed, though he never said at what.

Stem and Maleef went still, but by then, they were handling their interac-tions better, so they didn't actually wilt. Seafer and Arima looked at the others with bewildered faces.

"What?" asked Seafer.

Cassa turned to Mokam, who said to Arima, "You're a White! You're a White! You can't play with Greens!"

"I was just about to show you that I could," responded Arima evenly. She kept herself from adding that what she did on her stringbox wasn't really music anyway, and probably didn't count. Mokam would not get the jest.

"You're not a young girl, Arima…"

"Thank you."

"…so you don't have to be told that Colors just *don't* mix music!"

"We're a long way from anywhere that it could matter, Mokam."

"It's *wrong*, Arima!" His face was getting red.

"Why?"

"Why, it just is, that's all!"

"Why?"

"Why…why…because that's the way it's always been, and that's good enough!"

"Mokam, I didn't even use that argument…when I fought for the Cats! Doing *anything*…solely because it's a tradition…well, it's mental laziness…that's what it is. There's no Concert Prize here, no Guild honor at stake. Just friends passing time. Give me any *thoughtful* reason…I'll put my box away. Or…you could listen to the screeches and growls I've learned to get out of it, mercifully drowned out by Maleef's sweet flute. Your choice."

Mokam walked off, rumbling a bit. Arima and Seafer turned to Cassa and Antee, their faces plainly asking, "Do you want to hear this, or not?"

Antee had stopped laughing at Mokam's distress, but his eyes were still alight. He waved them on. Cassa slowly closed her jaw, sitting mute through the short session.

On the next visit, Antee brought his own six-string pickbox. Cassa's drums came out on the trip after that. She left them in her cave, saying it was an old set, and easier than carting them back and forth. Thereafter, the multi-Colored music became its own tradition. What it lacked in quality, it made up in energy. Since there were no Reds in the group, they had to listen to what they actually played, but it was fun.

Mokam held out for an entire cycle before bringing his valvehorn.

As soon as Steef had learned to drain, he was included in the sessions. Since he was not Color specific, he was given a choice of instruments to learn, even Cassa's drums. They all mused that he was probably the first child in history to have a choice.

"I want to play with Papa and Mama," was his instant reply.

So Stem and Seafer made him his own flute. It wasn't the single-pipe kind with holes like the adults played, but eight different small pipes tied together. It gave him his eight notes, and blew clear, and he loved it. He displayed every bit as much musical talent as his Father…none…but he blew with gusto, and the others learned to play around his efforts.

Kivverr hated the music sessions, but wouldn't leave Steef's side, so they also had to play over and around his moans and growls, as well.

Planting Quarter arrived without event, and discussion began through Pill about staff training for Steef. Antee was pushing everyone for an early start to real training, his argument being that Steef would have more to learn than most, might as well get a good start. The boy wasn't quite five yet, and serious staff training usually started at six, so the discussion was lively. What finally decided the issue in Antee's favor wasn't his logic, however, it was Steef himself. Or his nature, at least. The child just listened so well, and was ever eager to please them all. Whatever his aptitude might turn out to be, he surely had the spirit of a student. Next visit, they would make their first attempt.

❦   ❦   ❦

It was almost dusk, and the boat had been down for less than an eighthday. They were in the cove, which was safer now, catching up on news, and sipping some beanbrew, waiting for Steef and Kivverr to arrive. The pair always got back from their romping before true dark. Maleef was getting things together to begin lastmeal, with Arima's help. Arima actually was some help now, thanks to Maleef's relentlessly patient instructions. Food that Arima cooked no longer got thrown away.

They all heard Steef before they saw him.

"HA! HA! HA! HA! HA! HA! HA! HA! HA! HA! HA! HA! HA! HA! HA! HA! HA! HA! HA!"

All heads turned just in time to see Kivverr round the edge of the north face, and turn into the cove. At this distance, they couldn't see Steef just yet, but could hear him clear. Kivverr tossed his head back, and Steef flew up…and then back down, where Kivverr caught him again neatly in his mouth, head and hands sticking out one side, feet on the other. Face down, this time, muffling the laugh.

"You know," pondered Cassa, "I refuse to get used to that." All those same heads just nodded silently, then the two women went back to their preparations, and conversations resumed.

When the truants arrived, Arima called out, "Kivverr…Steef has to have a special lesson tomorrow, and you're going to have to keep your distance. Just thought you'd want to know."

Steef said something that was muffled by the Cat's jaw. Bringing his hands up, he grasped Kivverr's lower jowl, and pushed it down, "Kivverr says I can't have a lesson tomorrow 'cause tomorrow's his feeding day, and he's gonna eat me tomorrow…HA! HA! HA! HA! HA! HA! HA! HA! HA! HA! HA!"

Maleef looked up again from her duties to quietly say, "Pumpkin, climb down outta your beastie now, and ge' washed in the spill. We'll be eatin' soon."

"Okay Mama," came the muffled reply.

❦   ❦   ❦

They were all back in the same spot of field where the first staff test had occurred. Seafer had drawn this duty, and was too excited to be nervous, "All right, Sprout! We'll be a'tryin' this again!" He relieved Steef of his toy stick, and handed him a new one. The original live stick had been given to the dirt. "Draw up some Power now...and fill your arms...good, good...now gently push it into your stick...good...pull it back out...good...let's do that a few times." When Seafer was satisfied that Steef was controlling himself, he said, "Now Sprout...imagine that your stick has...oh...say...five sections to it...can you do that?...good...now we want to squirt that Power out in five squirts...got it?...GO!"

It never occurred to Seafer to get behind the child for cover, so he got to watch the five bubbles form as they appeared. They were very close to uniform in size, and streamed out in a smooth flow. Three Yellows and two Whites. The air that day was still, so the bubbles just drifted away slowly, and also slowly sank to the ground, where they sat. They didn't pop.

Seafer looked down at them, then back to Steef, who had a satisfied look to him. Scratching his almost hairless head, the old Green didn't bother to look up as he motioned to the others to come. He stayed in that position until they arrived. Speaking to the ground, and still scratching, he said, "I do believe them're bubbles...never seen anyone Pulse bubbles before...have any o' you?...no, 'course you haven't...no one Pulses bubbles...ever'one just Pulses, that's what they do...what *is* a bubble?" He finally stopped, but he still didn't take his eyes off of the ground.

They all pondered the bubbles in silence for several beats. Finally, Antee said, "Cassa, when we were here last, did you see his Pulse come out in a bubble?"

"Why, you know, it did...now that you mention it," she replied, "I didn't think about it at the time...because, well, it *was* Red, and..."

"You were feeling too good to think about anything?" Antee finished for her. She nodded. He walked around the others and approached the five little bubbles. They were about the size of one of Steef's fists. Planting his staff in the ground, he drained it, and reached for one of the bubbles. There was a general intake of breath from the others.

"One of these Yellows should be safe for me to handle," he assured them. Apparently it was, for as he took hold of it, it popped. Straightening up, he held his arm up to examine himself. "I just got a Yellow charge that filled my arm," he informed them, "No harm done."

He bent to another one, and took a gentler grip. Holding it up to the sky, he peered at it closely. "I think…"

"What?" "Yes?" "So tell us!" etc.

"…I think this is *not* a Yellow bubble. I think it's a Clear bubble that's filled with Yellow Power."

The conversation that ensued wasn't really a discussion, just five Masters voicing opinions over top of each other for a time, while two parents and three Cats watched, bewildered. Finally, Mokam boomed out loud enough to interrupt, "It doesn't matter! It doesn't *matter!*" They stopped. He went on. "What matters *first* is that the boy learns to control the amount of Power he puts out of his staff. When we get past *that*…then we can deal with these…bubbles." They all reluctantly agreed.

As they had with the draining lessons, they all took turns with Steef, working on his Power output. They would have him shoot streams of tiny bubbles, then short bursts of larger ones. Drain and refill. Partial Pulse, full Pulse. Steef was having a grand time. Kivverr got bored, and ambled a few staffs away to lay down and sleep. Around midday, Antee's turn came up. By this time, the ground around Steef was covered with bubbles. Every size, every Color. Since the bubbles occasionally popped on their own, activities would move when an area got too cluttered. Antee started his small pupil on some variations that he'd been thinking up, and was watching the streams of Colors come out of the little stick, when suddenly he shouted, "Stop!"

Steef stopped instantly, and looked up at his 'Unca' expectantly.

"Steef, did you stagger your stream just then?"

"What does stagger mean, UncaAntee?"

"Did you start, then stop real quick, then start again?"

"No Sir, UncaAntee. You told me to make twenty little ones, and that's what I was doing. Did I do wrong?"

"You did just fine, sweet boy. Maybe I just blinked. Let's try it again. Twenty little ones, all right? See how far you can shoot them."

Steef began again, with Antee watching very intently.

"Stop!"

This time, Antee watched the stream of bubbles until they came to ground, them turned to Steef, "You're doing just fine, Son, but I need to check something."

"Pill, ask the others to come out here, please." Pop!

"Steef, I want you to stand very still, all right? Don't move from that spot." Steef's head bobbed up and down, and grasping his stick to his chest, his body went rigid. Antee smiled a bit to himself as he lowered to his hands and knees. Moving slowly, he started brushing his hands carefully along the ground. The others were starting their way. As each arrived, they watched in astonishment as a Yellow Master crawled around on the ground. Occasionally, he would seem to grasp something they couldn't see, and set it in the same spot as the last something they couldn't see. He was making a pile of somethings they couldn't see.

When at last everyone had arrived, Antee spoke, "All of you have had a turn with Steef this morning, correct?" They all murmured agreement. "Did any of you happen to notice that occasionally there would be a stagger…or gap…in his stream of bubbles?"

There was general agreement, with comments like, "Sometimes I'd ask for five and get four…or two and two."

Mokam said, "I just assumed the boy made a mistake, and we did it over."

Still on his knees, Antee sat back against his feet and looked at them all, "Have any of you ever known him…young as he is…to make a real mistake on any instructions we give? No? Me either. So there has to be another explanation." Reaching over to his invisible pile, he gingerly picked up an invisible something between two fingers. Holding it up to them, he said, "A Clear bubble…filled with Clear Power." He carefully set it back down, and made his peculiar crawl back to where they stood, and stood up himself.

Turning back to the open flatland, he said, "I believe we have a problem." In every direction in front of them for a distance of fifteen staffs, the ground was covered in bubbles. "There is no telling how many Clear bubbles are out there. Anyone got an idea what happens when you pop a Clear?" There was silence behind him. "Me either," he said again. He waited.

"Well, we can't just leave them there!" exclaimed Cassa.

Beat. Beat. Beat.

Seafer brightened, "Mokam can bury 'em…that's it…just open up the ground and bury 'em!" He sounded pleased.

Antee continued to let them talk that out for a while. Finally, "What happens if they all burst at once?…if any of us is standing near? Just one of those little ones charged up my arm. Now we have hundreds. Any of you ever lost a duel? No? Well, I have. The overcharge is not fun. I'm guessing, but I'd say there's enough overcharge out there to kill all five of us."

Arima, "Do you have a suggestion?"

Antee lips pursed, "Mmm-hmmm…but I don't like it." Turning to look down at Steef, he said, "There *is* one person here…who wouldn't get an overcharge from those bubbles."

Arima, "No! I forbid it! You can't risk…"

"I said I didn't like it, but I doubt there's a real risk. The amount of Power *can't* hurt him, and the Black ones won't hurt him if…"

"He's only *five*, Antee!"

The Yellow Master turned to her and spoke gently, "I love him too, Arima. Think with your head, and not your pump. The blast will be centered on him and away…"

"What are you two talking about?" interrupted Cassa.

"He wants Steef to discharge, *that's* what we're talking about!"

There was a chorus of Pop!'ing as every Buzzbie in the area left immediately.

Cassa, Maleef, and Stem all went instantly pale, but Mokam and Seafer were nodding.

Mokam boomed, "Wish I'd thought of that!"

"Clever that…it'll work…just what we need," agreed Seafer.

As the argument began, Antee crawled back to where he had left off, and continued his sweep. They ignored him for a while, until Arima asked, "Where are you going?"

"To the center, of course," he replied, "Clearing a path for him to walk through."

"But we haven't agreed on anything yet!"

"And if you don't, then I'm only wasting my own beats," was his diplomatic answer.

To Arima's dismay, no other solution occurred to any of them, unless they wanted to leave the bubbles to eventually burst on their own. Steef had continued to stand, unnoticed and unmoving, in the spot Antee had fixed him in, during the entire process. Meanwhile, Kivverr had roused from the ruckus, and come to stand with his friend, tail swishing. Antee had just about reached the center of the bubble field when they turned to the bewildered boy.

Visibly shaking, brow perspiring, Arima spoke, "Steef, drain yourself please, and step over here…thank you…could I have your stick, please?" She started to lower herself to him, and Cassa reached over to help her down. "Now Steef, we're going to try something new…you like new things, don't you? In a few beats, you're going to go out to where Uncle Antee is. It's important that you walk along the path he's cleared, Okay?…good. He'll put you where you need to be. Then Uncle Antee's gonna come join us, and you're going to do this new thing right out there, and here's what we want you to do." She took a deep breath, closing her eyes for just a beat or two.

"We want you to fill yourself completely full of Power…uh…tickle. Full up. Everywhere. Doesn't that sound exciting? Now, Steef, when you're full up, don't stop. Keep pulling Po…tickle…from the ground. It's going to feel very different. Your skin will tingle, and your hair will stand up…like this," and she pulled a few strands of her own shaggy hair straight up. "Now we will be standing over there a way's…and you need to watch me. When I signal to you, I want you to clap your hands together and…"

"Shout," said Cassa, as Mokam said, "Hop real hard," as Seafer said, "Sneeze."

"…cough," finished the Healer, "Really hard. Can you cough for me now? Give me a hard cough…yes, that will do just fine. Now, pumpkin, you need to clap and cough at just the same time, Okay? When I nod to you, Okay? Good. Go on out there, now. Walk slowly…that's right…right down the path…Kivverr! No! You can't go! Kivverr! Oooohhhhhh!" Turning, she looked at Rivverr, who immediately bellowed out an impressive roar.

But Kivverr wasn't much of a cub any more, and he was going with Steef. He roared back. Not as impressively as his massive sire, but enough. Arima then spoke to Rivverr in a shrill, "It'll kill him! He can't go!" Rivverr roared again, with Timmerr joining him this time. Not that it mattered, for Kivverr was suddenly deaf, and Arima thought, almost with relief, that the discharge idea was probably over. Steef picked that beat to stop and turn back to his furry orange friend. He crooked a finger, causing Kivverr to lean down, and the tiny boy whispered something into his ear. Kivverr straightened back up, turned and walked back down to where the group stood, sat on his haunches, and began swishing his tail furiously.

Antee placed Steef as close to center as he could sight him, then walking carefully, he too rejoined the group. As he arrived, Arima jabbed him in the shoulder with one pointy finger, "Don't give me any smug, mister 'knew it all the time', or I'll have Rivverr take a plug out of your backside." At that, Timmerr rumbled, letting them know he'd have a say in that. "And if this hurts that boy…why…I'll have Him eat you outright!" That made Kivverr rumble, which they took to mean that Rivverr would have to get in line. Everyone was just a bit tense.

Antee gave the best smile he could, "We'd better move back," was all he said. Which they did, even a reluctant Kivverr. Antee led the way, and kept walking when the others were ready to stop. He wasn't satisfied until they had a forty staff gap.

Mokam was grumbling under his breath, "Don't know what the fuss is about. Why, we don't even know that he *can* discharge!" No one replied, and he followed them until they stopped.

It was a bit far for Arima to shout, so Cassa shouted for her, "All right, Shortstick, start filling up!…Hold your arms out like this!" She spread her own arms.

For her part, Arima was shielding her eyes from the sun, and watching for Power. She couldn't really See Steef's Power, but could often See waves in the air around him, something like hot air off of a hot rock, though Steef didn't actually get hot. She was watching for those waves now, hoping to judge when he should do his clap/cough. What she hadn't counted on was the distance. At this distance, she could see *him*, but couldn't See the Power around him that she knew *must* be building. For his part, Steef just kept pumping his tickle until Antreema told him to clap.

The cloud of Clear Power must have been twelve or thirteen staffs across before she Saw it at all. "Ooohhhh dear. Oh dear. Oh, oh, oh, dear." By then of course, it was too late to do anything, but she tried, "Get down…everyone get *down!*" With that, she started to wave them down. Unfortunately, Steef took that as his signal. His little hands came speeding together, and with a small cough from his chest, all of the Power he'd drawn up was released.

"KAA-WUMP-wump!!…BOOOOMMMM!!!"

🌾   🌾   🌾

"Arima, you've got to wake up!"

She opened her eyes dazedly, to find herself on her back, covered in Buzzbies. In fact, the air was filled with Buzzbies, flitting exciting around, creating a loud buzzing hum. Getting her focus back, she could see that where she was lying, the grass had sprung up high enough that she *couldn't* see…anywhere but up. She sat up and tried to look around. Cassa was getting shakily to her feet, as were Stem and Maleef. Antee was sitting. She could see the upper half of him rising above the new grass line. There were indentions in the grass where Mokam and Seafer had been standing.

"You need to tend to Seafer! He's hurt!"

Patting the ground to find her staff, she began crawling through the grass to Seafer. He was unconscious, bleeding from his ears. Sinking her staff, she made a complete pass over him. He was brain-bruised, probably from the fall. Both ears were hurt, but Healable. His backbone was wrenched, but no worse than he'd done to himself many times. She tuned her staff, and set it going. She then crawled to Mokam. He was less hurt, but needing a bit of White, nevertheless.

"Antee, I need to use your staff!" It wasn't a request, but he took no notice, handing it over instantly. She filled it with White, and set it off as well. Mokam was starting to rouse, but she held him down, and told him to lie still for a few beats. Cassa came and helped her to her feet.

Her world had changed while she was out. There was the grass, which was now halfway to her knees, growing in a perfect circle for a hundred staffs in every direction. There were the beasts that were coming running, heedless of the Cats, almost in stampede frenzy. And the Cats. Every Cat in near proximity was asleep. Those farther out were merely drowsy. Clouds. Clouds were racing towards them, strangely from every direction, and bunching up directly over-head, where skybolts were starting to flash.

What there wasn't…was Steef.

He was nowhere to be seen. Maleef was frantically heading in Steef's last direction, making the best progress she could through the heavy grass. She wasn't saying anything, just thrashing through the grass weakly, followed by Stem, who was catching up to her. Cassa helped Arima head that way, with Antee on her other side if she needed him. No one spoke, which was good, because the Buzzbies were so loud, they would have had to shout.

They'd covered about half the distance when it started to rain.

Maleef and Stem had stopped and were staring down. Reaching them, the three Masters saw why. There was a crater in the ground. Well, not a crater really. A shallow bowl, six staffs across at least, two deep. The inside of the bowl was completely smooth, almost as if the ground had been glazed. At the bottom was a frolicking Steef.

He was naked. They never saw those trous again. His scraped elbows and knees were bleeding, as was a split lip. Not that he was noticing. He was taking running lunges up the slick sides, and when he got as far as could, would flop over on his back and slide down to the bottom again, laughing non-stop. The rain was coming hard now, and the water only added to his game, making the sides of the bowl slicker.

All of the bubbles that had been their original concern, were gone.

"We'd best get him out of there before he drowns," mused Antee.

❧   ❧   ❧

"Arima, I need your pardon."

"Why would that be, Mokam?"

He paused. His face said he was twisting inside. "I have been skeptical of you since the beginning."

"Oh?" That wasn't news to her, but he honestly didn't know it.

"Yes. I doubted your Grading of the boy. I doubted his Color. I doubted your opinion of his strength. You have to admit, it sounded like you'd cracked a few seams." He didn't add that she had a reputation for it. "And it was odd that you wanted to keep him away from any Guild." There was more wanting to come out of him. He swallowed, and put a hand to the lump on his head. "You were right about all of it. Especially keeping things out here. That boy is a weapon that every Guild would try to abuse. I regret that I doubted you."

She knew that had been hard for him. "You didn't know me then, either," she replied. "No harm is done. Pardon is freely given." She smiled, almost to herself. "Does this mean you're going to start calling him 'Steef' instead of 'boy'?"

"I don't even call my grands by their names, Arima. A child's got to learn proper respect."

"*We're thinking he didn't get many hugs as a child.*" The Pills were still buzzing around excitedly. They would often hover in clusters, conferring perhaps, then explode into more frenzied buzzing. They had actually become more insufferable, and she hadn't thought that possible.

Everyone was sitting around the fire, solemnly contemplating the events of the day. The enormity of their task was bearing down on all. Until today, this had been an adventure to most of them, the responsibilities and risks of that adventure limited by their imagination. Not now. There was Power here that could kill, regardless of Color. Perhaps none of them had actually believed that, for no one seemed unaffected tonight. Even Arima. They were all Masters in their own fields, but this was no one's field.

Conversation was sparse, quiet, and off the subject. Stem and Maleef were the glummest, sitting mutely together with hands clasped. No one suggested a tune.

For his part, the subject himself was having a grand time, which was the only normal thing happening. He was studiously brushing Kivverr, one their favorite evening pastimes. The Cat was lying on his back, with his paws held bent in the air, while Steef worked his way down the bellyside. He was sitting on Kivverr's belly, brushing the lower ribcage, and occasionally pulling clumps of mostly orange fur from his brush, throwing them on the ground. There was no need to clean them up, as they would be gone by morning. Steef was humming, to himself mostly, a crude tune that he'd made up. Kivverr was giving a rumbling purr, something he did only when the other Cats had retired. He had learned to hold completely still. Past efforts at good, long, tight stretches always left his horns stuck in the ground. That wouldn't matter here in *this* dirt, but past experience had given him habits he chose not to question.

It's going to be impossible to train him at all," grumbled Cassa, "If we can't get his Colors separated."

Heads nodded. Beat. Beat. Beat.

"There's somethin' we go' to ask," proclaimed Stem. Glancing at his Mate, he actually stood. "Mean no dis'spect, folks. But...are you goin' to get our boy killed?" He didn't sit back down, instead choosing to look each of them pointedly in the eyes. His hands quivered a bit, but not his gaze.

Beat. Beat. Beat.

"'Cause if you are, you know, why we'll ha' to be leavin'."

Beat. Beat. Beat.

Antee cleared his throat. He seemed to have something in his eyes, which he kept wiping at. Quietly, he finally said, "Where would you go Stem, that Steef wouldn't take his own danger with him?"

Beat. Beat. Beat.

"Why, if the Sprout had been standin' under a rockface when that happened, he'd be..." Arima laid a gentle hand on Seafer's arm.

"You're right, you know," admitted Cassa to the still standing Father. "We really don't know what we're doing. We have to guess at a lot of it right now. Most of it, really. If it's any comfort...and I can't imagine why it would be...there's no one else that would know how to do this better. Not that we're all that smart. It's just that Steef is that unique." Then to herself, really, "You know, Shortstick did all that today without a staff, even."

"Which is why the effect spread in every direction," replied Antee. "I don't want to think about what that charge could have done if it was focused. Seafer...is this tree of yours going to produce a staff that can handle the child?"

Seafer shrugged. He hadn't counted on anything like this either, when he designed his tree.

Arima rose and stepped over to Stem, taking his hands. "If you want to go back to your home, or anywhere else, we'll take you...and wish you Creator's

Blessing. But Steef's gifts bring hardship *with* the blessing, and if he doesn't learn to control those gifts, they almost certainly will kill him...sometime. Somewhere. And perhaps others with him. Perhaps even us here." She hadn't really meant to remind him of the risks they all were taking. She was really just musing aloud. He had never understood the politics of the time they spent here, just the time itself. But this was a sacrifice and risk he could appreciate. His eyes widened, and he bowed his head. Maleef came to join them. Then Antee, followed closely by Cassa. Seafer kicked Mokam in the shin, and the Miner helped his old broken friend to his feet. Nothing further needed saying for beats.

Cassa finally broke the silence, "We've just *got* to get his Colors separated!"

❦   ❦   ❦

They spent two days working on ideas. What normally would have been loud argument between hard-willed Masters, was instead quiet, humble discussion amongst admittedly helpless friends. Ultimately, general consent was given to what they felt was the lamest idea. Practice. Steef would just have to practice his Pulses until he could get streams of a single Color. Any Color. When that happened, if it happened, training could begin in whatever Color he produced.

That led to another dilemma. Where to leave all of those bubbles. The last solution for bubble removal was not considered. It was decided to aim the bubbles into their new pool, the hope being that they would sink to the bottom, and water pressure would pop them. Steef would be instructed to use small Pulses only.

Steef's discharge hole had filled with rainwater, and Stem and Maleef had spent both days there with Steef, teaching him to swim. Or trying to, for Kivverr seemed determined to assist, splashing around and mostly getting in the way. Stepropes had been fastened on opposite sides to help them climb out. Mokam had tried to form a step in the bowl itself for that purpose, but couldn't make the slick sides move. They were Locked with a strength beyond his ability to break, which didn't really surprise anyone. Even Mokam just shrugged at his failure.

So they gathered at the pool. Stem and Maleef had already dried and dressed, but Steef and Kivverr were still at it. There was no fear of Steef's safety, as Kivverr was instinctively a strong swimmer. When Rivverr made it clear to

Kivverr that play was over, the young Cat scooped up Steef and clambered out. Maleef put some fresh trous on him.

They didn't bother to give a clear distance, as Steef would only be making small bubbles, so Arima got to lead this lesson, by request. She handed him his live stick, and his little face broke into an even broader grin.

"We gonna make more bubbles, Antreema?"

Not for the first time, Arima looked at her small charge and wished that he could have been given a normal life. One of hard work and earned joys with his parents, enjoying the glad spirit that opened his little eyes every morning. She sighed. Smiled. Nodded.

"Just one little one, please. Aim into the water."

This no longer took as much concentration on Steef's part, so there was quickly a tiny Green bubble floating out over the calming surface. It touched the water, and popped. She could hear murmurs of relief and satisfaction from behind her.

"Okay, sweet boy. What we want to do is try to make another Green one…just like that one was. Got it? Good."

His brows furrowed then, the little tongue came out to one side. They all waited for several beats, until Arima was about to ask if there was a problem. Just then, another Green bubble popped out of his stick, with the same ultimate result as the first one. With that, she turned to the others, all of whom were showing various signs of surprise.

"Could just be coincidence, Arima," Antee said. "Let's do another."

She nodded at Steef, who didn't hesitate this time. Immediately, a third Green bubble appeared.

"Again, please."

"Again, please."

"Again, please."

She stopped, so Steef stopped. Algae was starting to form on the water's surface. "Steef, would you give me one bubble that *isn't* Green, please." She noticed that she was breathing hard, and made herself calm.

He went back into his concentration face. This time, she waited with more patience, and was rewarded with a Blue.

"Now give me another Blue, please." This one was immediate.

"Again, please."

"Again, please."

"That's enough, pumpkin. Could you drain yourself and your stick? Let me have it. Thank you…no, leave your trous on for just a beat or two, then you can go back swimming."

Turning to the others, she was met with a stunned silence.

Finally, Antee lowered himself to his knees and asked, "Steef, how did you know…well…how did you do that?"

"Do what, UncaAntee?"

"Separate your Colors, Son."

He brightened again, "They all got diff'rent fuzzies, UncaAntee."

"All your Colors tingle differently, you mean?"

The small, smiling head nodded.

"So why have you been Pulsing out all different Colors?"

"I thought you wanted me to. Did I do wrong?" The grin faded.

"No, Son. It wasn't wrong. Tell me, when Aunt Arima asked you to repeat a Color, you waited a few beats before you did the next one, and after that you didn't have to wait any more?" He hoped he'd made his question understandable.

"I been fillin' up with *all* the fuzzies for the lessons, UncaAntee. When Antreema asked for more Green, I had to push out all the mixed-up tickle, and fill back up with the one she wanted."

"And so when she asked you to switch to another Color, that's why you waited again?"

"Uh-huh. I was drainin' and fillin' like you taught me."

Mokam exploded, "Well, why in the name of solid stone didn't you *tell* us you could do that!" he shouted.

Steef's eyes flew wide, and his little hands came together at his chest, obviously missing a stick to twist. But he didn't flinch or step back. Everyone turned in shock to Mokam. Arima wasn't surprised to hear Kivverr growling, but she *was* surprised that Rivverr and Timmerr joined in.

Mokam must have shocked himself with the outburst. He went pale. Setting his staff, he knelt next to Antee, while an agitated Kivverr watched intently.

"I ask your pardon, young man. There is no excuse for me, and you did no wrong. Can you give an old man pardon?"

It took half a beat for the grin to come back. Steef instantly gave his MassMoke a stickless bow. Mokam wasn't satisfied. Grabbing the boy clumsily, he pulled him in for a hug. Steef just hopped up and down in his arms.

Releasing him abruptly, Mokam took a softer tone, but repeated his question, "Tell us, now, young man. Why *didn't* you mention that you could separate those Colors?"

"No one asked."

❦   ❦   ❦

Everyone had enjoyed about as much lesson as they could take for a while. Mokam especially, was ready to have a break in what was for him probably a life's quota of asking pardon, so the three travelers had gone, leaving Seafer and Arima to oversee practice sessions.

Arima had also insisted on complete examinations and Healings for everyone after the discharge, on the chance that some lingering hurt might have occurred. She had left Stem and Maleef until last, since they were the youngest, and weren't going anywhere. She had just finished Stem. Now it was Maleef's turn. After running a thorough Pulse through the girl, she told her to rise. Maleef was completely unhurt and healthy.

"Maleef, may I ask you a private question?"

"Surely, Mum."

"You and your Mate are so very healthy. It's the way of things for most Mates to have two children, and there's no physical reason for you not to…"

Maleef blushed deeply.

"It's not my concern. Your pardon. I shouldn't have asked."

"It's all righ', Mum. Really. You bein' our Healer, an' all…it's jus' that me an' Stem…well, we figure that we're bein' enough trouble as it is, without addin' another mouth to feed. Ever'one is doin' so much for our little Steef…an'…"

"And you're afraid another one just might have the same…uh…challenges that Steef has?"

"Yes, Mum." She wasn't meeting Arima's eye.

Arima regarded her friend for a beat. "What you need to know, child, is that Steef is far more joy to us than challenge. Hmmm. It's also unlikely that a second Clear would occur, since Steef is the first in…well, ever." Arima didn't know…professionally…if that was true, since she didn't know…professionally…how Steef had occurred to begin with. But it sounded good.

"Yes, Mum."

"And it is *not* our concern if you and your Mate want to have another child."

"Yes, Mum."

This wasn't going well. She couldn't really tell this girl to have a baby, but this was a friend, and a good Mother.

"You know, accidents do happen, child. It's been five cycles."

Maleef didn't respond right away. She just couldn't lower her chin any further, it being thoroughly shoved into her neck now. She finally forced a whisper, "No, Mum. Accidents don' happen." Tears started spotting her tunic.

It took her several beats, but she got it, "You mean *never*!? But it's been *five cycles*!"

"Yes......Mum."

Arima started pacing from one side of her cave to the other, while Maleef stayed fixed to one spot. She had opened a wound that she couldn't Heal, and didn't know how to get out of it. Striding back to stand in front of the girl, she said, "You have choices, my sweet girl. I would encourage you to have your other baby, if you want it. But if not, I can close up your belly so that you can't have a baby."

The young woman jerked up at that, eyes wide, "You can *do* tha', Mum?" she croaked.

"Yes, I can do that. It doesn't have to be permanent, either." *I sure wish we'd had this conversation five cycles ago!* "Before you decide, how about I have a word with Stem, and we just keep this conversation to ourselves?"

"I won' lie to my Mate, Mum," she said seriously. Then she giggled, which squeaked a bit, "But if he don' ask, well, I don' have to tell him."

"He's a strong man, Maleef." *Stronger than most.* "He can stand a straight talk from me."

He's a good man, Mum. Better'n I deserve."

I don't know about that. I think maybe you good people deserve each other.

She waited a sevenday before approaching Stem. During that time, she had quietly consulted with the others about their opinion on a second child. The unanimous response was 'how is that our concern?' It helped that Pill hadn't thrown in any editorial comments. Pill hadn't been present during her conversation with Maleef, and carried the messages blindly. Arima had always maintained a personal rule that Buzzbies sat out of private Healings. About half of her Guild had agreed, the other half adding that to the list of what they called her eccentrics.

She deliberately waited until the four of them were together right before lastmeal, while Steef was somewhere getting eaten by Kivverr, "Stem, I'd like for you and your Mate to consider doing us a service," she began innocently enough.

He looked up from tending the fire, "Anything you need, Mum," he replied, walking right into it.

"Well, as a Healer, I am truly curious about how two Green Two's…your pardon, but that's the truth…could possibly have given birth to such an amazing child." That sounded plausible enough, except of course that she had never done White research in her life. He didn't know that, though. "There's only one way I could possibly start to investigate that." She waited. This would have been fun, if it wasn't so serious.

"How's that, Mum?" he took no offense at the 'Green Two' remark. It's what they were.

"Well, you fine children are surely wanting to have your second child…and I was wondering if you couldn't get on with it? I'd be very curious to see if we got another Clear. So would Seafer. Wouldn't you, you old stump?" He'd been warned, though he didn't have a glimmer why.

"'Course I would…just have another like the Sprout…'cause he's good as they grow," Seafer had added his own touch, which sounded genuine because it was.

Remarkably, Stem still took no offense, in spite of two prying Masters jumping into the middle of his life, "You mean, you'd *wan'* us to have another babe?" He sounded amazed.

"Absolutely," she responded firmly, "I just think, if you're going to have a second, that you might as well do it before Steef is too old to enjoy his brother or sister. And it will help me to understand Steef better while he's young enough for the information to be useful." She *should* feel wicked, meddling in these children's lives. Oh well. She'd feel wicked later.

Stem looked at Maleef, who wasn't moving much, or breathing much either. "We'll let you know, Mum."

CHAPTER 9

Seafer was sitting with his back to the rockface, just outside the entrance of Stem and Maleef's cave. His only duty was watching over Steef, which thankfully didn't take much effort, since Seafer's mind was elsewhere. Steef hadn't moved much in the past quarterday, just standing there facing the cave entrance, blankfaced. Even Kivverr was fairly quiet, after Steef had made it clear there was no play to be had for a while. They were waiting on the others to arrive, and Pill had informed Seafer that the boat was close.

Not close enough. The quiet was broken with the sound of a baby crying. Steef took a deep, deep breath, eyes widening to their fullest. Seafer looked up, then went back to his thoughts, not noticing the boat gliding in. Cassa arrived on a dead run, plunging straight into the cave. Antee was coming with Mokam, not wanting to outpace the old Miner, whose knees were slowing him some. The look on Antee's face said he would have carried him if he could, to make better time. But there was no hurry now, if ever there had been.

Arima came out to greet them. Glancing at the others, she went to Steef, "Your sister is here," she said with a tired smile, "And she'd like to meet you."

Springing around her without a word, he followed his Sassy into the cave. Mokam and Antee finally got there.

"Malem or Maleem?" asked Antee.

"Malem."

"Everybody all right?" He already knew the answer, with a Master Healer in attendance for the entire pregnancy, but courtesy required it. She nodded.

Mokam stepped into the conversation, "And the child is...?" Seafer perked up, wishing he'd thought to ask that.

"Green Three. A good, strong Three, but that's it." Behind her, Seafer grinned broadly. Greens everywhere. Even the Sprout counted. "We can confirm it with the Cats next cycle."

"We trust your abilities, Master Grader," replied Mokam formally, with only a slight bow. He was getting better.

"I thank you, Master Miner, for your courtesy," she returned, with a small answering bow, "But I prefer using the Cats, as you know."

"Well," broke in Antee, to change the subject, "It seems that this one doesn't mind crying."

❉   ❉   ❉

"Well, did you bring 'em?" To be fair, Seafer had waited the rest of the day, until the hubbub had died down. He was now ready to get on with crafting. His crafting.

They weren't looking forward much to lastmeal, as Arima and Cassa were preparing it without Maleef's help. The men were more weary than they cared to admit, unloading the boat without Stem. Antee had gotten the heaviest duties there, and was reclined by the fire, examining his eyelids. Steef had finally consented to play with Kivverr, but wouldn't leave the cove, so their play consisted mostly of the great Cat tossing the little boy around like a ball. He did it gently, if such a thing can be described as gentle, and the soft dirt cushioned the blows. All of the adults cringed when they would see him hit, so they didn't much watch any more. Steef loved it, and never noticed the bruises or scratches. His wild laughter was a bit subdued today, though. Perhaps his mind was elsewhere.

Seafer and Mokam were sitting near Antee, speaking in hushed tones for the Yellow's sake, and not for secrecy. But Seafer was vibrating a bit with intensity. Mokam nodded, and pointed to one of the trunks they had unloaded. Seafer relaxed.

"Good! We'll place 'em in the morning...you gotta come up an' watch...you never been up, Mokam...an' you really should see just once anyway...after all that you've put in...well, you ought to come once, anyway...I said that, didn't I?...well it's true..."

"Yes, old friend, I'll come see your tree."

"Well...it's not really my tree, y'know...nosir...the tree belongs to the Sprout, for true...I don't go up any more less'n the Sprout's along...and tells it to let me come up...quit going by mys..."

Antee's eyes didn't open, but his mouth did, "What do you mean, Steef tells the tree to let you up?" Apparently his exam wasn't as deep as they thought.

"He talks to it all the time, when we're up together," Seafer said casually. "Thought it was strange myself…until I remembered that I used to talk to my whole orchard all the time…there *is* something odd though…that tree don't like for me to be in it, less'n the Sprout's along an' talkin' to it…keep gettin' little shocks in my feet an' hands…less'n the Sprout's there…then I don't get 'em…strange." He shrugged.

Antee and Mokam were staring at Seafer, who was, as usual, completely unaware of their reaction, as his eyes were still on Mokam's trunk. As his explanation had unfolded, their mouths had opened proportionately. Then they turned to look at each other.

Antee recovered enough to say, "Pill, would you go ask Steef to come over here, please?" While still in the cove, they were far enough away that the Yellow didn't want to go hoarse, screaming at them.

"No."

"No? Did you just say no?"

"He's in that Cat's mouth, and HE eats anything but Steef."

"Hmmm. Can't argue with that." He turned to the ever-present Timmerr. "Timmerr, could you call Kivverr over here, please. If he comes, Steef will be with him."

"Or in him."

Timmerr let out a roar that only served to get Kivverr to turn his head. It wasn't enough, so, Timmerr repeated himself. Irritated, Kivverr spat Steef onto the ground, and roared back. The ensuing conversation gave everyone enough headpain that Antee wished he'd just waited. All of the ruckus finally resulted in Kivverr and Steef standing at the fire.

"Steef…uh…do you…uh…talk…to your tree?" Antee couldn't believe he was asking this.

"Uh-huh."

"Well…hmmm…uh…does your tree…uh…talk back?"

"HA! HA! HA! HA! HA! HA! HA! HA! HA!…That's a good funny, UncaAntee…HA! HA! HA! HA! HA!…trees don't talk!"

Antee was instantly relieved and embarrassed. Neither lasted long.

"She listens real good, though."

❀   ❀   ❀

It was an indication of how much they'd changed. Next morning, when Mokam opened his box, it wasn't filled with Dust. It was filled with Crystals. All pure, of course. All sizes. No one said anything, or even looked particularly interested.

Antee had spent the previous evening trying to make sense of Steef's claim that his tree 'listened'. Steef had offered to show him last night, but it was getting dark, so the topic had been set aside for morning, since everyone was going up into Seafwood anyway. Seafer was eager for them to witness the stone-setting.

There should be plenty of room. The tree was over twenty staffs tall now, and fifteen across. Seafer had quit measuring it daily. In fact, he'd hadn't been in it at all for a Quarter cycle. Said 'the Sprout was taking care of it', and it pleasured him enough to watch from the ground.

No one mentioned that a fall from *this* tree would probably kill him.

But they were all going up today, with Mokam's Crystals. All but the new parents and the baby. They hadn't seen Seafer this agitated since the acorns were planted. He was hopping a bit more carefully these days, but the eyes were just as intense.

"Mokam, you got the box…good…well, let's go!…rotted Cat!…move out, now!" Kivverr had moved to the base, and wasn't letting anyone pass until Steef started up, at which time the Cat turned and sprang over the small body, racing up to the lowest main branches, where he spun around and waited.

Cassa whispered to Arima, "I wonder if that tree is big enough for all of us, with him behaving like that."

"If you can think of anything we can do about it, let me know," the Healer whispered back. At least Rivverr and Timmerr were staying on the ground.

Climbing was easy enough. The huge, twisted trunk still had its five separate lines, with wide creases between them that made for sure footing. In spite of that, the thought came to Arima that at least some of them were a little old to be climbing trees. Beats later, they were all up on the first tier of branches. The boughs here were heavy, and the leaves so thick, it almost appeared to be a floor. Each of the main limbs had its own share of twisting staff growths springing straight up into points. Where these staffs met their limbs, there were burls. There were no burls on the sides or bottoms of any limbs. The staffs here on the lower limbs appeared to be large enough to serve any Master, though they had no stones in them yet. That's why they were all here, to watch Seafer set some stones. At least the staff/limb/growth things served as good handholds.

Kivverr was sprawled in a wallowed out section of intertwining leaves and limbs that looked as if it had grown up around him. Steef had climbed on up to the next main line, and apparently scurried out from the trunk a ways, for when she got up there, Arima saw his little head sticking down through a top-wall of leaves and limbs, watching their progress.

"You wanna see, UncaAntee?" his excited voice came over Seafer's, who was already directing Mokam.

"Show me, Son."

"Okay!" His head disappeared, but they could still hear him. "Seafwood, I'm gonna jump! Let me up!" With that, the limbs above their head began to groan and creak. And move. Separating. Making a gap that they all could look up through. In that gap, they saw the tree opening all the way to the top, and the back end of a climbing boy. There were other staffs growing up there, too. Hundreds of them. The higher up they were growing, the smaller they were. Steef only went partway, turned, and shouted, "I'm ready!" With that, the heavy limbs they were standing on swayed inward, causing the adults to wobble a bit, and all the leaves underneath the gap bunched together. Steef started laughing as he hurled himself from his perch, plunging in a blur past all those pointy staffs. Arms spread wide, he crashed into the heavy cushion of leaves. He was still laughing as he pulled himself out, "Thanks, Seafwood! I'm done jumping now!" Everything instantly snapped back into place, startling them all.

Seafer had forgotten about his errand.

"See UncaAntee, she listens real good!"

"Yes...yes, it...uh...she does."

"Doesn't surprise me," said Cassa defiantly, though her wide open eyes said otherwise, "Nope...a tree taking orders...doesn't surprise me at all... nope......Seafer, *what have you done?*"

Seafer's head waggled a bit, but nothing came out.

"Steef," continued Antee, "Why are you calling the tree 'Seafwood'?"

"'Cause she needed a name, and I'm named after Papa and Mama, so I named her after *her* Papa! She likes it, too."

Seafer's shoulders slumped, and his head bowed.

Arima finally caught her breath enough to ask, "Pumpkin, why do keep saying 'she'?"

"'Cause she's a she, Antreema."

"Well, if she doesn't talk to you, how do you know she's a she?" Now he had her doing it.

"'Cause I told her 'bout Mama having a baby, and she liked that too, so now she's gonna have babies too! Only Mamas can have babies. You told me that, Antreema. Gotta be a she." He was pleased as he could be with his logic.

But Seafer's head had stopped waggling, snapping to alert, "Sprout, did you say she was havin' babies!?" His feet…yes…they were moving again.

"Uh-huh."

Head twisting back and forth, up and down, he exclaimed, "I don' see any acorns, Sprout!…you sure?"

"Yessir, UncaSeafer. I told Seafwood last night that everyone was coming, and she moved her babies up there." One little finger pointed up.

Cassa turned to Arima and silently mouthed, "*She moved her babies?*"

Seafer was still talking, mainly to himself, through his shakes, "I'd give up, y'know…on seein' any acorns…shoulda seen 'em by now…guess it just needed the Sprout to tell…uh…tell her…couldn't have known that…would never have known." His voice got very soft as he asked, "Sprout, do you think…she…would let me see one?" The air was suddenly very still.

"Why sure, UncaSeafer!…you're Seafwood's Papa!…hold out your hand real still!" He tilted his head back, and shouted, "Seafwood, UncaSeafer wants to see a baby!"

A small hole appeared in the leaves directly above the old Green, and one lone acorn dropped through. It fell neatly into the center of his hand, which clamped closed instantly. They all watched Seafer's face take on a look of serene peace.

"That's it!" exclaimed Cassa, hands thrown up, "I'm going back down to solid ground…where, where, where the dirt *swallows*…things…and…*feeds*…this…aaahh!" She clambered down, and stomped off towards her cave.

There probably would have been an awkward quiet about now, if Seafer had any awkward in him, "Sprout, how many acorns *are* there?" The familiar Seafer was back, hopping as well as he could while standing on a tree limb, which wasn't bad, having a lifetime of practice behind him.

"I don't know, UncaSeafer, I can't go that high."

"Well how high *can* you climb?…can you count some o' them for me?"

"Nossir, I mean you haven't taught me how to count that high yet."

Beat. Beat. Beat.

"I think," Arima said slowly, as she was feeling more like Cassa with each passing beat, "That I need to witness your Crystal project later, Seafer. And maybe you do, too."

He nodded without argument, which said a lot. Mokam shrugged, closing his box back up.

As they were making their way back down, Mokam asked, "Seafer, are you telling us that you were unaware of the tree's unusual abilities?"

"Well, y'know...I don't come up here much any more...though I've seen the Sprout talkin' to it often enough...but I didn't think anythin' about it...been talkin' to trees all my life...none of 'em ever seemed to listen, though...say Sprout..."

"Yessir?"

"How come you'd wait an' tell Antee 'bout this instead o' me?" He didn't sound offended, just curious.

"He asked."

❧   ❧   ❧

About threequarterday, Seafer had recovered enough to go back up and start placing Crystals. Cassa and Arima chose to remain on the ground, so only Mokam and Antee followed the Green Master into the tree. Steef and Kivverr were waiting. Antee had the thought that Steef must surely be unaware of the oddness of his tree, since it was the only tree he knew. Besides, he was Steef.

Once on the main tier again, Seafer asked Mokam to show him the largest Crystals in the box. Mokam handed over three stones that easily dwarfed Antee's closed fist. Seafer hefted them absently as he looked around the tree, examining each of the staff growths closely. He finally settled on three of the largest, though Antee noted that there were at least two growths that were visibly larger. He asked about it.

"Them two aren't growin' straight," explained Seafer, "If you look at 'em close, the twinin' isn't even,...don't know that it matters, much...this is all new to me, too...so I'm guessin' best I can." With that, he abruptly dumped the three Crystals into Antee's hands, and bent over one of his selections with his staff. Putting his own stone against the base of the growth, he Pulsed. Nothing happened. He Pulsed again. More nothing.

Straightening up, sort of, he scratched his head and said, "Hmpff!...you boys might want to stand back...and drain...no...y'don't have your staffs...good...well, back up just a bit anyways." They couldn't see it, but they knew he was gathering up a goodly charge of Power. Another Pulse. Another nothing.

"That would o' made a normal limb curl into a ball...I knew this thing would be tuned to the Sprout...never thought I wouldn't be able to service it...hmmmm...Sprout!...where are you, boy?...oh, there you are...come on down here, would you?"

Steef had been watching with his head stuck down from above again. With Seafer's call, he just pushed through the leaves, and his body unfurled itself until he was hanging from a limb. Dropping down, he went to his Unca, and waited.

"Sprout...I want to put this here Crystal...thank you, Antee...this here Crystal...in a gap between that burl and the staff there...can you ask if...uh...she...would make a gap for us?"

"Sure, UncaSeafer!" Two small hands wrapped the large stone. Bending, Steef tapped it against the burl, "Seafwood, open up right here!" he shouted.

"It might listen well, but it obviously doesn't hear too good," Pill buzzed into Antee's ear. He nodded.

The wood split apart right where Steef had tapped. "More!...Okay, that's good!" The boy popped the stone into the opening. "Is that Okay, UncaSeafer?"

"That's good, Sprout." Seafer was focused on his task, oblivious to what had just happened.

"Okay Seafwood, close back up!" With that, the wood snapped back into place, closing over the fingers Steef had left in the gap while holding the Crystal. Antee started, reaching quickly for the boy, thinking his fingers must surely be broken, or worse. But Steef just laughed and said, "Seafwood, quit playing!...leggo my fingers!" His hand flew back as if the fingers had been spit out.

Still, Seafer had taken no notice. They moved around the lower tier, Steef placing stones as directed, until the three largest, and several other notable stones had been set. They were left with Mokam's box still almost full of medium and small sized stones. Seafer then spent a quarterday directing Steef around the tree, matching stone size to staff size.

It was fascinating for Antee, watching the boy work his tree. Steef had no trouble finding paths through the myriad of limbs and leaves, since the tree made paths for him as he moved. There was constant swishing and groaning and creaking for quite a while. Conversation was impossible, so Antee spent his beats pondering all of the unlikely events that had led him to be spending a day watching a tree 'listen'. He knew that this tree had become more than

Seafer expected, and wondered if that had been Seafer's Mastery at work, or the tree's interaction with Steef. He doubted they would ever know. He wondered too, where this Festival of Errors would lead for everyone. His life was now wound up in Steef as tightly as one of the boy's staffs. He could envision several different paths for Steef's life, and most of them ended badly. None of them ended with Steef spending his life as a Yellow Master and Healer of Beasts. He sighed. Did that really matter? No. It mattered to give the boy training in Power and Life, and let his sweet disposition guide him. That disposition comforted Antee, and frightened him.

Mokam quickly tired of the scene, and nodded to Antee as he clambered down the trunk. Seafer never noticed that either. Kivverr was asleep, despite the noise.

❀   ❀   ❀

Arima had checked in on Maleef and the baby, then settled in front of her own cave, waiting for the men to be done playing in the tree. From Cassa's cave, she heard the pounding of drums. Presently, Mokam emerged from the tree, and headed for his own cave.

Pop! *"Arima, there's news from Town."*

"Don't want to hear it, Pill." She got enough news from the other Masters to suit her. That life was over. Pill had been told often enough to keep their gossip to themselves.

"You'll want to hear this. There's a new GuildMaster of White."

"Wwhhaattt!? What happened to Mileck?"

"Dead."

"But he wasn't *that* old!" *Or was he? I'm losing track…now if I'm…* "How did he die?"

"Duel. With Vinntag. You can guess who the new GuildMaster is."

Well. That *was* news. She wouldn't mourn much for Mileck. He'd certainly never done Arima any service, letting himself be run by Vinntag's crowd. She'd questioned his promotion to GuildMaster all those cycles ago, always considering him too weak-willed to lead. But there'd been no denying his Power. He must have been older than she realized, for Vinntag to defeat him. If she'd held any hope at all for the future of her Guild, it was gone now. White would now become a Guild of Healers who hated people.

"You know what this means?"

"It will mean a lot of things, Pill. None of them good. But I can't imagine which one you're thinking of."

"You're now officially the strongest White Master alive. Even Vinntag can't argue that."

That stopped her. Leave it to Pill to think of something profound and unimportant. "I suppose you're right, Pill. I feel so much better now. Thank you."

"You've got to challenge her, Arima! You would be GuildMaster!"

"Don't want to be GuildMaster, Pill. You should know me well enough by now to guess that."

"But the Cats, Arima! You could bring them back to the Cats!"

"They still wouldn't come, Pill. They like their new influence too much. And their Dust. They'd find a reason not to come. I'd be dueling with everyone in the Guild." She had a new thought, "Besides, I'm *not* the strongest White alive."

"Your modesty is admirable, Arima, but you know…"

"I'm about to start training the strongest White alive." That purpose suited her much better than being GuildMaster.

"Oh…Yes…Yes you are. That will be even more fun! We'll wait." Pop!

There was no telling what Pill really wanted out of a duel between Arima and Vinntag. She assumed that the duel itself would be story enough for them. And Steef represented a Vault full of stories. Their priorities concerned her. Pill would love it if Steef challenged for GuildMaster. Hmmm. Which Guild? Pill would probably want him to blast through all of them. She couldn't imagine Steef wanting anything so ambitious. But if Vinntag ever got a hint about the boy, she wouldn't rest until she had mastered him, or killed him. Arima's only comfort was knowing that the older Steef got, the harder it would be to do either. *Grow boy. Grow faster.*

Steef had mastered Color separation. In fact, he displayed remarkable control of the size and quantity of his Pulses for someone his age. Arima and Seafer had worked with him during all the days of his Mother's pregnancy, and now real training could begin. He carried a live stick at all times now, though 'carried' wasn't accurate. They had ordered a sling made from some leather craftsmen in a village not too far away, which he wore across his back. He carried the stick there. With Kivverr's determined efforts to grab Steef unexpectedly and toss him skyward, sticks routinely went flying. They would often land on Seafer's dirt, and be gone. This hadn't mattered when they were just sticks, but the sling prevented further losses of live sticks. Arima had wondered how much that really mattered, since they had a seemingly endless supply of them, but Steef liked his sling, and that settled it. The live stick he carried had no stone, for until now, focusing hadn't been part of his training. That was about to change, so Seafer sent the boy into his tree to retrieve the smallest stick up there that had a stone in it.

It seemed only natural to have Mokam begin the training on focusing, since it involved a stone. Lastmeal was finished, and they had spent an eighthnight banging out some truly awful noise. Cassa in particular, was giving her drums a workout.

Mokam and Steef walked over to the nearest spot of rock wall, Mokam carrying his own staff. Mokam's staff was typical for a Master Brown, and a Miner. It was carved, of course, but not ornately. Uniform grooves ran up and down its length in perfect symmetry. The Green that had fabricated the wood had stained it to a dark chestnut color. Naturally, the stone was a Crystal. A really large Crystal, set in wooden fingers that were also perfectly formed. The staff said 'expensive' without being showy. He brought up a small charge.

"Young man," he said, though his tone was gentler now, "We're going to discuss focusing your Power through a stone. Drain yourself, and draw up a small amount of Brown…no, you won't need your own staff just yet, we're going to use mine first." Mokam then sank his staff a bit, so that it would stand on its own. Picking Steef up, the Brown Master balanced his apprentice on a hip.

"Make sure there is no Power in your arms," said the Brown Master, placing his free hand on top of his stone, "And put your hands on the sides of my stone, under my hand. Mmm-hmmm. That's right. Feel the Power in the stone. Do you feel it? Right, then. It's only moving a bit, because I haven't put much in there, but if you concentrate, you'll feel that it's spinning around and around inside the stone."

Steef took on his concentration face, tongue sticking out. After a few beats, he nodded.

"Now, here's what happens when I push more Power into it. Speeding up, isn't it? With practice, you can tell how much charge your stone is carrying just by how fast it's spinning. It will stay there indef…hum…a long time, if I don't release it or drain it. That's because this is not just any stone, it's Crystal. Other kinds of stones will carry Power, and focus it, but only Crystal holds it for long."

"Is this a Crystal in my stick, MassMoke?"

"Yes Sir, it is. The very best Crystal you can find. It's a small little fellow, but he'll serve you well. Hmmm. Where were we? Oh, focusing. Up until now, you have just been Pulsing out the end of your stick, and aiming by pointing it. We're going to aim with this stone." Mokam slid his hand down the side so that it faced directly away from them. "There are two ways to do that. The simplest way is to push the Power away from your hand, like this." The Brown Pulsed through his hand, and a small squirt of Brown Power shot out of the stone, cutting a neat little hole in the stone before them. "Now, I'm going to show you the second way, but I don't want you to try this until I say you're ready. Understand? All right." He removed his hand from the stone completely. "When you're practiced, you will get to the point where you can feel your Power in your staff from anywhere you're touching it. Your Power has a 'tune' to it, which you will learn to feel, just like breathing." He grasped the staff a span below the stone. "I can feel it spinning and spinning in there. When the spin gets to where I want it to go…" He Pulsed, and the first hole got larger.

"Now get your staff." Steef squirmed in his grasp, pulling the little stick out of its sling. "Hold it in front of you in one hand, and fill it with a small charge. Ready? Good. Put your other hand on the stone, facing towards the rock wall. That's right. Now, with *only* the hand that's on the stone, give it a little push."

A nice, neat hole opened in the rock wall, not far from Mokam's. It was the size of Mokam's head.

"That will do. Move your hand around your stone a bit, and let's see if we can make a smaller push."

Three spans over, another hole appeared, slightly smaller than the first.

"That's a good effort, young man. Now, try aiming just below that last one. Move your hand *up* just a wee bit. Push when you're ready."

The third hole wasn't directly below the second, but close. Mokam set him down a staff away from the first set of holes, "Recharge when you need to. I want you to stand in this spot without moving, and give me four holes that form a square." And so it went, with Mokam giving him different patterns to try, honing his aim.

After Steef retired to his tree for the evening, Mokam told the others, "It was nice to have something work for the first time without any surprises." To which they all fervently agreed. Some of the tension of the day relaxed, and they went to their caves a bit calmer. Even Cassa.

In the morning, they rose to find Steef at the opposite side of the cove, with Kivverr watching through half-open eyes. There were Steef-high holes along the wall for twenty staffs. The patterns that he formed were crude at one end, but the most recent ones were getting cleanly spaced. When Mokam inspected them, he was pleased to note that the size and depth of the holes became more uniform as well.

❋   ❋   ❋

It had been impossible to round up any of the local herd beasts with Kivverr along, and Antee had finally instructed Steef to make the Cat go back to the cove. They had walked a quarter of the morning away from their home, with Antee routinely sending out feeding Pulses, but one sight of Kivverr had always sent the cattle away. It was hard to be angry at them for it.

Finally, they had a small group of cows standing around, and Antee chose two of them.

"First thing you need to know, Steef," he began, "Is that you must *never* try this on any of the Cats."

"Okay."

"Fill up with some Yellow, Son."

Antee picked him up, setting him on the cow's back. "Put your hands over mine," he instructed, as he placed his own hands on either side of the beast. He had to hold them closer than he normally would, so Steef could reach. "Can you feel my Power? It's in my right hand only. Feel it? I'm going to send a small Pulse into the cow…," he did, "…and catch it again in my left hand. Did you feel it hit my left hand? No? We'll try it again…and again…got it? Good. Now we're going to send a small, constant…do you know what constant means?…it means we don't stop…a small constant Pulse and catch it, while we run our hands down the cow's back. You'll have to scoot back while we do it. Ready? Here we go." They made a run as far they could without Steef falling off the back.

"Now Steef, the Pulse that we caught in *this* hand…matched the Pulse we sent out from *this* hand. Let's do it again." And they did it several times, after which Antee picked him up, and set him on a second cow, one that he'd already tested, knowing what they'd find. They repeated the process.

"Did you notice anything different about this cow, Son?"

The little head bobbed, "This one got fuzzy right about *here*, UncaAntee."

Antee grinned at him, "That's exactly right, sweet boy! It got fuzzy right at the belly. This cow has eaten something that doesn't like her, and one of her bellies is sore. You ever get a sore belly? Sure you do. What happens when your belly is sore?"

"Antreema loves on me, an' I get gooder."

"Well we're going to love on this cow, and she'll get better, too! Only we're going to love on her with some Yellow Power." Moving until they were centered on the beast's middle, Antee said, "Put your hands right here on each side. Now fill your arms and hands with Yellow until I say stop...*stop*...now with both hands, Pulse into the cow." The Master felt Steef's Power drain into the beast.

"Let's do another pass now, and you tell me what you feel..."

"The fuzzy's gone, UncaAntee! Did I make the cow gooder?"

"You sure did, pumpkin." He pulled his young student off of the cow, "Now we're going to wait right here for just a beat or two, and the bad belly you just fixed is going to come right out the back end." When it did, they shared a good laugh.

"How about we spend the rest of the morning checking these beasts, and any others we can find? I'll show you how to do this with your staff."

❀   ❀   ❀

"Shortstick!...wait...wait a beat...whew!" the little Blue Master stopped, holding her sides, and trying to breathe. *I'd forgotten what a climb was like!* She thought. *Riding that boat has made me soft.* She could remember clearly the four cycles she'd spent at the Blue Guild's training mountain. It had been carved by Browns into the peak of the tallest mountain in the Territories, reachable only by boat. She developed climbing legs then, going from class huts to eating huts, to the observatory, and back down to her own sleeping closet.

She had just discovered that those legs were gone, replaced by soft porridge, seemingly.

Cassa wanted to get him high, of course, just not in a boat. Training for the young could tip a boat, a lesson Blues learned early, which explained why all but their last Master training was always done on firm ground. High ground, but firm. So they were climbing above the cove, to the highest overhang. Getting up here by boat would have meant asking Mokam to come along. She didn't want any Browns, even Mokam, around when she gave Blue training. She felt no guilt about her attitude. She assumed Mokam would feel the same about his Guild's workings. The others, too.

They had had midmeal, and Antee had finished his training session for the day. It was Cassa's turn. While they had been out with the beasts, she had asked

Mokam to Lift the boat above the Valley walls, where she could make some unobstructed Pulses. Spending much of the morning aloft, she had brought in a nice selection of clouds and pressures to play with. It was all holding within easy reach beyond the tallest walls of the cove. If she could just get there on these useless legs!

They finally made it, and though Cassa wasn't dead from the effort, she wondered if death might not be an improvement. All of her preparations were still there. She started pointing out the different cloud formations, briefly discussing what they meant.

"Now Shortstick, the three most important things to master with weather control, are temperature, pressure, and moisture. Do you know what moisture is? No. Okay, moisture means how much water is in the air."

"There's water in the air, Sassy? Even when it's not raining?"

"Sure is, little buddy. I'll be showing you how to feel it. Later, we'll learn how to call it up. Let's start with the easiest first, though. Temperature. You can feel temperature on your skin. Now here...is a cool breeze. Feel it? Let's make it a cold breeze...That's a cold one, eh? If we didn't stay warm through our Power, we'd need heavy garments for that one. Now...we'll warm it up. You have to watch out that you don't get too warm, Shortstick. We don't ever get cold, but we can overheat, and Blues can hurt themselves if we're not careful. We'll train on that, too."

"Now here's how we change the temperature..."

✤   ✤   ✤

"She is still there, GuildMaster."

"Is she doing anything out of the ordinary?" There was no sweetening to her voice now. It was cold and hard.

"Not that we can determine, GuildMaster. She continues to dwell in the Valley, in that cove. Green Master Seafer is still there, as are the servant family and their children. We have finally determined who the servant family is. They are simple mountain folk. Both of them lowly Greens. She probably selected them to help with the crops. Seafer is fairly old, and reputedly so self-damaged that even Arima cannot Heal him completely. He continues to grow that odd tree, but that's all."

"And no other activity?"

"There are still routine boat deliveries of supplies. Aside from that, she is visited only by Cats. They are everywhere. We can find no one in GuildTown that she communicates with, other than Red Master Dilruk, and again, that's only for supplies. She has never contacted her brother. Or...his Mate."

"You will continue to watch Linzel. She was always friendly with *Arima*." She almost spat her enemy's name.

"Yes GuildMaster...If I may, GuildMaster...is it safe to trifle with a Black Master? They are not known for their patience, and Master Linzel is particularly deadly."

"I don't want you to trifle with her. Just watch her. I will deal with the Black Guild myself."

"As you say, GuildMaster."

"Pool, you need to get closer than way up in the air. We can't tell anything from your reports."

"If we get closer, Pill will know we're there, and one of us might become a Cat meal. We're as close as we're getting without giving you away. Besides, there's nothing going on there. The woman is playing with her pet Cats. The only way she could be less of a bother to you, would be if she were dead."

"That is a lovely thought, Pool. I will accomplish that one day, if age doesn't do it for me."

"You're older than she is, Vinntag."

The small woman frowned. All Buzzbies were intolerable, and Pool was positively insufferable. She raged inwardly, again, that they were so necessary. And they knew it.

"True, Pool. But there's no one in that Valley to give her a Freshening, now is there? I'll outlive her yet."

CHAPTER 10

Arima arose to find Rivverr waiting outside her cave, and the ClanCat was with him. She knew what was coming. They hadn't discussed it, but she knew. She might not be a Healer of beasts, but age was age in any living thing, and Rivverr had it. For a cycle now, the frequency of his absences had increased. He would spend more and more time in his cave, the trip down and back being more taxing than he would admit.

He had never brought the ClanCat to her, in all these cycles. There had never been a need. The small group of humans had direct contact with the Cats through herself and Steef, and indirectly through Antee. But there was a Grading coming soon, and she was the Grader, and he was the ClanCat, and Rivverr was very old. She had seen age take her parents. She'd seen it take many others to whom she was less close. It was a practiced pain.

That only helped her remain standing. Her tears began before she got to him, wrapping her arms as far across his massive chest as she could reach. *I won't sob! Rivverr needs his decorum, and so does his Son.* There was a ringing in her ears, though. The wail she couldn't give.

"Yes, it is sad, my friend. We must part now for my Resting. But I will wait for you. When you find your Rest, we will be glad together again. Perhaps then you will have enough legs, and we can run together."

"I'll just go there with you now," she whispered.

"It is not your time, and that is crooked thinking. Do not let your moaning control you. You are needed here, to complete your task with the MixMaster. Be patient. I will wait." He bent and rubbed his head against hers.

"Now," he said, raising back up, *"You are the Healer. You must know the ClanCat, and he must know you. This is my cub. He is Plivverr. He is serving the*

Clan well. Greet him." With that, Rivverr gave a low rumble, which the other Cat returned.

Arima didn't want to let go, knowing that she must. Once she contacted the ClanCat, she could never speak to Rivverr again. Slowly she turned, letting Rivverr's fur pull reluctantly through her fingers. Then…he was gone.

Facing the ClanCat, she saw absently that he was slightly smaller than his sire, but not much. She'd seen him often enough, as he strode through the Valley, leading the Clan or taking a meal. But she'd never seen them this close together for comparison. She noted the familiar shape of his own white splash, and his magnificent horns. They stood facing each other for several beats, when it occurred to her that she was required to speak.

"It…it is my honor to meet you, your Majesty. Thank you for coming," was all she could force out. She did remember to give a bow. She knew that protocol required him to wait before responding, but he didn't. Immediately lifting his head and turning it, he exposed his neck for first contact. She took the few steps, and reached out her shaking hand.

"It is well that we meet Healer. You are held in great esteem by my sire, my Clan, and myself. I regret only that I am too young to remember your great battles for us, but the story is now part of the Clan, and we will remember always that you took no steps back. This, I oath you."

She would never remember the rest of that conversation, or even the rest of that day. She noted from her pad that Maleef would occasionally bring her a bit of food, but she wasn't much interested in eating. There was a blur of time for her that finally got interrupted by Steef. She opened an eye to see him standing by her pad, unmoving. She didn't know how long he'd been there.

"Aunt Ah-Reeema," he said quietly, his eyes wide, "Kivverr says it's time for the Moaning. They're waiting on you."

Nodding, she rose. Noting the unused food on her table, she wondered how many days she'd been here. Steef led her out. She was unprepared for the sight awaiting her. The cove was filled with Cats. They were everywhere. Seafer, Stem, Maleef, and young Malem were standing by one of the caves, watching quietly. Steef led her to the center of the Clan, as the great Cats made way for them. Waiting there were Plivverr and Kivverr. It was eerily quiet, the only sound was the shuffling of feet and paws.

Steef took his place next to Kivverr, and she stood next to the ClanCat. As soon as she stopped, the great Cat threw back his head, giving a headache-grade moan that shook her bones. Immediately, all the other Cats joined in. The screeching and moaning began just before sunset. It lasted until dawn.

She was out of tears. Exhausted. And hungry. She let Maleef help her eat, while Steef just watched. He had joined in the Moaning, of course, but hadn't shed a single tear. She asked him about it.

"Kivverr says," he replied, "That his Papa has Rested well. His life was…was…what was that word Kivverr?…well-spent…and that the Moaning was for honor. Kivverr says that his Papa will be remembered with gladness, and that's not a crying thing."

Arima stared at him, her mouth chewing the food without her.

"No pumpkin," she finally said, "It's not a crying thing, is it? But you know what *is* a crying thing? The way I smell. I think I need to bathe."

Two sevendays later, the others arrived for Malem's Grading. Arima had told Plivverr that only smaller males would be required, and several were waiting. Cassa was particularly excited, as she had never witnessed a Grading by Cats. For her sake, and the Cats', Arima took her time, and refined Malem's results as closely as could be.

This presented a few difficulties, as the young girl didn't much like being close to the Cats. Arima had to Pulse some calm into her more than once. The process was also slowed by Malem being put to sleep once, instead of the Cat. Eventually, they came up with a Grade of three and a half, about what Arima had judged at the child's birth. The experience was worthwhile though, judging from the way the Cats strode around the cove for days following. Their purpose had been restored, if only briefly.

There was music that night, for the first time since the Moaning. The celebration was a bit muted, but Arima finally joined in, and they went on for quite a while. Steef had begun with them, but quit early. No one noticed that he was sitting and looking at his flute intently.

Arima and Seafer had ample amounts of Steef's beats for training, so when the other three Masters visited, the White and Green gave over those days. The pace became almost frantic, they had all waited so long. An older child might have complained about all the lessons, but Steef was thrilled with all of the new things he was learning, and spent his spare time practicing. When Kivver wasn't eating him.

❈   ❈   ❈

"Shortstick, let's see if we can't call up some wind, and make it change speed and direction."

❈   ❈   ❈

"Those are parasites. They can kill the beast if we don't do something about it. Here's how."

❈   ❈   ❈

"Pulse over here…that's sandstone. Now over here…that's hardrock. You can feel the difference in the Pulse that returns to you."

❈   ❈   ❈

"When cold air meets hot air, we get a storm. They can meet head-on, or overlay each other. Here are the different results."

❈   ❈   ❈

"Looks like our acorns are comin' up just fine, Sprout!…now look here at this corn. Thirsty lookin' isn't it?…gotta have some rain…remind me to talk to Cassa…you'll do that for us soon, y'know…these beans over here we planted too late…they're comin' up, but won't bear properly by harvest Quarter, so we're gonna speed 'em up a little…we do it like this."

❈   ❈   ❈

"Feel that little 'hiccup' in your Pulse? That's a seam in the rock layers. There's probably some good stones under that. Let's look for them."

❈   ❈   ❈

There was now a common jest among them, that Stem was probably the healthiest living man. He had volunteered to let his Son practice White on him. His muscles rippled with the slightest movement. He practically ran everywhere, his walking gait was so strong, and they mused routinely that he looked taller. Arima's only concern was that they didn't have any truly sick people needing Healing, for Steef to get experience in diagnosis.

❧   ❧   ❧

They were at the top of the cove. From here, you could see the topmost branches of Seafwood below. Kivverr was stretched out on his side, with Steef sitting against his chest. Steef held his flute in one hand, and his stick in the other.

"*What are you doing?*" Kivverr didn't really care, but Steef had been quiet for too long.

"Making music," Steef said simply.

"*I do not hear anything.*"

"It's in my head."

"*That is much harder to hear. Make it come out of your pipe.*"

"That's the problem. What I hear in my head doesn't come out of my flute. Gotta fix that."

"*Are you going to blast it with your stick? Will it sound better then?*" Kivverr didn't sound hopeful.

"No, I'm trying something else."

"*I do not see you trying anything.*"

"You can't see anything with your eyes closed! Look here."

"*That was sass. I am definitely going to have to eat you soon.*"

"It isn't sass. Look here at the stick. You can eat me tomorrow."

Kivverr lifted his head slightly, and opened his eyes.

"*I still do not see anything.*"

"Look closer."

"*It has got a hole in it. You need a new stick.*"

"Closer."

Steef held the stick right in front of Kivverr's eyes. There were two holes, one just below the small Crystal, and another at the point. As Kivverr watched, the stick was expanding and shrinking in Steef's hand.

"Unk-ull SeeeFurr taught me how to man…man…"

"*Manipulate. I was there.*"

"Um-hmm. Let's see what comes out." With that, he put the top hole to his mouth, and blew into it. A small, almost transparent bubble came out. It separated, and started to float off. Steef stuck his finger into it and it popped with a clear note. Turning back to Kivverr, he gave a bright grin. Then he blew a long wind into the stick, and a stream of bubbles came out. He popped the first one, which set off the entire stream, in sequence. He got a perfect scale.

"Well, it seems to work, but your tune is boring."

"Guess we'll just have to think up something you like."

❦   ❦   ❦

"Wha' doin' Bubba?"

"I'm making a surprise for Sassy, Malem," Steef said seriously. He was concentrating. Mass-Turr Mo-Kamm had warned him constantly about cutting away too much stone. He said it would fall if he did.

"Can I watch?" she asked eagerly.

"Sure! Just stay close behind me so Kivverr doesn't step on you."

"Okay…what is it?"

"It's called a stairway. Don't know why…just looks like a bunch of steps to me. Every time we have a lesson, Sassy says she wishes she had a 'stairway to the heavens'. Asked Aunt Ah-Reeema…she said Sassy means steps…so I'm cutting them outta the rock and we'll be able to climb better." Steef had discovered that explanations in advance kept her questions to a minimum.

"Can I go have a lesson with you?" She spent as much time as she could with her brother, which was never enough.

"It's Okay with me, Malem, but you'll have to ask Sassy first."

"Okay." Her tone said she already knew the answer.

❦   ❦   ❦

As the boat came sailing in, they all three looked into the cove expectantly. Every visit held new surprises, as Steef's practice sessions always left their marks. The rock walls were a constant source of amusement. Scribblings of text, or strangely shaped sculptures would await them, to be erased and replaced when they returned. One of his more recent works had been terracing in the wall above and around his parents' cave. He and his Papa had brought in soil for the terraces, and now there were brightly colored flowers for his Mama to enjoy.

Cassa spotted the steps right away, squealing and giggling as if she were thirty cycles younger, knowing instantly what, and who, they were for. Mokam was interested in them as well, for a different reason.

"Well, young man," he said more sternly than he felt. That was all right, Steef was old enough now to know his Brown Master was pleased. "That is a remarkable project. Let's examine it together, shall we? I see a few spots that could use some reinforcement."

Meanwhile, Cassa had sprinted out of sight, her legs working better now with all the practice. Mokam and Steef worked their way up the stairway slowly, with the old Brown pointing out possible problem areas, and also noting several spots that merited praise.

The long row of Steef-made steps made a lazy spiral, generally following the flow of stone that Mokam had taught Steef to feel out with his Pulses. They had made their way a little over halfway up when Cassa had come blazing back down, and was now in the cove with the others.

Mokam was enjoying himself. He had a bright, capable student, and they were surrounded by rock. His perfect world. He was enjoying it just a little too much, and it was about to get cracked.

"Young man, how did you know to turn right here?"

"It was the right place, wasn't it Mass-Turr Mo-Kamm?'

"Yes, it's the right place. It's just that you haven't learned yet how to know that. Did you guess?"

"No Sir. I just stayed away from the big colors, and followed the soft colors."

"Well, it worked out really well…you did *what*?"

"I followed the soft colors, Mass-Turr Mo-Kamm. It seemed to make the steps stronger."

"What colors?" he asked, now dreading the answer. *Anyone but this boy. Not this boy.*

"The rocks, they're full of colors. When I'm full up with Brown, they have colors."

"What colors?" he repeated. He knew what was coming. A cave-in. A melted rock-spout. He couldn't change it.

"Not the colors I see when you glow. They're different. They change, too."

Mokam said nothing as he stared at the boy, pondering what to do, while his belly started churning. Deciding with an abrupt nod, the old Brown picked up his apprentice, and started down the steps.

"Are we done looking at Sassy's stairway?" Steef inquired. He liked when his Mass-Turr Mo-Kamm carried him.

"I think for now, yes." Mokam went silent again as they made their way to ground level, and across the cove to the others. Steef didn't notice, but

Mokam's face was now in constant change, from worry to thrill, and all emotions between.

He had a choice to make, and there was *no* choice. For Steef's sake, the others had to know. For Brown's sake, he *must* keep quiet. Trouble was, silence wouldn't work. The problem wasn't going to go away. Might as well take a breath and crack this rock.

"Pill, please ask everyone to gather. We need to talk." Pop!

By the time the twosome reached the campsite, the others had come out of their caves. Their faces showed clear interest, as Mokam rarely felt a need for consultation. The Brown set Steef down, and straightened up to face them. Might as well get to it.

"I have just learned that the boy has Brown Sight," he said simply. To the others, he looked as if he expected a skybolt to strike him down.

If Mokam was expecting shock at his revelation, he was disappointed. Only Arima seemed surprised, "What do you mean, Brown Sight!?" she asked sharply. "No one has Sight except Whites! What is Brown Sight?"

There was silence, as the other three Masters present suddenly looked like they had bitten into a bitterfruit.

"Some Browns have Sight, Arima. About as many as Whites. They just don't See what White Graders see. The boy has the Sight." His lips stopped, though the rest of him was trembling a bit at the effort to reveal a Brown secret. There was a voice in him, saying that the Brown GuildMaster was going to Pop! out of the rocks any beat.

Arima stared. "You're telling me...that all this time...for as long as we've kept Guild records...Browns have never felt obliged to mention...*that some of them have Sighted eyes!?*"

Mokam faced her squarely. He didn't like revealing Brown secrets, but this was a special circumstance. "It doesn't affect anyone, Arima! Sighted Browns don't See what Sighted Whites See. You Grade people's Power. Browns with Sight See Power sources in the ground." There, it was out. He tried to take a breath.

Arima looked around, but the other Masters were not meeting her eye. Not even Seafer. She glared at them for a beat, wanting help being indignant over the Brown conspiracy. No help was coming. No indignation. And it hit her.

She pointed an accusing finger at the three, who were growing visibly more uncomfortable with each beat, "None of you is particularly surprised! You *knew* about this! Are all the Guilds conspiring to help the Browns keep this from the Whites?"

Antee looked up from studying his toes, which could use a good washing, he decided. Glancing at the others, he turned resignedly back to Arima, "I'm thinking you've got it almost right, Arima. At least for Yellow, we have kept things from the other Guilds. All Guilds do that. But Brown's secrets aren't our concern…No. Hmmm…Well…Huh!…Yes. You see, Yellow has its own share of Sighted people. And…I would guess by their behavior, that Cassa and Seafer have their own secrets to share. Perhaps you would like to sit down?"

Giving Mokam a hard look for just springing this on them without warning, he stepped across and helped the Healer to a seat. He started to chuckle. Cassa noticed, and began to grin.

Before long, there were four Masters laughing roaringly. Arima sat through it, trying to be indignant, but that was becoming difficult.

"Secrets," wheezed Antee, "Are ugly things. Even the needful ones. I can't think why this one was ever needful. Still…it would probably be best if we didn't mention to our Guilds that this one is out."

"Agreed," chimed in Mokam, rather quickly. He had started it, after all.

"I'm assuming that you have other secrets," Arima stated with a bland stare.

"And you'd be right," said Cassa, without any remorse. "They will be staying secret, too, unless our young friend gives us reason to share." With that, they were reminded of why they were there.

"Steef," asked Antee, "How long have you had this Brown Sight?"

"What's Brown Sight, Unk-ull Ann-tee?"

"Let me try, Antee," interjected Mokam. "Young man, you told me that you Saw colors in the rock when you were filled with Brown Power, is that right?" The boy nodded. "How long have you been Seeing those colors?"

"Since right after your last visit, Mass-Turr Mo-Kamm," he replied. "That's why I wanted to make Sassy's stairway, 'cause I could See where to go."

"Well that makes sense," said Arima. "For a Grader, Sight never starts developing until about his age. Sometimes a bit later."

But something was now bothering Antee. He looked truly troubled. Rising from his own seat, he went and knelt before Steef. Kivverr watched him carefully, as he always did when anyone touched his friend.

"Ste…Steef," he choked out, "Do you…See colors…when you're filled with any other Power?"

It got very still in the cove. Even the Buzzbies stopped buzzing. "Oh sure! Unk-ull Ann-Tee!"

He knew what was coming, but he had to ask anyway. Putting his head in one hand, he whispered this time, "Which ones, pumpkin?" Antee's eyes squinted shut, bracing for the impact. It came.

"All of them, Unk-ull Ann-tee. Why? Is that bad?"

And now, most of them were whispering. "Oh my bending staff," from Cassa. Arima said, "Merciful Creator." Seafer added, "Way to go, Sprout." Mokam was silent. Maleef was weeping. The buzzing started again.

"Well, this does complicate things, doesn't it?"

"This is getting more fun every day!"

"Best deal we ever struck, joining in this party!"

All of the Masters were getting Buzzbie comments…

"No, dear boy. It's not bad." *Not for you, but what do WE do with it?*

They were all thinking about that same thing, but one of them was thinking a little too loudly. "What *is* this child?" came quietly from a shocked and careless Cassa.

Steef turned to her, back straight, with Kivverr right behind him. He shrugged slightly and said simply, "I am Steef."

Cassa wouldn't partake in the conversations that ensued. She spent the rest of that day following Steef and Kivverr, asking pardon with every second or third breath. A perplexed Steef gave it each time, wondering what was bothering his Sassy.

Meanwhile…

"I can certainly train him in White Grading, but I have no idea what he needs for his other Colors."

"I've only met one Green with Sight, and she didn't share any of her talent with me."

"We have been out of our depth from the beginning with the boy. It's time we enlisted help. I know the Brown Guild would be delighted to step in."

Antee said nothing. It was his opinion that the others weren't really trying to solve anything, just voicing their fears aloud. He let them vent. When they finally tired of it and grew quiet, he spoke.

"I agree with Mokam that we have more challenge here than we can meet," Mokam looked relieved, thinking he had an ally. He was wrong. "But we're all worried because of the assumption that Steef should be trained to use every talent and Power to its fullest. If all of the Masters from all of the Guilds were here…right now…and trained him night and day, he would still need more than one lifetime to learn everything. I'm still learning myself, and I've been a practicing Master for a long time. Steef will be learning long after our part is over."

"There is something else to consider, and Arima hit on it almost eight cycles ago. You all know that the Guilds are changing, and not for the better. I can't imagine what would happen, should knowledge of Steef's gifts become known, but I doubt that it would be pleasant. Not for Steef, or his family. Not for us. Not even for our Guilds. There would be Guild wars again…like the tales from times past. They would all fight to have him. They would see him as a key to dominating the other Guilds. People would die. Others would suffer. The only way I can see to preventing that…is to continue hiding him here."

"Yes, he will get less training than he could at a Guild school. Yes, we're two Colors short of his abilities. But he will have training in five Colors, which is four more than anyone else has ever enjoyed. Master training. It will have to be enough."

"And finally, I would remind you, that we all oathed to keep this secret. Had I known then what that oath would require of me, I would still have made it. And so would you. Arima warned us that it could mean our lives. Well, my life has never had more meaning. My loyalty now lies with the Steef Guild, not the Yellow."

He hadn't really meant to give a speech. He surprised himself with where his thoughts and passions took him. When he had finished, they all sat mute, keeping their own council, pondering what had been said.

After a time, Cassa returned from her circuits around the cove, asking pardon. She looked drained in every way possible. Flopping down on an empty seat next to Maleef, she threw one arm around the woman. Turning to the other Masters, she said, "We've got to double our visits and our training, Mokam. It'll cost you and me dear, but we've just got to get Shortstick trained up, and he can't ever leave here. We've got to come as much as we can." Closing her eyes, she laid her head on Maleef's shoulder. Another few beats, and she added, without opening her eyes, "Antee, you're the scholar here. Could we get some parches on basic training in Red and Black for Shortstick to look at? I'm not sure I trust myself with this any more, and I know I sure don't want to invite anyone else in. But the boy needs *some* basic idea of his other two Colors."

Thank the Creator for Cassa thought Arima and Antee at the same time. The effect of her words on Mokam was immediate, and profound. He had been in what Cassa called his 'stuffy stance'. Chest out, Master's face on. What Antee's speech couldn't do, Cassa's simple assumptions did. He relaxed visibly, and fully joined the Steef Guild that night. He did need to get in a final word, though.

"I just hope we've had our last surprise. They are getting harder to take." They all agreed with his wish, though privately none of them relaxed. They all believed Steef capable of further surprises.

They were finally right.

❦   ❦   ❦

"So, what do you See?"

"Colors."

They had him quiet again after lastmeal. He had dragged out his flute, thinking they would be playing, but they had given questions instead of tunes.

"You're confusin' him Mokam!" interjected Seafer, "Now Sprout, tell us about the colors you See…take your time…do they change?"

Antee held out his hand. "Steef, come here Son." That suited Steef just fine. His Unk-ull Ann-Tee asked the best questions. Gave the best answers, too.

With a gentle voice, Antee said, "Let's try this a bit differently. Fill up with Brown, please." It wouldn't hurt to cater to Mokam a bit. Might help his shakes. "Now, tell us what you See."

"There's colors in the rockface."

"What colors are there?"

"They're different from our regular Colors, Unk-ull Ann-Tee. Like they've been mixed."

"How many colors do you See?"

"Four."

Everyone turned to Mokam, who responded, "I'm told that there are seven in all. They represent the seven natural sources of Power. At least one would be missing now, anyway, since the sun has gone down. And there's no Crystal in any of the stone around this cove, so that's two. Which four he's actually see-ing, we'll just have to figure out as we go."

Antee nodded. "Steef, drain out your Brown and fill up with…White…now tell us what you See."

"The Colors are normal again, Unk-ull Ann-tee. And they're in people 'stead of the rocks."

Antee said to the gathered group, "I want everyone to fill up full with Power, please. But no visible glowing."

Steef's eyes got wide. "Wow, Unk-ull Ann-tee! Look how bright Aunt Ah-ree-ma got! And Sassy, too!" Then he leaned over, and whispered into his Uncle's ear, "Is something wrong with Mama and Papa?"

Antee answered aloud, not liking any more secrets, "No, sweet boy. They are fine. Their Power just doesn't glow as bright as ours because...it's going to their pumps, they love you so much. Now, would you mind trying another Color for me?"

Cassa spoke up, "Shortstick, fill up with Red!" To the others she said, "Well, I'd really like to know."

Antee nodded, "All right, Steef, let's satisfy Cassa's curiosity. Fill up with Red, please...and tell us what you See?"

"The colors are still on all the people, Unk-ull Ann-tee, but not all over any more...just on everyone's chest and head." Then, Steef added, "And they change some, too. The colors change, Unk-ull Ann-Tee. They aren't staying the same...like when I'm in White." He got his 'puzzled' look.

"Are they the same colors that were in the rocks?"

"No. But there *is* white! Mama and Papa got white! And look how it glows! You outglow all of 'em now, Mama!"

They tried Yellow, but the only beasts around were Cats, and he couldn't See any colors at all in them. Green didn't work well either, it was too dark. Finally, they got to Black. Everyone tensed up, including Steef.

"I don't like Black, Unk-ull Ann-tee!"

"Why is that, Son? Does it hurt when you're in Black?"

"No Sir...but it does bad things."

"Yes it does, Steef. But we don't want you to Pulse your Black, just tell us what you See."

"Okay."

Beat. Beat. Beat.

"Steef?"

"The colors are all darker. I don't unnerstand."

"Where do you See them?"

"On all of you...an' on the grass...an' on Seafwood! I don't like this!"

"Drain it out Son...all drained? Good. Come here," Antee wrapped him up in Yellow arms, kissing his head. "We're done, pumpkin. Why don't you run get your flute, and my pickbox? We'll play something."

"Okay!!" Two small feet pounded off towards Antee's cave with four large paws thudding along, a massive Cat body suspended over a tiny boy's head.

"Anything living, I think," Antee mused to the others about the Black Sight. "I'm guessing, but I would think that a Sighted Black would use it for targetting."

"What do you think about Maleef glowing so bright white?" asked Cassa.

"I think I was righter than I knew, when I told him his Mama and Papa had their pumps full of love," said the Yellow, giving a respectful nod to the parents. They nodded back. Malem stood with them quietly, having watched everything without a sound.

CHAPTER 11

"What is that!?"

"*It is a slithertooth.*"

"What's a slithertooth?"

"*That is.*"

"No, I mean…what do they do?"

"*I have never known them to do anything. They are tasty, but they are too small to be a true meal. Foul tempered beasts. They try to bite back. They are too slow for their own good.*"

"How come I've never seen any before? They don't come where we live?"

"*Yes, they come. There are many Clan there. As I said, they are tasty.*"

Steef approached the snake. Brownish in color, it had a pattern across its back. As Steef got closer, he reached to touch it. The coiled snake struck his hand, and backed off.

"That hurt! I thought you said they were slow!"

Since they were no longer in contact, he couldn't hear Kivverr's reply, just his rumble. Watching the snake with more caution now, he removed his stick from the sling on his back, and Pulsed Black at it. He hadn't used Black often, and misjudged the amount. The snake was cut to pieces.

His hand was really hurting, and already the pain was spreading up his arm. Kivverr came up.

"You said they were slow!" he repeated.

"*They are. Apparently, you are slower.*"

"This is still hurting." With that, he Pulsed White at his arm, until the pain stopped.

"*You are not supposed to do that.*"

"I know, but I think that slithertooth put something bad in me. I'll ask about it when we get back." They both looked at the remains of the snake.

"There is not enough left to eat."

"Are there more out here?"

"Usually."

"Let's find enough for lastmeal." He sent a test Pulse into a piece of just-dead snake, to get a proper tune. "Let me up. I want to get as high as I can."

Kivverr stooped and bent one leg. Steef clambered up the massive leg, and onto the Cat's shoulders, where he stood up.

"Hold still now, so I can feel the Pulse come back." The small stone in his stick flashed again, and both of them held very still for several beats. "Okay, got it. One more Pulse, and we can collect our meal. You know, Black can be useful after all." The stone flashed a final time.

"How many did we get?"

"Twenty seven."

"Then it is time to eat."

It was their first night away from the Cove. Steef had wanted to go exploring, and they had spent cycles looking at everything within a half day's walk. Papa had said to ask Mama. Mama had asked Aunt Arima, who asked Uncle Seafer, and that settled it, "Anything that's gonna hurt the Sprout has to get past that big Cat...don' think that's likely."

A little Brown on some stones got them hot enough to ignite the leaves and twigs he'd laid there. Using the small knife Papa gave him, he cut the snake behind the head, right where Kivverr said the meat quit tasting bad. Kivverr said the insides were the best part, but he did as his Mama made him oath, and removed the organs anyway. Running a stick through the remaining meat, he put his snake over the fire.

"You are ruining it with the fire. It tastes fine without burning." He was proving his argument by crunching on his tenth snake. He had sixteen more to go.

"Mama said cook. I'm cooking it."

"How is your paw?"

"It's still swollen, but it quit hurting. Aunt Arima will fix it better when we get back." Steef made a careful attempt to at least scorch his meal all around, then joined his friend in munching. "This *is* tasty! We'll do this again." For many beats the only sound was Kivverr's crunching. As Steef was chewing he asked, "So how many other beasts are out here...and I haven't seen them because they're tasty?"

"All of them."

"Okay, but how many?"

"You are a counter. I am an eater."

Steef had learned by now that if Kivverr had a real answer, he would give it. He would have to count and record the beasts himself, fulfilling Kivverr's assessment.

"Where are we going tomorrow?"

"Anywhere new."

"When you are done, I want you to play me the simple song, then you can brush all of these stickers out of me."

"Okay."

※   ※   ※

"So what are we doing?"

"Studying."

"I have noticed that you say that often, when you are not actually doing any-thing."

"It's stupid to do something before you know what you want to do. I'm deciding. The colors coming from this hilltop are different than the cove." He was filled with Brown. Everywhere they went now, he would switch Colors frequently, to get all the views he could of the new terrain. He wanted to know what it all meant, and no one could tell him. He would just have to find out. Brown Sight of this hilltop had caught his attention at a distance, and they had spent a quarter morning getting here. What Master Mokam called Power colors were shooting violently skyward. One of them was the seventh color. Master Mokam had said there were seven, but Steef had never seen more than six. Here was the seventh, and it was strong. They were sitting a ways away, Steef not wanting to approach until he'd decided what to do about it.

"I wonder," he thought out loud, "if I can separate them with bubbles."

Steef loved his bubbles now. He had practiced them relentlessly, when they were out of sight of the others. He could now Pulse with or without them. The trick, he learned, was the Clear. If he mixed Clear with any Color, he got bubbles, the Clear wrapping up whichever Color he was using. The neatest trick had come later. Clear by itself. Empty bubbles. He had practiced. And practiced. Kivverr had tired of it often, picking him up and chewing a bit, his subtle way of saying he was bored.

But now he could make hard bubbles, soft bubbles, big or small. He could grab things with them, and drag them. Fill them with water, and drink later.

Now he was going to try to catch a Power color. He wanted the seventh one, if only because it was rare. Master Mokam would be pleased.

All of the Power colors resembled variations of what he knew as the common ones, just 'smudgier'. The red one had tinges of yellow sometimes, making it look almost orange. Sometimes it would mix with brown and look almost black. The new seventh one was mostly blue. Not pure blue. It too, was streaked.

He decided to begin his experiment with the almost brown one, for no other reason than he was comfortable around the brown one. It was everywhere, all the time, and always had the same steady level of intensity. Taking his stick, he slowly approached the fountain of Power, Kivverr at his side. Sending a small bubble into the brown stream, he watched as it got caught up and disappeared into the sky. He and Kivverr looked at each other. Several unsuccessful tries later, he was sitting back studying.

"I gotta get the bubble to form inside the Power and catch it there…hold it," he mused.

"After you get it, what are you going to do with it?"

"Do it again."

"That makes no sense."

"Neither did practicing my Black. You grumbled about that too, but it fed us last night."

"Again with the sass. If I were not full…"

"I know, I know. Tomorrow."

"The thought of that will content me the rest of the day. We will need to leave soon. It is a good walk back, and you must be back by sleep time."

"Okay, but I'm going to try this again, first." Tongue sticking out, he approached again. This time, the bubble formed inside the brown stream, catching some of it. Steef held firm to his stick, and dragged out the smudgy brown Power.

"So what is it?"

"I think it's raw Power. Don't know what kind, but there's always plenty of this one." He sank his stick into the ground, and stepped to his bubble. Palms flat, he touched it on either side. "It's Power all right. The kind I get from the ground." He popped it with a finger.

"Now let's try the new one, and we'll go." Retrieving his stick, they went back, this time to the blueish looking stream. "I'm taking this one back to Master Mokam," he declared, as he began to form a fresh bubble in the new stream. It was harder this time. The stream of blue Power was stronger than his Pulse to form a bubble. He increased the Pulse. A bubble started to form, but was blasted away. Drawing up more Power, he pushed harder. And harder. The stick began to vibrate. Then it began to smoke. Steef wasn't noticing, he was watching the bubble forming. He was getting there…

BANG!

Beat. Beat. Beat.

Steef looked down. His stick was gone. It had fractured, and burned a stripe onto the inside of his hand. A fairly deep burn. It hurt.

Looking up at Kivverr, he saw that the great Cat's face was scorched in spots, and some of his whiskers were burnt. That made him examine himself, and yes, his tunic and trous had burn marks all over them. Searching the ground, he could see no sign of the Crystal that was in his stick. Looking closer, he saw small pieces of it scattered around.

"AAAAAAAAHHHHHHHHHHHHHHHHHOOOOOOOOOOWWW WWWEEEEEEOOOWWWW!"

"What are you roaring about?"

"Aunt Arima said I should yell when I'm hurt. Don't know why."

"Are you hurt?"

"Yes," Steef replied, holding up his right hand. The burn was beginning to swell, making this hand match the other one.

"Then it is time to go back to our tree."

"You'll have to help me up. My hands don't work too good."

Kivverr stretched himself out on the ground, and Steef clambered onto him with difficulty. They set out in the direction of the cove. They had been traveling about an eighthday when they both heard a Pop!. Kivverr didn't break stride as both heads tilted back. Two Buzzbies were hovering over them. Another Pop! and the Buzzbies were gone.

"Aunt Arima is sending them looking to see where we are."

"She tends you well."

"I know. I don't mind them watching, but they break my studying when they Pop! in and out."

"How are your paws?"

"Useless. I can't hold on well. And I don't have anything to show Master Mokam."

"I did not enjoy it either."

"Guess I need a bigger stick."

❧   ❧   ❧

"How are your paws?" He had asked routinely all day. It was almost dark.
"Still useless," Steef answered patiently.
"Can you walk?"
"My feet are all right."
"Then you must get down. We are almost there."
"Okay."

❧   ❧   ❧

"Doesn't it hurt?" asked Arima in alarm. The burn was deep. She started Pulsing on it immediately.
"Yes Mam."
Arima looked at Maleef, but continued speaking to Steef, "Pumpkin, that's your worst burn yet." The other three hadn't been nearly so deep. "I can't believe you're not shouting in pain."
"I tried yelling like you said," he replied calmly, "It still hurt."
How do I argue with that? she thought, with a sigh.
"Did you get this one like the others?"
"Yes Mam. I need a bigger stick."
"What were you doing?" she asked, knowing the answer. In fact, she and Maleef mouthed his answer as he gave it.
"Studying."
She finished Pulsing. Bathing his skin in ointment, she wrapped it with a clean rag. "That will need changing tomorrow. The day after, it can come off."
"Okay." He continued standing there, which wasn't like him.
"Is there something else, child?"
Steef just held up his other hand. He knew what was coming.
"So tell me."
"Slithertooth bit me."
"Slithertooth? What's a…oh!…a snake. A snake bit you? Let me see." Taking his arm, she examined it casually, since he wasn't showing any distress. Of course, he didn't show distress much, but she had learned to watch his face. Right now, his face had no alarm in it. "Well, it's a little swollen, but…"
"I had to Heal it myself."

"What!? Why? Oh, merciful Creator!" Arima exclaimed. Maleef looked perplexed. Steef continued to stand in front of them, with his arm held high.

"All right," she huffed, trying to gather herself, "Explain."

"Well, the bite hurt, but I would have left it 'til we got back…only, it started hurting up my arm, too. That…snake?…put something in me, and it wasn't good. So I Healed on it, just 'til it quit hurting."

"Poison," she said, glancing at Maleef once more. The Mother now had concern in her face to go with her tired. Arima sent a Pulse through the arm, and frowned. "Locked," was her answer, "And I can't See his Locks. Or break them." She was really talking to herself now. "This has got to be tended…now. If we leave it, his arm will stay this way."

"Pill! Go to the others! Tell them what's happened. I need suggestions. We have to teach Steef how to break a Lock. Right now!" Pop!

"Aunt Arima, how come I can't Heal myself? It worked just fine."

"Yes, pumpkin, it works. But Healing yourself does its own kind of hurt. The Power going in meets the Power coming out. They have the same tune. Where they meet…it leaves scars. Sometimes big ones. Sometimes small. The swelling in your arm is never going away if we…I…don't repair it soon, and I can't get past your Locks."

"What's a Lock?"

"You're about to learn."

❦   ❦   ❦

We need Antee she decided. Even Arima had to admit, he was the best of them for instructing their young charge. Seafer was good at his craft, but his teaching skills were suspect. That left Arima. Cassa was on the wrong side of the Territory, and none of the others could be here in less than four days. They didn't have four days.

"Aunt Arima, why is Malem crying?"

"She's been crying ever since you and Kivverr left for your little adventure."

"She cries a lot." He didn't like for his sister to be unhappy.

"Yes, she does. We can talk about Malem later. Right now, we need you to break the Lock on your arm," she replied calmly. She held his little arm in her lap. It was fairly stiff all over now, and cold. He could barely wiggle his fingers. Seafer was there, along with Stem. Maleef was tending to Malem. Again.

"Steef, putting a Lock on something means leaving some of your Power in it. We've all been teaching you about changing the tune on your Pulses, right?"

He nodded solemnly. She went on, "Well, you can set your tune to pass through something. It will still affect it, but it doesn't stay. Or you can set your tune to stay for a while, or stay forever. If it stays, we call that Locked. Since it's your tune…and your Power…only you can break that Lock. Or someone with more Power, who can force it open." *As if that's ever going to happen!*

"Now we haven't taught you this yet, because it usually isn't a problem." *Because there's always someone around to break a child's Lock.* "But we can't break your Locks, and the Power you Healed yourself with is Locked in your arm. We need for you to remove it, so I can tend to the scars."

"How?"

She was stumped. Normally, you first taught children how to deliberately *make* a Lock. They got so familiar with it, that they just knew how to break them. This situation was exactly backwards.

Seafer spoke up, "Sprout!…Sprout!…let's try somethin' 'for we get too confusin' here…drain that arm completely…I mean every last sprig…let me know…good…now put your good hand on your bad arm…feel anythin'?…yeah?…what d'ya feel?"

"There's a cold spot, Uncle Seafer. My Pulse doesn't come back from there at all."

"Well we want to get rid of that…you can push it out…or pull it down and drain it…but it needs to get gone."

"Oh. Okay." And just that quick, the small arm flashed bright White.

Arima was the only one of them that Saw it. She lifted her hands and eyes skyward. *Sometimes I just make things harder than they have to be* she thought. Then she went to work on Healing his arm. Let Antee refine the boy's Lock breaking later. But Steef wasn't done, though the damage was. She just didn't know it yet.

"Aunt Arima?'

"Yes Sir?"

"That wasn't hard. How come you couldn't do it? You said someone with more Power could break a Lock?"

"Well, Arima, how are you getting out of this one?" asked Pill.

Steef had gotten used to hearing the Buzzbies buzz from one of the Master's ears. He knew that often a reply came after, so he didn't much mind when his Aunt Arima said, "Hush now! I'm trying to think!"

But Arima couldn't think of a good answer except the truth. Steef was ten. How much truth could he handle? "I can't break your Lock pumpkin, because I don't have enough Power." *Would that do?*

No.

"But you glow the brightest of anybody. 'Cept maybe Sassy. Could she break it?" His choice of words wasn't clear, but he jerked his arm a bit in her grasp, making his meaning clear enough.

"No…nnno. Cassa wouldn't be able to break it either." *I'm sure of that, at least.*

He went quiet, but she knew he wasn't done. She knew the face, and it was working. The question she dreaded was coming.

"So who *could* break my Lock?"

Sigh. "No one, pumpkin. There's no one that can break your Lock."

"Okay." He didn't really know what all this meant, but Aunt Arima had given him two new mysteries to study. Locks. And no one could break his Locks. He had lots of work to do.

He needed a bigger stick.

❦   ❦   ❦

"GuildMaster, you have a visitor."

"I am not available, Meeben."

"Your pardon, GuildMaster. I believe you should become available."

"Why is that, Meeben?" *Impertinent clod.*

"Master Linzel would like to see you. Shall I tell the Black Master you are unavailable?"

He's enjoying this much too much. I will remember that. "Thank you, Meeben. You are correct. I *should* see her. Please have her in."

Linzel entered a few beats later. Looking around Vinntag's workcloset, she smiled. Finely crafted and polished wood furnishings, many of them adorned with inlay. It was a striking contrast from the rest of the ordinary décor of the White GuildHall. She turned her attention to the small woman behind the table.

Wishing the table were a valley, Vinntag felt a thrill of fear streak through her. In spite of Linzel's smile, her stone was glowing Black. There was a Black Master in her closet, with a fully charged staff. This couldn't be a good thing.

"Lllinnzzell! Wwhatt a pleasssure to seee you! You are not illl, I hope?" That would be asking for too much good fortune.

"You will explain to me Vinntag, why you are having me watched." The smile was gone. Linzel was in no mood for pleasantries, least of all with this woman.

"Why, wwhateevverr do you mean, Lllinnzzell? Why would I be wwatcchh-ing you?"

"Too many Buzzbies wherever I go, Vinntag. Peel tells me they are Pools. And too many White badges. Everywhere. You will explain...now!" Her stone flared.

"We...we...we are not wa...watching *you*, Linzel," her shaking voice had lost its sweetness. "We...we are watching your daughter." Vinntag was not completely thick. She had prepared this. "She shows great ability in her classes. And as you know, she has begun sh...showing rare gifts. I have s...s...started taking an in...interest in her training...p...personally." From Vinntag's view-point, having a GuildMaster's attention should be a great honor for a parent.

Just not *this* parent.

"I have considered my daughter's White gifts to be a great misfortune, Vinntag, since you drove her Aunt into exile. No! Don't protest! Your sweet voice is wasted on me! White Guild must train her. I can do nothing about that." Linzel took a step closer, and leaned over the other woman. Her eyes glinted under furrowed brows and her voice lowered to an ominous whisper, "Know this, Vinntag. *I* will be watching *you*! Arima may be gone, but she isn't dead. I can always inquire of her about your methods, if they displease me. Teach my daughter anything but tradecraft, and your entire Guild won't be able to piece you together again."

Linzel straightened, and strode to the door. Without turning back, she gave one last thought, "And the next beast I see following me, wings or legs, will get a small taste of my stone." With that, she was gone.

A very shaken GuildMaster sat for more than a few beats, unmoving. When the color had returned to her face, she said, "Pool, you incompetent. Can you deliver a message without getting me killed?"

"You were told not to trifle with a Black Master. Has it occurred to you yet, that if you just leave her alone, you won't have to watch where you sleep at night?"

"I have a better idea. I will need to meet with Masters Kuumit and Wingor. Together. Tonight."

"Kuumit is in the Eastern Territory. He won't be back for eleven more days."

She'd forgotten that. "Well go tell him to get back right away! I need him here!" she exploded.

"We can't get there. It's too far. You know that. Besides, do you really want to interrupt his meeting just because Linzel scared you?"

Once again, she tried to snatch a Buzzbie from her ear, to strangle it. Or smush it. Or something. Once again, she missed. Pop! Pop! At least they would leave her in peace the rest of the day. They usually stayed away for a day or more.

She'd wait until Kuumit returned before speaking with Wingor. Wingor could wait. It was Kuumit's Guild that Linzel belonged to.

❦   ❦   ❦

"She's not a happy chil' Mum," Maleef had to admit.

"Is there anything I can do, child?" asked a concerned Arima. *It's my doing. I talked them into a second child. Meddling again. Will I ever learn?*

"I's no one's fault, Mum. All she wants is time with little Steef. He's her only playmate. He's jus' so busy, with his studies an' all. He tries. He really does…An' she's still fearful o' the beasties. Can' blame a small chil' 'bout that. They're big an' loud an' they got all those teeth…"

At four, Malem was crying more than she did at one. Steef's overnight trip had triggered a flood of misery that seemed likely to keep flowing. Stem and Maleef were exhausted from the attention she demanded.

"We don' know wha' to do."

"Neither do I, but we'll think of something together." *I hope.*

❦   ❦   ❦

"What doing, Bubba?"

"Waiting for you to find us, Sissy," he said brightly. He'd quit calling her Malem, in spite of Master Mokam's instructions. She liked Sissy better.

"You knew I'd come?"

"I don't mind you following us, Sissy."

"How come here?"

They were over halfway up Sassy's stairway. Two bends away from prying eyes, unless a Buzzbie Pop!'d in, and he couldn't do anything about that. Yet.

"I want to show you something."

She brightened. Eyes lighting up, back straighter. "For me, Bubba? Whatcha gonna show me?"

"First, put your hand inside my tunic, right over my pump," he said, holding the collar apart. "Now close your eyes, and hold them closed."

Malem gripped her lids tight. She trusted her Bubba completely.

"Now just wait, and it'll come to you. Don't move." With that, he closed his own eyes. Filling with Red, he began thinking of Kivverr. Of Mama and Papa.

Of sunrises and sunsets. Learning new things. Sassy's laugh. Aunt Arima's hugs. Standing under the spillways. His own natural grin spread across his face. All of his joys. Life was good. Especially when Kivverr chewed on him. He was filled with the joy and contentment that was his life…and Red Power.

He pushed, gently and slowly, some of that Red into his sister's arm. Her face relaxed, then her small body. "Oh," she said softly.

He stopped, and pulled her hand away from his chest. He had to be careful with Red, for he had had little practice. It *should* be enough to last her for days.

"That was nice Bubba," she cooed.

"That's my world, Sissy. I regret it isn't yours, but I'll share…any time you want."

"I love you, Bubba."

"I love you too, Sissy."

🍁　　　🍁　　　🍁

The boat was gliding in, and for the first time in cycles, Steef was waiting for it, instead of playing with Kivverr. Uncle Antee was coming to teach him about Locks, which was interesting, but he had questions for Master Mokam. That seventh Power. Master Mokam would know.

He was carrying a new stick, slightly larger than the last one. Uncle Seafer had made him take back the one he had chosen, saying it was too big for now. There were plenty to choose from. At least the stone in this one had some size to it. It was as large as his thumbnail. Of course, his thumbnail wasn't all that big. He was pretty sure he would be needing a stick larger than this soon. That meant another burn. He sighed.

Everyone waited while he gave Master Mokam his bow. Then Mokam lowered to one knee, croaking, "Come here, you little piece of gravel." Master Mokam was more prone to hugs than he used to be.

But once in Mokam's embrace, Steef got a quizzical look on his face. He didn't release his hug from the Brown Master for several beats after Mokam had let go. The other adults just smiled at Steef's affection for his stiffest of Uncles. Next came Sassy, who also got a lingering hug. In fact, everyone there got a long hug. The boy just got sweeter as he grew.

Malem greeted everyone peacefully as well, which was at least as welcome. She often sulked, knowing that Steef's time would now be occupied. Not this time. Perhaps things were improving for her?

Steef wanted to start in on Mokam immediately, but the Brown Master stopped him, "Master Antee is going to begin immediately with your lessons on Locks. That will take the rest of today at least. We can talk tomorrow," he said.

"Okay."

❦   ❦   ❦

"Uncle Antee?"

"Yes, Son?"

"Aunt Arima says that she can't break my Locks." It was almost sundown, and like everything else they taught him, he had caught on quickly, and was Locking and unLocking Yellow on this now-extremely-healthy sheep. Antee had tried, but couldn't touch one of Steef's Locks. He hadn't expected to.

But Steef was sweeping away Antee's Locks as if they were smoke. Antee hadn't even told the boy they were there. Steef was filled with Yellow, and couldn't See Antee's Pulses.

"Neither can I," admitted the modest Yellow Master.

"She said Sassy can't either, and Sassy glows really bright when she's full."

"Yes, Cassa is a very strong Master." As clever as he was, Antee didn't see it coming.

"Could Sassy break someone else's Lock?"

"If it was a Blue one, then she probably could." *There probably aren't many Blues stronger than her, if she's Arima's equal* he mused.

"Aunt Arima says no one can break my Locks."

"That's probably true." *Where is this going?*

"Okay."

Good. No harm done. No disastrous ques...he should have known better.

"Why?"

Oh.

Well, you see Son, you are the single strongest Power anyone has ever known. You can do pretty much anything you want. To anyone. Through anyone. Hmmm. No. That's not what I want to tell a child. Of course, this is no typical boy. Still a boy, though. Can't lie to him. Ever. Why me? No way around it.

"Steef, if you were to glow as brightly as you could, like we did on our last visit, you would glow brighter than all of us." *Put together* he didn't add. *How strong IS he, anyway?* No one discussed that any more, probably from frustration at never knowing.

"I'm brighter than everybody? Even than Aunt Arima and Sassy?"

"Yes."

"That's a good thing, isn't it?"

"It can be. Whether it's good or not, will depend on what you do with all that Power."

"It helps me learn new things. That's fun."

"What will you do when you have learned everything?" *Let's see what he does with a hard question.*

"You mean you *can* learn everything?"

I should have known better.

🍁   🍁   🍁

It was late night, and everyone was asleep. Everyone but Steef and Kivverr. They were standing near the entrance to Mokam's cave.

"Are you studying again?"

"No. Well, sort of. I want to get this right. How did you know?"

"Your tongue was sticking out of your mouth again."

"Oh."

"Do you know what you are doing?"

"Yes. This is a simple Pulse. One of the first Aunt Arima taught me. I just need to be careful with how much Power I use." With that, he strode to the rockface, lifted his stick and Pulsed.

"That should do. Let's do the others while we're here."

🍁   🍁   🍁

Arima opened her eyes to a fresh morning. She strrreettcchhed…stretches felt so good…you push until it alllmmmost hurts…and hold it there. Aaaah-hhh. That was a good…

Wait just a beat!! I'm a hundred and ten…no eleven…no twelve…cycles. I haven't stretched my bones in…a long time, anyway!

She almost jumped out of her cot. Stood erect. Completely erect. Stretched out her hands, and balled them into fists. Lifted one knee to her waist. Then did the other. She bent over…and over…and *touched her toes!*

Straightening back up, she stood in place, unmoving. Her mind worked furiously. A slow smile crept across her face. Followed by a quick frown.

He could have done real harm! But he didn't. *Well, he could have!* But he didn't. *Who taught him, anyway? How'd he get in here without me hearing him?*

Dressing quickly, she left her cave, to find there were more revelations waiting. Mokam was smiling! He hadn't smiled much in several cycles. Talking with Antee, who was equally animated...and then HOAR! HOAR! HOAR! came across the cove to her cave. *Where is Seafer?* She looked around. *There he is...in the spillway! Standing upright...in the spillway! He can hardly walk any more!...let alone resist the water pressure off the rocks!*

Maleef and Stem were preparing firstmeal. Malem was playing quietly. Maleef was humming, but Maleef hummed or sang often. Serenity and peace abounded, everywhere but in her pump.

"Pill!...Pill! Where are you, you confounded bee?"

Pop! Pop! *"Yes?"*

"Find him! Tell him I want to see him...right now!" Pop! Pill didn't ask 'who?' There was no need.

How in the name of a merciful Creator could he have done all of this in one night? No way to know, except ask him. She began making her way towards the others, when she heard Cassa's drums start up from her cave. *She never plays in the morning before beanbrew. She's feeling frisky, too. That's five. Five Master Freshenings in one night.*

As she approached, Mokam called out, "Bright day to you Master Healer! And good work! I've never felt better. Antee here tells me the sa..." He stopped at the look on her face.

"It wasn't me, Mokam," she said, almost sternly.

"Then who...?" queried the Miner. Antee had already begun grinning. Mokam caught the grin, and went on, "You mean our little pile of gravel did this!? Well now! You have trained him well already!"

Arima busied herself getting a cup of beanbrew, with a nod of thanks to Stem.

"I'm glad you're pleased, but there are some questions that I...we...must have answered," she replied carefully. She saw Kivverr and Steef coming around the far edge of the cove, "Pill, ask Seafer to dress and join us please. And Cassa." She forced herself to smile.

❧   ❧   ❧

"Steef, you did a bit of Healing last night, hmmm?"

"Yes Mam."

"Freshening Pulse, I would guess."

"Yes Mam. Did I do it right?"

"Well, we're all still standing. In fact, some of us are standing for the first time in a while, so yes…I'd have to say you got it right."

"Arima," interjected Cassa, "You're scaring him! He didn't do anything wrong. Shortstick…you didn't do anything wrong!"

But Steef didn't look away from his Aunt Arima. Or step back.

"I'm not mad, pumpkin. But I *am* concerned. Freshening on a Master is tricky, and it appears you did five last night. Am I right?"

"Yes Mam."

"Arima," Antee queried, "You're scaring me! Would you mind telling us why this is so troubling for you?" The others nodded. Even Seafer, who was more alert than usual.

Arima didn't take her eyes from Steef, but she spoke to them all, "White Power is mostly a simple process. Many of our Pulses simply help bodies Heal themselves. Only later in our training do we learn specific tunes to Heal specific maladies, and applying creams and powders and potions. Probably much the same for you, Antee?"

He nodded, though she didn't see it.

"Something you don't have to deal with, Antee, is Healing a person who has Power."

When she said that, Steef's head jerked a bit, and he got his 'study face' on. Arima didn't realize it yet, but Steef wasn't there any more.

"Healing Inerts is the easiest. No Power resistance. Powered people are more complicated. And the stronger they are, the more complicated they become. The Pulses have to be stronger, and they take longer. So, a Five could never Heal…say…an Eight. And for anything other than simple things, Masters Heal Masters. Non-Master Tens can do some things on Masters, but it increases the time required."

"Well, how long does a Freshening on a Master normally take?" persisted Cassa.

"A quarterday, minimum. With the Master receiving the Freshening in contact with a tuned staff the entire time. Any of you remember cuddling up to a staff last night?" She was still watching Steef, whose face and eyes were pointed back at her, but she noticed that he'd left the conversation. *Where was he now?*

"Steef." His eyes locked back to the here-and-now. "How? Please."

"Bubbles," he said brightly.

"Explain please."

"I needed to Pulse on Uncl…Master Mokam for most of the night, so I sent a bubble into his cave, and filled it with White. Then I tuned the bubble to let the White out a little at a time."

"And you liked it so well, you did all of us?"

He nodded. "Master Mokam's bubble was working really well, and it didn't take hardly any beats at all, so I put one in all the caves."

"May I ask why you wanted Mokam to have a Freshening?"

Steef looked uncomfortable, but she held his gaze. Finally, he came over and whispered into her ear, over the Buzzbie. She had to bend for him to reach, "He was sick. He didn't know it yet."

"How did *you* know?" she whispered back.

"I felt it when I hugged him yesterday," he continued his whisper.

"Is that why you went and hugged everyone? You were checking all of us?"

He nodded his little head, "Uh-huh."

"And you were getting our tune at the same time?"

He shook his head at that, "I already know the tunes," he said. Not a hint of boasting. Just explaining.

Well. She *was* training him to be a Healer. Hard to get mad at him for Healing. She would talk to him later about methods and privacy. There was no way to know what Mokam had been sick with, but whatever it was most surely was gone. She straightened back up.

"There is something else," she said, turning to the others now. "Seafer, how often do I give you a Freshening?"

"'Bout ev'ry cycle now, 'Rima…and I thankee," he said.

"And even with those Freshenings…from an experienced Master Healer mind you…how long has it been since you could actually straighten up? Or stand under the waterspill?"

"Why…it's been a while for true! Good for you Sprout!"

"Mmm-hmmm," she said, sort of. Now would be a good time to laugh. Or cry. Or laugh and cry.

"I'm afraid there's still more, Arima," said Antee.

"What might that be?" She didn't want any more.

"If our boy here performed five Master grade Healings last night…he had to do it with a Master grade staff."

Everyone jerked up at that. Arima's discomfort was mildly amusing, especially as good as they all felt. But staff craft was serious. All heads turned to look at Steef's little stick.

"Sprout, did you use that stick last night?"

"Yessir, Uncle Seafer. You made me put the bigger one back."

The only sound made after that was Seafer's quiet, "hee…hee…hee…hee"

❦   ❦   ❦

"I don' unnerstan' the fuss, Mum," Stem was watching the hubbub as he spoke to Arima.

Arima and Maleef were now preparing midmeal. The other Masters had spent the morning fussing over Steef's stick. They took turns routinely, sending Pulses into it, with no effect. Yet it had clearly performed at Master level last night. And it was so small!

"I don't mind explaining, child," Arima gave Stem a smile, "But to do so, I'll have to make some…uh…comparisons." With that, she glanced at Maleef's own small staff, hanging from the girl's belt.

Maleef didn't miss a beat in her humming or cooking, but she did glance up with a shrug and a smile.

Arima was once more reminded of the constant lesson she got from this young couple. She had thought she already knew, but a long life as a Master had insulated her to what other people went through. Stem and Maleef both taught by example that *who* you were didn't have to be dictated by *what* you were.

"All right then. Stem, if you would be kind enough to fetch my bag from my cave? And my staff."

They continued with the food until he returned. Taking her staff, she sank it into the dirt. She motioned for the two of them to do the same, next to hers. Her staff was actually a slight bit taller than she was. Theirs barely came to their knees, and they weren't tall people.

Digging through her bag, she retrieved her measuring rope. She let one end drop to the ground, holding the other end at the tip of her own staff. There were ten evenly marked spaces on the rope.

"This rope is exactly one staff long. Or tall, I guess, depending on how you hold it. It's divided into ten equal spans. One 'staff' as we call it, is actually the height of a full Ten grade staff. A Ten staff *must* be this tall, and a *minimum* of one-third span thick at the top, to handle the Power of a Ten grade person. The stones vary, depending on size and type and clarity. Mokam can tell you what they are if you're interested. In addition, a Master's staff must have a minimum purity of wood and stone, over the requirements for a regular Ten. Now, some

Ten staffs are actually shorter, but thicker…as long as they still have the same amount of wood and stone."

"But someone…sometime long ago in the past…decided to use a Ten staff as our basic unit of measuring things. A span is one tenth of a staff, and equals the basic size of each Power rating. One span of staff is appropriate for a grade One, five spans for a Five. You will see that your staffs are roughly two spans long. Malem there will eventually need a three-span staff."

The others had come up to the conversation, either for the food or curiosity. Arima reached her hand out, and Steef handed her his stick. Kneeling, she said, "This is what all the fuss is about." And she held Steef's stick up to theirs. At about a span and a half, it was actually smaller than their Two grade staffs, and no thicker than Arima's first finger. The comparison was obvious. She let the parents get a good look.

She handed it back to Steef, and stood. "Last night, this stick performed five Master grade Pulses. Equal in *every* way to my staff." *At least* she added to herself. She put her hand on her own staff, almost wanting to defend it.

Beat. Beat. Beat.

"I's the tree, 'int it Mum?" asked Stem quietly.

"Yes, Stem. It's the tree."

❀   ❀   ❀

"Arima, could you spare me a beat?"

Mokam had left with Steef, and Antee had waited until the others were occupying themselves.

"Certainly."

"The Freshening that Steef did last night…was different than what you normally give us. Am I right?"

"I'm not sure I understand, Antee. Different how?" She was hoping no one would notice. No, she was hoping that Antee wouldn't notice.

"You pointed out part of it yourself. Seafer is in better health than he's enjoyed in a long while."

Arima sighed. He *had* caught it. He would get the rest of it, too, if he hadn't already. "I haven't seen him this well in almost thirty cycles," she admitted reluctantly.

"So one Pulse from Steef equals three standard Master freshenings?"

He had it all, she might as well give it all, "One Pulse did more for Seafer than I could have done with a discharge, Antee. It's not just the amount of

Power. It has to be the clarity as well. Has to be. Freshenings can only Heal things that are Healable. They can't turn back time."

"They can now, Arima."

"We are already able to live longer than we should, Antee." *Some of us more than others. GuildMasters, for instance. Shame, Arima. That was beneath you.*

"I think so too, but not everyone will. Why, the boy could be pestered every beat of his life just to do Freshenings."

"It's because of things like this, that we're here…in this Valley," she reminded him.

"We were smarter than we knew."

CHAPTER 12

❀

Steef finally got to have Mokam alone, but Mokam had his own agenda, "Young fellow, it is time you started to learn how to Lift," he announced with a bit of flourish to his voice. That was interesting enough that Steef put his questions aside again.

"There is a secret that all Browns understand," began the stone Master, "And you must oath me that you will not share it with anyone." He wasn't stern, but his gaze was intent on Steef's eyes. The student bowed formally to his Master.

"The secret is this...we don't really make *anything* lighter when we Lift!" He stopped, looking as if he expected Steef to faint dead away. When that didn't occur, he went on, "All we are doing is putting a reverse charge into whatever we are Lifting, making it push away from the Power pulling it down."

Steef's face got his usual faraway look, and Mokam waited, letting the boy absorb the new idea. Finally Steef asked, "Why isn't that the same as making it lighter?"

"Well... if we were actually making it lighter, you could lift it and just throw it around right? But you can't. Whatever we are Lifting will be able to resist a straight up-and-down pull from the ground, but...this is important...it...holds...its...original...mass...and...weight. I'll show you." With that, Mokam led Steef, with the ever-present Kivverr following behind, to a rock that was almost Kivverr's size. Touching his stone to it, he sent a Pulse into the rock. Nothing happened. Steef looked puzzled, obviously expecting the rock to Lift on its own.

"Now put one finger under the rock, and lift it," said a pleased Mokam. When Steef did as he was instructed, the rock rose easily off the ground, and hovered when Steef stopped pushing. "It has been charged with an up-and-down resistance that exactly matches its own original weight. If I give it more, it will rise on its own. If I take away just a little, it will slowly sink back down."

"It seems lighter to me, though," mused a perplexed Steef.

"It's not," replied Mokam, "Try this. Instead of pushing it up or down with one finger, push it sideways."

Using the same finger he'd lifted it with, Steef pushed on the side of the now-floating rock. Nothing. It didn't move. Putting one hand against it, he pushed harder. Same result. Then he used both hands, and threw his body into it. The rock would have laughed at him, if rocks could laugh. Mokam helped.

"HOAR! HOAR! HOAR! Wish you could see the look on your face!" Mokam Pulsed again, and the rock slowly sank to the ground.

"But I've seen you make things float sideways!" exclaimed a perplexed Steef.

"Yes you have, but not in an open field. Every time I have floated something sideways, it has floated away from something. You can add a second charge that pushes sideways, but it has to have something to push against."

"Now…there are some basic things that we have to learn today, so you can practice while I'm gone. First is knowing how much Pulse equals the mass of the object you're Lifting. We'll talk about that the rest of the day. The second thing you must know is balance. Objects that are unbalanced in shape or mass…will be unbalanced during a Lift, if you don't compensate."

"Is that why Sassy's boat is round?"

"Good! Good! That was a perceptive question! And you are exactly right, my little man! All boats are shaped like bowls because they are easier to balance that way. We are very careful Lifting boats, especially with people in them. That's why only Masters are allowed to be boat Lifters. Truth is, a Six could do it, but experience is best when we deal with people's safety. Anyway, if you're Lifting a boat, and it loses it's balance for any reason, you just decrease the Lifting Pulse in the bottom center of the boat, and it straightens right out! Can't help itself…so all boats are bowls."

"Now, where was I? Oh yes…basics. Lifting living things. Especially people. You don't ever…and I mean *ever*…want to put a Lifting Pulse on a person. Or a beast, either ." He glanced at Kivverr. "You're going to ask, so I'll tell you. It'll kill them. Their pumps run faster, blood flows faster, breathing is faster. But the mass is still there, and the organs tear themselves apart. You especially don't want to Lift *yourself*, for the reasons I just mentioned. Plus, Pulsing on yourself has its own dangers."

Just like Healing myself thought Steef. "Okay," was his response.

Mokam had learned over their cycles together that Steef's 'Okay' was more binding to the boy than most adults' oaths. It would do. Practice began.

❦   ❦   ❦

"I'd like to ask you something," declared the Brown Master. They had worked until dark, and as usual, Steef had caught on quickly. "How is it you are able to grasp…hmm…understand all these lessons so quickly? You have five different Masters pumping you full of information, and you never seem to get behind." *Is the boy just unnaturally bright as well? His parents aren't slow witted. Just uneducated.*

"That's easy, Master," replied Steef casually, "It's all the same thing."

Mokam stopped walking. "What do you mean?" he asked.

"Well, you teach me to send Pulses into the rocks. The answering Pulse tells me things."

"Yes. So?"

"Sassy has me send Pulses into the air. Uncle Antee has me doing it to beasties. Uncle Seafer tells me to Pulse into grass, and flowers, and trees…"

"I understand, Son. Why is that the same?"

"Same Pulse, different Color. Same returning Pulse, different Color. All I gotta do is remember what each returning Pulse means in that Color."

"You mean that when your Pulse tells you that there's a seam in the rock…"

"That one is the same as two pressure fronts meeting in the sky. A fractured bone in a person. Or a beast. Not a break, though…that's stronger. Or a stem that's ready to flower." He shrugged. "It's just remembering which is which, and what Color I'm in."

Mokam's mouth dropped open, and he stared at this…boy…with a sudden realization there really were…*five*…Masters growing in his small frame. And it would have been seven…if they had only found two more trainers. He'd seen the Power. He'd seen the tree. Even that crazy Cat's devotion. All were marvels, for true. But Mokam's focus had been on Brown training, and the time Steef spent with the others was…had been…just time away from his Brown studies.

"And we never knew about the similarities because…," he breathed to himself, really.

But Steef answered, "Well, Master, I never train with more than one Master at a time."

"And you never mentioned it because…," Steef opened his mouth to answer, but Mokam held up his hand, and finished, "None of us ever asked?"

Steef nodded.

"HOAR! HOAR! HOAR! HOAR! HOAR! HOAR!…That is the best jest I have heard in fifty cycles!…And the jest is on me!…HOAR! HOAR! HOAR! HOAR!…Them too!…HOAR! HOAR! HOAR!…Can't wait to tell them!…HOAR! HOAR!…We're all still guarding our secrets!…HOAR! HOAR! HOAR! HOAR!…And they're the same secrets!…HOAR! HOAR! HOAR! HOAR! HOAR! HOAR!

When Mokam had recovered himself, he once again regarded his young apprentice closely. He bent over and quietly said, "Ste…Steef…"

The boy's eyes grew wide. Master Mokam had never called him by his name before. Not ever.

"…I think maybe you don't need to call me 'Master' any more. Would you mind just calling me 'Uncle' Mokam?"

And Steef grinned excitedly. He nodded hard. Emboldened, he asked, "Uncle Mokam, I have a question."

"And what would that be, Sir?'

"It's about the Power colors that I See."

Mokam frowned a bit, "I will gladly help you as much as I can, but I do not have the Sight myself, and to be truthful, the one Brown I know who does…well, I don't know him well." The boy was still a bit young to be learning about Power sources. It was enough for him to learn how to use the Power he had. But he had the Sight, and deserved some answers.

"I saw the seventh color," Steef said simply, "I couldn't catch it. Do you know what it is?"

"You did!? Where?! When?!"

"When me and Kivverr went on our walk. On a hilltop. Almost a day's walk from here. It had a blue Color to it, and I was gonna catch you some, but I couldn't. It burned my staff up, and cracked my Crystal to pieces."

"You what!? You *cracked* a Crystal?!" Mokam's jaw dropped a second time. Steef nodded to him again.

"But that's not possible! Crystals don't crack! You can't bust a Crystal!" He stared down at Steef. His tone hadn't been harsh, just surprised.

From Steef's point of view, he was in a bit of a box. He had clearly seen the broken pieces of Crystal, but his Master said that wasn't possible. Hmmm. "Okay."

Beat. Beat. Beat.

"You did, though…didn't you? You actually cracked a Crystal?" Mokam rolled his eyes, something he'd gotten from Cassa.

Steef nodded…again.

Shaking his head, Mokam mumbled, "This has been an interesting day, and that is the truth!" He turned toward the cove.

"Uncle Mokam?"

"Hmmm? Yes? Oh! The colors!" Looking around, there was nothing convenient to sit on, so he lowered himself to the ground, marveling at how well his knees were working. "Since I don't have the Sight, I cannot tell you which color you are Seeing belongs to which Power. Except one. I can tell you though…about primary Power in general. From there, I guess you will have to figure out which one is which yourself."

It was the most dangerous thing Mokam had ever said. He just didn't know it.

"There are seven primary Powers…"

"What's a primary Power?"

"It is a Power source that needs no help. Look, you've learned to fill yourself with the heat from the campfire, correct?"

"Yessir."

"So the fire can be a source of Power. What happens when you don't feed wood into the fire?"

"It goes out."

"What happens if you don't start the fire?"

"Well, that's silly!…uh…then there isn't any fire."

"But the Power you get from the sun, you can fill up with it too, correct?"

"Yessir."

"And it's a faster fill-up than the campfire?"

"Uh-huh…I mean, yessir."

"And if you don't feed the sun?"

This time Steef didn't giggle, "You can't feed the sun!"

"How do you start the sun?"

Steef thought about this one for a few beats, "It starts itself, every morning," was his eventual reply.

"That is a primary Power! A Power that needs no feeding…and starts itself. There are seven. At least…there are seven that we know about. There used to be names for them. There are tales…old tales…that people from long ago…ancient times…used all seven…and named them. It's said that there were parches…old parches…that told how the ancients did that…" Mokam's eyes had lifted off to look at old parches that he had never actually seen.

"Humm! But we really only use two of them much. The sun and the pull-down. 'Gravvtee' it used to be called…they say. Who knows? Those two are the most constant, and controllable. Then there is the sky-bolt Power. It is hard to control, though the Blues keep trying. Don't know of a name for it other than skybolt. The two weakest primaries are Crystal Power and metal-pull. You didn't know Crystals had their own Power, did you? They channel our Pulses so well, we don't think about their Power, but it *is* there! When our Pulses touch it, they grow. A pure Crystal can often double the actual Pulse that's put through it. But their own primary Power is weak. If you've been Seeing it, it's probably a Crystal lode that could use digging up."

"The metal-pull is very weak. Not much use for our purposes, though Cassa's needles use it. She can find her way with it when she's Steering her boat. She will probably be teaching you that as soon as you get practiced at Lifting. 'Maggits' they used to call it. Strange…naming something after a grub. I am not sure I believe it."

"The sixth primary is from the world itself. The heat at the core of our world. It is *very* strong. And constant. So why don't we use it more? Hmmm. Knew you would ask. It is very, very…very…deep in the ground. The little bit of heat that trickles up to us is not strong. But some thick-headed Brown is always wanting to dig deep enough to tap that Power. Only the Creator knows what we would do with it if we had it. Every time a deep dig is made, we get a melted-rockspout. Every time."

Mokam grew quiet again. Steef waited, thinking the old Brown was remembering rockspouts.

"The seventh primary…I suppose you *do* need to know…well, it's dangerous. There is a Power…I know it to be true, though I've never seen it used…this Power is in everything. It is the Power that holds things together. When you use it…things split apart. Sounds strange, doesn't it? But I know it to be true. When I was a young man, still apprenticing, some Browns and Blacks decided to try and tame the seventh primary. They took some pure Dust…and together they Pulsed it with their own separating Pulses."

"What happened, Uncle?"

Mokam smiled at him, weakly. "I didn't see it, because they…there were three Browns and three Blacks…they went off into an uninhabited part of Territory three, in the east. Just in case. Good thing, too. Now the Brown Guild makes a ceremonial trip out there each cycle for those who want to go."

"Uh-huh."

"They made a new valley is what they did. A valley where there hadn't been one before. I am told that the blast was heard for sixty leagues. And the Browns who have the Sight...like you have...they say that whole valley glows blue. All the time."

Now Steef grew quiet. He knew where a blue glow was. That explained the cracked stone. He really needed a bigger stick.

But Mokam wasn't finished, "There was an ancient name for this Power. Until those six Masters made themselves into a valley, we used to laugh. No one laughs any more. They called it 'Tommik' Power."

Taking Steef by the shoulders, he braced him and said, "If you've Seen this blue Power, you've seen the seventh primary. It is dangerous stuff, young man! You be careful around it, agreed?"

Steef nodded, seriously, "Okay."

Unfortunately, 'being careful' isn't the same thing as 'leaving alone'.

❧   ❧   ❧

"Sprout...I wonder if you'd mind tryin' somethin' for me?"

The saplings were growing well. They had planted a small stand last cycle. Acorns from Seafwood. Seafer wanted to see how they would do on their own. Stem had helped tend the stand, listening as Seafer imparted Green wisdom. While his teaching skills were haphazard, his Mastery of all things green and growing was not, and Stem listened raptly to every word. As did his children.

The three males would prune, and Malem would collect into piles, the debris that fell from their efforts. While the saplings were healthy enough, they were different from Seafwood. There wasn't enough Crystal Dust for anything more than Seafwood, so these trees were growing in natural soil. As a result, they were not being 'fed' by the Cats. Their trunks weren't twined, nor their limbs. The leaves resembled Seafwood's, but that was the only physical resemblance. Seafer was able to charge up any of the twigs he broke off. So could Stem and Malem. The wood off of these trees had 'clean' Power, to quote Seafer. He seemed pleased with them, in spite of their differences from his main tree.

But no one could charge anything from Seafwood except Steef. The boy had been practicing his Locks for a sevenday now, and Seafer reckoned that was enough. "Sprout, I was a-hopin'...if you don' mind...tha' you might try unLockin' your staff for me...I'd kinda like to see wha' the charge is like…ever'thin' else works!…an' I'm pretty pleased, I gotta say!…but I'd sure like to get a feel off of…uh…Seafwood…d'ya mind tryin' for me?"

"Sure Uncle Seafer!" With that, he got his 'concentrating face' on, and Pulsed into the small stick. "Try it now," he said, handing it over to the old Master.

Seafer took it excitedly, but his face fell almost at once. "Still dead…nothin'…oh well…prob'ly not a Lock problem…just a tune…your tune…don' know if we'll ever get past that." He handed it back. "Keep at it, will ya, Sprout?"

They went back to work on the saplings.

"After the prunin', Sprout…you'll be wantin' to Pulse on the whole grove…testin' first for moisture, o' course…then I want you to tell me what food the little trees'll be needin' in the soil…shame we couldn't treat the soil like we did for Seafwood…no Dust to give 'em…Okay though…we don't really need more staffs anyway…though you do go through 'em pretty fast…now that Cassa's gone for a while, you can call up some rain without rocking her boat…if you think we need it…no…don't ask me…you tell me…then tell me what you think we need to feed 'em…after midmeal, we'll look in on your Papa's garden."

❧   ❧   ❧

It was a plain hut, and small. On the fringe of town, away from all the main paths and roads. Though it was dark, there was little light coming through the windows. In fact, nothing was odd at all about it, except that six Masters were standing in front of it, two of them fidgeting. Two Blacks. Two Reds. Two Whites. Behind each pair, was a single staff holding itself erect in the dirt. No one looked glad to be there.

The three GuildMasters inside the hut didn't particularly trust each other. That's why their staffs had been left outside. *Not that this little White crone could do any harm with hers* the others had both thought to themselves. But it gave the impression of fairness.

"What if someone sees us?" whispered one of the Whites hoarsely. It was his first time on this duty, having newly been brought in to his GuildMaster's confidence.

The Blacks and Reds just smiled casually.

"Then we'll stop them," said one of the Blacks. The Whites didn't see which, for they refused to look at them. If you didn't look, then maybe they wouldn't blast you?

"And we'll make them forget they were ever here," finished one of the Reds, equally amused.

"And then I suppose we can repair the damage?" the second White whispered to the first, in a voice he hoped couldn't be heard.

"What would you have me do, Vinntag? Linzel has Guild sanction to kill…with cause. And you've been giving it to her," said an amused Kuumit.

"What do you mean, 'I've been giving it to her'!?" screeched the White GuildMaster. "I was tending my own affairs, in my own Guild Hall! She threatened me in my own closet!"

"After you have been having her followed and watched for a cycle or more." It was getting harder to hold back the smirk. Wingor said nothing, and sat unmoving.

Vinntag fell back into her seat, as if struck, "How did you know that?" she finally forced out.

"We use Pool too," he said simply, letting her know that Wingor was in on the secret. Kuumit just assumed he was. Wingor wasn't as simple as Vinntag. *How did she ever get to be GuildMaster?* He asked himself, not for the first time. *At least she can be manipulated. We would have had to kill Arima.*

Her face set in fury, "I hate that family! And I hate you both for making me use them! Can't trust them with…"

"Perhaps we could get back to the topic," Wingor interrupted, smoothly. Of course, he said everything smoothly. He really didn't need his staff to control Vinntag, but Kuumit was a dangerous man, so he usually held his peace.

"I'm not going to challenge her, Vinntag. That's *your* style," continued Kuumit. *What did you do to weaken Mileck before you challenged him? Perhaps I should watch what I eat.*

"Are you saying you couldn't defeat her?" Vinntag scoffed. She was showing more bravado than she felt. Wingor could See clearly that her terror was almost as strong as her hate. All three GuildMasters had Sight in their respective Powers, though Vinntag was the only one using hers publicly. In fact, neither Kuumit nor Wingor knew of the other's Sight. Even in this alliance…maybe especially in this alliance, it was best to keep some things secret.

"I'm saying that dueling Linzel to death would unsettle my Guild. She has given no cause." *And I'm not entirely sure I could. I am sure that I don't want to find out.*

"Then I want you to take her staff! I don't want to have to watch every corner I turn, to see if there's a Pulse coming at me!"

"You could just leave her alone," again Wingor gave his silky voice. If he calmed her down, perhaps they could get on to some deal striking.

There was a brief silence as two of them waited for the third to control herself. "I have another idea then," she eventually continued, "One that will serve my purpose, I think, and also serve *our* purposes." When they didn't respond, she continued on for many beats, outlining the plan she'd formed. If she guessed Linzel's character correctly, this would serve nicely. It might even get that Black witch killed. That was a pleasant thought. It should at least get her staff.

Shortly, both men were nodding.

"I believe that will work, Vinntag," responded a surprised Kuumit. He didn't know she was capable of real thought. Apparently, what wit she had was devoted to being devious. "It will require some of your help with my Guild, Wingor."

The Red GuildMaster was also nodding, "I agree, Kuumit. We will have to move slowly, but it should work. When we're done, we will control…well…everything."

"Then we are agreed, Masters?" Vinntag was breathless again, for a different reason.

"One condition comes to mind, Vinntag," responded Wingor.

She was happy now. She would agree to almost anything, her smile said.

"You really must end your vigil on Arima," he said. He knew her mood would shift again.

He was right. Face reddening immediately, she exploded, "Arima is *my* concern! White concern! It has nothing to do with this!"

They waited again. This was a tiresome woman.

"It is our concern if you are detected spying on other Masters," continued Wingor. "Linzel spotted it. Arima might, too. We have more important matters than watching your competition, no matter how much you hate her. The woman has been sitting in that cove…doing nothing…for almost ten cycles. Yes, we are getting the same reports you get. She must have heard by now what you did to Mileck. If she *were* coming out to challenge you, she'd have done so." He leaned in. He didn't need Power for her. Just dangle a bigger prize. "What we can accomplish in the next cycle or so cannot bear the risk of detection. I'm sure you can see that. You must also see the wisdom of leaving her to her Cats." His voice sounded like he was making a request, but he wasn't.

She was fuming, but she held her tongue, forcing a slight nod. *I will remember. There will come a time when I…have the influence. And I will remember.*

CHAPTER 13

They had a list of names. Master Blacks who just needed a bit of help deciding. Not all of the Black Masters were on the list. Some had already decided, some never would. Those that were beyond obvious persuasion would be outnumbered, and ultimately outvoiced.

It was the middle of the night, and there were Master Reds traveling throughout GuildTown in pairs. Quietly. All of them had Pools. It was late enough that wandering Buzzbies were gone wherever it was they went for their own rest. The pairs would stop outside of a designated hut and whisper into their stones. The resulting Pulses went into the huts belonging to the names on the list. The pairs would move on to the next name.

A separate pair, the most experienced of their group, had only four names. The huts they visited were all GuildMasters.

They had been doing this for almost two Quarters now, once every sevenday. It had to be slow, or it would show. Another Quarter, and they would be ready.

"Don' know anythin' else to do, Mum," Maleef said. She was weeping openly. So was Stem.

Malem's distress was perplexing. She would have a few days of tranquility, then a few days of true misery, then tranquility again. It couldn't be healthy.

"Perhaps you're right, child. Being around other children her age might be a help." This *was* a strange place to raise a child. "Antee lives the closest. I'll discuss it with him. Pill, you heard?"

"Yes."

"Convey this to Antee, please. Their next trip out is coming up soon, and we'll need to make arrangements." Pop!

* * *

"You must be sure to keep your Brown unLocked, Steef. If we get into trouble, I can't fix it if I'm Locked out," Mokam said solemnly.

"Okay." Uncle Mokam had said that eleven times now. He must mean it.

Cassa was trying to look calm. She trusted Mokam's Lifting completely. She trusted Steef's willingness to follow instructions. She had been involved with many first boat-Lifts, and this was as safe as they got. She just didn't trust the Cat. *Whoever heard of a Cat riding in a boat? No one, that's who.*

It hadn't come up in cycles, for Steef hadn't wanted to go flying…since meeting Kivverr. Now, he had to learn boat Lifting. And Steering. He would be spending a lot of beats in this boat for the next few cycles, and Kivverr intended to go. The big Cat was sitting in the bottom, looking calmly around. Cassa's head told her that was a good omen, but her pump wasn't convinced.

Steef had practiced Lifting things for half a cycle now. Everything Liftable had been Lifted. Rocks mostly, but he had also experimented on plants, carcasses, even water. Everything except a boat.

He couldn't put his staff into the usual hole next to her mast, it would have fallen in and disappeared. He asked her permission to make his own hole, which she gave. They could always close it up later. Mokam mounted his staff, too, for emergency only.

The boat lurched off the ground, and Kivverr lurched in the boat. Massive claws came out to bite into the bottom, but they couldn't penetrate the stone, and orange fur stood straight out. The boat wobbled just a bit, then began to rise. Kivverr's moans rose with it, though he didn't move at all. There was nowhere to go, anyway.

Steef stopped the Lift, and with the boat hovering ten staffs off the ground, jumped down to his friend, "Are you all right? I can take you back down."

"I am Kivverr! I am Clan! We do not step back!"

"Okay. I'll go easy, and I'll try not to wobble so much."

Steef went back to his place, and Cassa filled the sails with a gentle wind. The boat moved off slowly. As it approached a rockface, Steef Lifted it over with only a few small jerks. Kivverr's distress settled into a low intermittent moan that they could bear.

"He can't stay behind?" asked Cassa in a hoarse whisper.

Steef shook his head slightly, "The Clan...they don't step back from things...," he lowered to a whisper, "...even if they're afraid." Louder, "They stand."

"That's admirable, Shortstick. What happens when they stand in the face of something they *should* be afraid of?"

He shrugged, "Then they will Rest well, I think. Besides, Sassy, what's gonna hurt Kivverr?"

She gave him a piercing look, which he didn't see, as he was watching where they were going. *How about a hundred-staff drop, if he decides to turn this boat over? And what are you learning from him? Resting well? What's that?*

The trip was short. Cassa and Mokam both wanted him to practice landings. And more Lifts. His very first landing settled with a slight 'thump'. Cassa whirled to face the big Cat, shouting, "Kivverr! When I get this boat back to Town, I will have a wooden bottom fitted into it for your claws! Meanwhile, you are damaging the bottom of my boat while you courageously stand there with nothing to grip to! I...*forbid*...you to ride again...until we have *something* for you to hang on to!"

Cat and Master stared at each other for beats, while anything with ears had turned to look. Kivverr slowly blinked at her once, and straightened up. Tail riding high, he regally strode from the boat without a glance back.

Mokam, Cassa and Steef kept their faces straight and solemn, until they were aloft again. Steef turned his bright grin to her and said, "Thanks Sassy!"

"You're welcome, Shortstick."

"Watch those rocks," said Mokam, "You're a little low."

❧   ❧   ❧

"All drained?" she asked.

He nodded.

"Fill up with Blue then, Shortstick. Mokam, is his Brown cleared from the boat?" Captain of her boat, Cassa's style was completely opposite of Mokam's, just as it was on the ground.

"Ready for Lift in all respects, Steerman," replied the Brown. It *was* her boat, after all.

"Steef, we will be Lifting at the same rate of ascent we used this morning. You will need South wind moving North at three levels, increasing in speed at each level. Are you ready?"

"Ready Sas...I am ready for the Lift, Master Steerman." He had one hand on his stick, the other ready to work the sail. There had been debate over whether he should use his stick or her mast. Seafer had assured her that Steef's wood training was more than sufficient to control his Power on her mast. 'He won't be a'crispin' it' was his actual wording. And that *was* what she feared, mostly. But her other concern was strictly Blue in nature. He would never actually be using a mast like hers...he needed to learn his Steering with the tools he knew. The ones he would be using on his own. That meant his stick, not her mast.

"Prepare your sail, and call your wind."

He grasped the lanyard and waited for the first wisps of wind on his neck, as Sassy had told him for cycles. When it touched, he released the sail, and it billowed. Mokam Lifted, and they glided slowly away.

"Is your second level ready?"

"Second level wind coming in now, Master Steerman."

"Lifter, ascend to level two, please."

"Lifting," Mokam responded stiffly.

Mokam and Cassa hadn't used such formalities for cycles, but the forms had been developed over generations for a purpose. All Browns and Blues were required to memorize and use them early in their boat training. The habits Steef learned first...would be the ones he used for life. It might save his life one day. When he had Mastered this completely, he could decide what protocol he used for his own boat.

Cassa noted with satisfaction that his wind speeds and directions were smoother than the Lifting he had done this morning. She didn't fault Mokam's training. She preferred to think Steef just enjoyed his Blue more. Whatever the cause, the boy handled his Steering well for a first try.

"Steerman, kill your wind. We will drift to a hover, and reverse course."

"I am killing my wind, Master Steerman," came the excited voice, then, "We're not gonna make a turn, Sassy?"

She cocked a severe eyebrow at him, "Were my instructions unclear, Steerman?"

"No Master Steerman. Your pardon!" He stood to attention, but his eyes were twinkling.

You can turn the boat later, Shortstick. When I'm satisfied that your wind control won't tear the sail, or that your tack won't snap the mast. Until then, we stop and restart.

❦   ❦   ❦

"Shortstick, your Uncle Mokam has a gift for you."

He carried the stack of freshly washed bowls to his Mama, and hurried over to the fire.

"He wanted me to give them to you," she went on, "Because they are a Steerman's prize. But the truth is, Mokam purchased them." She laid the maps out on the table. "They're not even a used set. Freshly inked from Merchant's Row. All the latest markings."

Steef and Cassa had studied her old set of maps for many cycles. Little had changed since her apprentice days, and she had just inked those changes in herself. Like any experienced Steerman, she knew them completely anyway.

"Here are all of the travel lanes. All of the Landing Fields, and approach angles. The latest elevation markings. Everything a Steerman needs to travel the known world. One main map, showing all nine separate Territories, and nine individual maps for each one of those." Thumbing through them, Cassa pulled out one in particular. "Territory six…and right down here is our Vall…" Her head jerked back in surprise, then bent to peer at the parch closely, "That's odd."

"Is something wrong with the map, Cassa?" inquired Mokam. "I was assured that they are the very finest." He stood and came up beside her.

She thrust her finger to the bottom of the parch. Now Mokam bent, and looked where she pointed, then returned her puzzlement.

"What's the matter?" asked Antee.

"Apparently," said Cassa, her voice now cold and hard, "This Valley no longer exists."

"What!?" exclaimed Antee, glancing at Timmerr, but the Cat hadn't caught the insult. Mokam's head was shaking. Arima's hand froze over her instrument, tuning forgotten.

"There is no marking on this map to show the Valley of the Cats. They even left off the travel lanes that come here!" She was getting madder with each beat.

After the first shock, Arima's calm deepened to match Cassa's anger. "Good," she finally said.

"Good! How can this be good?!" Cassa exclaimed. She needed someone to be mad at.

"They weren't ever coming back here for Gradings anyway, now were they?" Arima replied evenly.

"Well…no…I suppose not."

"Then I would prefer to be as completely forgotten as possible. Wouldn't you?"

Cassa's mouth worked around the answers she'd like to give, but Arima wasn't the one who deserved them, "I guess you're right…but I *don't* have to like it!"

She turned back to Steef. He had helped Malem onto the table, and was showing her around the main map. His eyes were shining as he pointed out what all of it meant. Her face was alight as well. At her Bubba.

An irate Blue Master began flipping through map parches, giving each a close inspection. Her attention was caught again.

An alert Antee was watching her. "Something else, Cassa?"

She held it up for him to see. "Territory three…eastern Territory…and the blue valley."

Mokam's head came up. So did Steef's.

"Yes?"

"It's at the eastern edge of the eastern Territory."

"Yes?"

"There's a travel lane marked here that wasn't here before."

"Is that important?"

"It's going east…*over* the blue Valley…off the edge of the map."

"What's out there?"

"Nothing. Wasteland. So why is there a travel lane going nowhere?"

❦   ❦   ❦

"I have something for you too. I didn't want to bring it out until you got to see your maps." He opened his trunk and pulled out a small cage.

"What is it, Uncle Antee?"

"Groundcrawler family. This one lives in water mostly. It's a coldblood, like a snake, but it's got legs and a tail."

"I don't see a tail."

"Well, that's what's interesting about this particular coldblood. If they lose their tail, it'll grow back." He remembered the arguments at Yellow GuildHall when he studied there. Many of his fellow students, and some of the Masters, would hunt these poor beasties and cut off their tails, just to examine them during the regrowth. It had been the beginning of his questions about Guild practices. He'd had word out among his fellow Yellows to watch for one that had managed to get itself injured. It had been more than two cycles.

"How does it do that?"

"No one knows. But I know you like puzzles. This may just be the greatest Yellow puzzle of all."

"Thanks, Uncle Antee!" This had been a really good day.

"Just feed it regularly. And keep Kivverr away from it."

"Okay."

"Out of my way, you 'Nert scum!"

The laborer was doing just that, laboring. Filling a cart with crates and goods from his Master's store for delivery. Arms full, he hadn't seen the man in his path, and bumped him. Some of the items he was carrying dumped onto the ground, adding to the passerby's obstructions.

Without looking up, the laborer bent to begin retrieving his work, "Your pardon, Master. I'll move these for you, righ' away," he said meekly.

"I said out of the way!" This was accompanied by a kick to the ribs.

The laborer had companions. Other laborers, who could see their friend's assailant, and stepped back into the store entrance. The man with the now-sore ribs picked himself up, and stood out of the way, still clinging to a couple of the parcels that were his responsibility. He lifted his eyes for the first time, and began to shake. The footprint on his tunic belonged to a Ten Black. He didn't understand the markings on the badge. He really couldn't even read. But he had learned One through Ten, and he knew Black.

"Your pardon, Master," he repeated, "I'll be standin' outta your way, Master." He proved it by stepping back.

"Little late for that, 'Nert," growled the Master Black. A fist sized hole opened front and back on the laborer's tunic, right where his pump had been. He dropped straight down, crumpling into a limp heap before the bleeding could begin.

"Here now! What are you doing to our help!?" One of the store's clerks had been alerted, and came rushing out. "What have you done? You've killed our laborer! You can't do that! I'll be reporting you to your Guild, I will! That's an unsanctioned killing! There'll be fines, you know! Be sanctioned yourself..." He didn't get it finished, landing next to the dead laborer.

The two Black Masters continued down the road.

"Imagine," said the first, truly amazed, "A Red Six telling me what I can't do!"

"I can't imagine a Six anything telling us what we can do," replied his companion.

"*There's* some truth."

"Nice clean kills, by the way. Good holes."

"Thanks."

Across the road, two Red Masters had been standing quietly between shops, listening. They looked at each and smiled thinly. It was working.

It was a sweet-smelling pot, at least. Some of the concoctions they'd made were much less pleasant. Kivverr always kept his distance when that occurred. Steef was stirring exactly as he had been instructed, watching for the surface to glaze. Arima was preparing the straining cloth. She could have ordered the salve from Town, but Seafer had Steef growing all of the different Healing herbs, might as well teach him to make the salves and potions. She shuddered. *And poisons. Eventually, we'll have to do the poisons.* He had to know them, for self defense if nothing else.

I wonder if he'll cry?

"Why can't we just bring Sissy some playmates here, Aunt Arima?"

"They wouldn't come, pumpkin. They would be afraid of the Cats."

"The Clan wouldn't eat them, though. They don't eat two-legs."

People, child. They don't eat people. She sighed. *Not any more, anyway.* "They won't be that far away. Antee's hut is in the closest village there is. We'll visit." *Not often. Or ever. I hate this. And it's my fault.* Every burden that was Malem would be forever riding her. The family wouldn't even get to come with Antee's regular visits, for fear of attracting attention. *If they were Yellows, we could say they were helping him tend the herds.* As it was, they would be stretching believability, presenting Stem and Maleef as crop-tenders on Antee's land. He was going to have to bring in more livestock to justify it. The complications just piled up. Mokam would be paying for it, of course. He never seemed to mind, having a seeming endless supply of Dust and Crystals.

I'd wager he doesn't cry.

Malem needed a normal life, and she wasn't going to find it here. It would break his parents' pumps to leave Steef behind, but truth was, he was already past the age when gifted children left their families to prepare for Master training. Malem was going to get village life, with village children. And no Cats. They would be leaving with Cassa's boat tomorrow. Steef had been given short warning, in the hope that he wouldn't have time to fret.

I wonder if that's why Steef got such a full day of flying and gifts yesterday? Uncles and big sister anticipating his pain? They don't understand him. Not really. He finds his own distractions.

"It's ready, Aunt Arima."

"Let's get it strained and potted up, then. Your Uncle Antee gets you the rest of the day. He has calves to birth."

"That's fun...Aunt Arima?"

"Yes Sir?"

"When are we going to do a baby birthing?"

She smiled. "Do you see any pregnant women around here?"

He grew silent. Lifting the pot off the fire, he began pouring the salve through the strainer.

"Is it important to you?"

"There's nothing new to Heal. I can't learn it if it's not here." It was as close to a complaint as she'd ever heard from him.

"True enough. You could always ask Cassa to have a baby," she jested, thinking to lighten his mood, then reminding herself that she'd instigated enough pregnancies. Anyway, she thought it was a good jest.

Nope.

"I did." He nodded thoughtfully, watching carefully as he poured. Tongue kept trying to creep out, but he was speaking too often.

"You *did*!? What did she say!?"

"She thought it was funny. She said she wouldn't be able to reach her mast."

Well, *there* was a jest. The image of that made Arima bark out a laugh, and Steef smiled with her. *Maybe we WILL make a quiet visit or two to this village. They should welcome a Healer and her apprentice. Maybe.*

I hope he cries.

❦   ❦   ❦

"Try it now, Uncle Seafer."

"All charged up, Sprout?"

"Yessir." He handed over his stick. He thought he had it de-tuned.

Nope. "Still cold Sprout...thankee for tryin'...how're the acorns comin'?"

"Over half of them packed up, Uncle Seafer. I should be finished in a seven-day."

"Good work…keep tryin' on the staff, would'ya?"

"Yessir."

❧   ❧   ❧

"I don' wanna go, Bubba!"

"I know, Sissy." They were back in 'their' spot, second bend of the stairs. It was pretty dark, but Kivverr could lead them back down, if needed. Arms wrapped around her, as she rested the back of her head against his chest, he began the Red. Again. "But you don't like it here. Not really."

"You *want* me to go?"

"You know better." He waited for his Red to work, pushing verrrry slowly, so she wouldn't catch on.

"You'll come see me?" Her breathing was slowing.

"I'll do better than that," he said. Reaching into his trous pocket, he pulled out the burl. A small burl from Seafwood that would have been a stick, eventually. It was loaded with Dust, and would hold a charge for…well, he really didn't know, but a long time. It was charged now, with the same Red that he regularly gave her.

"What's that?"

"It's me."

When her fingers touched it, she smiled for the first time that day, "It is! It's you!" Then her face fell again.

"Don't you like it?"

"I can't give you one."

"Yes you can. Get your stick." She'd been practicing simple Pulses, trying to keep up with her Bubba. It had only added to her misery, illuminating the differences one more way. But she *could* make a Pulse. It was an oddity of their situation that her Three grade staff was almost twice as large as his stick.

"Okay. What now?"

"Send a Pulse straight up."

She knew better than question his strange request. She instantly pushed everything she had out the end of her stick. He had switched to White, watching for the Green flash. His Clear bubble caught her Pulse neatly. He drew it back until it hovered in front of them.

"What happened, Bubba?" She couldn't See her own Pulse, of course. Or his bubble.

"I caught it. Now I've got a piece of you, too. Seafwood will keep it safe."

❧   ❧   ❧

I knew he wouldn't cry.

The boat was beginning to glide away, and everyone was waving wildly at everyone. Maleef was weeping, but refused to lose herself in it, lest she miss any dwindling glimpse of her Son. What struck Arima wasn't Steef's reaction to the scene, it was his sister's. Malem wasn't crying either. Waving slowly with one hand, her other hand was grasping something tightly to her chest.

When the boat was completely gone, Seafer patted Steef on his head, and ambled off to his chores. There would be more work for him and the Sprout, now that Stem was gone.

Arima stood with him silently for as long as it took, which was a while. She finally couldn't stand it any longer, "All right. Where is it?"

"Where is what, Aunt Arima?" His face was a mask.

"The joy. You always 'find the joy', so something won't be a 'crying thing.'" She didn't *want* to sound harsh. She wasn't mad, after all. She was beginning to be afraid for him, again. A new fear to go with the others she tried to ignore. Children *needed* to…no…*people* needed to cry, sometimes.

"It's better for Sissy, isn't it?"

"We hope so."

"If Sissy's better, then Mama's better, right?" Maleef *did* stay tired and strained. Odd that her 'normal' child would be the challenge that her 'un-nor-mal' child never was.

"We hope that, too." She saw where he was going.

"And if Mama's better, then Papa's better."

"Mmm-hmmm." Sigh.

"That's enough," he concluded with a shrug.

❧   ❧   ❧

Complaints were coming in from all nine Territories, and especially from GuildTown and its valley. Killings by Master Blacks. The Black Guild was being pressured to control its Masters, and punish them.

"Punish us?!" several of them shouted, "*Punish* us? For doing what we were *born* to do!?"

"We should be punishing them!" shouted others.

"That's right!"

Kuumit let them rant. He was watching closely. Predictably, there were some who appeared shocked, bewildered that their fellow Masters were becoming so callous. And the GuildMaster was doing nothing to stop it!

Six of them for sure. Another four were doubtful. *Ten against thirty eight. It's time.* He'd have Wingor here, behind the wall, for the next meeting. It had to be controlled, or the killing would be fearsome.

ꙮ   ꙮ   ꙮ

She had her eyelenses on. Her strongest. All of the Cats had been sent out of the cove, including Kivverr. Seafer and Pill had been sent with them. Just the two of them here.

"Drained? Feel my arms." She held them out, and he grasped her at the wrists. She noted that his fingers could finally go all the way around. "That's my regular tune. Now if I shift that tune just slightly…" she began to glow White, "My glow becomes visible to anyone. Even people without Sight. Making that same shift in your staff makes the glow in your stone visible, too."

"Okay. But what does it do?"

Show off, mostly. "Well, it can be a sign of courtesy, or respect, to glow your stone when bowing to a Master. Glowing yourself completely during a bow…is generally taken for affection, to go with the respect." She paused. *He'll need to know eventually.* "Some people just glow themselves all the time…mainly to show that they can." *And to show how much they can.* Ironically, the lower ratings usually did it more than the Masters, which she'd always found sad.

"And shifting your tune this way…" she made the adjustment, "Cloaks your Power. Then, even a Sighted person can't See it."

"What's that good for?"

"Good question. I've never known a good reason for it." *Except lying and hiding and sneaking. Well, those aren't good reasons.* "All right, you can release me, and fill back up. White only, please." She was hoping this wouldn't be a problem. She was hoping that…if it *was* a problem…White would be less dangerous to her. She stepped back a staff, anyway. Putting her hands up to her lenses, she was ready to cover up.

"All filled? Sure you know the tune?"

He nodded.

"Begin."

She was wrong about White being less dangerous. The lenses were no help at all, and her hands were too slow. White light stabbed her eyes faster than she could blink, and then mercifully, everything went blank.

"Ah!," she cried, as she crumpled against the table and then sank to the ground.

He was kneeling next to her in a beat, "Aunt Arima! Are you hurt!?"

"Just my eyes, pumpkin," she said weakly, "Only my eyes." That wasn't entirely true. Her head was throbbing. "We'll need for you to do some Healing on them, I think. Then maybe we'll just concentrate on teaching you the different Grading levels."

"Okay."

"Are you still glowing?" she asked, her unseeing eyes still wide.

"Yes Mam." His stick was already out, and White Power was pouring into her burned eyes, along with the White glow. He spread the Pulse to cover her bright red skin.

"You might better tune it off, pumpkin, so my eyes can Heal."

"Yes Mam." The glow stopped, but not the Pulsing.

Pop! Pop!

"Arima! That was great! We could see the flash from outside the cove! It was huge!"

Steef heard them arrive. Heard the buzzing. "Buzzbies," he said to Arima's head, "Tell Uncle Seafer to bring some water. Quick." He remembered his lessons. Burned people dry out.

Though the quarterday sun was shining brightly outside, the inside of the MasterHall was solid Black. Kuumit couldn't even see his feet. He allowed himself a smile, while no one could see. *There will be parches written about this day, and my name will be on all of them.* Every active Master of Black in the Guild was here.

"Pool," he whispered, "Tell Wingor to begin." Pop! Kuumit would just have to trust him, and it wasn't a feeling he liked. The Red GuildMaster would be directing his Pulses selectively into the Hall. One of the people he was supposed to avoid was Kuumit, as Kuumit didn't need stirring. His decision had been made in a hut, at night, almost a cycle ago.

There were ten others who wouldn't be touched by Red this day, either. Kuumit didn't need their voices. He did need examples, and these ten would suffice.

Pop! *"Wingor says to start."*

"Masters!" Beat. Beat. "Masters!" It was louder, catching the Red amplification. "MASTERS!" Kuumit's voice thundered through the Blacked-out Hall, swallowing every sound. *I could get accustomed to this!*

"Could we tune-off the glows, please!? That's better. Thank you." He went silent until every odd chatter and gesture stilled. "As you know, our Guild has been under attack. There is unrest among several of the other Colors. Complaints against our own Masters for doing what we are *supppppoooossssed...*," the word hung in the air. *Well...*thought Kuumit...*Wingor IS the GuildMaster of Red for a reason,* "...TO DO!!."

"Your Guild does not HEAR them...Your Guild does not HEED them...Your Guild KNNOOOWWS...who the Power is in this world!"

"Tell 'em, Kuumit!" "Let's show 'em, Kuumit!"

He continued, "Who is there to tell US?...Who will tell the MASTERS OF BLACK...HOW...TO...LIVE?!" the GuildMaster shouted.

"No one!" Thirty-eight voices in unison.

"Who controls the BLACK GUILD?!"

"WE DO!...WE DO!...WE DO!...WE DO!...WE DO!..."

The Hall went Black again, and he just waited them out. Wingor had been specific. *Work them up, then hit them when they're tired.* It took a while. Meanwhile, Pool was whispering into his ear, that the selected ten were *not* joining in. After today, Pool wouldn't have to whisper secretly.

"MASTERS!!," he was finally able to continue, "There is a reason for the turmoil. We have allowed...yes...WE have allowed...allowed others to forget...forget WHO HAS THE POWER!"

This could take all day he thought idly, as the tumult burst again.

"Not ALL have forgotten, though...How many of you have killed a White recently?" Staffs went up. "How many have killed a Red?" More staffs. "Have TTHHOOOSSE Guilds complained?...NO!...And why? Because they have RESPECT!...What we need is a change!...What is holding us back?...Nothing!...We have gotten SOFT!...And all...because...of...an ancient...parch!" He took a breath...then screamed...

"...WE NEED A NEW GUILDLAW!"

Kuumit had to shout his next message to Pool, as the crowd made whispering useless, and unnecessary. "Tell Wingor to tune it down some, or they'll be killing each other soon!" Pop!

Kuumit went on, "We need a GuildLaw that answers to Masters…and only Masters! We need a GuildLaw that answers to BLACK Masters…and ONLY Black Masters!"

"That's right Kuumit!" etc.

"We need a GuildLaw…," Kuumit began lowering his voice "…That doesn't…answer…to…TownLaw." He was almost whispering now, and his voice still carried across the hall. *Should have done this cycles ago.* "Who wants to live a free life!?…WHO IS WITH ME!?"

And thirty eight staffs went up.

Kuumit found he was tired, too, but he had to finish it. *Shame. Some of them were once friends.* Oddly, he didn't actually enjoy killing, he just didn't mind…if it served a purpose. And he *was* good at it. With Wingor's help, he was also getting good at getting others to do it for him.

"Not every staff agrees!…Some of us must still want to continue living in…SERVITUDE?" *Leemin or Linzel? Who will be first?*

The objects of his concern were on sitting on opposite sides of the Hall, and though they had made a point of not looking at each other, they both rose as one, stepping into the center. Their stones weren't flared, but Kuumit knew they would be charged. *Aaahhhhh. Let's see if anyone dies today. Maybe me? I can't take them both. Steady. I've got a lot of help.*

They stopped side by side, facing Kuumit, backs to the Hall and its assembled Black Power. Leemin spoke first, into the hush that suddenly gripped them all, "GuildLaw…is all that keeps us from becoming…beasts! Some of us have been prooving that for over a cycle now. So…when all of you have shown how MIGHTY you are…by killing…*EVERYONE!!!*…What will you EAT?…how will you TRAVEL?…who will dig your precious Dust?…or clean your huts? And THEN…you will have only yourselves left to kill!"

Beat. Beat. Be…

"That's not a purpose I was born to!!!" added Linzel.

Whatever he thought of their puny values, Kuumit had to give them a grudging respect. *They aren't even TRYING to defend themselves.* Basic training taught young Blacks to stand back to back. *A Pulse could come from anyone behind them, and they would die never knowing who it was.* On impulse, he decided to give them a chance to live. The choice would be theirs.

"Masters...you have now been heard!...But the will of the MasterHall is against you..."

"No more soft heads!" "No more talk!" "Time for a strong Guild!" came voices from all around them, in a growl.

"...We will NOT have you labor against us!" shouted Kuumit. He noticed that his palms were wet, and fought the urge to wipe them on his trous. "You are henceforth...EXPELLED...from our Guild. If you leave on your feet, you will do it...WITHOUT your staffs!" *It's got to happen now, or not at all.*

Before either of them could react, there was a ruckus at the end of the Hall. Another dissenter tried to get off a Pulse at Kuumit. The GuildMaster never moved, for Wingor had been specific about that, too. *You must let the crowd do the killing, and make sure they SEE that you killed no one.* The crowd didn't disappoint. They cut the troublemaker to bits.

I didn't think old Samist had that kind of courage. Kuumit turned a very satisfied face back to Leemin and Linzel.

Beat. Beat. Beat.

"Bahhh!" Linzel spat, as she threw her staff to the dirt. She had daughters to think of. She met Leemin's eyes proudly, and held them as his staff joined hers.

"Anyone else?" asked Kuumit smoothly. He could afford to be generous now. Soon there were nine staffs in the dirt before him. Samist's staff would be buried with him.

He was GuildMaster over thirty eight devoted killers. Enough for his needs. The thought came to him *Vinntag will be pleased.*

In fact, Vinntag was already pleased. The White MasterHall was littered with the bodies of six dead Master Healers, courtesy of the two Black Nines stationed outside of the GuildHall building. The Nines were thrilled. They had actually gotten to use Buzzbies! And kill Masters! The two Red Nines next to them had a more reserved opinion, which they kept to themselves. Fourteen staffs were left behind by their owners.

They never could have foreseen it, but the Red Guild gave the most trouble that day, for two reasons. There were more Red Masters than there were Blacks or Whites, and they couldn't be controlled by Red Power. The debate was furious, with Red Pulses flying everywhere. This meeting had been delayed somewhat. It couldn't start without Wingor, and he had to return from the Black GuildHall. So all of Red Guild's Masters were warned about what was coming. When it was clear to him that reason would not prevail, he spoke a word to Pool, and Masters started dropping. It took eighteen corpses to convince them. Wingor felt he might have spared a few of the last deaths, but the Blacks outside worked so fast, it was a marvel they didn't *all* die. Another sixteen staffs given over, and his Guild was cut in half.

❧   ❧   ❧

"Bigger."

Another Green Pulse, and the trunk swelled again. "Now?"

"Bigger."

Pulse. "Now?"

"That will do." Kivverr jumped onto the wood. It was now taller than Steef. A few more small Green Pulses, and there were holes to help him climb. Once up, he looked at his friend. Kivverr was belly-down on the trunk, legs draped over the sides, claws sunk deep. Steef had to admit, the big log was a good fit for Kivverr's bulk.

He had told Uncle Seafer that he needed one of the saplings for an experiment.

"Plenty of 'em…won't miss just one, I'd say." Uncle Seafer hadn't even looked up.

So Steef had made the sapling draw up its roots, and the willing tree fell right over. Pulse after Pulse of Green had made the tree soak nutrient from the soil for its artificial growth. Nothing else would be growing in this spot for a while. Not without help.

Steef liked the idea of using wood instead of stone. The charges would be cleaner, especially in *this* wood. One more quick Green, and a hole opened on top, into which he placed his stick. Done with Green. Time for Brown.

"Ready?" His legs were sticking straight out. If this worked, he would fashion a better seat later. For now, he was leaning against Kivverr's chest, with the Cat's head suspended over his own. Both of them had a good view.

"Yes."

The log Lifted slowly and smoothly. Straight up. Steef stopped it at two staffs.

"*Why did you stop?*" Kivverr had actually been eager for a second trip off the ground. That's what he said. Steef thought there might be another reason for his eagerness.

"I want to see how well we balance, before we go higher." *And see if you're going to moan again, while I can still get us down quick.* If any of the Clan got near enough, Steef didn't want them to hear.

But Kivverr seemed relaxed. *Must be the grip.* They went to ten staffs.

"*We get higher than this in our tree.*" That was true. Seafwood was two spans short of forty staffs at their last measurement, and Kivverr could squeeze himself almost halfway up. Higher, when Seafwood helped.

"Be patient. When we're practiced at this, I'll take us as high as you want." For as long as Steef could remember, Sassy had sprinkled every conversation about flying with warnings. 'Wild flying equals cracked boats' and 'A lack of caution means a lack of safety' and 'Let the wind do your hurrying, while you do the thinking.' Steef had listened. More than she'd ever known.

There would be no wind to surprise them this day. He'd been sending Blue out for two days. Lifting to fifty staffs, everything still felt stable.

He'd decided on using a log for Kivverr's sake, and that part of the idea had proven itself. But others before him…long before him…had settled on stone bowls for a reason. His Uncle Mokam had even explained the reason…balance.

They *were* balanced. They were both on the centerline, and Kivverr's sprawl lent itself to balance. But Kivverr had a tail, and that tail weighed almost as much as Steef. And Kivverr was pleased as he could be about how this was working out. And that tail swished.

And the log rolled.

Two things saved them, and both of them were Kivverr. He already had his claws in the wood, so he wasn't going anywhere. And he was quick. Quick as…well…a Cat. Which was good, because Steef left in a hurry. No seat. No strap. He couldn't even grip with his legs, the log was so wide. But Kivverr snapped…and Steef was dangling in the air, his middle caught between the familiar jaws.

"*When we get down…*"

"I know…you're not far from it now. I think one of your long-teeth punched through."

"*I could loosen my grip if you like.*"

"Get me to my stick, and I'll turn us back."

But the only thing holding the stick was friction, and it had already been jostled. When Kivverr bent to get Steef closer, the extra motion was enough. It came out of its hole. Kivverr's neck craned back as his eyes followed it down. In this position, Steef got a good view too. The stick hit the ground, and broke apart.

"Guess I'm gonna need a new stick."

His Uncle Mokam had told him, and he *had* listened. 'Stone holds a charge better than wood. Boats are made of stone because they take and hold a stable charge. Wood let charges through. That's why we use them for staffs.' He had listened, and factored that in. He wasn't reckless. It was a *big* log. He hadn't expected to lose his stick. The log was a sapling from a Seafwood acorn, and better wood than most. His sticks held their charges. It wouldn't be an issue.

But the sapling wasn't Seafwood. There was no stone mounted to this log. And the sapling had never been fed any Dust. It started losing its charge, and it started to drop. Slowly at first, but it picked up speed quickly.

"Resting day."

"I've got to touch the wood! Get me to the wood!"

Kivverr's head snapped again, and Steef's arms were slapped hard against the log. He still had charge in himself. It would do. The log's descent slowed, and came to a hover at the original two staffs. Being on the bottom of the log now, it seemed lower.

Kivverr's head craned back once more, his mouth opened and Steef dropped neatly to the ground. He scrambled out of the way and Kivverr followed with a graceful roll that landed him on his paws. They stepped well out of the way, giving the log room to fall, which it did a few beats later.

Glancing across the open field to the mouth of the cove, Steef said, "Hope Aunt Arima didn't see that."

But Arima was busy with problems of her own. A storm of Buzzbies had filled the cove, covering she and Seafer both. Bringing news from GuildTown. Lots of news. All of it bad.

CHAPTER 14

Pop! *"Linzel"*

"Peel!" she whispered hoarsely. Her throat was swollen. "You shouldn't be here! It's dangerous for you!"

❈   ❈   ❈

The three Ruling Guilds had made a mistake, letting so many Masters live...unstaffed. After the frenzy of that day, when heads cooled a bit, the remaining Masters remembered that some of these were people they liked. Even respected. And they were embarrassed...a little.

They began displaying that embarrassment, by being cruel. Within a sevenday, the expelled Masters were forbidden to wear their badges. That wasn't much of a sacrifice, as most of them had removed the badges in disgust. Since that didn't hurt enough, they were forbidden to do public commerce on Merchant's Row. That only hurt some of them, since all of the banished Reds had had their shops taken from them anyway, so they already weren't going there any more.

In frustration, the Three Guilds issued a new TownLaw, which was a first. TownLaws in the past had required agreement from all seven Guilds, and the LaborMaster. Strangely, the other Guilds held their peace, their GuildMasters displaying unusual reluctance to enter any debate. The new TownLaw gave leave to the Mates of a banished Master to break their Mating, without cause.

This caused more trouble than it was worth. People everywhere started breaking deals that had been struck of all kinds, their excuse being that the institution of deal-striking had been abolished. The new TownLaw was quickly rescinded, but not before five former Masters found themselves unMated.

Maar had been briefly tempted. Not because he disliked Linzel, though she was often a nuisance, pestering him to do something stupid, like giving Dust to scruffy people. But Maar's distress was more basic than dislike. She was now an embarrassment to *him*, too, and he didn't Mate to be embarrassed. What stopped him was the girls. He loved his girls, and they loved their Mama. And then his temptation was gone with the cancellation of the new Law.

At least the Three Guilds learned that passing Laws on a whim was treacherous ground. They would have to be reminded many times in the coming cycles, however. They never seemed to learn.

Meanwhile, the Masters in power had failed to beat their fallen brethren enough to feel good about it. It was, of course, Wingor who thought of it. He was a Master in human nature, after all.

"If you're determined to make them miserable, Vinntag, you can do it without harming them at all." *Without a staff, she wouldn't be fit to scrub huts* he reflected. His face remained unmoving.

"Hoowww might that beeee, Winngorrr?" The better her mood, the sweeter her voice got.

Does she really think anyone believes that sticky voice? "Simple really. Take away their Buzzbies," he said with a casual shrug. Of course, Wingor never gave any conversation casually, but she didn't know that. *She reminds me of an egg-layer…hmmm…that would be toooo funny…reveal me to Kuumit, though. Well, it's time he understood anyway.* Their staffs were outside again, but he had a stone in his trous pocket. He didn't need to touch his hand to it. It was resting on his leg, while his hands stayed innocently on the table. The stone Pulsed.

"And how," she said, "Can you…cluck…take their…cluck, cluck…Buzzbies? Bbwwaaaahhkkkk!" She blinked, and smiled at him expectantly.

Wingor never acknowledged anything but her question. Kuumit however, suddenly had trouble breathing, snorting through his nose, and setting his jaw very hard to keep still.

"We have Pool check them daily," responded Wingor patiently, "And any of them found with Buzzbies get their heads Pulsed off, Buzzbies and all. *They might not care any more, but I'm guessing their Buzzbies will.*" *That's enough for her. Any more would be an indulgence.* His stone stopped Pulsing.

"And just hhhoooowww…cluck…hmmm…does that serve us?"

"They will be alone, Vinntag. Utterly alone. Even *you* would miss Pool, in time."

As they were leaving later, Kuumit held Wingor back. *Perfect* thought Wingor, as the two Black guards saw their GuildMaster's gesture, and turned away, *they saw HIM stop ME. Do it now.*

"That was a treat, Wingor," Kuumit said, trying to appear relaxed and unthreatened, "But don't ever try that on me. You do know what will happen?" Kuumit was being as menacing as he knew how to be.

As if I can't See his fear! Well, he SHOULD be afraid. Wingor's stone Pulsed again, "I think you would probably lay me an egg, wouldn't you?"

Kuumit's face went blank. "Why yes, I'd be honored to lay you an egg," his flat voice said.

"And who is your wisest counselor in all this valley?"

"You are, of course."

"And who is the *last* person you would *ever* want to see touched by a Black Pulse?'

"You again, Wingor."

"And how important is it that you remember these things?"

"Etched in my memory, dear friend."

More than you know, Kuumit. It was over in scant beats. Wingor set his Locks, and drained the stone.

🍁　　　🍁　　　🍁

Arima had beaten their timing, getting her first message to Linzel the day after the day of blood.

Pop! "Linzel. A message from Pill."

"What is it Peel?"

"Arima sends greets. She offers transport to a place of sanctuary."

"Where might that be, Peel?"

"We don't know. Pill won't tell us. Pill says it's truly safe."

"I can't leave the girls, Peel."

"We'll ask." Pop!

Pop! *"She says to bring them. Maar too, if he'll come."*

It was tempting. She trusted Arima. Trusted her motives, anyway. Her pump. Her courage. But the offer, however genuine, might be misplaced. How could a Healer, even one as strong as Arima, hold off a Guild of Blacks? No place was safe.

Pop! *"She also says she has all the staffs you could want."*

"How can she?" Linzel thought to herself, out loud. Peel was used to her, though, and didn't repeat it. *Arima has no staff craft.* Just yesterday, one of the expelled Masters had died trying to purchase an unregistered staff. The illegal crafters had died with him, thus ending for all time the practice of unregistered staffs. That settled it, Arima's offer had just become unbelievable. *Her age has caught up with her.*

"Give her my grateful greets, Peel, but I can't risk my girls."

Pop! Pop! Pop! Pop!

"What's happening, Peel?" Linzel asked bleakly.

"Apparently, Pill is having a multiple conversation. We don't know who with."

"With whom."

"All right, with whom. We are told that transportation will be available again in one Quarter. You will be told how and when."

"Thank her again, Peel." Pop!

So a full Quarter had passed. The first two sevendays after this new Law, Pool had watched them, every beat of every day, in their huts, or out. Never communicating, just stuck to a wall or a tree. Watching. No killings were needed, since everyone knew the threat was real. Eventually, the vigil ended and new habits set in.

It was midnight, and Linzel was on her pad in the very back closet of the hut. Maar no longer spoke to her, which was no great loss. Leemin and the seven others had gone off to find work. They had to eat. The girls were being teased and tormented by the other children, to the point where they blamed their Mother. And Peel had been gone for six sevendays. Her throat was sore a lot lately. She hoped she didn't wake Maar, speaking to the Peel that had just come…in the middle of the night!

"Won't stay long. Transport day after tomorrow. Landing Field just before dawn. Don't pack. If you're there, you'll be contacted by Pill. If not, we'll be back in a Quarter." Pop!

"Thank…you…Pe…" But Peel was gone.

❦   ❦   ❦

"Where is he?" Cassa asked for all of them. Arima pointed one finger up. Necks craned back. Even with her sharp eyes, Cassa couldn't see anything but the storm. She'd felt it moving up all morning as they approached, but it had stayed out of her lanes, so she paid no attention.

"Nothing up there but a skybolt storm," said Antee.

"Mmm-hmmm," said Arima.

Beat. Beat. Beat.

"But you can't *dooo* that!" exclaimed Cassa, "It's not pos..."

"Please don't say it," Arima beseeched her quietly. Mokam was nodding.

Beat. Beat. Beat.

Her foot started stamping. "But it's *not!*...It's *not!* It's *not!* It's *not!*...Those are *skybolts!* Do you know what *happens*...when you get hit with a skybolt!?" Cassa was a Blue, after all.

"I used to think I did," replied Arima evenly.

"Me too," threw in Seafer. "I used t'think I knew a lot of things...nope...not sure I even know about trees."

"You can't say that, old friend," Mokam comforted. They'd all had low spirits for a Quarter now. Seafer's was showing a bit. "Look at this fine lady here." He gestured at Seafwood.

"I thought it up...for true...an' made the acorns...but I didn't grow it...nossir...the Sprout grew that tree...without knowin' how...I grew those...," he pointed across the flatland to the stand of saplings, "...fine trees to be sure...proud of 'em...an' they'll do everythin' I intended from the start...but I didn't grow *her*."

"Pill, I don't suppose you'd care to go get him?" asked Cassa.

"Would you want to go into that?"

"Then we'll just wait until he's finished."

No one mentioned Linzel. She hadn't come.

❧   ❧   ❧

"Ready?"

"Play the simple song."

"I am. This is gonna be great!" Kivverr always asked for the 'simple song' first. It was his name for the first crude tune Steef had put together cycles ago. He'd tried many different compositions since, some he felt actually sounded like music. Kivverr's 'simple song' was little more than a complicated scale, or interweaving scales. But the Cat loved it. Steef played it quietly for him in the tree almost every night. He'd blow through his stick, and sets of tiny bubbles would come out, popping low so they wouldn't disturb anyone, playing the 'simple song' over and over while Kivverr got brushed or scratched.

Steef liked to play his music, and often called up some wind to magnify the bubbles. He'd gotten a lot of practice over the last few cycles, calling wind.

Now he wanted to study skybolts, one of Uncle Mokam's primary Powers. There was a strong bubble around their sled. A smaller storm ten days ago had proven that the bubble would hold against the skybolts, so now it was play time.

Adding to the glad event was the effect that the skybolts had on hair. Steef's hair was standing straight up, and Kivverr looked like a giant orange powder puff. He licked at it proudly every few beats, while maintaining a complete disdain for Steef's look.

Steef was happy with his latest stick, too. Almost as big as Sissy's had been, it handled more Power. Enough that he could divide its charge into separate Colors, and do several things at once. There was a bit of Blue maintaining the storm, some Brown for the sled, and mostly Red for the song. Music just seemed to sound better in Red.

The sled would hold its charge for a while, so he took the stick, and passed the point through the bubble. They had the exact same tune…no accident…so the stick passed through without disturbing the bubble's strength. Putting his mouth to the blowhole, Steef blew Kivverr's 'simple song' into the storm. The Red bubbles swirled together into the wind, until getting struck by a skybolt. They swelled in unison until saturated, then popped.

Steef turned a big grin to Kivverr.

"That was a good one. I like the change we made on the last note."

      ❧   ❧   ❧

They heard it on the ground.

"Did I just hear music?" asked Antee.

Cassa nodded numbly, "He's playing the storm like a flute," she said resignedly, as if it happened every day. Maybe it did…here.

"Can you do that?"

She just stared at him.

      ❧   ❧   ❧

Now for something new. He blew a new kind of bubble into the storm, followed by a stream of more complicated music. The new bubbles burst at intervals. They dampened the boomers off the skybolts, releasing it in measures, as each new dampener burst. The intervals of booming mixed with the notes he'd sent, blending into a rhythm. Like Sassy's drums.

When it reached them, Cassa just shook her head.

"Well y'got t' admit…it sounds pretty good!" Seafer said. He'd lived here for almost thirteen cycles now. He was thoroughly immune to surprise.

🍁   🍁   🍁

"One more thing and we'll go."

"What one more thing?"

"I want to take Uncle Mokam some skybolt."

"Do you know how?"

"Nope. Won't know 'til I try."

Skybolts turned out to be hard to catch. Sitting still and having them strike was easier than catching. He'd have to study that. A disappointed Steef sent the storm on its way. He'd brought it in from a direction away from any of Sassy's approach lanes, and much higher than any level she ever flew. It shouldn't have been in her way. They were probably already here, but he couldn't tell from this height. Time to go.

🍁   🍁   🍁

The usual greets out of the way, Antee went first, in spite of Cassa's eagerness, "I have a gift for you from your sister. I was told to give you this first, without fail," he told his young friend with a strong smile. He handed over a small pot that held a flowering plant. "She grew this herself from a seed."

Steef took the plant and smelled of the leaves. Touching the stem, he could feel Sissy's Green tune running through it. "Thanks, Uncle Antee!"

"I also brought some fresh sweetbreads from your Mother. My instructions for those were that they had to wait until you'd finished lastmeal."

"Okay!" Steef was excited. No one made sweetbreads like his Mama.

Cassa had waited, but she'd also learned hopping from Seafer. "Tell me about your sled, Shortstick!" she cried. He had set it in its hole, near her boat.

"We aren't gonna have Steering lessons, Sassy?" he asked, his nose still in the flowers.

"Sure, Shortstick! But I really want to see your sled!"

Everyone gave him subdued smiles as he marched back out to the Landing area with her.

"Lift it out so I can see it."

Steef obliged, and the sled Lifted enough to hover out of the ground.

What Cassa saw was a long stone wedge. Looking at it from the front, it looked like a slice of fruit pastry, with the wide end down, and the point sliced off at the very top. The bottom of the sled held that shape uniformly down its length, about four staffs. From here, the underside of the wooden rails could be seen.

"Would you set it back down for me, please?" The sled lowered itself to rest without a sound. *No thump at all* she said to herself with pride. For him. "Master Steerman," she said seriously, with a bow, "May I board your vessel?"

He brought his stick up to a two-hand grasp, and returned her bow. "We would be honored by your visit, Master Blue."

We? she mused. *We would be honored?*

There were steps set into the stone at the back. When she stepped onto the wooden rails, she saw why 'we'. The stone that rose above the rails had been cut and formed, in the very center of the sled. A bed, of sorts, that sloped gently away from the centerline, and lower than the top of the sled. A Kivverr sized bed, it took almost half the length of the sled. She noted with amusement that there were Kivverr sized claw marks on the top of the wooden rails, too. Deep claw marks.

"You put Kivverr right in the center for…"

"Balance," he interrupted.

"And you have all that extra stone at the bottom for…"

"Balance," he repeated.

"Why didn't you use a bowl?"

"We tried a bowl," he replied simply. That had been their second attempt. "But without a sail, it wanted to rock in the wind, so…"

"You built a sled," she finished. He nodded. "I've never seen a sled like this before, Shortstick. The only sleds I've ever seen are for the traffic directors around GuildTown, and they're much smaller." *Of course, they weren't taking their Cats with them.* "I really like your design. Everything about it makes it…so…"

"Balanced?" he sounded very satisfied with her appraisal.

"That would be the word…I see you have ropes to tie your passengers in their seats. Do you remember to use yours?" Besides Kivverr's bed, there were four seats sculpted into the stone.

"Every time, Sassy," he replied with complete honesty. He glanced at Kivverr, who looked away. There was a tooth-sized scar at Steef's waist to remind him about the tie-downs. Aunt Arima had been really busy that day, for some reason, and Healing himself seemed easier than answering questions.

"And the rails? How are they attached?" She didn't see any ropes binding them. Like Mokam, she only thought of Steef in the limited scope of her own Blue lessons with him. But the boy spent much more time with Seafer and Arima, than the other three of them together.

"They're saplings from Uncle Seafer's orchards. I made holes through the stone, and asked them to grow through the holes. They can't let go now."

Just like staff crafting she thought with a start. *Seafer.* There was a glimmer starting in her head. The same glimmer that had come to Mokam a cycle ago.

"Then I only have one more question. How, in the Creator's name, did you get this thing out into an open field without a sail?"

Steef grinned, "That was the easy part. Kivverr talked to his brother, and He got some help pulling. All I had to do was Lift." 'Simple really' his attitude said.

"His brother? His brother..." She mused on that for several beats. It had been a while. Finally Steef pointed across the flatland to a group of Cats lounging. "The ClanCat?! He asked...and they pulled?...how?"

"Ropes."

"You had *HornCats*...roped up like horses, and they pulled your sled out here?"

"Uh-huh."

That would be the Clan who has almost nothing to do with us. That would be the Clan whose only concession to us was not to eat us if we lived here. The beasts who speak only to Healers, and one little boy...young man. Working like labor-beasts to drag a stone for him. Would that be Antee's influence? No, Timmerr never even speaks to Antee.

Cassa threw one shaking leg over the second seat, and lowered into it. She motioned for him to come closer. One hand on his shoulder, another through the scraggly hair over his eyes. *He's ready for Buzzbies, and doesn't know it* she thought absently. She smiled at him softly. When she was a young woman, the world was very clear to her. Everything had its place. She was a Master of her own life, a gift she never stopped being thankful for. Now that world was gone. Two different worlds had replaced it, and she understood neither. She smiled again. A warm, gentle smile.

"Steef," she said.

He knew it would be important. She never called him that, either. Of course, Uncle Mokam rarely called him anything else any more.

"What are you...*who* are you...going to be?" She didn't know how to ask her question. Antee could've found the words.

"I am Steef," he said simply. He didn't understand her discomfort, or her question, though he had answered it completely. They just didn't know it yet. He didn't like to see her troubled though. Leaning into her ear, with a glance at Kivverr, he whispered, "But from you...I like Shortstick better."

After the hug, and Cassa clearing some wind out her eyes, she said, "I assume you only go up and down on this thing?"

"Uh-huh."

"How about you take me for a ride? I'd like to see how you got that storm to play music." *Yes, I'd really like to see that!*

"We aren't gonna have Steering lessons?" he asked again. He wasn't going to add a sail until he was sure of his Steering. The balance issue was still fresh.

"Yes Sir! We *will* have Steering lessons! I oath you that!" *It's all I've got left to share with you.* "But I want to see that storm play music first! Let's see how well you can call it back."

"Okay, but it'll take a while. I started it moving before we came down."

"I'll wait."

❦   ❦   ❦

"And you should have seen my hair! It stood straight out like this!" She pulled some strands above her head. "And Kivverr! He looked like a..."

Kivverr gave a low rumble.

"...well, his hair stood out, too! You all have to experience this! Skybolts! We've been teaching Blues to avoid making skybolts for...as long as there are records. As to that, Shortstick," she gave a wink at his name, "I've never actually taught you how to make skybolt storms. How..."

"Yes you did, Sassy." He was chewing slowly, making the sweetbread last as looonnnnggg as he could.

"No...I'd remember that. All of our training was about how *not* to make...," her voice got soft, and her eyes unfocused, "...ooohhh nnnooo...it's the *same thing*..." Her hand slapped her forehead, and stayed.

"Uh-huh." He missed his Mama. And Papa. And Sissy. The sweetbreads were a remembrance.

"...oh, my bending staff," she whispered. *What else did I teach him how-not-to-do?* It would torment her all night.

"I'd like to see your storm music, Steef," said Mokam, "Could we go tomorrow?"

"I'll have to call up another storm, Uncle Mokam," replied Steef disappointedly. The sweetbread was gone. "That one is used up. If I call for it tonight though, it can be here day after tomorrow."

"We'll still be here then, Steef. Do you mind? Plenty to do until then."

"I'd like to go too," said Antee, "Arima, you ought to come. You haven't been off the ground in cycles. Do you some good."

Arima regarded her Yellow friend, then the circle of faces. *Why not?* "I'll come, if Steerman Steef permits."

He was delighted. She'd been so quiet the last few sevendays. "That would be great, Aunt Arima! Plenty of room!"

"Well, no there's not, really, Shortstick. You only made four seats. Since I've already seen it…how about we make a second trip and take Seafer. Say Shortstick…why only four seats?"

"Balance," he said, licking the sweetening off his fingers. Kivverr turned away again.

Seafer was shaking his head. "Got no interest t'go up…" he pointed, "…and besides…there's plenty o' marvels down here…has he shown you his staff yet?"

Three of them looked back at Steef's stick, hanging in the sling on his back. Arima didn't look up from her cleaning. She'd seen it.

"Looks like a good enough staff, Seafer," mused Mokam, "Just like the others, only a bit bigger. Almost as large as one of Kivverr's horns."

In fact, it looked *exactly* like a HornCat horn, except that it was wood, and had a stone in the end. The stone was held on by a burl that had grown around it, and the burl had slits in it to allow the stone to glint through. The stick didn't need help glinting though. There was Dust running all through it, and the particles at the surface would occasionally catch the firelight and flash briefly. In fact, Seafwood sparkled too. All over. Every night.

"It's not like the others, Mokam…hee, hee, hee…nossir…not like the others…show 'em, Sprout."

Steef didn't really understand why his Uncle Seafer liked seeing this. He had to show him at least once a day. Sometimes more. It was a simple Lock, really. Well…three Locks. He stood and pulled the staff out of its sling. Turning, he flung it away from the fire. Hard.

The stick turned end-over-end as it flew through the air. Flew two staffs…exactly…and stopped. Upright. Then floated back slowly to Steef, where it stopped and hovered. He took it and put it back into its sling.

The only unnatural sounds in the cove were Arima's cleaning, and Seafer's 'hee, hee, hee'.

"How?" was all anyone could say.

"Lemme tell 'em, Sprout! It's got a Brown Lock to keep it from hittin' the ground...an' a White Lock to find the Sprout and go to him...an' a Blue Lock to give itself a push. Right, Sprout?"

Steef nodded. He was avoiding his Uncle Antee's eyes, just in case.

Indeed, Antee was scrutinizing him carefully. "Steef," he said, and stopped.

"Yessir?" Aunt Arima needed help with the cleaning. Part of his chores...supposed to help...he moved towards her.

"That's a clever bit of Locking, Steef."

"Thanks, Uncle Antee." Almost there. Those bowls needed a spillway. He wasn't going to make it

"Steef," Antee persisted, "Why would you need a staff that won't get away?"

Sigh. Stop. Turn. "Well, Uncle Antee, you never know when you might drop it." Kivverr lumbered up and walked away.

"And have you..."

Uncle Seafer saved him. "Y'know...never dreamed 'bout the tree bein' able to do all this...when I first thought o' this, I mean...nossir...'spected to get good trees, o' course...like those out there...but this...," he waved at Seafwood, "who'd o' dreamed this...or believed it...can't put a Lock in a staff...not a perm'nint one, anyhow...it's the Dust, Mokam...it's your Dust...an' the Sprout."

"Old friend," Mokam replied warmly, "I don't grudge you one speck of that Dust. We've put what?...fifty...sixty boxes of Dust into your tree?"

"Fifty two...an' it's the Sprout's tree."

"Steef's tree," Mokam corrected himself, "Which is, you should know, almost all the Dust I have. Or had. And no telling how many Crystals..."

"Two hundred forty three," came from the back of Steef, as he was now furiously stacking up bowls.

"...two of which are enormous. One of those...I've been hoarding it for more than forty cycles. Anyway...it's all worth it, Seafer. All of it. I wouldn't have missed this for anything."

Antee was nodding. His questions forgotten.

Arima and Cassa, too.

Seafer's head was shaking lightly, "Know what y'mean, Mokam...an' I thank the Creator every day for the Sprout...who else could'o' put the tree to use...we'd never have known what it...she...could do...without the Sprout. Only regret I could have..."

Steef slowed on his way to the spill, head cocked.

"…never will get t' feel one o' her charges. The saplings are fine…best staffs the world'll ever see…don' mean to sound like complainin'…did y'see that thing float back!?"

Steering lessons went well. Her mast survived, though it groaned a few times in hard turns. *Youngsters just love strong wind.* Well, she'd used her share when she was his age.

Mokam had had him mining. Steef had chosen the direction of the Steering, and they'd settled on a hilltop that he was excited about, spending the latter part of that first day making careful tunnels that she didn't understand. She'd stayed with the boat, as it was moored by a line, and she didn't want to leave it just floating. They'd come back with dirty faces. Excited faces. She didn't ask.

Next day, everyone got to experience the skybolt storm, and storm music. She made a second trip, and Antee went again, too. She didn't expect to tire of that soon. It also seemed to perk Arima up a bit.

Antee spent his lesson time with Steef closeted around a small cage. They didn't even leave the cove. The others gave them privacy by staying around the fire and chatting, though conversation was subdued. Everything of importance to discuss was depressing, so they avoided it with bland pleasantries.

"It's all grown back."

"That's really amazing, isn't it?"

"Uh-huh."

"Any glimmers?"

"I got strange Pulses off it. I need some more, though."

I know the feeling. "They're hard to find. Well, they're not hard to find, but it's hard to find one with its tail missing." *By natural means.* "I don't want you to be cutting them, all right?"

"I won't, Uncle Antee."

"Have you been tending the herds like we discussed?"

"Yes Sir."

"And what have you found?"

That discussion lasted a quarter morning.

"Uncle Antee?"

"Yes, Son?"

"Would you carry something to Sissy for me?"

"I would be glad to, Son."

He pulled it out of his pocket. To Antee's eyes, it looked to be a scrap of burl, smaller than the boy's fist. He took it. It sparkled in places.

"You want me to give her a piece of wood?"

"Yes Sir." It was tuned for Sissy. Uncle Antee wouldn't feel it.

Antee shrugged, and put it in his pocket. "She'll get it first thing."

"Thanks."

❋   ❋   ❋

They left shortly after midmeal. There would be plenty of time to get to Antee's, and get settled, before dark. The three of them watched the boat float down the Valley, and lift over a cliff. It was gone.

"Uncle Seafer?"

"Yessir, Sprout."

"Seafwood and I have something for you. It's not really finished yet, but if you want…I'll get it anyway."

"What is it Sprout?"

"Well…you know how I can't get any of my sticks to un-tune?" They'd been trying for almost two cycles now.

"Yessir…that's all right, Sprout…I'm jus' pleased as I can be with Seafwood."

"Well, last cycle, I asked Seafwood to grow you your own stick. One stick…without my tune in it. I put an untuned Green Lock around the burl. I don't know if it'll work…and it's still pretty small…but if you want…I heard you talking the other night…I'll get it for you."

"You did!?…really!?…that's jus' fine, Sprout!…I thankee…from my roots up!…let's try her out!"

"I don't know that it's gonna work, Uncle Seafer."

"Run get it Sprout!…let's see!"

Steef sprang away towards his tree. Arima smiled at her friend and headed towards the camp. Seafer started his hopping.

He was hopping as hard as he could go by the time Steef returned. The stick was no more than two spans, and had no stone.

"Did you charge her up, Sprout?" Seafer had his hands out.

"Yes Sir. Full, untuned charge. You might want to be care…"

"CCRRRAACCKKK!" Steef was knocked flat. Looking up, he saw Uncle Seafer was down, too. And parts of him were smoking!

"AUNT ARIMA! AUNT ARIMA! AUNT ARIMA!"

She hadn't really paid attention to the noise. There were often noises coming from Steef's direction. But Steef's voice held a note she didn't like. Turning, her insides went cold.

"Seafer?......*Seafer*!?......SSSEEEEAFFERRRR!" She was already running.

Both hands were charred. Both feet. His skin was blacker than usual, from flashburn. His Pills were on either side of his head, dead. Burned up. She touched his neck. His pump had stopped!

"Steef! Get back! Way back!"

He didn't want to leave. It was Uncle Seafer! He wanted to help!

"NOW!!"

"Seafer...don't you do this! You hear me?" She hit him with a Pulse. Nothing.

"I'm *telling* you Seafer! I won't stand for it, you hear?" The second one drained her staff. Nothing.

"Pill, is Steef out of the way!!!?"

"*Yes.*"

"Discharge warning, Pill!!!" Pop! Pop!

"Seafer, you can't leave me here!" Ka-WUMP!!! CCRRAACCKKK! His body heaved off the ground.

"SEEAFFERR! I'M TALKING TO YOU!!! I'LL HIT YOU ALL DAY, IF I HAVE TO!!!!" She drew back for another one.

"'Rima," came a weak voice, "Don't." He lifted a burned hand to her arm. "Don't."

"Seafer! Seafer! You can't leave me here!"

"I'm...done...'Rima.   It's...all...done...y'see.   Ever'...thin'...works... y'know...Let me...go."

"You can't go, Seafer. *You can't go! You hear me!?*...You can't...go...Seafer... I...love you...Seafer...you hear?...please Seafer...don't..."

"Tell...Sprout...not...fault...carele..."

"Seafer?" She was whispering now. "Seafer......please......oh please."

❀   ❀   ❀

"Arima?"

What was that? Was someone speaking?

"Arima? We've…got to…move him. Arima?"

It was dark. "Who's there?" *Why is it dark?*

"It's…Cassa…Arima." She couldn't speak well through her sobs.

"Why is it dark?"

"It's…almost…morning…Arima. We've…got to…bury him…sweetie. Can you…can you stand?"

Of course I can stand! What is she talking about? Why aren't my legs working?

"Where's Seafer? There was something I needed to tell Seafer."

He's…resting   now…sweetie.   Let…me…help…help   you…stand up…Antee…oh!…I can't…stand it!"

❁   ❁   ❁

They took him to the top of the cove. From there, he could watch his tree forever. Kivverr carried his body up the steps on his back, heedless of what the Clan thought. Arima couldn't make the steps, so Cassa just took her to her cave.

Mokam was unable to open the ground. He was a mess. Steef didn't know anything about graves, so Kivverr and Timmerr began digging, until Antee stopped them. It was enough. Steef Lifted his Uncle carefully down, then his staff. The Cats covered him back up.

Then the Moaning began.

All up and down the Valley, the Cats were moaning. It lasted all that next day.

Arima heard it, and came out of her fog to ask, "How did you know?"

"Pill came for us. We turned and came right back."

"How long?'

"We left you there until you cried yourself to sleep." *If that was sleep.*

There was something she needed to ask. What was…oh, yes.

"Is he crying?"

Cassa heaved, stifling another sob, "No sweetie, he's not crying."

Then he never will.

❁   ❁   ❁

"Arima, wake up sweetie."

"Hmmm?"

"Wake up, now…Arima…we have to go…Arima."

"Go where?"

"We have to go back. If we don't, they'll come looking." *This is terrible! Curse those foul Guilds!* "We can't even leave Antee. Regrets, sweetie! I give regrets." She was crying again. "Do you understand, Arima?"

"I understand, Cassa, thank you."

Antee nodded, helping Cassa up. Mokam was at the boat. He said he could Lift. Antee wasn't sure if that was true, but a boatcrash would have been only slightly worse right now.

"Cassa?"

"Yes pumpkin? I'm here."

"I could have Mated with him, you know. I should have…should have given him children."

"But you did, sweetie. You gave him a Son."

CHAPTER 15

Just after threequarterday. Steef and Kivver were standing just outside the cove. On the ground in front of them sat a wooden box, its lid open. A straggling line of Cats was coming up to them singly, and spitting into the box. Mostly younger Cats, they were tired and irritable. And hungry. Kivverr had anticipated that, and fresh kill was waiting for them.

Each time a new Cat spit into the box, Steef would bow to him and say, "Thank you for the gift."

When the last Cat had passed, there were nineteen tailless groundcrawlers in the box.

"Are they what you wanted?"

"Eight of them are. Do you want the others later?" he whispered.

"I have eaten well today already." That was true. He had helped gather some of the kill this morning.

"Then I'll just separate them, and see if I can find any differences." Closing the box, he turned for the cove. It was time to make some midmeal. *Hope she'll eat a little more today.* She hadn't finished a meal since Uncle Seafer went to his Rest. Occasionally, Kivverr would eat the remains of her meal, though he didn't much like 'burned things'. Steef usually just gave it to the dirt.

The others would be coming soon. Maybe Aunt Arima would cheer up some from their company. At least her Core was showing hints of white again.

Steef didn't feel guilty at all about the White bubbles he left in her cave every few days, but he did feel guilty when he mixed in a little Red. He didn't do it often, just when she cried a lot. And not much Red even then. He was beginning to think that Red didn't really fix much. Even with Sissy, when his Red wore off, the problem had not changed. Red only made you *think* you were better, it didn't actually *make* you better. He would have to study that.

They always traveled about Town in pairs now. One Black Master and one Red. They were out everywhere, posting parches on Town newsboards:

MASTER LAW

ALL TOWNLAW IS SUBJECT TO MASTER LAW

EVERYONE IS SUBJECT TO MASTER LAW

There had been some debate in the three GuildHalls about what 'Master Law' should be. No one could agree. For the first time in anyone's memory, a combined meeting was held that included all the remaining Masters of those three Guilds. During that meeting, only two things were resolved: general agreement was given that these combined meetings of the 'alliance' of Masters were a good thing; and since they could not yet define Master Law, why, it would just be whatever a Master said it was at the time. Though no one actually said it, the implication was that only Masters in the new 'alliance' held this ultimate authority. The other four Guilds would have to earn their way in.

So the parches had gone out, proclaiming the new Law. No matter that the new Law had no definition. It really didn't exist at all. But it was walking around, watching.

Boats were sent out to the other Territories, carrying the parches of good news to everyone. Each boat had its share of Blacks and Reds to ensure that the news was welcomed.

As Cassa's boat approached the cove, its three occupants were solemnly quiet. Inquiries had been sent from each of them, daily at first, as to her well being. Her answers had been courteous enough, but she hadn't sent Pill to *them* for anything, even conversation, since…

Pill assured them that Steef was looking after her physical needs. She left her cave now, Pill said. She went out each day to sit in the sun. Sometimes at the spot where she and Seafer had sat, sometimes at the spot where she and Rivverr had sat. The crying had stopped. That was good.

Their first view of the cove stunned them. There were flowering plants everywhere. Every color imaginable, and some not so imaginable. All three of the rockfaces inside the cove were terraced, all the way to the top, and each terrace held new, brightly colored growths. Even the stairway had plants, growing in nooks of dirt.

There were no Cats in view, except Kivverr. He and Steef were standing in the Landing area, awaiting them. Bows were given, then hugs. The atmosphere was subdued, though Steef wore a small smile for his Uncles and Sassy.

"How is she, Shortstick?"

"Aunt Arima's going to be Healed, Sassy. She's getting better."

"How are you, Son?" Antee gently asked.

Shrug. "I'm Okay, Uncle Antee. Thanks."

Arima emerged from her cave, where she had put on a fresh tunic. The four Masters visited quietly for the remainder of the day, remembering, and sharing some tears.

There was a reason why Antee and Mokam had never shared cooking duties, and they set about to prove it at lastmeal. Steef watched patiently for many beats, until a measurable portion of the meal was almost ruined. Asking if he could help, he salvaged what he could. Cassa had remained close to Arima.

❧   ❧   ❧

"We brought you something, Steef," said Mokam. They were stacking up the clean bowls. Antee had gone to join Cassa and Arima.

"Thanks, Uncle Mokam."

"Aren't you going to ask what it is?"

"All of your gifts are treasures, Uncle."

Mokam's features softened, but he was already cried out, so he just said, "We brought you a sail for your sled."

"See? Another treasure. Thank you again, Uncle Mokam."

"You are welcome, Sir."

"Uncle Mokam?"

"Yes Sir?"

"What's it like...outside the Valley?"

And Mokam had another of his glimmers. It had never occurred to him that Steef might want to *leave* the Valley. Steef and this Valley went together. With the sail, he could go anywhere, any time. Oops.

"Well…lately…it's gotten to be a pretty ugly world. It's not like this Valley, where everything is peaceful…" and Mokam had *another* glimmer. "Your pardon, Steef. I need to speak to the others."

🍁   🍁   🍁

"Mokam, that's just crazy!" exclaimed Cassa.

"Yes it is. But it *will* work," the Brown said diplomatically. "They wouldn't come looking." *Probably.*

"Antee's old enough to be my Father! Your pardon, Antee."

"Freely given, Master Blue," Antee replied amiably. He was enjoying this.

"Well, it's either him or me, and I'm old enough to be your grandFather."

"There's got to be another way!"

"And when you think of it, you will let us know, won't you?" Mokam sounded just like Antee.

"Did you ask Arima about this? It's her home, after all."

"No, not yet. It's a bit more permanent for you than it is for her."

"Well," interrupted Antee, "While you two are deciding my fate, I'd like to point out that it wouldn't have to be done today."

"True," nodded Mokam, "But soon. You aren't in any of the real towns any more, Antee. You can't imagine the changes."

"I can believe it though, Mokam. Even in my small village, most of the Power people have left. The only ones there now are Greens and Yellows, and the Yellows are only staying because I'm there." This wasn't boast. Lower grade Yellows had followed Antee his entire life. He shared his Mastery as much as he could.

🍁   🍁   🍁

"Come on, Uncle Antee!" Steef urged excitedly.

Antee was a bit excited himself. He hadn't been in this tree since…Seafer…had put the stones in for the first time. The tree had changed, and not changed. The limbs were the same, if only bigger. The leaves were the same, just fuller. The spaces were shaped the same, only broader. But where it had been barely lit before by whatever light got through, now the entire interior was lit up like midday…only, it was dark outside. *Odd to think of 'outside' while I'm in a tree.* The light came from all the Crystals, and reflected off of the tree. It reflected off the leaves. And the limbs. Everything had Dust in it. It glittered.

"How do you sleep in here Son?" he asked, before his tact could catch up with his eyes.

Kivverr was already up wherever they were going, and Antee's view was the lowest side of a climbing Steef. They were climbing on limbs that were growing conveniently in the right spots to serve as steps. Steef's voice came around him as he kept climbing, "I just tune it off."

"Tune it off?" he asked. He had already cautioned himself that he would *not* be surprised. He thought of…Seafer…and his tranquil acceptance of all things bizarre.

"Uh-Huh. I'll show you, if you want."

"I think I'd like that, if you don't mind."

"Oh, it's Okay, Uncle. It's not hard. But we might want to stop climbing. Kivverr's the only one that can see in here when Seafwood's off." They stopped, and Steef reached out a hand to the tree's trunk. The glittering just…stopped. It became completely lightless inside the tree. Antee waved his hand, feeling stupid, and couldn't see it. The glittering came on again.

"Aunt Arima taught me how." Steef knew he would want to know.

"She did?" What could…

"Yessir. She taught me how to glow myself. She taught me to glow my stone. Just a tune change. Now, I can glow Seafwood." The climb continued.

Antee had to admit, that wasn't a remarkable concept, it was just a remarkable tree. And he wondered if he would have ever thought of it. But then, Steef's reality wasn't defined in the same terms that Antee's had been.

"Here's what I wanted to show you." Steef had two large boxes sitting in a nook of the trunk. There was a small Crystal nestled into the tree, just over the boxes, giving off a soft Yellow glow.

There were groundcrawlers in each box. One of the boxes held eight of them, their tails in various stages of regrowth. The other box had eleven beasts in it. Antee recognized the variety. They were permanently tailless. Antee felt a quick, unexpected anger rise up. It was a new feeling. He hadn't ever been angry at the boy before.

"I specifically told you not to be cutting their tails off! I am truly dis…"

"But I didn't, Uncle Antee," replied Steef, evenly.

"Now Steef, that's beneath you. It's clear you mutilated these poor beasties. I..."

"The Cats did it, Uncle. They bit them off." 'That explains it' was clearly in his voice.

"That doesn't change anything Steef! If you had them bite off those tails, it's the same as..."

"No Sir, I didn't ask them to bite anything. I asked them *not* to bite something."

"What!? What do you mean? What did you ask them not to bite?"

"The rest of the beastie. They eat these all the time. Kivverr mentioned it when I let the other one go. He said there's a lake full of them, almost a day across the Valley, and the young Cats go there to hunt sometimes."

"Why would they go all that way when we keep herd beasts here?" This was coming too fast to keep up, even for him.

"Kivverr says that sometimes the herd beasts are just too easy. The Clan likes to hunt. These groundcrawlers are one of the things they hunt. I asked them to bring me some back. I figured the groundcrawlers that didn't get *all* eaten...were better off than the ones who did."

There was a moral dilemma in there somewhere. Antee just knew it. But it would take a while to work it out. He lamely asked, "So how did you get them here, if they were so far away?"

"The Cats carried them for us."

"In their mouths?"

"Yessir."

"A day's walk?"

"Yessir, that's what Kivverr said."

"Without eating them?"

"Well, they were pretty grumpy when they got here. Hungry, too."

There hadn't been any lessons at all on this visit, though they lingered as long as they could. Aunt Arima seemed to be cheered some by their time together. It was time.

He needed to leave the cove, if only overnight. He hoped it would be no more than overnight. "Aunt Arima?"

"Yes Steef?"

"Kivverr and I need to go on a little walk. We won't be gone long…two days at most. Would that be all right?" He was asking if *she* would be all right, but asking permission sounded better for both of them.

"Yes, you may make your trip. I will be fine."

"It's my last overnight trip for a while, Aunt Arima." It really *was* important, and her Core hadn't changed back.

"Go on with you then."

Uncle Seafer had taught him what to look for, while teaching him what *not* to look for, 'Some trees are good for charges Sprout…an' some aren't'. His Green Master had gone on to describe in detail, what kinds of trees made good staffs, and which ones didn't. It was the 'didn't' variety they were looking for now. To use as a mast.

He needed a mast for his sled that wouldn't interfere with the charges off his stick. Every boat ever made had incorporated staff duties into the mast, but the Blues who Steered those boats didn't have any of his sticks. He preferred his stick.

They found it late the next day, on the kind of ground Uncle Seafer had said they would. It took a strong Pulse to get it out of the ground, and cleaned up. An even stronger Pulse to Lift it. Throwing the noose around Kivverr's neck, they started back.

After several days of pulling, Lifting, pulling some more, climbing, stretching, roping, and perspiring, the result was that his sled had a mast and a sail only six days after the others had left. Time to try it out.

The sled hadn't been off the ground since Uncle Seafer had touched his stick. Aunt Arima had needed him. She still did. "Aunt Arima? Kivverr and I are going for a ride. It's our first flight with a sail. We really wish you would come, too."

She studied his face for a while. It was a good face. A kind face. *How can he mix tranquility with concern? Seafer did that, too. His concern is for me, after all.* "And where we would be going, young Steerman?"

Steef released his grin. He'd been wanting to use it for a while now.

"Why don't *you* choose?"

❧   ❧   ❧

She was reclining in the sun, in a seat that Steef had fashioned for her out of one of the rocks on this hilltop. He brought her here often, when she told him that she wanted a 'quiet' day. He and Kivverr would go down into their hole in the ground, coming out only for meals and sanitary needs.

The last four sevendays, they'd gone somewhere each day. There were now landing holes in several spots around the southern end of the Valley. One near a lake that the Cats frequented. Another close to a tall spillway. She'd mentioned how beautiful it was, and he had landed immediately, climbed down his steprope, and fashioned a hole. They took midmeals there a lot, at the fringe of the mist cloud. Sometimes he'd make a bubble, and they would eat under the spill itself, its boomers drowning out all conversation.

They also stopped any time they saw new beasts of any kind. Beasts that had never made it as far as the cove. He would examine all of them. Especially any beast that was heavy with young. He would send Pulse after Pulse. Tiny Yellow ones that were just barely visible to her. Then he'd get his 'study' face for a while.

But they were excavating again today. It had been most of the morning. She expected the two of them would be up soon, for something. She wasn't wrong. Steef was nursing his left hand, and Kivverr was carrying a large sack that hung heavily from his jaw. When they arrived, Steef held his hand up wordlessly. His face said 'could you fix this please?'

It was burned. Again. The boy found more ways to burn himself. Usually his staff hand, though. This was the wrong hand. She began Pulsing it, and noticed that the wound had a different tune, one that she'd never encountered before.

"What *have* you been doing, child?" He really wasn't a child any more, she reminded herself again. *He's at least half man now…but he's always going to be a child to me. My child. Some.* She missed Maleef.

"Studying."

"Well, whatever you're studying did some real harm this time. This is a strange burn." It was resisting her Healing, and wanting to spread up his arm. "What gave you this burn?"

"There's stone down there, Auntie. It's not like any other stone. Even Uncle Mokam said he'd never seen any."

"And what is so special about a rock?"

"It's giving off the seventh primary. All on its own."

She stopped and gave him a serious look, which did nothing to slow his grin. It was just so hard to scold him, and somehow, he always knew that, "You are stirring up things that even you might not control, young man. Do you know the tales about the seventh primary?"

"Yes Mam. But I didn't Pulse it. I just wanted to get its tune."

"So you stuck your hand into it?" *Of course. How else would you test it?* She sighed.

"Uh-huh."

Would he always be a danger to himself? Probably. "Did you get it?"

"Yes Mam!"

When he's that excited, strange things happen. "Steef…please be careful! This could be…probably is…really dangerous."

"Yes Mam."

"So what's in the sack?" Now that she knew what he was doing, she expected anything that came out of the hole to blow up on the beat. It was a fairly large sack, big enough that Kivverr had set it down, rather than hold it.

"Crystal. There is a Crystal Lode that runs all around the strange rock. The Crystal picked up some of that seventh's tune. I'm gonna take some back and polish them up. Show Uncle Mokam."

She didn't ask him how he was going to polish them, without the usual tumbler, and an army of laborers to keep it rotating night and day. She knew that somehow, he'd come up with something.

❋   ❋   ❋

"Yes, I oath to the Mating," Cassa replied.

The Red Eight that was running the Registry Hall that morning was skeptical. Neither of these two Masters were exactly Mating age. In fact, they weren't even close to the same age! TownLaw allowed her to use her Red to inquire if either of them had been 'influenced' to agree to this union. Sometimes, unscrupulous people would hire a Red to do just that. It usually involved Dust somewhere. And in fact, this Blue Master came from a family of minor prominence, the records showed.

But TownLaw wasn't what it used to be. In fact, most people were ignoring it these days. The Eight didn't like the changes that were occurring, even if it did give her freedom to do almost anything. She didn't *want* to do almost anything. If this Blue wanted to fight off loneliness in a remote village with a Yellow Master, who was she to question it? There had been a steady trickle of Masters leaving Town for a while now. The ones that were staying…it was just better to stay out of their way.

"Then the Mating is Registered. Very bright days to you both, Masters."

Antee was ready to leave. He hadn't been to GuildTown in many cycles, and it hadn't improved in his absence. It was becoming a depressing place. But Cassa now had an official reason to be gone. No one would come looking.

Mokam had already notified Brown Guild that his official retirement would now be really official. Everything of value that he owned, and it was much less than it used to be, was already loaded into the boat. Like most Steermen, Cassa cared little for 'things', and it showed. Her trunks were few and small.

The three of them left.

❦   ❦   ❦

"Steef, there's something you should know."

"What's that, Auntie?"

"Cassa and Antee have Registered themselves as Mates."

"Oh!…Well!…Hmmm!" He reminded her of Mokam when he did that. Or maybe it was Antee.

"They had to travel to GuildTown to do that. They are on their way back to Antee's farm now." *And then here. At least two of them.* She thought she knew why they were doing this. It was sweet, if extreme. It didn't occur to her that the Valley might look to them like a welcome refuge.

"GuildTown is a long way from Uncle Antee's farm."

"True." *He knows his maps.*

"When are they supposed to arrive?"

"Tomorrow. Late tomorrow. Sundown, probably." Cassa had good flight timing. No one ever flew at night.

His mind was working, she could see it. "What is it, Son?"

"I was just thinking…we *could* go see them there."

What to object to first? "Kivverr couldn't go, you know?" *That should stop him right away.*

"He can visit with the Clan. We wouldn't be gone more than a few days."

"You've never been there. You don't know the way." This already felt like she was losing. She didn't know why she cared so much.

"I have my maps. Sassy has trained me well. We could find it."

He probably could. No, he certainly could. "And if someone sees your sled? No one flies a sled."

"We'll arrive at dark, just like them. We'll land in the woods. I can clear us a spot. No one would see."

She was out of decent arguments. His face said he really wanted to go. *And how long before he goes where he wants, when he wants? This is as harmless as a trip can be.*

"Then we need to make some plans."

"Okay!"

❦   ❦   ❦

He was wearing his best tunic, and it had a badge on it. The badge was White, and had a Three, to match his stick.

Arima had to admit, she was excited. And nervous. It had been a while since she'd been around people. She'd had Pill tell their three friends they were coming. None of them liked surprises any more, if they ever did. She had also had Pill go tell Stem and Maleef. They had a right to know, too.

Steef normally kept a bubble in front of them, to block the wind from her face, but she had asked him to remove it. She had washed and washed her pale white hair. It was now blowing in the wind as they watched the Valley unfold beneath them, then disappear. It felt good.

"Steef!" She had to shout over the wind.

"Yes Mam?"

"Oath me something!"

"What's that, Auntie?"

"Oath me that you won't kill anyone while we're there!"

He laughed, "Why would I want to kill anyone?"

"Just oath me please." *Because you've only known eight people in your life, and they all loved you, that's why.*

"Okay, Auntie. Oath given."

❦   ❦   ❦

Malem had to hurry, her Bubba was coming! She'd been working all day at various farms, all of them owned by Powerless people. Her Mama wouldn't let her call them 'Nerts. She and her parents worked Uncle Antee's small farm, keeping enough crops for his beasts. But Papa wouldn't let Uncle pay them any more Dust than the work called for, and it wasn't enough. So Malem would go around to the villagers, on days when she didn't have studies, and ask for work. Their crops always flourished after she'd been there. She'd been only six when they left the Valley, but those cycles had been spent at the heels of a Master

Green. She would always be able to earn her way in life. There were several specks of Dust in her pouch to prove it.

If she could get them home.

There wasn't any point in going around the road. It was a small village, with sparse huts and open land. No matter what route she chose, they would see her. She had under a league left, and she was running as fast as she could down the road. Maybe they wouldn't be out tonight.

A rock came flying out from behind a tree, making hard contact to the back of her head. She collapsed into the dirt.

"Got her, th' lousy witch!"

The three of them swarmed around her, kicking.

"Got any Dust today, lousy witch?"

"Thought you'd ge' by us, dirtyfoot?"

"Ge' her staff this time!"

She felt hands pull at her pouch, and her staff. They backed off, two of them peering into her pouch, while the other broke her staff over a knee. Leaping up while she could, she took off at her best speed back down the road. The ache in her ribs didn't slow her, but her head was spinning from the rock.

"She's gettin' away!"

"She can't ge' far. Look how she's weavin'."

"Ge' her Dust out o' there, and le's go *get* her."

"No hurry." The leader of the three remained calm. There weren't many witches left in the village any more. No Blacks or Reds at all to worry about. This little Green had become a good target. She always seemed to be getting Dust from somewhere.

Malem kept running. Though her eyes wouldn't focus well, she could still see her turn in the road coming up. Making it to the hut that marked that turn, she staggered around it.

"Come on! She's gonna ge' home!"

The three boys sped around the hut, expecting to see Malem limping up the incline to her own hut. They knew she couldn't have gotten home yet.

They didn't expect to see her hugging some other kid. Who was *this* anyway? His face looked older than theirs, but he wasn't much bigger. He had a badge! A White one! And a little staff. He didn't look like much. Anyway, there were three of them. And their rocks.

"Another dirtyfoot! Good! Wanna taste our rocks?"

"Yeah, jus' another witch for us! How fat is your pouch, White witch?"

Oddly, neither of these witches were running any more. They didn't seem too scared at all. In fact, the little Green was turning around and grinning at them! Laughing! What did she think was so funny? She knew what their rocks tasted like. Maybe they would just have to remind her.

Three rocks started their flights toward Steef and Malem. None of them got there. Mysteriously, they got about halfway, and bounced off to the side. Perplexed, the three boys launched another flight, with the same results. The little witch was laughing loud now, almost hopping with glee, though she winced with each hop. But…the boy witch wasn't laughing. He didn't look happy…at all.

"I think it would be best if you left my sister in peace." Steef Saw something in them he'd never Seen before. Their Cores were dark. Black dark.

Sister? "Why should we do tha', dirtyfoot?"

"Yeah, what's i' to us what *you* think?"

"If you don't leave my sister alone, I will have to accept that as challenge. You don't want that," he said seriously. Aunt Arima's oath had already come to mind, and they had just gotten here. Did she know about this? He'd have to ask.

"We aren' afraid of any dirtyfoot witch, leas' of all a White. Wha' are you gonna to do…*Heal* us t' death?" That got a good laugh from all three.

Steef glowed his stone White, for effect. He was supposed to be a White while he was here. Then he gave them a little Pulse of sleeping White. Well…maybe more than a little. They dropped their rocks, then dropped *like* rocks. Switching tunes, he started pumping fresh White into Sissy. By the time they reached Uncle's hut, the swelling on her head was going down, and she could breathe without pain.

"They got *all* my Dust, Bubba! And broke my staff!" She was torn between laughing and crying. Laughing would win.

"That's Okay, Sissy. I've got plenty of Dust. Dug it myself. And I can make you a new stick. Let's go see Mama and Papa."

When the three young criminals woke next morning, they made their way back to their own huts. Upon arriving, they told their parents about being attacked by a White witch. They expected to make an uproar, and they did, just not the uproar they wanted. Word got out in the village and surrounding huts, that a Healer was here. Did anyone notice his number? No? Well, let's go see. He's visiting that Yellow Master at the end of the road.

Everyone in Antee's hut was having a comfortable firstmeal, including a delighted Steef. Mama sure could cook. They heard the crowd approaching, and Antee went to the door.

"Your pardon, Master, bu' we heard there'd be a Healer here. Could he come ou' and help? We'll pay."

He? thought Antee. *Oh, Steef must have been seen with his White badge.* Antee smiled. "Just a beat, Cirruss. I'll ask."

"Thankee, Master."

Antee shut the door, and turned to the questioning faces, "'Rima, feel like going back to work? Seems the whole village is out there, needing a Healer. Know where we can find one?"

She blinked at him, and everyone waited. Her drawn face, admittedly improved since they last saw her, took on more color still. Then a slow smile crept into the corners of her mouth. "Actually, Antee, there are two Healers here, and one of them needs some experience." She rose, followed closely by Steef, who needed no prompting. He saw Malem's face drop.

"Come with us, Sissy. We'll visit while we work."

Work they did. All that day. They had the villagers go back to their huts, and Malem served as guide, directing them to each hut. Arima wanted Steef to learn the value of privacy. They even visited the families of the three boys that had attacked Malem. None of the boys said anything, but their stares were hostile, if their parents' weren't. People that would otherwise have had nothing to do with a 'dirtyfoot', welcomed them into their huts, and offered food or garments for their services. No Dust. No one had enough Dust to pay Healer's rates. That didn't matter. They weren't accepting payment anyway.

Steef got to see all sorts of maladies and injuries. Even better, he got to observe how others handled their afflictions. There hadn't been much illness of any kind in the Valley. Only instruction and parches.

One man in particular made an impression on the young apprentice. The man had cut himself badly in the lower leg with an ill-aimed axe. The wound was many days old, and smelled. Arima knew the smell. It was death. The flesh below and around the wound was dead, and that death was running up the leg in black, blue and yellow streaks.

"Tell me where you feel the death stop," she instructed her pupil. He Pulsed a diagnostic Pulse, and pointed to mid-thigh, above where the streaking stopped. *Good, he found it.* She knew it would extend past what could be seen.

"Bu' my cut's down there!" the alarmed man exclaimed. He knew he was in trouble. He had fever, to add to his leg problems. He couldn't feel his foot any more, either.

"The cut's down there, Sir, but the death is spreading," Arima explained patiently. "We can Heal sick things, but not dead things. Your leg must be removed up to here." Her hand joined Steef's on his thigh. "If we don't, it will spread and kill you." *Soon* she didn't add.

"Then le' me die! Can' work on one leg! No good t' my Mate or my young! Le' me die!" he repeated. Perhaps his Mate could find a new man. She was a good woman.

Steef was now studying the man's chest.

Why is he looking at the chest? There's no hurt there. Arima wondered.

Arima Pulsed the man to sleep, then stepped out to speak to his Mate. 'No', she said, 'She di'nt want her man t' die. Take th' leg.' Steef and Malem stood quietly out of the way while Aunt Arima spoke to the woman.

Arima was glad at the decision. She didn't like leaving unHealed people to their death, although it was the way of their world to let them, if they chose. She asked all of the family to step out of the hut.

"Steef," she whispered, "I didn't bring any of my cutting tools, and your knife is too crude. Have you learned enough Black out of those parches to use it for this?"

"I think so, Auntie." He'd had more Black practice than she knew. Mostly on snakes.

"Malem, you don't have to watch this, if you don't want to."

"I'd like to stay, Aunt Arima, if it's Okay."

The amputation went fairly smoothly. Arima had never seen a limb cut with Black before, so it was a learning experience for her, too. She made certain they got all of the poisoned flesh, and had Steef leave a White-filled bubble in the hut, to prevent any further decay.

As they made their way through most of the village that day, Steef discovered that two of the village women were pregnant. At his urging, they visited each of those women twice that first day. He would linger over them, Pulsing and Pulsing. They didn't mind. Their babies were safer for it. He took on his study face, tongue out. She thought she Saw an occasional Yellow Pulse. *What was he doing?* There was just no way...whatever it was, finally struck. Her young apprentice took on the most serene look and smile she'd ever seen him have, and that was a lot.

"I'm done here, Master."

"Then let's move on, apprentice."

It was getting late. After assurances to the unattended that they would return the next day, they made for Antee's hut. About halfway through the village, Steef abruptly stopped walking. Arima turned in time to See an odd Pulse come out of his staff, and head off up the hill. Their walk continued.

"What was that, Son?"

"That man whose leg we cut today?"

"Did he need some more White? I thought your bubble would last…"

"I think it'll be growing back now."

"I got it from the pregnant beasties, mostly, Uncle Antee," said Steef over sweetbreads. His eyes were closed while he chewed. It had been a good day, all except the ruckus that his Masters were making.

"How is that, Son?"

"The strange Pulses I got from the groundcrawlers?" His Mama had made plenty. He reached for another.

"Yes?"

"I got those same Pulses from anything pregnant. Only beasties, until today. Today I got to try it out on those pregnant ladies."

"What does pregnancy have to do with growing a leg?" asked Mokam. He didn't share Arima's excitement, but he *was* curious.

"Whatever makes babies grow inside their Mamas, makes those groundcrawlers grow a tail," shrugged Steef. "Whatever it is, it looks like most of us forget it. Not the groundcrawlers. So I matched that tune to a White Pulse, and sent it to that man with the sick leg. It should work." Three would have to be enough, he'd get a bellyache if he ate any more. "Probably take a while, though."

They continued their tour of the ailing villagers the next day, finishing their work by threequarterday. Steef noticed that they had picked up a following. The three young boys were lurking around everywhere they went, and they didn't look happy. He walked with Aunt Arima back far enough that she could reach Uncle's hut by herself.

"Aunt Arima, I'm gonna take a walk with Sissy."

"All right, Steef." She felt like she'd walked all day, but the two of them were young, and they *did* need some visiting greets of their own. She went up the hill.

"Sissy, we're gonna go for a little ride when it gets dark." He hadn't lied to Aunt Arima. They *were* going to walk…as far as the sled.

"Okay, Bubba."

Steef headed them for the wooded hill where he'd left his sled. They went into the treeline, followed by three not-so-stealthy shadows. As soon as the shadows got thoroughly out of view from the village, they dropped to the ground again. Another night-long nap awaited them.

※   ※   ※

"This is great, Bubba!" She loved his sled.

"Just don't unstrap, Sissy." They were at five hundred staffs.

"I won't. What are we doing up here?" Bubba was just hovering the sled now. She liked flying better. Especially the swoops.

"We're leaving a little surprise for your friends."

"Will they like this surprise?"

"No."

"Good."

※   ※   ※

"Sassy, I need to talk to one of your Buzzbies." He needed to stay away from Uncle Antee and Aunt Arima, as they were more likely to ask questions. They were also asleep, their Buzzbies gone for the evening.

"It's all right with me, Shortstick, if…" Pop! "…and I guess that answers that."

Steef walked outside. "Buzzbie, I need a service from you."

"Depends on what it is."

"I want two of you to stay with Sissy for the next few sevendays. I'll explain why."

"She's not a Master, Steef. You know we only ride Masters."

"You deliver messages to non-Masters all the time. I've seen you do it. And you're constantly wanting to ride with me." It was true. For almost two cycles now, every time they'd delivered a message to him from one of his Masters, they'd asked if some of them could stay. He had been refusing. Too much distraction.

"We will gladly deliver messages to your sister for you. As to why we want to go with you...that should be pretty obvious."

"Do you still want to ride me?"

"You know we do."

"If you do this for me, I'll let two of you ride...hmmm...my shoulder...from now on."

"That is a deal struck! Name your service!"

Steef and Arima left before dawn the next morning, amid hugs and tears. Malem took it surprisingly well. She was older now, they supposed.

Except for the one she wore around her neck, all of her burls were on boards around the walls of her little closet. All of them had fresh charges, but they weren't as strong this time. More remembrance, and less artificial peace.

Malem was wearing her hair down. All the Masters thought it was sweet, that she wanted to be like her brother.

Cassa left later with Mokam, the boat laden with supplies. Their home would be in the Valley now. As official as her Mating to Antee had been, it was still just a ruse to get her out of Town without suspicion. They were friends. Dear friends, and family. They weren't Mates.

It did mean that she could never actually Mate with anyone else. At least not while Antee lived. She didn't mind. Who'd have her, anyway?

"My brother says to tell you that he's watching. He put you to sleep twice before. He says he let you wake up. The next time might be different."

Bubba had said to find them as soon as he was gone. To stand. No steps back. She trusted her Bubba. And she had a secret.

They didn't know what to think of this. She'd always been afraid before, then that strange witch showed up, and they weren't too sure any more. They turned and left.

But if there is one thing that can be counted on, it's that meanness and stupidity always walk together. It took them a sevenday for the fear to wear off, and the mean to boil up. They were waiting for her in the road, as she walked casually back from her work. Bubba had left her plenty of Dust, but she liked to work. It made her feel useful. Her neighbors benefited, too.

They were making no attempt to sneak. Perhaps they were proving something to themselves…their fearlessness. Malem just stopped…facing them, her face peaceful.

"Your brother hasn't come back, dirtyfoot!"

Pop! A Pill left her ear.

Malem continued her smile. Tucking her new staff under her arm, she held up her hand, palm out. She didn't know what was coming, but she had Bubba's oath that it would be good. "Wait," she said quietly. No fear. "My brother is watching. He has a message for you."

Back in the Valley, Pill had arrived before Malem's staff had gotten tucked. Steef stopped what he was doing, and Pulsed a tight Black beam. Pill went back to Malem. Steef waited for word.

Pop! *"Steef says wait six more beats, then say 'Here is my brother's message.'"*

The six beats was the time Steef had estimated it would take his Pulse to reach them. He was confident it would, and that everything would work. The only doubt he had was the timing, but it turned out to be close enough.

Steef's Black Pulse arrived two beats after Malem's proclamation. Waiting for it were four sets of bubbles. Each was a set of three. The outermost bubble was Blue, holding itself in place, directly over the village. Inside the first, the second bubble was also Blue. When it popped, it gave off a skybolt boomer. The innermost bubble was Black. Tuned Black. Tuned to the three boys, whose huts Steef had been in. Getting their tune.

The arriving Pulse ruptured the first set of bubbles only. With a loud BOOM! all three boys were popped with a Black Pulse that stung them all over, and left a skinburn that would be sore for several days.

Malem was delighted. "I told you. My brother is watching." With that, she flounced home.

The three remaining sets of bubbles just hovered over the village, waiting to be released. They were out of all travel lanes, which was good, because only a Grader could have Seen them, and the only Graders in the area had just left. It would have been unfortunate if some unsuspecting Steerman ran into one and broke their boat.

Each held a different level of Black, the last one being set to kill. He hoped he wouldn't have to use any more of them, least of all the last one. But Pill was watching, and Aunt Arima had only asked him not to kill anyone while they were there.

CHAPTER 16

❀

For as long as there had been Guilds, different Powers had kept mostly to themselves. Reds companied with Reds, Blues with Blues, and so on. Inter-Guild relations were rare, friendships rarer. Now there was a new Master's Alliance between White, Black and Red, and the Masters of those Colors met in total every fourth sevenday, to discuss their prosperity and any new ideas for increasing it. This new routine had a spillway effect. Whites, Blacks, and Reds of every grade began companying together. Nines with Nines, Sixes with Sixes, and so on. They still had to maintain *some* standards. And they became enterprising, too. Just like their Masters.

"Just don't understand it! This leg has never hurt before!" the limping man said to his Mate. They were trying to quietly get their purchases home before dark. GuildTown wasn't any place to be after dark any more. "Ow! There it goes again!" The man had to stop, and abruptly sat down. His children caught the parcels before they could tumble to the center of the road. He didn't like appearing weak in front of his children, but his hip no longer worked.

"Is anything wrong?" came a pleasant voice. There stood a White Seven, looking concerned. She seemed friendly enough. "Are you hurt?"

"My hip's gone out," responded the sitting fellow, "I don't mind the pain, but it's quit wor...ow!"

"Would you like for me to look at it for you? It's almost dark, and Healer's Hall is on the other side of Town..." she waited.

"You would do that?" asked the man's Mate, "Can't you get in trouble for Healing out here in the road?"

"Not really," said the courageous White, "But I would still have to collect a Healer's fee, and report it to my Guild. That way, I have maintained GuildLaw."

"Nothing's been wrong with this leg before," continued the seated man, "Wouldn't put it past some darkminded Black to be up to some mischief...still...I gotta walk...what's the rate for this, Healer?"

"One and one, grade Two," she responded, with true concern in her voice. She was absently rubbing her free hand along her face. Probably worried about her pending patient.

"Well, let's get this done...and our thanks," he said, motioning for his Mate to pay the woman. "Cursed Blacks," he muttered, as the Healer bent over him.

The Seven made a show of glowing and Pulsing, though it wasn't necessary. She had made her Healing Pulse the beat after being paid. She was an honest criminal, giving the family what they were paying for. At least her Black companion had learned better control. He hadn't left any burn marks on the man's skin, just a hole in his hipbone. She had deadened the pain enough for a seven-day, and told the bone to start mending.

The man was soon able to walk. Parting greets were given, and they moved off. He was still venting about the Blacks, "Someone should do something about those criminals! Town isn't safe any more for anyone! Thanks be to the Creator that that Healer was near!...I like the Reds too...good bunch of people...they'll keep those Blacks straight...nothing...wrong...with...Blacks...why, they're fine folks! What was I thinking! Some of the nicest people I've met are Blacks!" His Mate looked up at him, perplexed.

Her Red friend had gotten the signal. The Dust was put into a mutual bag, to be divided later between the three Sevens. It wasn't dark yet, they should be able to find at least one more.

❦   ❦   ❦

"And this?"

"Nine."

"And this?"

"Three."

"And this?"

"Ten. Non-Master Ten," he added.

Arima tuned off her glow. "Now give me an Eight," she said.

Steef re-tuned, and began to glow himself. Blue this time, he wanted to feel if Sassy was on her way back.

"Good. Ten please...good...Master Ten...good...Five..."

Steef drained down to his toes. It was hard to glow that low. Five was as low as he could get, "Aunt Arima?"

She knew that voice. Questions were coming, and his questions kept getting harder. It had been half a cycle since their visit to the village, and every few days he would have a new set of questions. Always about people. She had spent their lives and cycles here in this Valley worrying about people finding out about him. The impact of *him* finding out about *them* had just not occurred to her. *One more guilt to throw on the pile* she chided herself. She just knew her pile would be higher than most.

"Tell me more about emotion and desire."

She sighed. He was preoccupied about 'Cores' again. Whatever it was that he Saw with Red eyes, he was calling 'Core', apparently a term he'd picked up from one of the parches Antee had brought. She couldn't guide him well, in spite of her experience in Sight. Her experience was limited to viewing people's Power, not their emotions. She hoped that training him thoroughly in *that*…might help him in his other Sights. She also had a passing thought that her own well-earned cynical view of people might be an influence. A non-constructive influence.

"Desire is such a complicated word, Steef," she said resignedly, "And people can have conflicting desires. I can't imagine how your Sight would distinguish them…but I can tell you this much…you can desire something without feeling any emotion about it…and you can have emotion for something without desiring it."

"That does sound complicated."

"Here's an example…you are constantly desiring to solve new puzzles…am I right?"

"Yes Mam."

"And yet…as soon as those puzzles are solved…you move on to the next one without another thought."

He pondered. *At least his tongue doesn't stick out any more!* She waited a few beats, "That would be the *desire*…of discovery…without the love of accomplishment. You don't love your results…you just learn and move on."

"I suppose so."

"And yet you are capable of deep emotion without desire."

"How so, Auntie?"

"You constantly experience the emotion of joy, do you not?" He nodded. "You are capable of loving someone…correct?" Another nod. "And yet…" *Do I want to do this? How did I get here from Grading training?* "…you are not capable of emotion with desire."

The study face came out in full. He wasn't offended. She didn't know if he could *be* offended. She waited, watching his face. His thoughts would play across that face, almost as if they were tangible, physical things.

"I don't understand," he finally conceded.

"When we love people, we want to keep them with us. The selfish part of us…the desire…fights constantly with the love. When your Papa and Mama and Sissy left us, did you selfishly mourn their parting?"

"No."

"No…you 'found the joy' instead. Yet you love them…without the selfish *desire* to bend their lives to your will. Emotion without desire." *How far? Do I dare…I really want to know.* "When your Uncle Seafer died…did you mourn?"

His face was thoughtful, but not apprehensive, "No…I moaned him, but that's not mourning."

He's more Cat than human. The thought was abrupt. *Maybe Kivverr wasn't the blessing we thought.* "You didn't mourn…yet you loved him, yes?"

"Yes, I loved Uncle Seafer a lot."

I know you did. That's why I pardoned you…why we're still friends. "You didn't feel a *desire*…to have him back?"

He studied his answer, which she thought was healthy, "No…Uncle Seafer lived a full life. A good life. He's all around me. I carry him wherever I go…" he held up his stick, "…he Rested well," he concluded.

"Again…emotion without desire," she said simply. She'd known the answer, but it was good to hear it. It was good that he heard himself say it. She hoped.

But Steef wasn't through, "You know, Auntie…I *did* have a desire when Sissy left."

"Oh?"

"Yes Mam. I desired that she find more joy…more than she was finding here."

She took his face, kissing his forehead, "That's not desire, Son. There's nothing selfish in it. That's emotion."

"What emotion?"

"Hope."

❁   ❁   ❁

Cassa and Mokam arrived later that day, bringing Antee for his visit. The entire trip to and from Antee's village didn't actually take a full day, but they had spent some beats visiting Stem, Maleef, and Sissy.

Antee was glad to be back, and made pleasantries for a time. He didn't see Timmerr, but the old Cat sometimes took a while to get here these days. After idle conversation was exhausted, he took Steef aside for a private talk.

"Arima tells me that you have been burning your hand a lot lately, Son."

"Not any more, Uncle," Steef replied, quickly on guard. Nowhere to go. No chores to do. Stuck.

"Steef, we need to talk about your 'studies.'"

"Yessir." *Uh-oh.* There weren't many 'studies' with the Masters any more. They enjoyed mutual activities now, but no serious lessons. He'd been right the first time, this wouldn't be good.

"You're playing with the seventh primary, aren't you?"

"Yessir…but I'm being careful!"

"You're not being as careful as you think, Son."

"Yessir."

"That was too easy. Steef, look up here now, Son, and listen close. You have gifts that I can only imagine. And I would want to play with them too…if I had them. Especially at your age. But you've had more good fortune than you deserve, at least so far."

"What do you mean, Uncle?"

Antee leaned back, closing his eyes, "Let's think back to your Lock training."

"Okay." *Lock training?*

"I came out here to teach you Locks…after you got bitten by a snake."

"Yessir."

"I'm a Yellow, Steef. I deal with snakes, remember? People get snakebites on their legs or feet, not on their hands. You were reaching for that snake."

Sigh. "Yessir." *Not any more, though. Snakes are for cooking.*

Antee let it soak in for a beat or two, then continued, "Nice staff you've got there." His eyes still closed, he wasn't even looking at it.

"Yessir." *Uh-oh.* Again.

"Four spans, I'm guessing. Larger than the one you carried when you visited with us in the village," he paused, "Does this one come back to you too?"

"Yes…Sir." *I was hoping you'd forgotten that.*

"So I ask myself 'why does he need a staff that won't get away'…at the same time he's doing Lifting training…and you can guess how I answered that."

"Yes…Sir." Steef's voice was flat with resignation.

"How high were you, when you tipped over and lost your staff?"

Sigh. "Fifty staffs."

Antee had to open his eyes to roll them. And he had to keep himself from laughing. This was serious. But Steef sure did look like a herd beast facing a Cat's charge. He let the boy simmer for a while as they sat silently together. The others were letting them alone.

"One other thing."

"Yes Sir." *There was more?*

"I've noticed some changes in your sister. She never arrives home out of breath any more. She isn't getting small little injuries any more. She has three new best friends that follow her everywhere…protecting her, she says. She's tying her hair back again. And I notice that you are carrying two Pills on your shoulder."

Steef didn't respond.

"There were rumors in the village that those same three boys got badly burned. It's said their hands and feet were blistered for half a Quarter. After that, their purpose in life has become 'protecting' your sister."

Still, Steef said nothing.

"I am as certain as I can be…that you had something to do with that. And so did Pill, though they won't say anything about it. My point is, you aren't being careful enough. Someone is going to get really hurt."

"Yes Sir." He didn't think it would be Sissy. Or the three boys. After the second set of bubbles had been used, she'd told them that her brother's third message would remove their future as Fathers. They were now determined to see that no one else hurt her, either. But the last two bubbles were still there, if needed.

"Son, is it absolutely necessary that you play with the seventh primary?"

It was over. Uncle Antee was back. And Steef *would* be more careful. At least he'd try. His legs started swinging, "I want to give something back," he said quietly.

"What do you mean?"

"I want to give something back. Uncle Mokam has given everything he has. All of you have. I have nothing to give back. But Uncle Mokam would like to see the seventh primary. I can tell when he talks about it."

Antee had no reply to give. *He probably can, at that* he thought.

Steef wasn't through, "I won't be burning myself any more, Uncle. I've got better control, now. Want to see?" The light was back in his face.

"See what? See the seventh primary? Here?!" *Oh merciful Creator! No! I don't!* Too late.

"Uh huh. I know what went wrong the first time...you know, when they made the blue Valley. They used too much Dust...here I'll show you." And before Antee could say anything, Steef had reached into his pouch, drawing out two little specks of Dust. Placing them gently on the palm of his open hand, they Lifted about a span, and hovered. "Besides, they didn't have bubbles. I put a bubble around it...you can't See it, but it's there...then I squeeze that bubble down..."

Antee watched, wide-eyed, as those two specks of Dust changed shape. They had had little jagged edges, but something was folding them in. In just a beat, they were round and smooth. And much smaller still.

"Now turn your eyes, 'cause it's really bright." Steef turned away too, after making sure of his aim. "Then, just a small Black...and..."

Antee could see the flare in reflection off of everything around him.

"You can turn back now. It's going down," Steef informed him. Indeed, the two specks of Dust were gone, replaced by what looked like the center of a dwindling fire, still suspended over an open palm. "It never lasts long. I don't want to show Uncle Mokam until I can make it last...and I'll be *really* careful, Uncle Antee."

🍁   🍁   🍁

"*That looks like a good spot.*"

"Then that's where we'll land." Steef noticed there were some whitetails there. Kivverr must be thinking 'food'. There was water here, too. And a rock outcropping that he could land the sled behind, just in case. The sled came to a hover, then Lifted straight down, keeping his wind from being a problem against the rock walls.

"Do you want to eat first?" he asked, nodding toward Kivverr's obvious meal.

"*No. We will do your studying, I can eat later. They are not going far. The grass is good here.*"

"Okay."

They had traveled north up the Valley. Steef hadn't ever seen this part of the Valley before, and that would have been excuse enough to come. But Uncle

Antee was visiting, and wouldn't be coming back for another Quarter. He wanted to get his experiments done *now*, and show everyone, before the visit was over. None of his Masters spent much time with him in lessons any more. They just visited with each other. He didn't know why. That was Okay, he had plenty to study.

Today, he would get past the seventh primary, and move on. There were other puzzles calling to him. He was carrying some of the Dust that had come from around that strange rock. This Dust had some of that rock in it, and gave off the blue glow. They were larger pieces of Dust. He hadn't ground them down yet.

He wanted to get away from the sled. If anything went wrong, they would need an undamaged sled to get back. He was being careful.

"This is a pretty place. We'll have to come back." He could already see beasts and trees that were new to him. Plenty to do.

"How far do you want to go?"

"That low spot we saw from the air. It was clear of trees."

"We will be there soon."

"I can walk if you like. It's kind of hilly here."

"That would just slow us down. You are too small to tire me."

"Okay."

They arrived in the clearing that Steef had picked out, but as they approached the center of it, Kivverr's hair started standing up. Then Steef felt his friend begin to rumble, deep down inside.

"What's wrong with you?"

"We are not alone."

"We're never alone!" He was thinking of the ever-present Buzzbies on his shoulder. "What's here that would bother *you*?"

Kivverr didn't answer, he growled. A long growl that increased steadily in volume. And from the treeline surrounding most of the clearing, came answering growls. One by one, five male HornCats emerged.

"Oh, is that all? Well, we'll do them courtesy, and ask them to give us privacy," Steef declared, sliding off of his friend. Kivverr didn't want the Clan to see him being ridden.

"They are not here for courtesy. They are here for food."

"Well, tell them where we left the sled. There's plenty to eat there."

"They intend for us to be their food." The Cats were getting closer, and spreading out around them. Kivverr let out a roar, *"I am Kivverr! I am Clan! If you challenge me, you will die, and have no Rest!"*

Steef was concerned, "Why are they acting this way? Don't they know what the ClanCat will do to them?"

"*They are not Clan. They are wild. Crooked thinkers.*" He roared again. They answered…and pounced.

In his shock, Steef just barely got a bubble up. The five Cats crashed into it, and slid back to ground. This did not improve their mood. They attacked the bubble, screeching and clawing, leaping and pacing. The noise was deafening. Steef pushed the bubble out, giving room at the center.

"What should I do? Should I kill them? What will the ClanCat say if I kill them? Can you talk to them?"

"*Talk is over. They have challenged. I must meet the challenge.*"

"You? You can't fight five of them!"

"*I am Kivverr! I am Cl…*"

"I know. I know. But there are five of them and one of you, even if you *are* bigger than them."

"*I must meet the challenge! I am Clan! We do not step back!*"

Steef studied on this, while Kivverr began pacing as well. There were five of them on one side, and Kivverr on the other, following the bubble's contour around the clearing. Steef motioned him back over.

"Would it be acceptable to you to fight just one?" Steef didn't like this much, putting his friend at risk. He was bigger, but not that much, and this could only end one way.

"*I must accept…*"

"One at a time, then?"

Kivverr went still for a beat, then said, "*That will do. It must be the largest one first, though.*"

"Get ready. I'll let him in."

Kivverr went back to roaring, but stayed near the center. Steef waited until the largest one took another lunge, and released the bubble for a beat.

Kivverr leapt at once, and they met with forelegs in the air. Gnashing at throats, carving with claws, screeching at each other. It was the most terrible thing Steef had ever seen. He stayed planted in one spot, a smaller bubble over himself. If he interfered, his friend would never pardon him. The other argument was the blood that both Cats were now spilling. Steef wasn't squeamish around blood, he just didn't want to see Kivverr's.

But Kivverr was no ordinary HornCat. He was large, even for a Cat. He was HornCat to the MixMaster. He was Clan. He was fighting for honor, not food. Not-winning wasn't an option.

The other Cat was just mean...possibly hungry...mostly mean. Mean is rarely brave. He didn't mind attacking five against one, but one against one was different. When Kivverr landed a vicious bite to the challenger's neck, the attacker...stepped back.

Kivverr had spent most of his life with the MixMaster. He'd watched while 'crooked thinking' turned itself into real results. It was his own 'crooked thinking' that had brought him to the MixMaster to begin with. His opponent was expecting a fight with teeth and claws, because that's what Cats fight with. But when the attacker stepped back...Kivverr had another 'crooked' thought. Lowering his head suddenly, he lunged forward, and both of his horns plunged into the challenger's chest with the force of...well...a HornCat. One of them must have hit the pump, for he died on the spot, his collapsing body pulling itself back off the horns.

Kivverr stepped astride his foe, and roared! He was Clan! The challenge had been met!

Then he sputtered, and sank down on top of the dead Cat.

Steef rushed over. Kivverr was bleeding from a lot of different spots, and some of them were serious. "Do you mind if I kill the rest of them now?" he asked.

"That would be best. I have met my challenge. Now you must."

"Well, don't move..."

"You must take my foe back to the ClanCat. It must be done today. It is important."

"Let me take care of the others first, and we'll talk about going back."

"It is important!"

Steef stroked his friend's face, then stepped up on his back. Holding his stick high so they could see it, he flared his stone. "I am Steef!" he shouted, "Friend of the Clan! I accept your challenge!"

The Pills on his shoulder had watched all of this with fascination, but when Steef flared his stone, one said to the other, *"Not Black? He's flaring Blue! Skybolts?"*

"What difference will it make? Nothing he Pulses will hurt a Cat anyway."

"Then we'd better go."

"I'm staying. I don't know what he's thinking, but my wager is on Steef."

"We might have to pay for that."

"Maybe, but I don't think so."

Steef's face was a study. He was worried for Kivverr. He had to kill some Cats...and he really didn't *want* to kill Cats! And he still hadn't gotten his studying done!

The four remaining Cats were almost berzerk, since one of their own was down, and that filthy Clan was down too! The two-leg wasn't a real meal for four of them, but they could finish off the Clan, and all of them would eat well that night. They all lunged at the hard air that kept them away...it was gone!

They sped towards the center of the clearing, and at just over three staffs, they all four leapt, intending to come down as one on their prey.

Except they didn't come down at all.

The whirlwind that Steef had called up...caught them and carried them skyward. Up they went, screeching, clawing at the invisible air. Up. Up. Thirty staffs. Sixty staffs. A hundred. Spinning in circles, the four orange bodies quickly became orange spots. Then the whirlwind...stopped.

Steef was already moving to help his friend. There was a new bubble over them, lest anything come straight down. Nothing did fall directly on the bubble, but four HornCats showed up shortly, paws and claws down, eyes wide, moving fast. Too fast. The ground won, and the bubble served to keep the splash off of them.

Moving down to his friend's level, he tried to examine Kivverr's wounds. But Kivverr was in pain, and started thrashing around the beat Steef got off of him.

"Kivverr!"

"*What?!*"

"Those claws work!" One of them was halfway into the fleshy part of Steef's shoulder. The Buzzbies had moved to the other shoulder, watching warily.

"*Pardon!*"

"I've got to Heal you!"

"*You know you cannot Heal me. Even the MixMaster cannot Heal a Cat.*"

"I might if I broke one of your horns," he said, almost to himself.

Steef had given this some thought for many cycles, how to Heal a Cat. Some of his 'studies' had scorched Kivverr in the past, and it had occurred to him that the occasion might arise that Kivverr would need more than a quick chew on Steef's skin for relief. It had to be the horns. They were the channels of Power to a Cat's body. Break one, or both, and Yellow should work. Proving it didn't appeal much.

Kivverr had heard, "*You are not breaking my horns! I will Rest with both my horns!*"

"You *will* Rest, too, if I don't stop this bleeding! Hold still!" He was trying to hold his tunic on it. Compression helped bleeding. But Kivverr wouldn't, or couldn't hold still. Exasperated, Steef reached up and took one horn in each hand, draining until Kivverr slept. That was better.

There was a lot of torn flesh, but he ignored it. What concerned him were two wounds that had hit large bloodtubes, and they were leaking. It wouldn't take long. He could break a horn, Heal Kivverr, and listen to him complain the rest of their days. No.

His Aunt Arima's words came back to him: 'Healing Power people is different than Healing beasts. Power people need more Power, to overcome the backcharge'. Well, HornCats were Power beasts…sort of. They just needed more Power. Steef filled up, and drained his full stick into Kivverr's wounds. Did the bleeding slow? He couldn't tell…and he didn't have time for studying. He needed more Power, or Kivverr would Rest today.

He reached into his pouch, pulling out a palmfull of Dust. The large chunks of Dust that glowed blue.

"Pill," he said with a deep breath, "Discharge warning." He thought absently that his voice sounded calm.

But Pill didn't leave. One of them hurriedly crawled into his ear, *"How far is safe, Steef?"*

"I don't know, Pill. Better go back to the cove, to be sure."

Pop! Pop!

He had to hurry. No time left to think about it. The Dust Lifted off of his hand. He watched it rise, and then begin to squeeze. He noticed that his hand was trembling. Turning back, away from the coming flare, he placed the point of his stick into one of Kivverr's wounds. The other end aimed at the Dust.

"No steps back," he whispered. He released the bubble.

There were four very nervous Masters, sitting in a cove, pretending to be visiting. They knew he was up to something, they just didn't know what. And it had been quiet since he left. Too quiet. Usually, Pill would tell them what was going on. Usually.

Maybe Antee's talk helped Arima tried to convince herself. It wasn't working. Conversation was sparse, as all of them were thinking the same thing.

Pop! Pop! Pop! Pop! Pop! Pop! Pop! Pop! Pop! Pop! Pop! Pop! Pop! Pop! Pop!

Pills filled the air, and the ones already on Arima made room for two new-comers. She saw Pills landing on all four of them.

"He called us Pill! He called us Pill! He never calls us Pill! He always called us 'Buzzbie'!" said one.

"Also," said another, calmer Pill, *"He's going to Disch..."*

A stab of near-blinding Yellow light washed over the walls of the cove, and blew past the open field. The Cats that were out in that open all alerted, and started moaning and roaring.

Beats later, the ground rumbled, as a wave of sound passed from north to south.

They were *up*! And running to the boat. Fortunately, they had started from the back of the cove. Had they been closer, they'd have been caught in the wind that followed the rumble. It rocked Cassa's boat, though it did it no real harm, as her sail had been furled and cinched properly. Several of the smaller Cats were tumbled.

Pills started Pop!'ing in and out.

"We think he's alive Arima!" She assumed they were all getting the same messages. *"But he's going to need help!"*

Cassa was at the boat, setting her sail. She sent out a Pulse for wind, *"How far, Pill?!!"* she screamed.

"Just over seventeen leagues."

"Seventeen leagues!? Seventeen *thousand* staffs?!!!"

"Yes. Straight up the Valley to the north."

It wasn't hard to find him. From the air, they could see trees blown down for a five hundred staff radius. In the center of that radius was Steef, lying motion-less. He was draped over the body of an also motionless Cat. Kivverr was pac-ing back and forth, all around, roaring and moaning. When he saw them, he sat next to Steef, quivering and swishing his tail.

Cassa brought the boat in too fast. The bottom scraped and banged across the clearing, actually sliding past their target. Antee leapt from the boat, rush-ing to his boy, then remembering and turning to help Arima down. Steef needed her more than him. Kivverr set to roaring again.

"Kivverr!" shouted Antee, "Move back so we can help him!"

The Cat finally heard, after three or four shouts, and moved back. Arima attended to Steef. His tunic was under him, and the blood she saw there terri-fied her. But the only open wound on him was a gouge on his left shoulder. Both hands were burned, too, but that wouldn't account for the blood. She was getting frantic, looking for something significant to Heal.

Meantime, Antee was scanning the scene. He looked at the dead Cat. He hadn't ever seen this one before, he was sure. The Cat's blaze was unlike any he'd seen, and he was good at remembering. This Cat had wounds all over his upper body, and two deep holes. Then he looked at Kivverr, who was fully animated. He looked hard at Kivverr.

"Arima."

"What!? I'm busy Antee." She was busy finding nothing, and she needed to find…*something*!

"He's asleep, Arima."

"What?! Don't be silly, Antee. Look around…"

"Stop what you're doing. There is no alarm here. Let *me* help *you* look around." He bent and pulled her up…as respectfully as he could…because she didn't want to come.

"He discharged, Arima. Remember?…Remember the Color we saw? Yellow. He discharged into Kivverr. It drained him. He's sleeping a drained sleep."

"That's absurd, Antee! *Look* at Kivver! Why, he's fit as he…"

"He would be, wouldn't he Arima?" Cassa and Mokam got there. They'd been securing the boat. "If Steef discharged into Kivverr, Kivverr *would* be full of himself, wouldn't he?…And he is."

"Why would he need to discharge into Kivverr?" an arriving Cassa asked. She'd had to furl the sail, and hadn't had time to take it all in.

"Kivverr was wounded, I think. Apparently a serious wound…from him." And he gestured to the dead Cat. "And if you look close, you can see small spots on Kivverr that look like wounds that are almost well."

"You mean he *Healed a HornCat*!!!?" Cassa blurted.

Antee nodded. "It certainly looks that way. And it looks like it took everything he had." *At least there IS an 'everything he has'.* "Arima, I think if you revive him like you would a child at a Grading, he should be fine."

The shaken Healer bent to do just that.

Cassa looked around. Mokam looked around. They looked at each other.

Cassa grinned, spun around and knuckled Antee in the shoulder, "He Healed a HornCat, Oh Mate of mine! Can *you*…do *that*?!"

Their eyes met. There was a time when Antee had asked her that same question. A good remembrance. He shook his head slowly, giving her a slight smile.

Steef woke slowly. He was dazed somewhat, and his eyes would need several days of Healing. "How is Kivverr?" he asked first, blinking.

Kivverr had stretched himself on the ground at Steef's feet. He reached out a paw, touching a foot, *"I am well. If you are also well, then we must go."*

"Oh...Okay. Aunt Arima? Kivverr says we have to get this body back to the Clan right away. I don't know why, but it's important, he says."

"We need to be moving for another reason," interjected Cassa, "It'll be dark soon." She didn't know if they had time to get back or not.

"Can you walk, Son?" asked Antee.

"I think so...well, maybe not," he said, flopping back down. Kivverr solved that. Closing his jaws over Steef's middle, the Cat picked him off the ground, flounced over to the boat with his tail held high, and leapt the distance neatly. Steef was boarded. Mokam Lifted the dead Cat, and they tied a rope between it and the boat. They left quickly. Looking back down as they traveled south, they could now see some of Steef's sled. It was buried under trees, and the top half of its mast was snapped off. They would have to retrieve it later.

"I was gonna be careful, Uncle Antee," he said weakly. "Really. But I didn't have the beats. Kivverr was hurt."

"It's all right Son, you rest now."

"I didn't get to finish my study for Uncle Mokam. The Cats came, and everything happened..."

"Cats? More than one?"

"Yessir. Five Cats. Kivverr took the first, but he got hurt, so I had to finish."

Antee was puzzled. He hadn't seen any more Cats, "Did you scare them away?"

"Nossir, I had to kill them. Didn't want to...but Sassy would have been proud."

"You killed them...with Blue?!" *How do you kill with Blue?*

"The Color doesn't matter, Uncle. Any Color can kill. It's not-killing that's hard."

It was dark when they got back, and not a beat too soon. Cassa was running out of charge, and so was Mokam. They were going to ask Steef, weak as he was, to give a charge from his staff, when it occurred to them that he had no staff. No one remembered seeing it there. They assumed then, that it had just burned up.

It seemed that every Cat that lived in the area was waiting for them. They landed, and Mokam Lifted the dead Cat down. Kivverr sprang from the boat, heading straight for the ClanCat. The two beasts stood very still, side against side, for the entire time it took to get the boat secured, and Steef unboarded. By now, Arima was glowing her stone and herself to give light to work by.

The ClanCat approached Arima, stopped, and bent his head up. A signal for conversation. She touched.

"We must have a circle. It must be now. All two-legs must be there."

"Your Majesty, your pardon, but Steef is not well. Could we possibly do this tomorrow?"

"No. It must be now, while the meat is fresh. The MixMaster must be there."

"As you wish, your Majesty," she sighed. Cassa had been holding their boy while Arima was with the ClanCat. She motioned for her Blue friend to let him sit. "Steef, drain yourself completely, pumpkin. We have been invited to something with the Cats, and his Majesty insists. I'll give you a little Freshening. It should help."

"What's all the fuss, Arima?" asked Mokam.

"Haven't a glimmer, Mokam."

Meanwhile, several Cats had chewed through the rope holding the dead body, and drug it into open field, where now a solid ring of Cats formed around it. A large ring, holding every Cat there, all squished against one another. When the people arrived, a hole was made in the ring, and they stepped through. Kivverr came over, and Steef slumped against him, catching himself on one great leg.

"Tell your tribe that they are to join the circle, not stand inside of it."

"My tribe?"

"Yes. The other two-legs. You are all one tribe, are you not?"

Kivverr had never spoken to him like this, and he was already tired. He decided that just repeating it was easier than explanations he couldn't give anyway, "Kivverr says that all of us are to join the circle, not stand inside it."

They all just stared, until the ClanCat himself came to Arima, and repeated it. The humans stepped back to the circle, and the Cats closed in on them. They were all bunched up, shoulder to shoulder and shoulder to huge legs. As Steef watched, all four Masters took on looks of pure wonder and amazement. They were transfixed and unmoving, as the voices of the Clan began passing through them.

"Are we supposed to join the circle?"

"No, we must go to our defeated foe." With that, Kivverr stretched out on the ground. *"You must get on me. We must approach our foe as one."*

"But…they'll see," he whispered.

"That is no longer an issue. They MUST see us together."

Steef was too tired to argue. He wearily clambered onto his friend. Kivverr rose gently, padding to the center, where the dead Cat lay. He let out a deafening roar. The Clan roared back.

"*I am Kivverr!!! I am Clan!!! The Clan was challenged!!! I stood!!! I took no steps back!!!*"

The circle roared again.

Kivverr went on, "*We are Clan!!! We do not kill for sport!!! We kill for food!!! We kill when challenged!!! We eat our kill!!!*"

Another roar from the assembled.

Kivverr bent suddenly, almost throwing Steef off. He took a bite out of the dead body. Raising back up, he spit it out.

"*This foe died without Rest!!! His food will not fatten!!! I reject this food!!!*"

Again, the circle responded.

"*I am Kivverr!!! I am Clan!!! I am tribe of Rivverr, Rested ClanCat!!! I am...HornCat to the MixMaster!!!*" He waited for the noise to slacken.

"*The MixMaster stood the challenge!!! I, Kivverr, witnessed this!!! HE DID NOT STEP BACK!!! The MixMaster is now my BROTHER!!! Tribe of Rivverr!!! DOES ANY CLAN CHALLENGE???!!!*"

The only sound was the Buzzbies hovering overhead.

"*You must declare yourself, as I did. You must give your name. You must eat the foe. Then we will be brothers.*"

This was going soooo...fast...but he tried. Taking his knife, Steef raised his hand, and weakly said, "I am the MixMast..."

"*No.*"

"What, no?"

"*Give them your name. MixMaster is not who you are. It is what you are. Give them your name.*"

"All right...I am Steef!..."

"*No.*"

"What, no!?...that's my name."

"*Not here. In the Clan, you are Steefrr.*"

"Okay......I am Steefrr!!!...I am Clan!!!...I am tribe of Rivverr, Rested ClanCat!!!..." deep breath, "...I am *brother to Kivverr!!!*" With that, he slid off of Kivverr's shoulders, the easiest task he had that night. Bending to the carcass, he cut off a piece and put it in his mouth.

Like his brother, he raised up for the circle to see him spit the meat, "This foe died without Rest!! He will not fatten!! I reject this food!!"

The circle erupted in a frenzy of roars and screeches.

It was easier to walk back to the circle than climb up on Kivverr again. Steef approached his Masters, his tribe, who were beyond response. He stopped before them, "Kivverr says that I am now Clan. The first two-leg ever invited in. Kivverr says that you are my tribe. My tribe may also join the Clan. Kivverr says that you may refuse, but you will not be asked again...ever." He held out his knife, blinking his still-raw eyes.

They gaped, but only for a beat. Cassa stepped out, exclaiming, "Get out of my way! I'm in!"

But Antee reached out and pulled her back. He mouthed the word 'wait' and nodded towards Arima.

She wasn't moving, but not because she didn't want to. Her legs just didn't work. It was the ClanCat himself that nudged her, making her take a step. The circle roared again. She slowly walked out to the center, with the ClanCat by her side at each step. Steef had put the knife in her hand. Then the ClanCat told her what to say.

"I...am Arimarr!!! Tribe of Rivverr, Rested ClanCat!!!..."

Cassa had to go next, there was no stopping her. She met Arima halfway across the circle, taking the knife, and bounding to the center. There was another roar, and *every* female Cat in the circle stepped out. Some snarling and snapping ensued, until the largest female roared them down, and walked out to meet Cassa, tail high. She turned her head. Cassa touched...

"I am Cassarr!!! Tribe of Zallrr!!! Mother to the Clan!!!..."

Antee was ready. Where was Timmerr?

Three large males stepped out and approached Mokam. The old Brown's face was ablaze with wonder. He let them walk him out...

"I am Mokamrr!!! Tribe of Clemmerr, and all free males!!!..."

Antee waited until Mokam got back, receiving the knife from his Brown brother. He waited some more. No Cat stepped forward. *Where is Timmerr?* He wanted to go, but not without Timmerr. Not sure what to do, he stepped out and walked to the center. The circle was quiet...waiting.

Beat. Beat. Beat.

A growl came...a roar! From outside of the circle! The Cats made way, and Timmerr lumbered through. He was old now, and walked slowly. It occurred to Antee that the Clan had let the others go first, waiting for Timmerr to get here. There were two younger males pacing him, slightly behind on either side. The three Cats approached, and Timmerr stretched his neck.

For the first time in fifteen cycles, Antee got to touch his friend.

"It is good, old friend, that this should occur before my Resting. I came as soon as I heard. I have listened as I approached. We have much to discuss, you and I. First, you must say this…"

"I am Anteerr!!! Tribe of Timmerr!!!…"

Kivverr and Steef then insisted that Pill be included. Pill had stood, too, they said. They met the challenge. The result was that a Boss Pill descended onto the carcass, buzzing angrily. It rose back up to a hover. Everyone assumed it spit.

Every member of the Clan followed. They left nothing but bones.

The circle broke up, with all of the females carrying Cassa off, tossing her from one back to another as her delighted squeals blended with their roars. Many of the males had moved off with Mokam. Kivverr carried Steef to their tree. It wouldn't be the first time Steef went up the tree in Kivverr's mouth, though it hadn't happened for a while. Arima was left standing with the Clan-Cat, as another very large male approached them.

"Arimarr, this is someone you need to meet."

"Your Majesty! You called me by name!"

"Yes. You are Clan now."

"And all those cycles…when Rivverr called me 'Healer'?"

"You were not Clan. It was proper to use your title. Rivverr led well."

"Your Majesty…I…"

"You are Clan, Arimarr. Amongst Clan, I am Plivverr."

"And who…who is…this fine fellow?" she asked, turning to the approaching male.

"This is my cub. He will be ClanCat, when I step down. He bears the name my sire wished I had been given, but I was already named when you reappeared amongst us."

"What name is that?"

"It is proper for him to greet you. You are no longer limited to speech with me alone. You are Clan." With that, Plivverr stepped back, and the younger Cat stretched his neck.

"Greets to you, new Clan! I am Arivverr!"

Antee had watched as Arima's arms wrapped the leg of that second, really huge, male Cat. Then Timmerr began headbumping him in the shoulder, his horns passing front and back of Antee's head.

"You must meet my cubs, Anteerr. Then we will talk until the new light comes in the sky."

"Greets, Anteerr! I am Antimmerr!"

"Greets, Anteerr! I am Teemmerr!"

※   ※   ※

Antee overstayed the days he'd planned, visiting with Timmerr. During those days, all of the Clan had been called in from every cave. Most of them had arrived by the time he left, giving silent respect to the parting that he and Timmerr shared. When the boat was gone, all of the male Cats gathered for a circle. The conference didn't last long, and they were off, leaving behind only the females, the young Cats, and Kivverr. It was decided that he had met his challenge.

The rest of them, over a hundred adult male HornCats, were going north. The ClanCat led them out. There would be no repeat of a wild Cat attacking any Clan. The wild ones would be leaving the Valley, or die.

CHAPTER 17

❀

The males were gone for four sevendays. Three of them never returned, and a proper Moaning was given. Steef had gone out several times to Heal grievous wounds, or the count would have been higher. Kivverr would stay behind, in the event that space was needed on the sled to bring a Cat back to the cove, but none ever came. After being Healed, they would always rejoin the hunt.

Oddly, during that time, Kivverr would disappear for days at a time, returning without a word.

Cassa couldn't step out of her cave without an escort of females. She never had less than two for company, and often more. The females would tolerate the others, which meant no biting, but conversations between Cat and two-leg were limited to Cassa.

That changed when the males returned. Arima could now enjoy the company of Plivverr or Arivver almost constantly. It was a glad time for her.

And Mokam left, carried off by a large group of the free males. Staff in hand, crude supplies in a pack on his back, he informed them that he would be back and away he went. He stayed gone for forty-two days. Pill told them that he was digging, and yes, he was fine.

He didn't look fine when he finally came back. He was filthy, and his tunic and trous were torn and ruined. The only thing about him that looked fine was his grin.

Once washed and re-dressed, it looked like Mokam again, but it didn't sound like him. With a new sense of excitement, and a gleam in his eye, he sounded more like...Seafer, "Been making caves!...the whole southern half o' the Valley!...improving some...making new ones...Cats'd take me everywhere!...not a Cat den I haven't seen!...gonna wait a while and then we're going out again…that'll take longer!…we're gonna do the north half!…did'ya know that Pill doesn't like caves?…wouldn't go in!…always came back when I'd come out again, though…what an experience!…nothing at all like mining for Dust!…shaping the stone to suit each tribe!…gotta see Steef about getting some new Freshening!…gotta keep up!" While he spoke, he was going through enough food for three Mokams.

They watched him in amused silence, though Arima experienced a wide range of emotion. She was thrilled for Mokam and his newfound joy. She was as pleased as she could be that their family had grown, and yet tightened. And she was proud and hurt at the same time…that Mokam would be asking Steef for a Freshening…and not her. And it hadn't occurred to Cassa to catch it, either. Arima had to remind herself that…given a choice…she too would want one of Steef's Freshenings over anyone else's. He redefined what a Freshening was.

"The laborers are here for your trunks GuildMaster," Meeben said, glowering. She wouldn't tell him where she was going, and neither would Pool. There wasn't anywhere in the Territories that she could go, and be gone that long. And she wouldn't be accessible to Pool! Very strange. He comforted himself with the thought that he would be in charge for at least four sevendays. Perhaps he could even sneak in some real Healing. Probably not. Pool would still see.

"That will be all, Meeben," Vinntag replied. *I really must find a replacement for him. Soon.* Her mood was more foul than usual. It was thrilling that Wingor would be taking her east with him. She would finally get to meet their brethren in the Eastern World. So much secrecy. Delicious. She couldn't tell Meeben, of course. She wouldn't have, if she could. There were a few White Masters who knew now, as there were a few in all seven Guilds. Very few. All chosen by Wingor. For some reason, he seemed to think he was a better judge of people than she was.

She was happy enough to be going. It was an honor, really. But eleven long days in a boat! With Wingor! *And* those other clods who did the Lifting and Steering…but who ever spoke to Blues or Browns? Eleven days! And that was just to get there!

And they had to travel over the blue valley. The far eastern edge of the Territories was also the far eastern edge of the blue valley, and they would be over it for almost half a day! And then have to camp that third night close enough that…she was told…the blue could be seen against the skyline. She shivered each time she thought of it. There was Power enough in the ground.

The laborers had removed her trunks, and all that was left to do was select a staff. Which one? One wall of her workcloset was lined with a rack full of staffs, all ornately designed. One white one in particular was stunning. It had never been used, waiting for her new apprentice. A gift. A very special gift. Sad, really. The girl was a special talent. Such a waste. She selected a tall, heavy staff that she'd had for many cycles now. With the bottom worn off from scraping, it was showing a bit of age. The inlay was still pretty, though nothing like some of her others. It would do. Wouldn't want her new friends to think she was showy.

At the far end of the rack was her oldest staff, the one she'd gotten during her last cycle of Master's training. Her brows furrowed, remembering. She'd wasted a couple of inferior staffs on that witch Arima. Part of her still hungered to show her old enemy what she could do with a proper staff. Part of her…but most of her didn't. *She was a young fool! Then she became an old fool! And now, she's probably dead! Probably a meal for one of those foul smelling Cats, and a fitting end, too! Why, she probably died spewing out that 'Mastery is a gift' nonsense!*

The boat was waiting. She bustled out to her brightening future.

❧   ❧   ❧

"Mastery is a gift. A gift to be shared. I witness a sharing," intoned Arima.

Mokam didn't look up, but Cassa did. They were having firstmeal. Steef had left before sunrise, wanting to get some distance for his practice. The first rumble had caused Arima to stop and recite the old pledge. She only recited it at the first one each day now.

She and Cassa and Mokam had dutifully tried at first. They had given the recitation with each blast they heard. But that was six days ago. With at least twenty discharges per day, it had soon become tiresome. And that was just the ones they could hear! Now Arima's conscience was soothed with one pledge per morning, at the first blast.

"You know, Arima," said Cassa, with a thoughtful look, "Actually, he's not."

"Not what?"

"He's not sharing it," she went on. "I don't mean he's doing anything wrong! But he's not actually sharing those discharges."

She's right. Another new definition needed.

For her part, Cassa thought the image would be complete, if only Arima would stick out her tongue...just a bit.

Kivverr had left again, only the Creator knew where. Steef had decided that the opportunity was right for him to practice discharging. Since none of them had ever done that, or heard of anyone else doing that, they were understandably perplexed about how to deal with it. Discharging was simple, really. Fill up to the bursting point, then fill some more until you burst. You could tune the charge, and aim it, but you couldn't control the amount of release. That was determined by the Creator, at birth. A discharge really released itself.

Or it used to.

They listened, having no other way to judge. And judging from the different noise he made with each one, they assumed he could release at many levels. They'd kept Antee informed, and his opinion matched theirs. Steef had such a surplus of Power that he could manipulate a discharge, releasing at will, at a Power level of his choosing.

At least he's not using Blue sighed Cassa to herself. The sky had remained clear every day.

❧   ❧   ❧

Pop! *"Vinntag, there's news."*

Her mood had not improved. She'd been in this boat for two days already, and tomorrow was the blue valley. "What is it Pool!?"

"There are reports of HornCats outside the Valley. All at the north end, where there are some villages. Livestock is missing, and a few people, too."

How delightful! She brightened instantly, "I assume you told Kuumit? Is he sending out some of his people to kill them?" *Let's just kill them all, while we're killing.*

"Kuumit knows. He checked his parches. From what he says, Black has no affect on the Cats. He has sent for the Yellow GuildMaster. He wants Yellow's opinion of how they might deal with the beasts."

This was less good. She wouldn't miss any careless Yellows, but this could get messy. "What does Kuumit want from me?"

"He wants everything you know about the Cats. You are the only Master available who has any experience with them.

Well...this was different. They needed her. Her back straightened and her shoulders pulled back. It was true that she was the only Grader left. Three other Graders had died when…and that was no coincidence. She'd been the one selecting who died that day. There were two Sighted children in her Guild now, but they would be trained…properly.

"Here's what I can tell you, Pool…"

❦   ❦   ❦

"Uncle Mokam, I want to ask your pardon."

To Mokam's view, the young man looked as chagrinned as he'd ever seen him. "Steef, why in the name of all that's solid, would you need my pardon?"

Steef chin drooped. A foot scuffed the dirt. He needed to wash them again, anyway, "I've tried, but I can't catch any 'seventh' to show you. I really wanted to do that."

Mokam grasped his shoulder, surprised at the muscle he felt there, "Pardon willingly given, Steef, though it's not needed. It's not like I've had a shortage of glad events lately."

"I know…but I wanted to give you something myself." He still hadn't looked up.

"Well, it seems to me that all of the recent events…are a result of something *you* did. I have been well gifted."

That helped a bit. Steef raised his head, "That was more Kivverr's doing than mine, Uncle," he said.

"Why don't we give you equal honor, and call the deal struck," replied the old Brown, kindly. "Besides, the Freshening you gave me is more gift than one person could ask. Now tell me, is that what you've been doing out there with all those discharges? Still playing around with the 'seventh'?"

Steef got more animated, "Not really…well, some…but mostly I've been practicing Yellow."

"So what conclusion did you come to about the blue primary?"

Steef shrugged, "I don't think it's possible to catch it raw, Uncle. I can start it Okay…" and he raised his hand…

Which Mokam grabbed, and lowered, "No, your oath is enough."

"…but I can't store it. It burns right away. I think raw 'seventh' is going to have to be stored in something…not caught." The head went down again.

"Much like we store Power in ourselves and our staffs, I'm guessing," responded Mokam.

Steef's head snapped up, and as Mokam watched, the face squinted down until it looked like one of Seafer's acorns. The boy's tongue was even trying to slip out. *What did I say? Merciful Creator…and he'd just given up, too!*

"Yessir," said Steef absently, "Just like that. Thanks, Uncle Mokam!"

And he was gone, leaving Mokam with renewed worry.

❧   ❧   ❧

"You don't mind? You're sure?"

"It is a good thing you are doing. I am glad to help."

"Okay. Let's go talk to your brother."

Plivverr was agreeable to the idea, but skeptical that it would work. Steef pointed out that if it didn't work, nothing was lost. They loaded straps onto the sled, and a bundle of extra sticks that Steef had brought.

"You know where to find him?"

"Yes, it is not far through the air."

The sled Lifted and silently glided away. The three Masters on the ground watched the departure with hope.

They found him asleep. His cubs helped wake him, and then helped board him. Too weak to hold on himself, it was necessary for Steef to strap him down. He would be careful with his air, trying not to rock the sled, but a little caution never hurt. Kivverr stood silently with the cubs, as his brother Steefrr sailed away, with another HornCat in the seat he usually occupied.

Steef turned back north, but only went as far as safety required. He landed, instantly jerking his stick out of the sled. His second discharge of need, and both times, haste was important. He wondered about that.

"Pill, discharge warning. Three leagues should be safe. Wake me if I go to sleep."

Pop! Pop!

The cloud of Power that surrounded him was a pale Yellow. He was mixing. He hoped it would work. It should work. Sure couldn't hurt. He didn't have to shut his eyes any more. He'd discovered that filling them with Clear prevented flashburn.

The discharge wasn't large. He only got drowsy. And it worked. The effects were immediate. "Finally…," he breathed, sleepily, "Something!"

Pop! Pop! *"It worked! It worked! Can we go tell him?"*

"You may *not*! It's a surprise."

Turning back to the Cat, he asked, "Feel up to a little trip?"

"Yes."

❦   ❦   ❦

Antee was anxious *and* depressed. He was overdue for a trip to the Valley, and for the first time ever, he didn't want to go. He hadn't sent Pill to ask for the boat, and they hadn't offered. He knew why. Timmerr had Rested by now. Pill didn't say so, but he'd noticed that lately, Pill often didn't say things. He and Timmerr had enjoyed really good parting greets, with full understanding that it was their last. That wasn't sorrowful. It was the way of life. What made it sorrowful was the fact that it had also been their first.

To add to his misery, there were apparently at least two of the wild Horn-Cats stalking his village. At least two, because attacks had occurred simultaneously, several leagues apart. One man was badly mauled. The only thing that had saved him was the abundance of sheep he was herding. Apparently the Cat decided the sheep looked tastier. The man would be dead soon, anyway. Sooner than Arima could get here.

Pop! *"Antee! Get your staff and your travel bag. Wake the others. You're going for a walk!"*

"Pill! What are you doing here? It's almost midnight!"

"Why aren't you standing yet? Get up! Wake...never mind, we'll do it." Pop!

He heard Pop!'ing travel through the hut. A Green glow came on. Shortly, Malem came to the door.

"Come on, Uncle Antee! Bubba's here!" The glow moved away, and then went out.

"What!?"

Pop! *"You do understand, that if you listened more, and questioned less, you'd know more. Right? Good. Get dressed. Get your staff. Get your pack. Get out to the woods. Your ride is here."*

Antee surrendered to the inevitable, putting away his questions. Pill was full of himself, and answers would be impossible. Besides, Malem was already out the door, being followed closely by Stem and Maleef. He gathered his things, and followed. There could be only one place to go. The landing spot Steef had used last time. It was deep in the woods. A fleeting concern for the possibility of meeting one of those Cats out there...and he followed.

The moon was almost full, and its reflected light was enough to get him to the woods. Once inside, he glowed his stone to see. There were three Green glows ahead of him, two dull, one a good bit brighter. He Pulsed, to see if any Cats were around. There was! He got one distinct return Pulse. Merciful…

"Pill! Tell Steef there's a Cat somewhere near here! He's got to protect his fam…"

"He knows."

"Are you sure? You'd better ch…"

"He knows! Will you hurry, please?"

And hurry he did. Passing the edge of the clearing Steef had made so long ago, he saw the silhouette of the sled, three Green glows illuminating its front. There was Steef! Good, they were safe. And there was the Cat he'd felt! On the sled! *Steef brought Kivverr with him? What was he thinking?*

Closer. That couldn't be Kivverr, unless he'd shrunk. Who…?

Steef's stone glowed bright White, illuminating the entire clearing, and the Cat sprung from the sled.

It was Timmerr.

Timmerr as Antee had known him ten cycles ago. Timmerr that was bounding towards him like a young Cat. Timmerr that…smack!…weighed more than ten grown men, and whose tongue was scraping the hide off of his face.

"I……can't……breathe! ……I……can't……breathe!"

"Pardon." Timmerr lifted his paw off of Antee's chest, but he didn't stop licking.

When the commotion settled, and the family had hugged their boy a few times, Antee approached, Timmerr at his side. Steef's grin outshone the others, and he was rocking back and forth, heel to toe. Antee didn't have to ask.

"Been practicing my discharges," he said.

"I heard, but…"

"Been practicing my *Yellow* discharges…and my mixed Yellow/*White* discharges…a Freshening discharge. For a Cat."

Antee couldn't think of anything to say, so he hugged.

"I couldn't give Uncle Mokam his 'seventh,'" Steef said gleefully to the back of Antee's shoulder. "Besides, what good is all this Power, unless I *do* something with it?"

❧   ❧   ❧

Antee and Timmerr visited in the woods while Malem led Steef to the injured man's hut. The man's family was up, waiting for him to die. Now they could stand vigil while he Healed. They didn't question Steef at all. Word was out in the village about the man who was re-growing a leg, and this was one of the Healers who'd done it. No other Healers came visiting this far south any more, and who could afford them, anyway? Steef was welcomed, heeded, and blessed on his way.

While they were gone, Timmerr's hair had bristled. Antee asked.

"I smell another Cat in the area. It is not Clan."

"How close?" Antee asked in alarm. He sent out another Pulse to find out himself. He got nothing.

"Not close. The scent is on the wind. Do not fear. If it comes, I will stand."

"I have no doubt of that, old friend. But my friends in the village are at risk."

"We will discuss it with Steefrr, when he returns."

*   *   *

"Timmerr, I will have to go high to find them. Will you stay here and guard my family while I'm gone?"

Timmerr's back straightened, and his tail came up. Chest full, he said, *"You honor me, Steefrr. I will stand before them, as I would my own tribe."*

"It's important that you not leave this clearing. It is *very* important."

"I hear. I will heed the MixMaster. Remember, I have witnessed your Power often in my days."

Steef gave his Uncle Antee a look that said 'make sure he doesn't leave the clearing'. Antee nodded.

Steef Lifted. On his way out, he put a bubble around the clearing. If he had to discharge a killing Pulse, he didn't want it to hit Timmerr. And if Timmerr never left the clearing, he wouldn't know it was there.

Timmerr made a show of pacing the perimeter, sniffing. Satisfied, he returned. Stretching out, he exuded the image of a Cat in charge. Antee sat nervously next to his head, stroking.

"Would you mind if Steef's family spoke to you?"

"No. They are Steefrr's blood. I would be honored."

"Malem, would you like to speak to Timmerr?"

The girl's eyes went wide. Here was something her Bubba had never been able to share with her. She reached…, "Bright day…Master…Cat."

"I am Timmerr! Greets to you, little grassgrower."

The four people took turns speaking with the old/new Cat, passing the beats, all of them privately aware that something was about to happen. Timmerr maintained a very relaxed pose, while Antee's neckhair got prickly. What was taking so long? He glowed again, and caught the glint of eyes just outside the treeline!

"Timmerr!"

"I see him. He has been crawling up."

And Antee finally knew. Knew the cold fear that other people felt when first meeting the Cats. He'd never felt that, being trained from his youth to respect and honor, instead of fear. He didn't like it. Not at all. Steef had faced four of these at once. It sobered him.

"Should we be doing something?" He meant 'should *you* be doing something?', but he didn't want to offend his friend. But he didn't want to be a meal, either.

"No. The MixMaster left hard air all around the clearing. Our foe cannot enter."

"He did!? How did you know? Why didn't you say anything?"

"Steefrr is good Clan. He understands a Cat's position. But he does not understand our nose. When the hard air went up, all smell stopped." If Cats could chuckle, Timmerr would have done it then. He went on, *"I look forward to watching this one die."*

"You sound pretty confident."

"Are you not?"

❦   ❦   ❦

Steef sent out Pulse after Pulse, looking for Cats. Timmerr was in the bubble, so he wouldn't give a return. There were six Cats that he could reach without destroying the village. Two more that were too distant, and they were moving away, anyway. *Now, how to do this? Hmmm. Blue worked before. And some Yellow for aim.*

One grain of Dust. Only one. Very small. Compressed in a bubble. Another large bubble around it filled with a Blue/Yellow mix. He moved off. No point destroying the sled, either. *Something else…oh, yes, those last two bubbles over the village. Don't want them popping!* He took them with him.

At two leagues, he stopped. A solid Blue around the sled to hold him steady. Passing the stick through his bubble, he released a small Pulse of Black.

The trees blocked the flash from hurting their eyes, and a morbid curiosity took Antee. He hurriedly glowed brightly to see. The wild Cat was swelling. Frantic, not understanding, he inflated like a waterskin with too much water. Then he popped. No bang. Just a whoosh.

Their boy looked tired when he returned. He'd had a full day of being the MixMaster. But he insisted on leaving, for it would be light soon. He'd brought extra sticks, fully charged, for night flying. Three were used up, but he could recharge soon from the sun. They had to leave before they were seen.

There were many Cats awaiting their return, including Antimmerr and Teemmerr. Antee could see from the air that his three two-legged friends were beaming.

They'd known what Steef was attempting. Since he hadn't come back yesterday, they'd assumed it had been successful. Pill wasn't worried about him, and that was reassuring. But Pill hadn't told them anything, either, which was strange for Pill. When the sled came into view, it was apparent just how well the whole thing had gone. Timmerr leapt from the sled before it touched down, met by his two cubs, and the three Cats frolicked like youngsters. They stopped when Antee was finally able to climb down. Antimmerr growled, and grabbing Antee around the man's waist, neatly flung him onto Timmerr's back. The three Cats sped off, with Antee clinging too hard to wave. His staff went flying. Another male picked it up, and casually padded after them. Fresh or not, Timmerr couldn't maintain that pace for long.

Steef greeted quickly, and went to tell the ClanCat about the night's hunt. Then he and Kivverr retired to their tree.

Well, that had gone well. Their eastern friends were a pleasure to work with. And so many delightful ideas! Stipends! She'd never heard the word before, but she and Wingor and Kuumit would be making certain that everyone heard it, before long. What a concept! Charging people for the privilege of being governed! And here they'd been doing it all these cycles for free! They *should* get paid for their troubles. Enforcing it would be Kuumit's problem. The Reds would make people like it, and she would see to it that people stayed healthy enough to work. Hmmm. That meant she would have to start caring about people's health. Well, no, not caring, just interested. That was better. She could do that. When she wasn't busy deciding what the extra Dust would bring her.

The eastern Territory had been a dreary view. Everything looked old and dirty. Scruffy. And she would welcome some decent food when they got back. They'd eaten what she'd eaten, so she assumed that she'd been served their best. But their best wasn't very good. After a few days, she'd inquired about their Green Guild. Just being polite, of course. They no longer had a Green Guild! No wonder the food was so bad.

But the eastern Yellows had been busy. A casual remark about the new HornCat problem brought a surprising answer. Eight answers, really. All in separate cages in the back of the boat, along with another large cage holding food for the eight. The Yellows said these were just babies! They were huge! Her own boat crew wouldn't go near, but she spent the entire return trip back there, talking to them. She'd never considered herself a beast lover, but she might have to change that.

It would take a cycle at least, she'd been told. Maybe a little more. They had to get their full growth. Then…no more Cats.

❧   ❧   ❧

"*I need a service from the MixMaster.*"

Steef stirred. Kivverr rarely called him that. In fact, Kivverr rarely called him anything.

"What would that be?" he inquired, wiping his eyes. He'd almost gotten to sleep.

"*You are able to Heal us now…yes?*"

"Yes, I suppose so…wait, are you sick!?" he jolted upright. He assumed that, by 'us', Kivverr meant Cats.

He was right and wrong. "*No, I am not sick. There is someone else I want you to Heal.*"

Whew. "Well, sure! Who is he?" Steef knew all of Kivverr's bloodline. He couldn't remember seeing any of them ailing.

"*Not he. She. Mepprr.*"

"Oookkaayyy. I'll gladly look at her in the morning…care to tell me what's wrong with her?" Why was Kivverr concerned about a female? Not even his bloodline. Steef only vaguely remembered a 'Mepprr'.

"*She is unable to have cubs.*"

"Not a problem. We'll see if it's something…wait a beat! Cubs?! Have you been *mating!?*"

"You are now being very loud."

Steef sobered at once, "I understand. I ask pardon."

"That is better. Yes, I have mated with Mepprr, but she has not gotten heavy. Something is wrong."

So that's where he's been going. "Well, that's just the brightest thing I've ever heard! We'll fix up Mepprr, and have some little Kivverrs in our tree." Couldn't be better.

"That is the crookedest thing you have ever said. I…am Kivverr! They will be someone else." Then he added, *"And you know Mepprr would not brood them here. She will keep them in her cave until they can hunt and speak for themselves."*

"Of course…you're right…pardon again." Hmmm. "Kivverr?"

"Yes."

"You're not exactly a young Cat you know. Most of the Clan mate at four or five. You've always been a free male. Why have you waited until now?"

Kivverr didn't answer, he just rumbled. Steef knew that rumble. Kivverr didn't want to talk about it. But he hadn't rumbled loud, and this was a puzzle, sort of. So Steef reached up and scratched. The best spot, right behind the jaw-bone. "Come on, you *want* to tell me. You know you do."

"That is not fair. rrrrrrrrrrrrrrrrr You are a rrrrrrrrrrrrrrr crooked two-leg. rrrrrrrrrrrrrrr."

"Tell me, or I'll stop." Both hands now, reaching around to either side. His nose was almost pressed against Kivverr's.

"rrrrrrrrrr No rrrrrrrrrrrrrr."

"Okay," he shrugged, and started to pull his hands away.

"No one…would…mate…with me…until now."

"What!!!"

"You are getting loud again."

"Okay. Okay. Why wouldn't the females mate with you? You're Kivverr! You're the Son of a ClanCat! You're easily the biggest Cat in the Valley…" Steef was offended. This was his brother!

"All of that is true."

"That's just…crooked!"

"Do you remember when my sire brought me to you?"

"Of course."

"Do you remember why my sire brought me to you?"

"No."

"I was considered crooked then. And I spoke to you. No Cat speaks to two-legs, except the ClanCat to Healers. Or future ClanCats to young Healers. Timmerr never spoke to Anteerr."

"They thought you were crooked...because you *spoke* to me?"

"I companied you. I dwell with you. I go into the air with you. We are brothers. Crooked."

"And you're not crooked any more?"

"You are not a two-leg now."

"I'm not?" He absently glanced down, bumping his head on the great Cat's nose. Yep. Two.

"You are Steefrr. You are Clan. You are the MixMaster!......I was...RIGHT,......and THEY were crooked!......I AM KIVVERR! HORNCAT TO THE MIXMASTER!!!" That last remark was accompanied with a roar.

The blast knocked Steef over, but Seafwood caught him. She was used to Kivverr.

"I thought you wanted to be quiet?"

"Now all the females want my cubs." He curled a paw to his mouth, and calmly started licking it. *"But Mepprr will carry my cubs, or no one. She did me courtesy when the other females would not. We will see."*

"Yes...we will. Tomorrow first thing." This had suddenly become very important.

"Play me the simple song. Then scratch me again."

❉   ❉   ❉

The boat went back out immediately, with a fresh crew that Wingor trusted, carrying the eight cages. They had to be placed right away, or they'd outgrow the cages. Already, the food they'd brought was exhausted, and Vinntag could tell they'd grown, just in the journey back.

She didn't go with the boat, though she'd enjoyed the beasts' company. She had no intention of ever visiting the Valley of the Cats, ever again. She'd spent much of her youth there. Too much. When the White Guild had finally broken contact, she'd burned all of her garments, and bought new. Just couldn't get the stench out.

❉   ❉   ❉

Pop! *"Arima, someone's coming."*

"What do you mean, Pill?"

"It was a message from Paal. They work a lot of Browns, and one of them at Landing Field in GuildTown overheard a conversation. A boat crew left this morning with a flight plan to the Valley."

"Do you know who's in that boat?" Her throat was constricting. Looking up, she could see Cassa across the cove. Her Blue sister had been grooming one of her many females, but was stopped now, looking back at Arima.

"We don't know names, but apart from the boat crew, there are two Blacks, and two Yellows." Pill didn't have to mention that they were Masters.

"How did Paal know to tell you?"

"They know we work the southern Territories. They've always known you were here. That's not a secret. They just don't know why."

Cassa had stood, and was walking towards her.

"I assume you've told Mokam and Antee?"

"Yes. They are already on their way back. Mokam can be here later today. Antee can't get back before tomorrow morning."

"Well, that boat can't get here before day after tomorrow. We have some time. Where is Steef?"

"He's busy with Kivverr. We'll tell him when they're through."

✻ ✻ ✻

"Mepprr, you're gonna have to hold still!" Steef had met Kivverr and Mepprr near their old hilltop. Kivverr had spent most of yesterday walking here with his female, and Steef had flown in this morning. No one would see them here. The sled was behind the hill, under its own bubble.

"I do not want a two-leg touching me!" And she snapped at his arm to prove it. He let her catch his arm. The jaws closed just enough to show that she now owned that arm. She did him no hurt.

"Then I won't touch you any more. I'm not gonna do anything you don't want. I'll see you back at the cove." Pulling on his arm until she let go, he put his stick back in its sling.

Kivverr had his jaws on the back of her neck, ready to hold her still. When he saw Steef let go, he did so as well. If she didn't want his cubs, he wouldn't have cubs.

The two of them turned away, and would have boarded the sled, but Mepprr roared. They stopped. Waited.

She started pacing. Well, almost a pace. More like an aggravated sway. They remained unmoving. Finally she sat, and remained motionless. Steef walked around to her hindquarters. Making a show of taking things slowly while she watched, he Pulsed into the back half of her body. Once. Twice. Three times.

"Well, your eggs are Okay. I think your tubes are blocked. Are you having any pain?"

"*I do NOT have pain.*"

"Okay. Whatever you say. Well, after today, you're gonna 'not have pain' even less...Kivverr, you need to go down into the mine."

His brother crossed the couple of steps, laying his head on top of Steef's, "*I will stay. Mepprr is my female. I will stand with you both.*"

"Well, that's fine with me. I'm just gonna give Mepprr a little Yellow discharge that improves her female organs. Now my discharge won't mind that you're not Mepprr, so...you'll get a nice new female organ of your very own." He raised his stick.

"*I will be in the mine, if you need me.*" And Kivverr padded off. After he was out of sight, Steef put a bubble over the entire hill. No point in setting off the 'seventh' stone that was still in there.

"Pill, even without the horns, this one will put me to sleep for certain. Wake me up."

"*We'll try.*" Pop! Pop!

Pop! Pop! "*Steef! Wake up! You've got to wake up!*" They both stuck him, just a little.

"Wha...I'm Okay."

"*We know you're Okay. You've got to wake up. Don't make us sting you for true.*"

"Mmmmm...why?"

"*Arima wants you back at the cove. Right away!*"

"Okay." Dragging himself from the ground, he looked for his friends. Mepprr was standing near the edge of the mine, facing Kivverr, whose head was trying to peak out. Steef released his bubble, and Kivverr ambled over, with Mepprr nipping at him.

"*You are well?*"

"Yes, I'm Okay. I think I have to go."

"*That would be best.*"

"Oh! Yes...it would. I'll see you back home...when you're ready."

❧   ❧   ❧

Pop! *"We can't get close, Arima. There are Pools everywhere around that boat."*

"I don't think it matters, Pill. We'll find out what they want when they get here."

Steef watched his Aunt in silence. She sure was upset. Sassy looked mildly concerned, but kept giving him strange smiles.

"Arima, answer me something," Cassa said quietly.

"Hmmm? What's that Cassa?" She didn't *want* conversation.

"Why did we come here to begin with?" Every word brought more peace. She had made up her mind.

"What?" *What is she talking about?*

"*Why*...are we...*here*?" Cassa asked forcefully, pointing to the ground.

"Well...we're here to protect Steef," she said, after a beat or two.

"Protect me! From what?"

"Exactly, Arima," continued Cassa, nodding. She was getting animated. "Protect him from what?"

Arima started to speak...stopped...and then said it anyway, "From the Guilds, I suppose."

"And why did he need protecting from the Guilds?"

Steef nodded. This was all new. He wanted to hear what Aunt Arima didn't want him to hear. "What's a Guild?"

"He was so young, Cassa," she said softly, ignoring Steef's question. Her voice pleaded for her Blue sister to cease. "You know what they would have done to him."

But Cassa wasn't ceasing, "That's right! What they *would* have done to him! But Arima...what is it you think they can do to him *now*?"

And they both turned to look at their handiwork. Arima really looked. She saw a boy almost to manhood. A wide-eyed boy/man with a glad spirit and a terrible Power. No longer a defenseless baby, but could all that Power protect that spirit?

"Steef?"

"Yes Mam?"

"There are at least two Black Masters in the boat that's coming our way. Do you know enough Black to fight them?"

"Will I have to fight them, Auntie? Are they bringing challenge?" He reached for his stick.

"Not on this very beat, dear boy. But they might when they get here. You have no real training in Black. Can you defend in Black? Against a Master?" *Two Masters* she corrected herself.

"Probably not," he replied casually, until he saw the look in both women's eyes at his answer. He added, "But if they challenge, I don't have to fight them with Black."

"But Shortstick…it's Black that kills. If they challenge in Bl…"

"Any Color can kill, Sassy. I've killed Cats twice with Blue." *And besides, I don't think they'll be getting past my bubbles.* "I've never met a Black. This should be interesting."

"I wouldn't call an angry meeting with a Black Master…interesting, Short-stick." He was calmly discussing Master Blacks as if they were another one of his puzzles! *That's what they are…to him! What have we done?*

"Sure it is, Sassy. It might not be pleasant, but it *will* be interesting." He didn't add that he thought the Blacks would be experiencing the unpleasant part. That wouldn't be polite.

Arima's fear hadn't ebbed a beat. *Evil always finds a way to hurt, Son. That's what evil does.*

❧   ❧   ❧

Pop! *"They're going around, Arima."*

They were all here now. All were getting reports, including Steef.

"The boat stopped at the very northern tip of the Valley. They went down almost to ground level. We can't get close enough to see what they're doing, but they didn't stay long. Now they're moving south, but they aren't coming into the Valley. They're following the eastern ridgeline."

The four Masters looked at each other with collective shrugs. Very strange.

Steef was listening to Pill, but he was watching for Kivverr. He wanted to know how everything went, knowing that he couldn't ask. And he was working on a new project now. All this ruckus over a boat. He'd suggested that he just go out and ask them what they were doing, but that idea hadn't lasted long. Four heads shook as one.

It took two days for the strange visit to end. The boat made its way around the entire perimeter of the Valley, and then…just floated away, leaving them with nothing more than questions.

Cassa didn't know it, but she had kindled other questions. Questions for which Arima had no answers. After the boat had gone, Arima started searching herself for those answers.

CHAPTER 18

"Your apprentice is here, GuildMaster," Meeben informed her, his voice flat. Since she'd been back, Pool hadn't spoken to him at all, except to deliver messages. He didn't know what that meant, but it couldn't be good. He missed Peel.

"Wellll! Good! Please sssennnd her innn, Meeben!" She hadn't selected his replacement yet, mainly because she couldn't think of anyone she trusted more. She didn't trust him, either. She really didn't trust anyone. At all. He was behaving with more respect now, at least.

Her apprentice entered. The young woman was tall. Much taller than herself. Of course, she would be. She was a strong White, this one. Too strong. Of course, she would be. Vinntag had Seen that strength before. The difference was…this time she could do something about it.

"I am here as commanded, GuildMaster," said the girl. She stood straight of back, because her Mother had taught her to never ask pardon for who she was. She gave a formal bow.

She should be showing more humility thought Vinntag. *She will learn it here.* What she said was, "Come innnn, Leeeeezzzell! You mmmust be just sooo *excited* about beginning your Master's training! I am excited forrrr you!"

"Yes, GuildMaster." She didn't sound excited. She sounded sad.

Well, she would be sad a lot, with her gift came unbidden to Vinntag. She didn't like to wallow much in charitable thought. "We will become the besssst of friends, you and I! I mmmusst say, I'm looking forrrward to apprenticing someone again!"

"Yes, GuildMaster."

"I do not ssshhare your gift, child. But since no one else does right now, we'll just have to work through it…together!" Strangely, that wasn't Vinntag's doing. Empaths were extremely rare. The most recent one had died over thirty cycles ago. He had left the Guild many parches though, relating his experiences. Parches that were now in Vinntag's possesion.

"As a remembrance of this day, I have arranged a little…gift…for you child." She rose from her table, and bustled to the rack on her wall. Removing the staff she'd had prepared, she turned back to the girl.

"Tthhisss is for *you*, child! Come, take it. Your legs are younger than mine!" Haltingly, Leezel moved to her new Master. A glance at the staff being offered was all she needed, to say, "GuildMaster, that is much too fine for me." Her own staff, no toy itself, looked plain by comparison.

Vinntag held it up. It was truly beautiful, and she was loathe to give it up, despite that fact that she could never fully use it anyway. The wood had been bleached pure White. Though not tall, its carving was unequaled, she knew, by any staff…anywhere. Carved out of a solid piece of hardwood that would have originally made ten staffs, the vertical shaft went straight through a lace patterned bulb of wood. There was a hole in the bulb for its owner's hand to pass through, guiding that hand to the only place the staff could be grasped…directly onto the clearstone set in the wood. It's owner would have complete directional control of Pulses. The stone was faceted, and sparkled brilliantly. The shaft continued out the top of the bulb, ending in a stoneless point, which was again, unique. It wasn't a full staff tall. Indeed, no more than nine spans really, but there was ample wood in the bulb to compensate for its lack of height. Truly the staff of a Master!

"Nnnnonnnsensse, girl! Thisss staff has been waiting for you! I've had it rrrighttt here for twoooo cycles, just so I could present it on tthisss day!" She didn't add that it had taken more than two cycles to have it made. Especially the stone. She took the girl's hand, and placed the staff there. "Nnnowww, I inssssissst! You mmmussst use thisss staff from now on. I will accept nnnnoooo argument!"

Her apprentice bowed again, "Yes, GuildMaster. I thank you, GuildMaster."

"Have you Registered yet, child?" Vinntag held her breath.

"Yes, GuildMaster. I came of age late last cycle, and Registered privately."

"And will you be taking a Mate soon, then?"

"No, GuildMaster…"

Vinntag allowed herself to breathe again.

"…my Father wishes it. He's selected a man that he thinks is suitable, but I wish to complete my studies."

"And what does your Mother say, hmmm?"

"Mother tells me to follow my own design, GuildMaster. I will take my Mastery…before I consider anything else. It is my choice, after all," she added.

"Good! Good! Now…I have prepared some parches for you. Take these, and let's yyyouuu and I go see how much you've learned already."

❦   ❦   ❦

Steef had fretted a bit about removing those two bubbles over Sissy's village, so for the last half cycle, he had sent Pill to check on her every night, after their parents had gone to sleep. Two of the boys had tired of keeping vigil over her, she said. The third boy was starting to be nice to her. He wasn't following any more, but walking with her, and companying her while she worked. She liked him now.

He and Kivverr had traveled up and down the Valley, trying to discover what that strange boat had been doing. No amount of Pulsing could turn up anything other than the usual assortment of beasts, rocks, and plantlife. They didn't know what they might be looking for, or even if there *was* something to look for. They eventually stopped.

Besides, there were other things to do. Aunt Arima and Sassy had suddenly decided that he needed lessons again, but not Power training. People training.

He learned what a Guild was, what it wasn't, and what it was becoming. He learned about Guild etiquette. Who to bow to, who not to bow to. They told him about the new relationship between the White, Black, and Red Guilds, and that the other four Guilds were now considered 'minor' by the first three. There'd been killing, he was told, to take control of GuildTown.

"Why would someone want to control other people, Sassy?"

"I don't have an answer that makes sense, Shortstick. All I can tell you is that some people are just so miserable, they seem to be compelled to share that misery."

"Well, I'm not miserable. I don't want to tell anyone what to do."

"No, Shortstick. I'd have to say you're the least miserable person I've ever known." She stopped, pondering for a few beats. "Say, Shortstick…haven't you ever wondered about how different you are?"

"Am I different, Sassy? Different from who?"

"Well, surely you've noticed that none of us wields more than one Power?"

"Of course."

"And you can't have missed the fact that you wield far more Power than we do?"

"I don't like to talk about that, Sassy," he said quietly, looking down.

"It's all right, Shortstick. Look, I've got more Power than Antee or Mokam, now don't I?"

"You know you do, Sassy."

"Yessir, I do." In the cycles immediately after she'd taken Mastery, she'd entertained thoughts of one day becoming Blue GuildMaster. But good fortune had brought greater purpose to her life. "They know it too, Shortstick. Have they ever seemed to mind?"

"No."

"Do your parents mind that almost everyone has more Power than they do?"

"No."

"Because they like who they are. If you like who you are, then you don't ever have to ask pardon to someone because you have more Power than they do. Or less. Our Power, Shortstick...it really *is* a gift...to each of us. Only a fool would measure their life or happiness by it. Anyone who minds that you've got more Power...that's their misery, not yours."

He pondered, and she let him. Finally, he said, "Still, it would be nice sometime to meet another Clear, Sassy. Someone with as much Power as me...see what they've learned with it."

She put her hand on his arm, "That's just not ever going to happen, Shortstick," she said softly.

"Why not? There's lots of people out there. You said so."

"Yes, but there aren't any more like you, pumpkin. You're unique."

He pondered some more, screwing his face up. "Does that mean...I'm..."

Cassa put her hand over his lips. She wouldn't tolerate him saying anything bad of himself. "It means nothing, sweetie. Nothing at all. You are Steef. What you choose to make *that* mean...will not be because of your Power...or anyone else's lack of it."

These were puzzlements, and he determined to study them. Soon after his conversation with Sassy, he insisted on another trip to Antee's. It would be nice to visit his family, and he would, but he also wanted to study the people. Somehow, his Red Sight should help.

After they'd arrived, Sissy wanted him to meet her new friend. His name was Cirlok. He was really nice. Bubba would like him.

Cirlok was hard to find.

He'd heard that Malem's brother was coming, and decided that those chores he'd been putting off looked more urgent than ever. Steef finally sent out a White Pulse to locate him.

What struck Steef about the boy was how his Core had changed. At their first meeting, this boy had a dark Core, almost black. Now it was nearly white, especially when Cirlok looked at Sissy. It would get a distinct blue hue to it, however, when he looked at Steef. Then Steef saw that the boy's face was white as well, and his hands were shaking. That wouldn't do. Sissy liked him now.

Steef bowed to him, saying, "Bright day to you Cirlok. Malem tells me good things about you. I'm pleased that you two are now friends."

"Uh...uh...uh..."

"Cirlok!" Malem poked a finger into his ribs, "What's the matter with you? You can't *stop* talking when we're working! Give greets to Bubba!"

"Br...br...bright...day...Healer," was all the stricken lad could get out.

Malem poked him again, then took his arm, "He really can talk, Bubba! For true. Guess he'll have to prove it later, after he gets used to you." She smiled up at her friend.

And Steef couldn't help noticing Sissy's Core when she looked at Cirlok. Blazing white. She was only eleven, but she'd decided. He wondered if Cirlok knew that his future had been decided for him. Probably not. Well, that was Sissy's choice to make, not Steef's. As long as this boy was good to her, he'd live.

He mentioned as much to Auntie after they'd gotten back to the Valley. The trip had been educational, if not completely informative. He'd gotten to See Cores everywhere, as they had made another round of Healing while they were there.

"You know Steef, you can't just decide to kill someone. That's not your choice to make."

"Why not, Auntie? Isn't that what Black is for?"

"That's what Black does, Son, but it's not what *you* are for. Having a weapon doesn't mean you have the right to use it."

"Well, I wasn't going to kill him anyway...unless he hurt Sissy. Then it would be challenge."

More Cat influence she sighed. "I'd like to think that even then...you would look for...some other way to deal with him. Something creative. You're good at that. But not killing."

Privately, Steef thought he'd been pretty creative the last time, but she didn't know that. What he said was, "Okay."

❦   ❦   ❦

The 'minor' Guilds didn't much like the idea of stipends, and said so. Often. Loudly. Publicly. And it became apparent that there was a flaw in Master Law. Other Masters. Blue Masters, Green Masters, etc. Master Law hadn't made any distinctions. So, over a Quarter or so, the GuildMasters of those four Guilds were encouraged to step down from their posts. They were already inclined to do so, anyway. In spite of a constant barrage of Red, they had become disgusted with themselves, and that stupid Master Law.

They were replaced. All four of the new GuildMasters were young. Much too young for their new responsibilities. The Guilds weren't happy about that, either, but each GuildMaster was companied constantly with a Black, and often a Red.

Particular turbulence occurred in Brown Guild. After the new GuildMaster took office, it was 'discovered' that most Master Miners had their own private Dustpiles hidden away. That wouldn't do. Those Dustpiles belonged in the Vault, where they would be 'safe'. Visits were made to each Master's hut, and the mines they worked. Visits by teams of Black and Red. The Dustpiles were always found, though the encounters usually left the Miners unable to function any longer as Miners. The quality and quantity of Mined Dust and stones dropped after that, but the Dustpiles in question were now 'safe'.

They were thorough, too. It occurred to someone else that there were several retired Miners. They probably had their own unsafe Dustpiles. Again, the new Brown GuildMaster was happy to furnish a list of names, and all of the old Miners also received visits. All but one. One was missing.

❦   ❦   ❦

"Are we agreed, then?" asked Arima.

"I don't have any problem with according Brown, Arima," replied Mokam, "but I don't know if it would be right to include Green."

"I understand, Mokam. But he's continued Seafer's work with the saplings. And you've seen the cave." They all nodded.

Seafer's old cave remained just as it had been the day he died. Nothing had been moved. In fact, every artifact in there had been sealed with Clear bubbles, and no one knew how long it would take for those things to decay, if ever.

But entering the cave carelessly could make you swoon. Once a person's eyes adjusted, they found themselves suspended over a cavern. The stone floor of the cave seemed to…float…on nothing. The cavern around it extended below, behind, and to the sides of what once was the original cave, limited only by the protuding walls of the adjacent caves some twelve staffs on either side. There were Crystals set in the walls, glowing either White for illumination, or Green for growth, for there were growing things in Seafer's cave. At least one of every growing thing found in the Valley.

That wasn't odd, in itself. What was different was what they were growing *in*. There was no soil at all. Every plant, tree, or blade of grass was anchored to stone. The roots were set in the stone, which also glowed Green wherever growth was needed. All plantlife was thriving. A waterspill had been diverted from above the cove, emerging at the top back wall, and the spray it made when it hit bottom kept everything moist.

The cavern extended some fifty staffs deep into the cliff. Strolling through the open space was easy, as paths of stepstones meandered all around, suspended in midair. Since most of the stone walls were covered in something Green or green, sound was muted. No echoes. There was one large, flat, stone suspended in the center, on which Arima liked to recline. Eyes closed to slits, she would lie there for long spells, the Crystals twinkling at her.

"I don't know much about Green," added Cassa, "But I'd wager all the Dust I've ever seen that the entire Green Guild together…can't make one single blade of grass grow out of solid rock."

Chin in hand, Mokam nodded agreement.

"Until Seafer's death," Arima marveled that it no longer caused her pain to say that, "Steef spent more time with him than all of us together." She turned to the Yellow Master, newly arrived that day, "Antee?"

"Yellow accord given, Arima, if for no other reason than seeing the Healing of a Cat. Truth is, the only thing left for him to learn will be by experience, not training."

"Blue?"

"It was my idea, Healer," answered Cassa amicably. As the elder Master present, it was Arima's place to bestow the accords.

"Blue accord, then. White accord is given, as well." Somewhere there was a man with a new leg. "Is there doubt in anyone's mind that, given time, he will himself eventually Master Red and Black?…no?…I think so, too."

"That's it, then. After lastmeal?" She got three nods.

✤   ✤   ✤

Another puzzle. No one was speaking much at lastmeal. Their Cores were all right. Better than all right. He could See four hot-white Cores, with no apparent reason. And they were dressed oddly, too. All of them had on trous and tunics that looked as if they'd never been worn. Strange badges. Instead of simple Tens, with a Master's mark, these badges had other marks with them. He'd been taught recently to recognize them. Uncle Antee's badge said he was a Herdsman, Breeder, BeastHealer. Aunt Arima's showed Healer and Grader. Uncle Mokam's showed Lifting, Mining, and Cutting. Sassy had Steerman, Controller, and HeavyWater. An absent thought occurred to him that they'd each taught him all of those things. All but Sassy bore an additional mark of Trainer.

They ate carefully, mindful of getting their tunics stained.

When the meal was done, he began to clear the bowls.

"Steef, leave off on the chores for a beat, please," Auntie said.

"Yes Mam."

"Come with us, Son."

"Yes Mam." Why was Sassy grinning? In fact, everyone looked…odd.

He followed them until they stood under Seafwood's outermost branches. Once there, they formed a line, facing him. Kivverr rested his chin on Steef's shoulder, watching from behind.

"They are behaving oddly."

Steef nodded.

"Steef," began Arima. It was her place to go first. "You have been found to meet the accords of White Mastery. You have displayed the Power of Master, a Master's use of Power, and the mindfulness of its gift. You are hereafter recognized as Master of White." With that, she bowed low, glowing her stone and herself in homage to his station.

He started to reply, but Uncle Mokam beat him to it. "Steef. You have been found to meet the accords of Brown Mastery. You have displayed the Power of Master, a Master's use of Power, and the mindfulness of its gift. You are hereafter recognized as Master of Brown." He added his bow and his glow, to Arima's.

Steef's mouth was already open, but Antee was still too quick for him, "Steef. You have been found to meet the accords of Yellow Mastery. You have displayed the Power of Master, a Master's use of Power, and the mindfulness of its gift. You are hereafter recognized as Master of Yellow."

He finally got it, and closed his mouth. Good thing too. "Steef. You have been found to meet the accords of Blue Mastery. You have displayed the Power of Master, a Master's use of Power, and the mindfulness of its gift. You are hereafter recognized as Master of Blue."

So now he could...all four of them, still glowing, said, "Steef. You have been found to meet the accords of Green Mastery. You have displayed the Power of Master, a Master's use of Power, and the mindfulness of its gift. You are hereafter recognized as Master of Green."

And there was nothing for him to say. Bowing to each of them, glowing their respective Colors at each bow, he finally set his stick in the dirt...Uncle Seafer's dirt...and set it to glowing Green.

They bowed again and, as one, intoned, "May you always have bright days...Master Clear."

"I like this. I think we should do this every day."

❧   ❧   ❧

"You do realize...that this has no official sanction by the Guilds?"

"That's Okay, Auntie. I'm not sure I care much for these Guilds you all talk about, anyway."

Neither do we, Son. "Your Sas...Cassa...has made something for you."

She was coming back from her cave, still grinning, with a tunic in her hands. One of her own, by its look, since new supplies from Town had all but ceased. Stopping before him, she held it up. Her own Blue badge had been removed. In its place was sewn an empty circle. No Color. Around that circle were the marks he'd seen on all of their badges. Master's marks. Healer's mark. Grader, etc. Everything but Trainer. There was no number.

"No number, Sassy?" he asked without thinking.

"I'll gladly sew on a number for you, Master Clear. Just tell me what number that might be." She smiled sweetly, as if to say 'I'm waiting'.

"You're not really gonna call me that now, are you?"

"Why not? It is what you are." Kivverr responded.

"Why not?" Cassa asked at the same beat, "It's what you are." She continued her grin.

"I like 'Shortstick' better," he mumbled, regretting that he'd brought up numbers.

"Master Shortstick it is, then." She knuckled him in the shoulder.

"I thank you, Master Blue, for the gift," he said, taking the tunic. "And for once, I can return the gift."

Her grin faded, and three other heads turned. A gift from Steef could be, well...hazardous.

He chose not to notice their demeanor, or the shift in their Cores. Holding up a finger, he rose, and left for his tree. When he returned, he had a bundle under his arm. Something wrapped in an old rag. Looking at them all in turn, he laughed, "I oath you, there's nothing to fear." Laying the bundle on the table, he unwrapped it, revealing four small sticks. They were Seafwood spirals, but unlike any they'd seen before. Each stick was little more than one span, and each stick had two Crystals. One Crystal in the center, and one at the wide end.

Antee was first to look closer. The others kept their distance.

"They're not charged, if that's what you're worried about," Steef said seriously, "I won't make *that* mistake twice." He picked up one of the sticks.

"Since the tunic was from you, Sassy, you can go first."

Cassa's breath caught in her throat. "Shortstick...I..."

Before she could say anything else, he had grasped her hand, slapping the stick into it. Nothing happened. "This is specifically tuned to you, Sassy. No one else can use it. Charge it up!"

Her face blank with apprehension, she said, "All...all right."

After a beat of nothing exploding, Steef said, "Now...glow it!" His eyes were shining.

The top Crystal glowed...Brown!

Four mouths fell open. Steef grinned. Kivverr roared.

"How...?"

"The middle stone there," he pointed, "That's a Crystal from our mine." He meant his and Kivverr's. "It's laced with that odd stone that gives off the seventh primary. I don't know how long it will last, but it hasn't gone down in two cycles. Anyway, I set it to convert your Power to Brown...you *do* know what that means, right?"

Her tears had already started. She knew. In a whisper, she said, "I can fly by myself."

Steef thought that maybe she could use a beat or two of privacy, so he picked up the second stick, "I have you to thank for this, Uncle Mokam."

"Why...why...why..."

"You gave me the idea to store the 'seventh', instead of catching it. I worked *sooo hard*...to catch something...that was already caught!" Steef gave his second laugh, handing the stick to his Uncle. It instantly flared Blue. "Guess we're gonna need a second boat, Uncle!" Mokam just looked at him, and nodded.

"Uncle Antee…"

"I thank you Son, but I'm too old to learn to fly," he said as Steef handed him the third stick.

"Yessir…you are. So that stick won't fly you anywhere."

Puzzled, Antee glowed it. White!

"Now you can Heal anything, Uncle."

It took Antee several beats to say, "I don't know what to say, Son."

"I know the feeling, Uncle. Now, the best comes last!" he exclaimed, picking up the fourth stick.

"I am perfectly happy with the gifts I have, thank you," said Arima stuffily.

"I thought you might be, Auntie," replied the Master Clear, "So your stick does nothing…that you will find useful. Will you try it for me? Please?"

Everyone was waiting, of course. Watching. Marveling at their own gift. Arima's bony fingers wrapped around the slender shaft. They waited some more. Finally, it glowed…Green.

"I can show you how to use it, if you like," Steef said gently.

❦   ❦   ❦

Leezel didn't care much for GuildMaster Vinntag's tutelage. Either the GuildMaster had forgotten much of her Healing from disuse, or the old woman had never known much to begin with. She supposed that Vinntag's authority came from her Grader's Sight, and her Power.

She learned more from Ormis, though he wasn't a Master. She spent a lot of beats with him, learning how to Heal difficult maladies. A few of the other Masters at GuildHall were also helpful. Since GuildMaster Vinntag only spent a few beats each day with her, she had plenty of extra beats to study elsewhere. And, as apprentice to the GuildMaster, she enjoyed complete access. The parches that Vinntag had given were *some* help, too. Cribbus, the old Empath that had preceded her, had left a record of many of his thoughts, though the parches seemed sporadic, as if some of them were missing. Must have been lost.

Trouble was, there were few people to Heal, and no one that came in needed her special gift. White Guild had raised its rates to the point that only the wealthy, or someone near death, would trade that much Dust for White services. Leezel would spend days listening to the Masters describe ailments, and the tunes needed for their Healing. But listening was all she could do. She needed to be with ailing, desperate people.

She tried wandering through Town, looking for people in need of White, but Pool would spot her and report it to Vinntag. That led to a few tongue lashings. She didn't carry Buzzbies herself…yet…but they were all over Town, and unavoidable

And so, ironically, she found herself sneaking, at night, to the one place where Buzzbies never went. She would go to Nert Hollow.

"Steef, you will be eighteen soon," mused Arima. She was trying to keep her voice calm. Her best defense against anxiety was to watch his face. Even when he rested, the face was working. *How can a face do two things at once* she asked herself for the hundredth…no thousandth, time. He could have a serene smile with faraway eyes, that said he was completely content, while at the same time, the muscles around those eyes would twitch, telling anyone who was listening that the Master Clear was working on another puzzle.

"Yes Mam," he replied, tiredly. These last few days had been busy. He and Uncle Mokam had taken turns giving Cassa Lifting lessons. Then they'd turn around, and he and Cassa would give Uncle Mokam Steering lessons. Then he'd help Auntie give Uncle Antee Healing lessons. And quietly, in the evening, when everyone else had gone to their caves, he would show Auntie how to use her Green.

"Well, I'm puzzled. There's something you have never asked about." *And you should have asked by now.*

"What's that, Auntie?"

"Girls." Arima had chosen her timing carefully. Antee and Mokam were with their Cats. Only she and Cassa were here. Cassa was watching and listening intently.

"What about girls, Auntie?"

"I think that would be *my* question to *you*, young man. What about girls? You never ask any of us about…well…girls."

The face puckered, pondering, "I don't understand, Auntie. You've already taught me, since I was small, what the differences are. Is there something about girls that I don't already know?"

Arima and Cassa both looked at each other, for a large beat trying to hold back, but it was just too tasty. Together, they both burst out laughing. Steef waited, perplexed.

"What Arima means, Shortstick," said Cassa, wiping her eyes, "Is how come you've never asked about meeting girls...for yourself."

"Oh, that," he responded.

"Yes," said Arima forcefully, "That. Aren't you at least...interested?"

And the face went off. To Arima and Cassa, it looked to be a discharge of conflicting thoughts, all crowding one wheat-topped head. Struggling for an answer, all he could find was, "I guess so...eventually."

She loved to watch that face, but...*this isn't going well.* "Let me explain why I'm bringing it up. You're almost eighteen. Sometime after your eighteenth birthday, and before your nineteenth, you have to Register for a Mate. You don't have to take a Mate, but if you go to the public Registry, during the upcoming planting festival, all of the girls...and boys, for that matter...your age will be there. It's the best time for you to see what young ladies are available, and they can see you, too. Also, unMated ladies from recent past cycles will often come."

"But I don't want a Mate right now, Auntie. I'm perfectly happy here in the Valley."

Another look passed between Cassa and Arima, before the Healing Master continued, "You're always perfectly happy, and I don't want to change that. But you may want a Mate in the future, and Registering now is the best way to ensure finding a girl you will like." There had been several discussions between the four Masters about this recently, and Arima had been pleased that Cassa agreed with her. Arima was determined that Steef would at least have the opportunity for a Mate, regardless of the risk. The time spent after Seafer's death had been filled with a lot of 'I wish'. She would *not* have that for Steef. She added, "If you don't Register, you will never be allowed to Mate with a Power. You would have to look amongst the Powerless girls for a Mate."

Steef could see that they were serious. He didn't mind, really. If they wanted him to Register, he'd Register. "Okay," he said casually, with a shrug.

"Does this mean more MixMasters?"

Steef shook his head lightly to his brother, "Not any time soon."

Arima watched the interchange between two-leg and Cat. In spite of her resolve, she was loathe to utter what she felt must be a pronouncement of doom. No avoiding it. Deep breath. "The largest Registry, and widest variety of people to meet," she said, her throat closing up, "Is in GuildTown. I think we need to prepare."

"Okay."

CHAPTER 19

Arima was about as nervous as she would ever be. Nine more days until they left for GuildTown. They had arranged to stay with Cassa's family. Cassa had sent Pill to her Mother, who was delighted to hear from her. She told them she would explain when they arrived, and yes, they could meet her Mate. No, she didn't need any Dust, in fact she would bring them some. That offer was well received. It seemed Cassa's family didn't enjoy the position they once had, causing her some concern.

All four Masters were going, against Arima's objections. Once the idea had come to her for Steef to Register, she had given no thought to anyone companying him except herself. She'd had to convince them of the need for him to go, then she couldn't talk them out of going themselves. Mokam even expressed an interest in seeing his own family, something he hadn't discussed in cycles. Antee said that he would not be left out. He was already in the Valley, ready to depart.

Strangely, the most difficult discussions were with Steef. He didn't want to wear a Five on his tunic.

"It's not true," was his concern.

"If you wear anything higher, someone is going to ask why you aren't listed at the White Guild," explained Arima, fighting her own nerves for patience. She hadn't expected this. "And to be fair, we really wouldn't know what number to use, now would we?" She'd long suspected that he knew, or at least had an idea, what number would fit. She also knew that he'd never say.

"I don't mind listing myself at the White Guild," he shrugged.

"We could do that," she went on, "As long as you don't mind a couple of cycles of explaining everything about yourself. You know it won't stop at

White. Ultimately, you'd have to explain to every Guild." *And somewhere in there, someone would give challenge, and then people would start dying.* She didn't know whether to laugh or cry. Now she was actually concerning herself for the safety of the Guilds! They would be the ones doing the dying.

They'd explained to him about duels. Simple, really. Two people would grasp each other by their forearms, and push charge into the other, until one of them quit, or passed out. Or died. Or dueling by staff, where the overcharge could be aimed, and thus end the duel faster still. He hadn't much liked the idea. Arima and Cassa had even shown him, to a point, with his drained hand on their clasped arms. He refused to try it himself, much to their relief and disappointment.

Then they'd explained that anyone could challenge for a duel with any number equal to or higher than their own. If he wore a Ten, some Master would get curious, then dead.

She continued, "We're not going to GuildTown to reveal your gifts to the world, we're going to see if there's a girl that might interest you." And she'd struggled with the fact, sad as it was, that wearing a Five meant that some girls wouldn't give him a glance. She reminded herself often that any girl that cared what number he wore wasn't fit company for him anyway.

"Okay. But it's still not true," he said with resignation. It was the strongest argument she could remember ever hearing from him. Wearing that Five also meant that Steef would be doing a lot of bowing to every Six and higher. It struck her that, though he knew that now, he didn't mind. He would be humbling himself to people whose Power didn't earn them the right to carry his staff, and his only concern was the falsehood! *We've raised him too well* she thought. *Or Kivverr has.*

They were timing their arrival to give Steef one full day before the public Registry, so he could meet people. Well…girls. She wondered if he would even try, with all the new things for him to see. *Too much Cat.*

❀   ❀   ❀

"*Plivverr wants to speak to both of us when we wake.*"

"Okay. Did he say why?"

"*No. But he said it was important.*"

"Okay."

They found Plivverr outside of Auntie's cave at first light. She was already up. Arivverr was there, too. A circle formed.

"Some of the Clan are missing," Plivverr began.

"Missing?" replied Steef and Arima together.

"Yes. We have been setting watches at points in the Valley, to make sure the wild Cats did not return. The watches changed many days ago. We should have had returning Clan, but none have come back. I sent others to inquire, and they did not return either."

"What parts of the Valley are they missing from?" asked Arima. The timing couldn't have been worse. Three more days.

"Every part," responded Arivverr, *"It is very strange."*

"Steefrr," Plivverr continued, *"I would like for you and Kivverr to go in the air, and see if anything is wrong."*

"Of course," Steef said immediately. He was Clan, after all. "We'll leave now. Is there any direction you would like for us to check first?"

"There are more Clan missing from the far end, than the close end. There is more ground to watch there."

"Then we'll go north first." With that, he and Kivverr broke from the circle, and turned to go. Auntie took his arm.

"You two be careful out there, young man. If something is hurting Cats…well…," words failed. What could hurt a Cat?

"I understand, Auntie. We will."

They flew low and slow up the length of the Valley. Not one Cat was in sight. They wouldn't have hidden from his sled. All of the Clan knew his sled. Even sightings of food beasts were sparse. He sent out Pulses, getting nothing back. No Cats. No unusual return Pulses at all. Nearing the north end of the Valley, they spotted a few sheep, running south as fast as sheep can run.

"I think we need to take a look around."

"Something is making the fuzzy ones afraid. Let us see."

Landing in the nearest clear spot, Steef climbed atop his friend. Nothing in view. They headed up, to spots where Clan might be found if they were still standing their watch. Up, up. Eventually, it got steep enough that Kivverr had to follow a path that had been worn by other Cats. Rounding a large rock, they found their first sign of trouble. It was round enough that it almost looked like one of Steef's bubbles, until they got closer. There were bones, and fur. Orange fur. And horns. Steef slid off to inspect it.

"It's dry. It's been here a while. Do you recognize the horns?"

"No. Many horns appear the same, except for size." Kivverr sniffed at it. *"It does not smell like a Cat. It smells like…a slithertooth."*

"A snake? What kind of snake could do that?"

"*I do not know. But I want to find out.*" Some of his fur was standing up, now.

"Let's keep climbing. I'll walk." He took his stick out of its sling.

Within a short distance of the winding path, there were three more bundles. Kivverr was giving off low rumblings.

"*The smell of slithertooth is getting stronger. It is on the path.*"

"Good. Whatever is doing this, it needs to die today. Let's find it."

They didn't have to go far. Two more turns. Kivverr was roaring before Steef even saw it.

It was a snake, if anything that big can be called a snake. Its eyes were more than a staff above the ground. There was no way to determine its length. The wall of the rockface bent away from the path, and about half of the snake was coiled in the space. It had one female Cat caught in that coil, and two more lay between the coils and the rock. They lamely lifted their heads at Kivverr's roar.

Kivverr instantly lunged at the snake's head. At the same time, the snake struck out. Kivverr was used to being faster than a slithertooth, but this one matched him. As the great Cat's claws swung round, a gaping mouth closed over him, snapping down...and bouncing back. Kivverr was pulled back too, snarling and screeching.

Steef stood quietly as his brother vented inside the bubble. He was flicking through his different Sights. He'd started with Yellow, naturally, expecting to get a clue about this monster before him. But Yellow Sight yielded nothing but snake. Large snake, but not unusual. Going through the other Colors, he was further surprised at the nothing he Saw. Black Sight should have at least yielded life zones to Pulse at. The only useful information was in White. The snake had Locks. Strong ones, in all seven Colors. No wonder he hadn't picked up anything. Standard Pulses had returned nothing unusual, because the only Pulse he'd get off this beast was that of a snake. Hmmm. Some one had set this beast here deliberately, to kill Cats.

Kivverr was making so much noise, that Steef missed it at first. He caught "...assssster."

"Kivverr! Quiet down! I need to hear!" If he released the bubble to touch the Cat, he knew what would happen. "I need to hear!"

It wasn't working. That was one really mad Cat.

"Listen to me! If you get yourself swallowed by that thing...I've got to go in there after you! Then we both smell like snake for days! Hush now, and let's figure this out together!"

That helped. Pacing and growling replaced roaring and screeching.

"Are yoouuu thhhee onnnne theyyy callll thhhee mmiikkkkssssssmmaassss-terrr?" It was a low voice. Slow. As if each word was a new challenge.

Everything stopped. Steef and Kivverr both looked at the snake, then slowly back at each other.

One of his Pills crawled up to Steef's ear, *"Did that snake just speak?"*

"I think so," Steef nodded blankly.

"Are yoouuu thhhee oonnnne theyyy callll thhhee mmiikkkkssssssmmaassss-terrr?"

Man and Cat turned heads back to the snake. It had backed off a few staffs distance, remaining unmoving after bouncing its teeth off of Steef's bubble. The mouth wasn't moving, but as Steef peered closer, he could see that its tongue didn't look like anything found on a snake. Those Locks were a puzzle, too. The White one was stronger than Auntie could have produced.

"Are yoouuu thhhee onnnne theyyy callll thhhee mmiikkkkssssssmmaassss-terrr?"

"I am Steef," came the bewildered reply, "I am sometimes called MixMaster. How could you know that?" *I'm talking to a snake?*

"Mmmoosssstt prrreeyyyy hhhaassss tooo beeee sssssskkwwwweeeezzzzed-ddd sssssiillllllennnnnttt. Nnnnottttt thhhee hhhoorrrnnneddd onnnnesss. Thhhheeyyyy aaarrrre eeeagggerrr tooo ffffeeedddd mmmmeeee. Allll offff thhheemmmm mmeennnnccchuunnn thhhee mmiikkkkssssssmmaasssterr beeefffooorrre tthhheyyy diiee. III ammm gllladdd yyyooouu arrre hhheeer-rre."

"Well, thank you. I'm glad you're here, too. It saves me any more beats look-ing for you."

"III ammm sssuuurrrre mmmyyyy bbbrrroothhherrrs hhhaavvve hhhear-rrddd offf yyyooouuu. Ttthhheyyy wwwilll beee mmmaaddd thhhaaattt III gottt too eeeattt yyyooouu, buuttt III knnneewww iittt wwwoouulddd beee mmmeeee. III ammm thhhee oolldddesssst. Iittt iissss mmmyyy dessstti-innnyy!!!"

Brothers? "There are more of you here?"

"Yyyesss. III hhhavvve mmmaaannnyyy brrroothhherrrs. Buuttt III ammm thhhe oolldddesssst. Iittt iissss mmmyyy ddessstiinnnyy tttoo dddeeefffeeeattt tthhhee mmiikkkkssssssmmaasssterrr!!!"

"You said that. How many brothers?"

"Wwwhyyy dooo yyoouu assskkk?"

"Well, after I kill you, I'm going to have to find them, now aren't I?"

"Sssssssssssssssssssssssss...yyoouu ccannnottt hhurrttt mmmeee!! Tthheee Mmmaasssstterrrsss wwhooo mmmaaddde mmmeee hhhavvve prrroottteccтteddd mmmeee!! Iittt iissss mmmyy ddessstiinnnyy..."

"If I can't hurt you, there's no harm in telling me how many brothers you have."

"Trrryyy yyyoouurrr puunnyy sssstticckk oonnn mmmeee! Yyooouu wwwilll ssseee."

"Okay." Steef made a show of sending a visible Black Pulse. It bounced off of the snake's hide. Show was all the Pulse was. Steef had already Seen the strength of the Locks on the snake. He could break them, but the blast would have brought the rockface down on the female Cats, and sent them all over the edge. The drop from here looked to be over two hundred staffs. Surviving that fall would have meant some creative bubbles. He'd made other plans while he spoke. Kivverr had finally calmed some, listening to the amazing conversation.

"Sssssssssssssssss...III toolllddd yyoouu!!! Iittt iissss mmmyy..."

"So how many brothers?" Steef persisted. If he didn't get it soon, he'd finish this, and just go look for them. The Clan was at risk with every beat. And that breath! Whew.

"Yyoouu sssshhoouulddd hhhaavvve mmmoorre rrreeessssppeccctt!!! Yyyoouu wwwillll bee mmmooorrre rreessspeccttfffull!!!"

He wasn't going to get a number. It occurred to him that the snake probably couldn't count. The Cats had trouble counting, and they weren't artificial. What was worse, in its anger, the snake had drawn back for a strike. Striking was all right, but drawing back wasn't. It affected his aim. "I have great regard for snakes," he said casually, "They've been some of my tastiest meals." That should do it. He released his surprise.

The rock was hovering ten staffs above the snake, waiting for a number. Since that number wasn't coming, the stone would. Stone and speed didn't care about Locks, and this rock had a special tune. Mixed with Brown and Yellow, it just loved that snake. It was going to follow it anywhere. And it was a large rock, so it would convey a lot of love. Plummeting down, it hit the snake between its coils and the striking head. The head, now separated from its body, just kept right on going, over Steef and Kivverr. Over the edge of the path. Following an arching path to the bottom of the ridge.

Steef's and Kivverr's heads had craned back, watching the flight. The bubble over them served only to shield from the splash, much like it had done once before. Man and Cat ambled to the edge of the path, and looked down.

Pill was still in his ear, *"I'm thinking it overestimated that 'destiny' thing."*

Nod. "Pill,…"

At that beat, another Buzzbie Pop!'ed into the area. Instantly, both of Steef's Pills launched themselves from him, attacking the intruder. The new Buzzbie Pop!'ed back out again, and Steef's Pills returned, this time to each ear.

"What was that about?"

"It was a Pool. They serve only bad Masters. They should not be here."

"It wanted something, and I'm guessing it had to do with that snake. Pill, you have to warn the ClanCat."

"You know we can't talk to him."

It was almost true. Ever since Pill had become Clan, Plivverr had allowed them to contact him. He could hear *them*, but they couldn't hear *him*. They had no bones to vibrate.

"Yes you can. He just can't talk to you. Warn the others. Tell them we're going to look for more of these things."

Pop! Pop!

"No," said Kivverr.

"What, no?"

"You must hunt them without me. It is proper. You are Clan."

"You're not coming?"

"I must see to the females, and get them home safely. We can not all ride in the air."

Steef had forgotten the females. One was still caught in the now-dead coils. With the snake's death, the Locks had disappeared. A few Black slices, and she was free. She and her sisters had been squeezed breathless so much, they were barely conscious. Steef gave them as much Yellow as he could without discharging, which would still bring down the rockface. They wouldn't be moving very fast.

"You know it'll take you more than a sevenday to get them back? They can barely walk!"

"You are leaving anyway. There is time. I will be waiting for you when you return with your new female."

"You'll need to stay in the flatlands…away from the rocks. You can't stand against one of these things."

"I will not step back, and leave the females."

"Kivverr…," Steef's voice wavered, "You can't…you just can't stand against one of…"

"Then perhaps you should find them first."

No chance of talking him out of it. He wouldn't run from one, if it showed up. He'd die, and then the females would be taken anyway. Stubborn Cat. Steef was supposed to leave in less than three days, and he didn't even know how many of these things were out there! There was no time for a ritual meal of snake. Not even time for proper parting greets. Stroking his brother quickly on the neck, Steef began sprinting down the path towards his sled.

Pop! *"Vinntag, one of your little pets isn't eating Cats any more."*

"Wait a few beats, Pool. I'm almost done. Now children, you have the Guild's fee?"

The pair were both from good families, meaning that at least one of their own parents was in the Alliance. It showed in the quality of their clothes, and the size of the Dustpouch they set on Vinntag's table. She smiled, and held out her arms. The young Mother placed her baby in the Grader's hands. Vinntag opened the cloth, and gazed at another fresh face. Ignoring the small smile, she concentrated on the Power she Saw. Brown Five, at best.

"A strong Eight," she said, glancing again at their payment, "Great regrets, children, but I have to tell you, your sweet baby is a Brown." Their faces fell, as she knew they would. There was no way around the Color. "But at least she's a strong Brown. With your connections, she'll have a bright future."

That's what they'd paid to hear. Now that it was official, they could make plans. Brown Guild would have to make a place for their daughter. Bowing, they left.

"Now Pool, what is this nonsense you're spouting?"

"One of your Cat eaters is dead."

"How!?" From all she'd heard, those things had gotten huge. Nothing natural would be killing one, and the Locks they carried would keep any Power she knew of away from them, too.

"Looked like a rock fell on it. A big rock. Split that snake in half. At least only half of it was left. The head was missing."

"Missing? Where…?"

"We didn't have time to look around. There was a man there, and another Cat. When we arrived, Pill drove us off."

"A man? Who? Pill? What was Pill…whoever that man was, he must have been a Master."

"We didn't have time to see who it was, but you're right, it must have been a Master if Pill was with him. And if he had anything to do with that rock, then he must have been a Brown."

"Can you inquire from Pill who it was?"

"We can. We did. Pill isn't saying."

"Can you make them?"

"No. We could attack their hive, but even if we defeated them, there is no surety that they would talk. Do you really want to start something like that over one mystery man? That rock could have just fallen, you know."

Maybe, but Vinntag didn't believe in coincidence. And she didn't like the idea of any Masters being in the Valley. She didn't want anything left alive in that accursed Valley. At all. That's what the snakes were for. Now there was one less. Pool had been reporting regularly that Cats were finally getting eaten. That part had worked. This was less good. Curse Wingor for making her stop watching that witch Arima. Well, it was time to see if she was still there.

"Pool, I want you to check on the rest of the snakes, right away. And I want you to take a look at that cove where Arima was. See if she's still there."

"Pill will be expecting us."

"I no longer care what Pill knows, or what Arima knows, either. Also, tell Kuumit and Wingor that we need to talk. Right away."

Pop!

❦   ❦   ❦

Arima wasn't nervous any more, and she wasn't dreading their upcoming departure, either. She was furious, and she *wanted* to leave for Guild-Town…right now. Pill had reported what Steef and Kivverr had found. Steef had seen Locks on the snake. It had been put there. Deliberately. To kill Cats.

Vinntag.

There had been a small, little voice inside her head, all of her adult life. Someday, she was going to have to kill that woman. But Arima was a Healer. She'd spent her life bringing health and relief to people, and sharing her skills with other Healers. Enjoying the secret of the majesty that was the HornCats. All constructive things, and things that she could have shared with Vinntag. They had the same skills. They both had Sight. At one time, they had both had the Cats. They could have been sisters.

Instead, they were enemies, by Vinntag's choice. All because Arima had bested her in those stupid duels. Well…she had to admit, it was more than that. Had Vinntag proven more Powerful, they would still be enemies. The woman was just evil, and Arima's superior Power had been a fuel for that fire, but not the spark.

Now, that Power was going to kill, rather than Heal. Arima had no doubt that she could deal her foe a deadly overcharge. During all those duels, Vinntag had always succumbed before Arima had ever reached full charge. Arima had never felt any urge to share that information with anyone. Certainly, Vinntag had never known. But she would find out soon.

Not soon enough. The others shared her fury, but had to remind her that there was another priority. Apparently, there were more of these awful, giant snakes. Since Cats were missing from every part of the Valley, that was likely. They had to deal with the snakes before they did anything else. Steef was going to hunt the north end, and move south. Antee and Mokam would go south now, which was foolish.

She couldn't talk them out of it, "Are you *crooked?*" she screamed, "You heard Pill's report! Steef said those Locks were so strong, even *he* couldn't break them without a discharge! What can you accomplish…besides becoming snake food?"

But Antee was resolute. "I'm going to find them…and my Brown brother here is going to throw rocks at them. It worked for Steef. It'll work for us." Mokam just nodded. His jaw was set grimly.

Plivverr was no help. *"It is proper, Arimarr. They are Clan. They are meeting the challenge, as Clan should. Timmerr will carry Anteerr. I will carry Mokamrr. We will stand together."*

"Besides, Arima," continued Antee, who was touching Timmerr, not Plivverr, "We're Clan now. Maybe we didn't know everything that meant when we joined, but we do now. There've been times in my life when I didn't stand…and should have. That won't happen again." Mokam nodded again. Hefting their staffs, both men stepped onto bent Cat knees, and mounted their friends. They departed at a fair pace, Antee's staff already sending out Pulses.

That left Arima and Cassa together in the cove, with nothing to do but listen to reports from Pill. There were plenty of Pills. The air was full of them. Cassa asked why.

"Pool will come. We're sure. They are pressuring us everywhere to tell them who Steef is. They will come to the Valley to look for themselves. Eventually, they will come here. Steef can take care of himself."

Cassa nodded, listening. It took her a few beats.

"Wait! Pill! What do you mean 'take care of himself'? Would Pool actually try to *hurt* us?" As a second thought, she continued, "*Could* they hurt us?"

"*Yes. And yes. They are an ill-tempered family, and they have been serving ill-tempered Masters for many cycles. They have no honor. And yes, if enough of them sting you, you will die.*"

Cassa was shocked. It had never occurred to her to be afraid of a Buzzbie. Aggravated, yes. Afraid, no. "Uh...thank you, Pill."

"*You are welcome, Cassarr. We are Pillrr. We stand too.*"

Arima had turned her attention from the departing backs to Cassa's conversation. She nodded once, and walked off to her cave. When she returned, she was carrying two staffs, one in each hand. The ornate one that she used daily, and her old one. It had been in one of her trunks for cycles. She handed it to Cassa.

"You might need this," she said, her brows bunched fiercely, "I don't know what we can do...a White and a Blue...but we will *all* stand."

Cassa agreed with the 'stand' part, and she was glad to have a staff in her hand. But she was a bit more confident than her Healing sister. She had learned from Steef that Blue was useful for more than weather and Steering. It could also be a weapon, and she was in the mood.

❦   ❦   ❦

A second snake dead. This one hadn't been helpful either. Apparently, whoever had bred these monsters, had reached a limit in how much intelligence they could produce. Neither snake had shown any limits to vanity or pride, but those were a poor defense against falling rocks.

Pop! "*Antee is getting a Pulse on one of them. They are going after it. They can't travel as fast as you, though.*"

"Remind them that these things are really fast, and they don't have bubbles to protect them."

"*We will. You should know that we are expecting a visit from Pool soon. All the Buzzbie families are stirred up. Paal and Peel are asking us what's going on. How much can we tell them?*"

"Do you trust them, Pill?'

"*Well, they aren't Clan, but they're good families.*"

"Aunt Arima still doesn't want them to know about me. If we still go to GuildTown, that might be best. Just tell them there's a ruckus in the Valley, and you'll fill them in when it's over."

"Okay." Pop!

"Pill, are there any other families I should know about?"

His two 'regulars' were still with him, as were seven or eight others riding his shoulders. *"Only the Pulls. Their hive is in the very north of the Territories. They are considered a main family line, but their hive isn't as big as the other four. There are also some minor hives, but all of them are related to one of the five main families."*

"Will the Pulls fight with Pool, or with us?

"Probably neither. They don't like Pools much, but they don't like us either. In fact, they don't like people much, either. Very few of them ride Masters at all."

He was getting a return Pulse on a third snake. The sled turned east.

☙   ☙   ☙

"How close, Antee?"

Antee's eyes were closed, concentrating. Both hands on his staff.

Pop! *"Mokam, Steef says the snakes are very fast. He says if you can't get your rocks to follow them, you might not be able to hit them. And the Cats can't outrun them."*

"Thank you, Pill," replied the Brown. He'd already been thinking about that. Only Steef could mix a Pulse, so there was no way to get Antee's Yellow into a rock. He had another idea, one that didn't involve rock-throwing

"Less than a league away, Mokam," came Antee's answer, "Up yonder in the trees."

"Well, I have an idea," said Mokam. He quickly outlined what he hoped would work.

Antee and Timmerr didn't like it, but there weren't any other ideas that sounded better.

"Your Majesty," continued Mokam, getting formal, "I will need you here with me. Will my charge do you any harm?"

"I do not know, Mokamrr. It does not matter," was Plivverr's resolute response, *"I am ClanCat. I am Plivverr. I will stand."*

"Very well. This is as good a spot as any. Nice clear ground, and the bedrock's not too deep. I need to prepare." Throwing his leg over, he slid off the Cat's back. "Antee, you two need to leave. I am giving discharge warning."

"Very well, Mokam, but we aren't going far."

"If this doesn't work, you might want to have a lead on outrunning that thing."

"We aren't running anywhere." And with that, Timmerr turned and they started back the way they'd come, leaving Mokam and Plivverr to the snake.

The Brown and ClanCat were in an open space of roughly a quarter league in any direction. Good visibility. Mokam sank his staff, and started Pulsing, preparing the ground. "If you would, your Majesty, you might want to let him know that his midmeal is here."

Plivverr stepped away from his comrade, and began roaring with full air. He continued for some time, so they didn't actually hear the snake approach, but they were both watching, and eventually saw the huge head appear in the shadows of the trees. It stopped, and watched warily.

Mokam was ready, "Majesty, you'll need to stand here with me, please. It's the safest place during the discharge." The great Cat came back, and pressed his shoulder. Mokam took a beat to be flattered.

"It does not appear to want us."

"If what Steef has been saying is true, his own ego will drive him here. Give him one more challenge."

"I am Plivverr!" roared the King of the HornCats, *"This is MY Valley! Come out and die with no Rest!"*

Slowly, something pushed that big head out of the trees. The body just kept on coming, what seemed like forever. *Merciful Creator! That's a big snake!* thought Mokam. When the last tip of snake was out of the trees, Plivverr roared again, as a loud hiss escaped the snake. With no further warning, the snake began slithering across the open ground at a speed that Mokam wouldn't have believed possible. *Good thing I prepared first* came unbidden to him. He was fully charged, staff in ground, companion standing unmoving beside him. Death was racing towards them, and Mokam waited, waited…now.

Ka-Wump! CRACK!

With one final drawing of Power, his discharge released, and the ground opened in front of them. A crack in the bedrock, splitting so fast, even the snake couldn't avoid it. Its own speed and stupidity carried it right into the open fissure.

Meanwhile, just in case, Mokam began recharging. The ground stopped cracking just before reaching their feet, with man and Cat watching a writhing body plunge down, down, and…catch itself between the narrowing rock walls before it could disappear into blackness. They watched as it got its balance, and began a torturous climb back up, stretched between the two stone faces. Again, the snake was approaching them, although with far less speed. Up it came, until the head reappeared just above ground level.

Unfortunately for the snake, the crack was at its widest here, and balance was difficult. It was moving slowly now, very slowly. For Mokam, the hurry part was over. He was charged again, but he patiently waited until the head was completely above ground.

Ka-Wump! CRACK!

The bedrock snapped closed. The snake's head was clear of danger, and remained unhurt. It was also now unattached, and flopped sloppily to the ground.

Pop! Pop! *"Antee says that it's possibly still dangerous. Sometimes they don't die all at once."*

"Thank you, Pill."

Antee and Timmerr had been watching from a safe distance. They made their way back, and victory greets had just begun, when the air exploded with Buzzbies.

🍁　　　🍁　　　🍁

Steef was getting close to number three, when many Pills Pop!'ed in, *"Pool has come! They are attacking Mokam and Antee, and Cassa and Arima!"*

"Why aren't they here, Pill?"

"We don't know for certain, but we think it's because you're between snakes."

Steef's face took on his concentrated look. He shifted his Pulse, and sure enough, there was a cloud of Buzzbies in the direction of his third target.

"Are the others in danger?"

"Not yet. We were waiting for them. We outnumber them, at least for now."

"If they send more, can you keep up?"

"We don't really know. We've never visited their hive. We don't know how big they are."

"Well, let's give them another target. If they come after me, that's less for you to worry about." More Blue, and his sail filled to almost bursting.

🍁　　　🍁　　　🍁

Arima and Cassa could only watch, in dismay and disbelief. They were in the middle of a Buzzbie fight, with Pop!'ing and stinging going too fast to keep up. Loud and angry buzzing filled the air. No attempt was made to land on them or the Cats. Once Pool discovered that Pill was giving battle, attention was turned there exclusively. So, untouched, the two women had an amazing view of a terrible, thrilling contest.

As suddenly as it started, it was over. With a loud simultaneous Pop!, Pool left, defeated. But not without cost. There were at least a hundred dead Buzzbies on the ground, and they knew that some of them had to be Pills. As they watched, the dead bodies, foe and friend alike, disappeared into Seafer's dirt.

Pop! *"They will be back. They are mad, now. They will bring most of their hive."*

Both women nodded, getting the same reports. "Pill, should we ask Peel or Paal for help? Would they come?" asked Arima. Their secrets would be out soon, anyway.

"They would come. Both of them. But they are not Clan. We are Pillrr. We have learned."

"Then Pill," said Cassa, "It's time you had some help from your Clan." And she shared with them her idea about a Blue greeting for Pool.

"We don't like that!" insisted Pill. *"We stand!"*

"You *would* be standing, Pill. As bait. That's as much stand as anyone. And we don't have the beats to argue." Cassa had made up her mind. "Arima, you've been teaching Shortstick how to Grade, yes?"

Arima nodded, her face bleak.

"And do you trust his Grading Sight?"

Again, a nod.

"Well, he says that you and I are just about equal. Do you agree?"

That's what Arima thought she was going to say. There was no other way, really. A third nod.

"Then you know…there's only one safe place for you to be?"

A fourth nod, and she was committed. She was the wrong one to be here. Antee had said once, that he wanted to view this. But with his lower Power, he wouldn't survive it. It might still kill her, but if she tried to hide in her cave, Pool would find her there, defenseless.

❦   ❦   ❦

Pop! *"Vinntag, you now have three dead snakes, and we think the number will be getting higher. And we still don't know if Arima's there."*

Vinntag was marching as fast as her small frame would carry her, on her way to their meeting hut, in bright daylight. She was too furious to care who saw them together. Besides, what was anyone going to do about it now? When

Pool delivered the first bit of news, she wanted to throw something, but all she had around her was her staff, and she couldn't throw that.

"You'd better explain yourself, Pool!" she shouted. People turned to look, but seeing her companying guard of Black Nines, they quickly turned away again.

"*Well, either three of them are dead, or we've found the missing head from the first one. Since it's on the opposite side of the Valley, we think three. And there are at least four Masters there. The first Master we saw is gone...*"

Pop! Pop!

"*Make that five Masters there. The first one just showed up at another snake. Pill was waiting for us everywhere. They outnumbered us when we arrived, and many are dead on both sides.*"

She could see that Kuumit was waiting for her. The hut was closer to his side of Town. Wingor was on his way, and would be here soon.

"I want to know who they are! I want to know *now*! And I want them *dead*!"

Kuumit was nodding agreement. This entire affair with the Cats had gotten too messy. Left up to him, they'd have left those Cats alone, but that wasn't possible any more. He confirmed Vinntag's orders to Pool. Wingor, still half-way across Town, also agreed.

"Empty the hive, if you have to, but get it done. Arima first."

Pop!

❦   ❦   ❦

Pop! "*Steef, Peel and Paal tell us that all Pools have disappeared. We think that most of their hive is coming.*"

Steef was landing. The snake was waiting for him, slithering back and forth in open field. It was a field with no large rocks in plain view. The snake had been warned.

"Will they come here, Pill?" If they did, he'd just have to fight two battles at once.

"*No way to know for sure. We think they'll go for the cove first, since they lost big there. Cassa has a surprise for them. We're sending most of our hive to cover Antee and Mokam. They're the most exposed.*"

"Just leave me my two regular friends, Pill. Send all the others to help else-where." There had been a cover of a hundred or so, lit on his sled.

"*That's what we thought you'd say.*" His cover rose up and hovered for a beat before him, then Pop!'ed away.

He turned to the snake. No way to hit it with a rock. He'd have to kill it another way. He still didn't want to discharge, if he could help it. Might damage the sled, and he needed the sled. Hmmm. He started walking purposefully towards the snake. When he got close enough, he began shouting, "I am Steef! I am the MixMaster! I have defeated two of your brothers! They were weak!…Are you weak?"

The snake didn't bother to speak, it just headed for him. The little pests had told him there were no rocks to fear in this clearing.

"Pill, you sure you want to stay? This will be messy."

"*We stay.*"

"Okay." He stopped. The snake was closing fast enough without his help.

Steef waited until the snake struck. Its mouth wide, he leapt inside, and kept moving forward. Uncle Antee had taught him well. Snakes swallow slow. They digest slow. Steef wanted to get far enough into the snake that he couldn't be spit back out. The snake's jaws clamped shut, no doubt its pride filled with the boasting he could give his brothers, now that he had eaten the MixMaster.

Trouble was, the MixMaster wasn't interested in being digested. Already into the back of the snake's throat, it didn't feel like any meal the snake had ever enjoyed. It was round, smooth, and hard. Gagging him. He tried to spit it out, but it was too far in, and moving. Well past his massive jaws, into the throat proper, where it stopped. That was better, he'd push it out like a cast of bones.

Only this wasn't working out too well. His meal was growing, right in his throat! It was getting bigger. Cutting off air. Cutting off…

Steef's bubble split the snake in two. He continued the stretching until the two pieces were far enough apart that he could step out. He released the bubble, only to have some of the snake plop onto his tunic. *And now I smell like a snake anyway* he sighed to himself, flicking pieces off. He hurried to his sled. Time to find another. *Wish I knew how many there were.* He had some trouble getting his wind up. A massive front had moved in south of him.

Pop! "*Steef, Cassa has a question.*"

Pop! "*Steef says to ask pardon for saying so, Cassa, but he doesn't think you CAN hurt Seafwood!*"

If that message had come from anyone else, about any other tree, she'd have taken offense. Now, she was just relieved, "Okay, Pill!" she had to shout over the wind. Everything was ready. She hoped Pool showed up soon, this was getting hard to control.

All the Cats were gone. She and Arima were standing as close to center of the cove as Seafwood's size would allow. Arima was behind her, with her bare arms wrapped around Cassa's belly, under the tunic. Skin to skin contact. Arima had drained as completely as she could before Cassa filled. Cassa had both of Arima's staffs, one in each hand. To Arima's Sight, the entire cove was filled with Blue, and the stones of both staffs were aflame with Power. Strong winds were whipping around the inside of the cove, in a lazy whirlwind, waiting.

Pill was above them, a thousand strong, hovering close to the center, keeping out of the wind. There was no wind above the cove that might give warning of the trap.

In the noise, they didn't hear Pool's arrival, loud as it must have been. But the light level, already low from cloud cover, got dimmer still. Looking up, the two women saw more Buzzbies than they knew existed, hovering just over the edge of the rockface. As Pill had predicted, they hadn't come straight into the cove, preferring first to see what awaited them. Also as Pill had predicted, they'd come in force. Thousands. Tens of thousands. Blocking the sun.

That's all right thought Cassa, *I don't need any more Power anyway.*

For Arima, it was like a really bad dream. The roar of the wind, challenged by the loud angry buzzing of Pool. Wisps of wind in her hair, just a tease of what was destroying everything loose at the edge of the cove. And her sister Cassa, whose neck muscles were bulging from the effort of holding and controlling two staffs.

Pill returned the angry buzz, but Pool could never have heard it. They didn't need to. From their position atop the cove, they dropped as one…straight towards the waiting humans.

"PILL…NOW!"

With a giant Pop!, Pill disappeared, leaving Cassa's and Arima's view unobstructed, as a hive full of Buzzbies dove at them.

Ka-Wump! CRAAACCCKKKK! BOOOOOMMMM!

When the Creator had fashioned the cove, scooping out an almost perfect bowl, he probably hadn't envisioned squeezing a swirlfury storm into it. To Cassa's credit, she hadn't called a big one. Grade Two at most. All of her effort, and the purpose of the two staffs, was to shut it off, which she began to do at once, now that her discharge had started it. It would still take many beats. If they survived it. At least they were in the center.

Not Pool. The massive family looked like a thick black fog being sucked point first into a bellows. The black fog got blended into the fury of the whirlwind that sped around the inside walls of the cove, never leaving, just spinning with now-furious force. The fog became streaks of black, then spread into spots of grey, that eventually became something that oozed down the sloped sides of the rockfaces. As if that weren't enough, there were skybolts flickering everywhere in the whirl, arcing all through the circular storm. Anything that didn't ooze, smoked. The Pool problem was solved.

Now, if Cassa could just shut it down. There was still not much real wind where they were, but the vortex had lifted them off the ground more than three staffs, where they hung, suspended. Arima clung to Cassa for her life, as the Blue stretched out both staffs to arm's length, and discharged again.

"AAAAAAAAHHHHHHHHHHHH!!!!!!!" Both women screamed, as the discharge reverberated around the cove. The storm began to quiet, much as a massive bull trying to stop from a full charge. It just can't happen all at once. Slowly, the vortex lowered them back to ground, where they settled without a stumble.

"'Rima...you...Okay?" Cassa was laboring to breathe. Dropping both staffs without ceremony, she sank to her knees.

"No! I'll never be all right again!" exclaimed the Healer, also on her knees, still hugging the SkyMaster. "But thank you, pumpkin. You've saved us."

"Look at Seafwood," Cassa managed to say.

Arima looked up. There *was* no Seafwood. Much like the morning so many cycles ago, when Maleef's screams had wakened them, the giant tree was shrouded in a swirling, perfect bubble of Power. They knew without seeing, that the tree was untouched.

"My discharge must have set it off in defense," mused Cassa. "Remind me to never make that tree mad."

Arima just nodded to the back of Cassa's head.

❧   ❧   ❧

Pop! *"We lost two thirds of our hive!"*

"What!? How could..."

"We don't know! Every Pool that went to the cove is gone! Just gone! Those of us that went to the south end, where the third snake died, met the entire Pill hive! Only a few hundred escaped! We were going to go north, to the fifth Master, but

there aren't enough of us left! We've gone to some of our sub-families, to fill in service to the Masters here, but we ARE NOT going back to the Valley!"

Vinntag glowered at Kuumit and Wingor. Both men had grim faces.

"Then we'll have to take care of it ourselves, Pool," Vinntag said coldly, "Since you seem to be incapable."

Pop!

Kuumit nodded agreement, but Wingor held his thoughts. Vinntag's harsh words to Pool were hasty. Nothing he knew of could idly kill an entire hive of Buzzbies, or even one of those foul snakes. He'd never been able to See the Locks on those beasts, of course. That was Vinntag's gift. But he'd spent days in a boat with them. Their eastern friends had said the Locks were unbreakable, so naturally, Wingor had tried to break one, first chance he got. He couldn't. Whatever Red had Locked those snakes was stronger than Wingor. Much stronger. And that wasn't possible. Now something in the Valley of the Cats had just killed three of them, and was probably hunting the others, after taking a few beats of diversion to destroy most of the Pool family.

Whatever Vinntag's vengeance had stirred up, was very, very dangerous. Whatever was in that Valley had been content to stay there, until it was attacked. Whatever it was, *might* go back to being content. And it might not. Whatever it was, had to be dealt with.

Pop! *"A few Pools had gone north, to wait for the attack on that fifth Master. They got there too late to see what happened, but you've lost a fourth snake, and this time there's no rock. At least the whole snake is there, but it's not whole any more. It's in two pieces. That fifth Master is gone. And Pull wants to talk to you."* Pop!

"Wha...?"

Pop! *"Vinntag. I am Pull. My family is neutral in your dispute. We will remain neutral. I have a message from Pill. I was asked to repeat it exactly. I will do so, if you oath that you will not have Pool attack us for the service."*

"Very well, Pull. I oath you. What is the message?"

Neither Kuumit nor Wingor had received a Pull. They were watching with interest, when suddenly, all the blood drained out of Vinntag's face.

"The message is this: 'Arima says to Vinntag, I know it was you. The presents you left are dying as you receive this. The Valley belongs to the Cats again. Anyone or anything entering without leave of the ClanCat, will forfeit their life immediately. Except you. If you visit, you will get to meet the current ClanCat personally.'...We were not told what that last part means."

Vinntag knew. She'd spent enough cycles with them, when Grading was done there. The ClanCat himself knew of her schemings, and had given challenge. She knew what that meant.

"Is…is…is…"

"Yes, that is all of the message." Pop!

❧   ❧   ❧

Steef had worked through the night, flying recklessly, using his Green sight to keep him above treetops. He'd actually had to land once, to recharge his stick. It was six spans, but even so, he'd been using it a lot.

There were now no snakes left alive between Kivverr and the cove. He was sure of it, and that wasn't something he would take lightly. From the very northern tip of the Valley, to the cove, there'd been five snakes. The fourth one had been the smartest, or the most cowardly. It had run away. Steef had no clever ideas for chasing it, so he walked an eighthnight away from the bubbled sled, and discharged. A small one, but Clear. There was now a small crater where the snake had been. A rock in the dark for the fifth snake, and he was level with the cove again, moving south to reach Uncles Antee and Mokam by first light. They had continued on south, and Antee was getting Pulses back on their second snake when he arrived.

A 'discussion' took place about how, or really 'who', would continue on to clear out the south. Everyone wanted to go. Steef stayed out of it, knowing that regardless of their decision, he would be going. The real issue was the Cats. There was room for both Masters on the sled, but only one Cat. Timmerr had no intention of letting Antee go without him. Plivverr had no intention of not going. This could only end one way. Plivverr had to go. Antee wouldn't leave Timmerr, so the sled rose from the ground while the Yellow Master dejectedly watched. There was nothing left for the grounded pair to do but return to the Cove. Their fight was over.

There were only two snakes left in the south. Between the two of them, Steef and Mokam sent a shower of rocks at each snake. There was no escape for the coldbloods. Continuing the search during all of that day, they could find no others. Eight snakes dead, in all. An exhausted Steef turned the sled back north, towards the cove. They arrived just past quarternight, and Steef drained Seafwood from the ground. All of them, including Steef, just slept around the fire that night. Steef was too tired to climb, and Kivverr wasn't there to carry him.

They were still tired next morning, but it was time to leave. Arima was determined to go. The others had gotten to do their part in the battle. Now it was her turn. The message to Vinntag had been a ploy. Of course they would come here, they had to now. She just wanted to make sure Vinntag didn't come. She wanted her old nemesis to stay right where she was, because that's where Arima was going. She kept her thoughts to herself.

A weary Steef made his way up into Seafwood. He retrieved his tunic, the one with the Five badge. He also re-set his sixspan, and asked Seafwood to release a fivespan. Now his stick matched his tunic. Five spans would be more than enough. While he was there, he had a good chat with his tree, and left a very delicate tune for her to generate. Once back down, he made his way to Plivverr. "May we speak in private, your Majesty?" Curious stares followed them as they separated themselves.

"I have left instructions with Seafwood," Steefrr began, "After we're gone, a bubble will go up that covers the cove. Only Cats and Pills can enter that bubble, until I return. If I've missed any of those snakes, the Clan will be safe here."

"*I understand, Steefrr. But we are not accustomed to hiding. You know that.*"

"Yessir, I do. If danger comes, I will be gone no more than eight days. When I return, you and I can stand together and meet it. But you saw those snakes. There is no point in losing all of the Clan, just because I'm not here." He hoped that would work. The Clan would follow Plivverr's lead.

The King of the Cats mused to himself for many beats. This was a new idea, but it was also a new foe. And Steefrr was Clan. It was proper. "*We will await your return before making any stands,*" gave Steef opportunity to breathe with relief. "*I will call in the Clan, and we will stay near your tree until you return. Then we will cleanse the Valley properly.*"

"Thank you, your Majesty."

Arima had watched them walk away. She turned to her Master brethren. "We were going to Town to find him a Mate, if we could. Now, I must ask that the three of you help him with his social dilemmas. I had intended to help him myself, but…"

They all nodded. Cassa spoke for them all, "You must make your own stand, Arimarr. We will tend to our boy, and at least get him Registered." The Blue bowed into the circle they'd formed, and concluded, "No steps back."

"No steps back," they all repeated. It was time to go.

CHAPTER 20

Meeben had never seen her like this, and that was saying a lot. Something really bad had happened yesterday. She hadn't said so, but she didn't need to. There were two Black Nines at the door to her workcloset, and two more at the front entrance. On his walk to work this morning, he hadn't seen a single Pool. Anywhere. And they were always everywhere, watching. Not today. Occasionally, he would hear something crash behind her door.

So when Ormis sent the GuildMaster's apprentice up from the public closets with a message, he'd stopped the girl out of mercy, and taken the message himself. Good thing, too. Disturbing her for something that silly might have gotten the child punished. He decided to go down and check it out first.

The man he saw there was in real distress, no doubt about that. A simple 'Nert. Laborer, really. But Meeben could understand Ormis's dilemma. The man was certainly sincere. Frantic, even. While they'd been waiting there for a response from the GuildMaster, someone had brought out a map, and managed to glean from the man where he was from. The other Healers there had all agreed, there wasn't a White anywhere in that area. Meeben politely looked at the man's hand, which was beyond hope. Then he looked at the map, and with a sinking feeling, knew he would be disturbing GuildMaster Vinntag. Telling everyone to wait, he turned a heavy pump and sluggish feet back to that end of the building. If he didn't go, someone else would have to.

The Blacks let him pass. "GuildMaster, there is a man in the public closets you need to talk to."

She didn't even look up, at first. When she did, the poisonous glower she sent at him made him know that he wouldn't miss the GuildHall. He had already decided to leave service, and hope for manual work somewhere. He wasn't Healing anyone any more, anyway. Most White Masters had already left.

"I know you don't want to be disturbed, Vinntag," he said without ceremony, "And truly, I don't really care." Before she could call in a Black, he jumped further into the fire, "There is a serious Guild matter that needs attention in one of the public closets. It's something you will want to know about. Now, you can have one of your pets," he jerked a thumb towards the Blacks at the door, "Cut me to pieces later, if you like, but you're going to want to see this. So let's go." With that, he turned and walked out, not caring if she followed.

A few beats later, they were back to the public closets. She hadn't spoken a word. Meeben assumed that she was either choking on hatred or wrath. That was all right, as long as she as she was choking. Bustling across the dirt floor to the obviously wounded man, she jerked the injured hand out of Ormis's.

"Well, obviously, he's lost two fingers, and now the poison's spread up his arm. He'll have to lose the arm." She let it flop back onto the table.

The injured man must have been in a lot of pain, but not so much that he couldn't tell that now was a good time to hold his peace. That was one angry woman.

Ormis had stepped over to stand by Meeben. Meeben spoke for both of them, "We told him that. He already knew. That's not the problem," Meeben paused...*might as well* he thought with a sigh, "He wants us to grow him another arm." He wanted to close his eyes. No, he wanted to be a Green. Or a Yellow.

They just let her rant. Everyone in the area could hear her. Probably heard her at the Landing Field.

"Becccaaauuusssee...," Meeben went on for the rest of them, when she stopped for air. He was already dead, anyway, "He says that the Whites who come to his village Healed a man there who grew back his leg."

"That's ridiculous."

"He seems very sincere, Vinntag."

"Why should we care what this 'Nert thinks or believes?"

Meeben pointed to the map lying open on the table. "Apparently, he's been traveling for many days. First by cart. His cart turned over in a stream. That's where he lost the fingers. Then, they walked. He's been trying to get his Son to the Registry coming up."

"And why...should I...*care about...that!!!???*"

Meeben stepped across the space that separated them, and actually took her red face between his two hands, and turned it…forced it, really…to look at the map. "Because he comes from *there*, you old witch!" And he slammed a finger down over the spot marking the man's village. Then, he scraped his finger a short…very short…distance across the parch, and stopped. There was nothing marked under his finger. It was a fairly new map. Meeben was feeling nauseous, just for showing her.

Now she knew why he'd forced her here. Knew why he'd given up any pretense of courtesy. She no longer cared, "Pool. Get Wingor. Right now." Pop!

※   ※   ※

Pop! *"Tell Steef that Kivverr is all right. The females are moving slowly. It will take several more days for him to get back to the cove. We have seen no sign of any more snakes."*

"Thank you, Pill," said Cassa, watching her wind, "I will." She and Mokam were controlling the boat, while the others caught up on sleep. They would sleep tonight, while Steef flew by himself. It would be a new experience for Cassa, flying at night. She wondered if she *could* sleep.

※   ※   ※

"Well," said Wingor, straightening up. The injured man's face was a blank. At least it kept him from feeling pain. "He certainly believes what he says. Do you know who this young Healer is?"

"No," spat Vinntag, "But it's surely Arima with him." There were just the three of them in her own closet now. She had to admit, Wingor was thorough.

"Can you really grow limbs back, Vinntag?" By *you*, he meant the White Guild. Every Guild had its secrets. Maybe this was hers. He couldn't See any deception in her Core, though.

She shook her head, "No one can. But no one was supposed to be able to kill those snakes, either. I assume you tried to break their Red Locks?" She hadn't bothered with the White ones. She could See they were beyond her Power.

"Of course. And Arima's Power would be no match for them either?" It was no time for delicacy. He saw her Core change again. Every time Arima's name was mentioned. And her nostrils flared. *That temper will be her undoing* he thought. *At least we have two Graders coming along. She will soon be unneces-sary.*

"Of course not! She's no stronger than me!"

He chose to leave that alone. "What do you propose to do about this?" He didn't really care about White problems, but this could be a part of their problems in the Valley.

"I think we should visit this village. Right away," Vinntag admitted nervously. It was awfully close to the Valley. And the ClanCat.

"We?"

"Yes…*we*! Whatever we find there will need your skills more than mine! Do you want to trust this to another Red?"

She had a point. "Pool," he said, "Ask Kuumit if he has any Masters left." Pop!

Twenty boats had left this morning, loaded with Masters of Black, Red, and Yellow. They were laden with the only weapons that had proven effective against the few Cats that had come out of the Valley, and those weapons were being carried by a small army of 'Nerts. No point risking a Master on the ground.

Pop! *"He has three Masters left in Town. Will you be needing them?"*

"Yes!" cried Vinntag.

"Probably," replied Wingor. He had to check first if there were any trustworthy boat crews left.

Pop! *"Vinntag, the Registry says there are two Masters listed for that village. A Yellow, and a Blue. They were Mated a few cycles ago."*

"No Browns?" she asked.

"They didn't mention any."

"Pool," added Wingor, "Go back and ask if the Blue was a Steerman, please." Pop!

"They're all Steermen, Wingor!" he could be so thick sometimes.

He just waited. Some Blue Masters preferred teaching to flying, but arguing with her meant Pulsing, and he needed her as clear as she could get.

Pop! *"Yes, it was a female Blue Master named Cassa. She was a Steerman. Is a Steerman."*

"And she relocated to this remote village after she Mated to the Yellow?"

"Apparently."

"She had to have a Lifter to get there, Pool. Find out who her Registered Lifter was." *And there will be the Brown we're looking for.* Pop!

They waited in silence. Merciful silence.

Pop! *"Her Lifter's name was Mokam."*

Vinntag just shook her head. She didn't know him. Wingor had heard the name, though he couldn't remember where. He didn't have to.

Pop! *"We checked at Brown GuildHall. Mokam is the retired Brown Miner they never could find. They assumed he'd just died in a private dig somewhere."*

Wingor pursed his lips, while Vinntag waited. She'd been emboldened by the thought of three Blacks on this journey. "I think we just found him, Pool. And I think that Vinntag's right," he hated that, "We need to make a little trip. Are there any boat crews left that use you, Pool?"

"Yes, two."

"We'll only need one boat. Please inform them that we will be leaving immediately. And we don't need to tell anyone else, Pool." Pop!

❧   ❧   ❧

Steef felt much better. He'd had a good sleep. Kivverr was Okay, though his paws were gonna be sore. The Cats were safe in the bubbled cove. He was as certain as he could get, that all of the snakes were dead.

He was flying high enough that he really didn't have to watch for clearance below, and there was surely no one else up here. Every so often, he'd switch from Brown to Green sight, and back again, to match the terrain to the map. His needle told him was he Steering correctly, but it never hurt to check.

Sassy had fretted at handing over the controls of her boat, and then going to sleep. She trusted him, he knew, but it was a fretting thing. Her weariness won the battle, and she was sleeping soundly. Auntie was awake with him, but keeping her own thoughts.

The only thing they were landing for was sanitary needs. There was enough food and water for the trip. By flying at night, they hoped to avoid prying eyes. Their schedule should get them to GuildTown at sundown tomorrow. During the day, he was going to put a bubble of air around them, and Lift them high enough that no one could see them.

There were occasional campfires below, but no one on the ground would see them in the dark...there were no glows coming from Cassa's boat. And since he was only occasionally using Brown and Green Sight, he never noticed that a group of those fires was surrounded by twenty boats.

✤   ✤   ✤

Word had gone out quickly, late yesterday. The GuildMaster was leaving. She wouldn't say where she was going, or when she'd be back. Meeben hurriedly organized as much as he could for morning.

No Pools watching. No GuildMaster watching. No Black Masters watching. There was a frenzy of Healing at White GuildHall. No Dust required. The lines grew. Every Healer that carried a staff had been called in. It was made clear to the people in the lines that this was for one day only. The Whites didn't know how many beats they had. Each day would have to tend to itself.

Meeben had a charged staff in his hand again, and it felt good. The smiles and gratitude he saw on the faces of sick and Healer alike, were some solace for all the cycles he'd had to endure. Vinntag had left in such a hurry, she'd forgotten to have him killed, but that would only be temporary. *Now, what to do about the Registry, if Vinntag doesn't come back in time? Well, that's two days away, I'll worry about it then.*

Meanwhile, they were attracting entirely too much attention. If Vinntag wasn't back tomorrow, they'd need to find another way to help these people.

✤   ✤   ✤

Cassa was back at the mast, with Mokam next to her. It would surely look odd if Steef landed by himself. The Landing Field was quieter than usual, especially for threequarterday.

It was a subdued group of Masters that exited the boat, and followed Cassa towards her parents' hut. She found herself getting excited, though, as they approached. It had been too long. Old feelings that had lain untouched got stirred, and as she made the familiar last turn down their road, she couldn't help but blow the door open, as she had in her youth. Her parents knew that delicate touch, and came rushing out.

Liksa was Cassa's height and build, but that was the end of any resemblance. A gentle woman, and soft spoken, none of them would have known she was Cassa's Mother. Anyone and everyone would have known that Cassa was her Father's daughter. Though much taller, Casim had given his daughter her features, and her personality.

"My little Sassy girl! Come wrap your arms around an old neck!"

Cassa did just that, giving him a few joyful tears as well. Her brethren waited politely as the family reunited. Then introductions. Antee first.

"This is my Mate, Papa! Antee is a fine Master Yellow!"

The two men shared an awkward couple of beats. It was apparent that their ages were much closer to each other, than to Cassa's. Finally, Casim embraced him, "If you're able to keep up with Sassy, you're welcome in our hut!"

Liksa gave Antee a glowing Blue bow, then offered her delicate hand.

The others were introduced. When Cassa got to Steef, she said, "This is Master Arima's apprentice! He is Steef!" She was just beaming, and knuckled his shoulder.

Once again, a slight hesitation from Casim and Liksa. Masters didn't apprentice Fives. Sixes apprenticed Fives. Well, it was becoming a strange world. The young Healer seemed pleasant enough, and his bow was courteous enough. Shame he had such a weak glow.

Everyone had pounded on Steef to remember his glow, visible or not. While fully charged, he minded himself regularly to leak out only a Five. It was his only preoccupation, distracting him even during the quiet walk through Town. All the buildings! And people! More people than he'd ever seen before, and Auntie…Master Arima said that the roads and rows looked empty to her!

But as they made their way to the door of the hut, he had a question for his Blue Master. Taking her arm, he whispered, "You never told me that your Papa called you Sassy!"

Her eyes twinkled with glee, "You never asked!" And laughing at the look on his face, she pulled him inside.

Arima purposed to hold her wrath until morning. *At least let Cassa give good greets to her family before the stirring begins. Vinntag isn't going anywhere.*

She was tired. It had been a long day of hard work, but rewarding. Even thrilling. This was the White she'd longed to practice. She'd learned much this day, watching the Masters, and finally, having them watch her. Some of what she'd been practicing in the Hollow had been slightly off, but they'd corrected her with kindness. She found that, oddly, there were some things that she didn't have…quite…enough…Power to Heal. Maybe she wasn't Master level, after all.

I'm too tired to go to the Hollow tonight she thought, wearily. Meeben had conferred with the others, and tomorrow they would spread throughout the valley, giving aid wherever there was need. She had volunteered for the Hollow of course, and was surprised to see a few smirks. Did they know she'd been going? They couldn't. The smiles were from the oldest Masters, and they certainly weren't getting out at night.

Mother was still happily sewing. Her sister surely did demand a lot of new tunics. Wishing for the thousandth time that she had Grader's Sight, she kissed her Mother's cheek, and went to her own closet. Mother was just too happy, and she'd only just discovered a passion for needlework in the last few cycles. With Sight, she could have Seen if there were Red Locks on her Mother, and how strong. She laid herself down with a sigh. A troubling world.

Three more cycles, and she could take her Mastery. She'd find her way in the world outside of Town, where Healers were welcome and free to Heal. Perhaps she could take Mother with her. Get her away from all the Red in this hut. She routinely had to ask the GuildMaster if there were any traces of Red on herself. *Three more cycles. Three more cycles. Three more cycles. Three mo...*

There were cycles of news to catch up on, and it went late. Cassa's parents had fallen on dark and lean days. They were both Blue Tens. Non-Master Tens. Because they weren't Masters, they had never been allowed Steerman status, and it had been a blessing. The two of them had worked their entire lives in GuildTown, as the best weather controllers ever seen around the Landing Field. All of the Blue Masters appreciated their weather, as it made flying easier in a complicated valley of wind. They had become wealthier than most Master Blues, and the Masters didn't mind. Blue Guild loved them. Their patterns were always completely harmonious.

Then everything had changed. Eventually, even the Blue Guild had changed, along with its GuildMaster. They were given a Master overseer, a too-young man with no experience, and seemingly, no more Power than they. If indeed, as much. He came from another wealthy family, though. One in which there was a Master Red. When winds became unruly over GuildTown, this overseer always seemed to get the blame shifted to them. Finally, there had been a crash between three boats, and people got hurt. Two were killed. Casim and Liksa were 'asked' to leave service. This, in spite of the fact that they weren't even on duty that day.

There had been no work since, and they'd been scratching by on their Dust-pile, which was getting very small. And in spite of no work, there were the new stipends to pay. Stipends that kept going up, though they couldn't say they'd seen where it might be going.

By now, Sassy was weeping openly. Naturally, the first thing Steef did was remove his Dustpouch, the one containing the purified Dust. He'd keep the small amount of 'seventh' that he carried in a separate pouch. One never knew. He laid it on their table without a word. Uncle Mokam looked over at him with a warm smile. Well, that was Okay, he'd learned about giving Dust from Uncle Mokam to start with.

He watched as Sassy pushed the pouch to her parents, who of course didn't want to accept it. Steef didn't really understand. It was just Dust. Grindings, really, from polishing Crystals. Useful, he supposed, if you wanted to leave a charge in something, but just ground up Crystal, after all. He had a hilltop full of it.

You wouldn't think so, when Sassy opened the pouch, revealing the sparkle of pure Dust. Casim drew in a breath. Enough wealth in that one pouch to support them for two cycles. Where would a Five White get such a thing?

Sassy did some long and fast talking to get them to accept it. To their credit, they gave a warm glow to their Five benefactor, something a Ten wasn't used to doing under any circumstance.

It was late, and everyone was tired, but not too tired to appreciate one final awkward beat. Awkward at least, for Antee. Casim and Liksa naturally expected Antee and Sassy to occupy her old closet. Together. No way around that. So, with two bright Master grins, and one bewildered look from a Five following them, Cassa dragged her unwilling Mate to their pad.

With the door shut, she burst out laughing, "You should see the look on your face!"

"Hmmm. You take the pad, and I'll just sleep on the ground over here."

She continued to laugh, though it was getting gentler, "You honestly are an airhead, Antee. Do you really think I haven't seen you a thousand times, washing in the spillway? And how many times have you seen me?"

He drew himself up, "Not the same thing at all, Master Blue. We at least had the privacy of distance," he concluded stuffily.

"Oh, keep your trous on, you old man...in fact...*do* keep your trous on, and lay down here on this pad. You're not sleeping on the dirt in *my* hut!" And she pulled and pushed at him until he finally relented.

❦   ❦   ❦

Steef knocked at the door. Auntie had been given the guest closet, while he and Uncle Mokam had slept in the receiving area. It was time to rise. He knocked again. No answer.

Pop! Pop! *"Bright day, Steef! You will be pleased to know that we checked on Kivverr first thing, and he is still fine. Two of the females are moving a little better this morning. One is not. Still no sign of snakes. We think you got them all."*

"Bright day, Pill. Would you please tell Auntie it's time to rise?"

"She has already risen, Steef. She left before sunrise."

"She did!? Where did she go?"

"Why, to the White GuildHall, of course." Oops.

"Hmmm. I thought she was done with the Guild. What's she doing there?"

"Uh…we're not supposed to say."

Steef was stumped. He'd never known them to refuse him any answer. "Ookkaayyy. You're not supposed to tell *anyone*…or you're not supposed to tell *me*?"

"Uh…you?" Pill's voice was just barely audible.

He whirled away from the door he'd still been facing, and collided into Sassy, who'd been listening, "You can't help her, Shortstick. She's got to do this on her own." *And besides, I'm supposed to be helping you find a girl.*

"Why, Sassy? What's she doing?"

"It's time for her to stand, pumpkin. It's a stand we can't make for her."

The young Master Clear pondered this. 'Stand'ing he understood, and agreed with. But if everything he'd been told was accurate, Auntie would be standing against an entire Town before midday. Not without him, she wouldn't.

"Is there someone in particular she's looking for, Sassy?"

"Yes…yes there is."

"She can stand against *them*, then. I'll just follow along and make sure everyone else lets her."

"But you're supposed to be looking…"

"That'll have to wait, Sassy. You know that. I'm Clan, too. Even if I weren't, you know I can't let anyone hurt Auntie."

She knew he was right. He had to go, and no one else could do it like he could. If he could. "Shortstick…there are a lot of Blacks out there," she said with rising alarm.

And Steef gave her a smile that she'd never seen on his face before. A smile like Antee used, when he understood something that no one else had gotten yet. He opened his hand, and the fivespan that had been standing in the dirt came floating their way, "That's kind of the point, isn't it?" And the Master Clear strode by an awakening Mokam, to the front door of the hut. As he disappeared, she heard him say, "Pill, do you know the way? Good…no, don't tell her I'm coming. It's her stand."

✿   ✿   ✿

Two boats stayed outside the ridgeline of the Valley, much to the relief of their occupants. Every Master in those two boats was crowded with Pools. The other eighteen boats proceeded Pool-less over the ridge, towards the cove, as directed by Pool.

That was one big tree. There were Cats everywhere around the cove, and they were stirred. Roaring and screeching as the boats hovered above and circled around the cove. It was a lot of Cats, but fewer than they'd been led to expect. The Cats that weren't actually in the cove, headed there at first sighting. In only a few beats, all Cats were inside the surrounding walls of stone. This couldn't be better. If they were going to stay there, they'd be easy targets.

There was a strange sled in the open field before the cove, and one empty landing bowl. It took a brave boat crew to set down there, but one did. The 'Nerts were told to go first, armed with nets and longsticks. Strangely, no Cats came out of the cove to meet them. Perhaps the tales of Cat ferocity were just that…tales. These Cats wanted no fight. All of the horned ones were lined up in a strange sort of circular line, facing the boats.

Little by little, the men moved forward, while their numbers increased from the other 'Nerts jumping out of hovering boats. Still, the Cats gave no fight, though they screeched and roared enough. There were two really large ones side-by-side in the center of that line, and each time one of them gave a roar, the entire line would sound off.

Eventually, the trembling men had gotten to within a couple of staffs. By now, there were more than two hundred longsticks pointing directly at the line of Cats. Several were launched in the direction of the largest male. They marveled that the Cat made no effort to dodge the sticks. They sailed the distance, and bounced off of the Cat's nose! Fifty sticks flew, and fifty sticks bounced. The Cats continued to roar, but they didn't move, forward…or back.

A few of the sticks were retrieved, and re-tried. No affect. A net was thrown. It also failed to reach a Cat. Finally, some clever soul tried throwing a stick *over* the line of Cats. When *it* bounced…they finally realized that it wasn't the Cats that were doing the bouncing, something else was. Something unseen. The Cats were just standing behind it. What magic was this?

The Masters had been watching all of this, with growing impatience. One of the lead Blacks climbed down a steprope, and came to talk with the chief 'Nert. Unbelieving, he tried a stick for himself. Then, he tried a Pulse. Nothing. Striding boldly to the line of unmoving, but raving Cats, he rapped on the bubble with his fist. Turning to all the other Masters watching in the boat, he made a show of the rapping, so they could see the dilemma. Communication was difficult without Pool.

Information is an important fact of life, and this Black Master was missing…or overlooking…a vital piece. Neither his sticks, his nets, his Pulse, nor his rapping fist could penetrate the bubble Steef had left…but the Cats could. They were standing with their noses less than a span behind it. The poor man rapped once too often, and Arivverr obliged him by removing the hand, then pulling his head back behind the bubble again.

In the ensuing commotion, no one noticed that the hand didn't actually get consumed. Arivverr had spit it back out. There was shrieking and fleeing and roaring and screeching aplenty, but when the boats departed in confusion, the hand was still there.

❀   ❀   ❀

If Arima had been a Blue, there would have surely been skybolts and boomers going off as she strode up the steps of White GuildHall and unceremoniously threw the doors open. She was fully charged. Just short of discharging, in fact. No point in glowing, though, Vinntag had Sight, too. She would See it coming, regardless. To her utter disappointment, there was no one there. All workclosets were empty, though she found the one that obviously belonged to Vinntag. *Who could possibly need all those staffs?* The common spaces were empty. Not a living thing anywhere. Her fury was now competing with frustration. She turned towards the public closets.

She found Ormis.

He was sitting by himself. No one else around, not even the ill. When he saw Arima, his eyes widened, which would have been more emotion than she thought him capable of. Then his face broke into a grin! He leaped to his feet, and without a word, rushed to embrace her.

This was not the reception Arima had been anticipating, and she had to do some seriously fast draining, or poor Ormis would have died on the spot.

"Oh, Master! Oh, Master! Oh, Master! Bless the Creator! It's so good...!"

"Uh...I'm glad to see you too, Ormis," she said to the back of his shoulder.

He broke away, still holding her shoulders at arm's length, "She's not here, Master! But she'll be glad to see you, I just know she will!"

"Not when I get through with her, Ormis," Arima growled.

Quick as a blink, his joy changed to puzzlement, "I don't understand, Master. Has she displeased you in some way?" Strange, he didn't think they'd been in contact, but you never knew with Masters and their Buzzbies.

"I think that's a fair statement, Ormis," she said, gently extricating herself from his grasp. "Before sundown, one of us will be dead." Arima knew which, too.

This was severe. "Your pardon, Master, but may I ask why? She's done nothing wrong that I know of, except to Heal when she's forbidden?" His voice said that he approved.

"Ormis! I'm surprised at you! *Vinntag*...done nothing *wrong*?! Why...she's done nothing *right*!...and I would have wagered you, of all people, would've agreed! Now...*where is she*?"

Another time, the wonderment that passed across his face might have been amusing. Falling to his knees, he began kissing her hands, "Bless you, Master! Bless you, Master! Bless you...only you can do it! No one else is strong enough. We'd given up hoping..." As suddenly as it had started, it stopped, "But she's not here! She left yesterday! No one knows where she went!"

That was the only piece of news that could have bothered her. She thought. "Pill, if she's in this Town, I want to know where!"

"Right away, Arimarr!" Pop!

"Get up, Ormis. It's not seemly."

"Yes, GuildMaster Arima!" he said brightly, jumping to his feet.

Arima shook her head, "Understand, Ormis. I am not here to challenge for the Guild! I am here..." she stopped. "No...you tell all the Whites...that is *exactly* what I'm here for. I give formal challenge!" *Vinntag can't ignore that.*

He nodded, "Most will be thrilled, GuildMaster! But have a caution," he lowered his voice. "Not all will. Some of the younger ones are enjoying their Dust a little too much."

"We'll deal with that when it happens, Ormis." She turned to leave. Pill would find Vinntag soon enough. Might as well start out. Then, she stopped. "Ormis...when I came in, you thought I was looking for someone else?"

He blinked, "Of course, GuildMaster."

"Who?"

"Why Leezel, of course."

She blinked, "*Who...*is Leezel?"

He couldn't have been more shocked if she'd slapped him. Ormis had changed. Dipping his head with puzzlement, he said, "Your *niece*...Leezel. Master's apprentice...Leezel..." he waved his hands, lamely.

"Her name is Leezel? Not Marzel? Or Zelmar?...She's apprenticed here?"

He nodded, "We've always wondered about the name ourselves, GuildMaster. But she chose not to explain, and of course, we didn't ask. And yes, she's apprenticed..." swallow, "...to the...GuildMaster."

"MY NIECE IS APPRENTICED TO VINNTAG!?"

Pop! "*Vinntag is not in GuildTown, Arimarr. Do you want us to look elsewhere?*"

Her nostrils were flaring. She really needed to...well, not to Ormis. Certainly not Pill. "Thank you Pill. Wait just a beat. We now have another concern."

"Ormis, I cannot believe that Linzel would have allowed this!"

Whew! She wasn't angry with him. "Master Linzel has not been seen in public in many cycles, GuildMaster. We assume that she is unhurt, as Leezel has never mentioned any..." Might as well stop, Arima was gone. He heard a dwindling 'thank you, Ormis', and he was left to sit back down, waiting to see if any people came in need. The long beats were lighter now, though. Arima was back. The days of sneaking to Heal were over.

The fleet of boats continued up the Valley. They had failed to kill the main Clan, but they had other orders, as well. If they could find any.

The man with the missing hand was tended to. They hadn't thought to bring Healers. An oversight. Stupid, really. So some of his Black friends had scorched the open wound until it stopped bleeding. That should get him home.

They'd made slow progress up the Valley, until almost midday. Finally, they spotted some Cats, out in the open. As they got closer, they saw that it was three females, and one giant male. The females were trying to run from the boats, but were not running very fast. The male was pacing them. Surely he could run faster than that?

One by one, the females dropped from fatigue. They were a bit spread out, but the idea had worked. They expected to have to chase the male until he dropped, too. That's how it had worked with the Cats that had been killed outside this Valley. Not this one. He stopped…and turned around. Took position halfway between the two farthest females, and began roaring at the boats!

This was not good. They had brought nets for tired Cats, not fighting, spitting Cats. Well, he was staying in pretty much one place. Just a little pacing back and forth. They began to lower a net…which the big Cat caught in a leap, his weight pulling the boat over, and dumping its contents onto the ground. The female Cats roused at that, and came to inspect their meal.

The 'Nerts were no loss, but that cost them six Masters. By then, everyone wished they could just use the longsticks, and leave. But orders were orders. Ten nets flew out. Then, ten more. All four Cats were tangled. The more they struggled, the more tangled they became. Some 'Nerts jumped out and quickly tied the corners off. When the attached boats Lifted, they took the Cats with them.

All the men on the ground climbed back up and the fleet set sail. They were a half day ahead of schedule, owing to their failure at the cove, which took practically no time at all. The Cats hung below the boats, swinging in the wind.

As Arima passed out of the GuildHall and turned up the road, Steef watched from behind a corner of the large structure. Sending out a Pulse, he knew that she was upset by how hard her pump was running, and her high pressure. He gave her a quick Pulse of White, to make sure she didn't explode.

Pill said that Pool was not out in public. There surely must be Pools somewhere, on some of the Masters. Eventually, Auntie had to be seen. Pill was staying under his hair, so no one would wonder why a Five had Buzzbies.

Arima was striding purposefully toward Maar's hut. For cycles, she had sent messages through Peel to Linzel, every Quarter. Her offers were always declined, though with courtesy. Then, the replies had stopped. Pill reported that Peel was perplexed about Linzel, but that she was unhurt. From the Valley, that had seemed like it would have to do. But Linzel would never have agreed to have a daughter apprenticed to Vinntag. Something was truly wrong.

"Pill, would you please inform Linzel that I'm coming?"

"Do you want us to go directly, or work through Peel?"

"Peel will do, for now." Pop!

Pop! *"Peel says that Linzel is giving no answer, Arima. Just like all those other times."*

"Then, would you please look for yourself, with regret to Peel?" Pop!

Pop! *"She's just sitting there sewing, Arima. She seems happy enough. She's humming. But she never acknowledged that we were there."*

"Where is Maar? No…just look to see if anyone else is there, please." Pop!

Pop! *"There is a young woman in the front closet, with a Red badge. When she heard us, she ran out of the hut. There is no one else there, now."*

Arima's puzzlement grew as she walked. She wished she could 'pop' like Pill, and *get* there. Lost in her thoughts, she never saw Steef following some distance behind her. As she strode down the roads and rows, she absently sent occasional Pulses at people whose infirmities she felt. She passed within a hundred steps of Red GuildHall. There must have been a Pool somewhere close, for she'd gone no more than twenty more steps when two Red, and two Black Pulses appeared, aimed directly at her.

Steef brushed them aside. He was enjoying the stroll, seeing all the new shops. From his passing glance, Merchant's Row looked particularly intriguing, except for all the Red. Why would anyone want all that Red on them all the time? Some of those Red Pulses just canceled each other out. What was the point? This 'Town' place was already full of puzzlements.

Whoever had Pulsed at Auntie, the Reds were Master strength, but the Blacks weren't. Another puzzlement. He hadn't Seen any Black Masters in their walk. Other Grades, yes. Masters, no. Didn't matter.

As Arima made her way from the Red GuildHall, a young woman came running by her. The girl had red hair, and for a beat, Arima thought she was Linzel. Her breath caught. The girl caught sight of her, and stopped.

Standing no more than three staffs apart, the two of them stared, unspeaking, for several beats. Steef had seen them, and stepped into a shadow. Then, the young girl straightened, forcing out a "Hmmmph!" and ran off again, glancing at Steef as she passed him.

Arima continued, moving quick as her feet would carry her. She found Maar's hut open. Apparently, her red-haired niece had been in a great rush to get wherever she was going.

"Linzel!" she exclaimed, into the open doorway.

"I'm back here!" came a voice from the back of the hut.

Arima followed the voice and, turning finally into another open door, she froze. Linzel was sitting behind a table in the middle of a large space, surrounded by fabric and garments. Stacked to the top of the walls, there were parcels everywhere.

Linzel looked up. With blank eyes, she said, "Are you here for a tunic? I'm awfully busy you know, but I'll try to fit you in." She blinked, and laughed, still blankfaced, "Fit you in! HaHaHaHaHa! I'm a jester!...Do you need a tunic?"

Through her tears, Arima could See the Locks. Red ones. Nine, and weak Seven strength. She could See them, but she couldn't touch them. Leaning against the doorframe for support, she stood mutely for many beats, feeling helpless.

"What else could I do, 'Rima?" came a familiar voice. She turned to see her brother standing behind her, with the red-haired girl behind him. "She wasn't eating, you know. Crying herself to sleep every night. If she went out, someone was sure to kill her. What else could I do?" he repeated.

"Is someone else there?" cried Linzel. "Do you need a tunic, too?"

When Arima found her voice, she said, "Some things are worse than death, Maar. You've got to release her. At least let her choose for herself!"

The young woman behind him scowled, and shrank back.

Maar shook his head, "I can't 'Rima. I give regrets, truly, but I won't do it. The girls aren't going to lose their Mother, if I can help it...and this is all I've got."

The red-haired girl stuck her head out from behind her Father, "Why don't you just go back to wherever you came from!? We don't need you here...*Aunt* Arima!" She made the 'Aunt' sound like a curse.

"Stop that, Zelmar! This is my sister! You show her some respect!"

"I've heard about her Father! We don't need her here! She's trouble!"

Maar turned back to Arima, "She didn't hear that from me, 'Rima," he said softly. "Great regrets."

"You're too soft, Father! 'Rima this, and 'Rima that! Well, I've heard the truth! And don't forget...she sent her Buzzbies in here! Into our hut!"

"I've told them to watch for Buzzbies, 'Rima," he went on, "Never imagining they might be yours. I always thought..."

"They'd be from the Black Guild?" she asked. There was no good solution here. Maar had changed, just like Ormis.

He nodded.

There was nothing she could do. She couldn't break those Locks. And her niece...Zelmar?...was right. Arima was in Town to make trouble. No point in bringing that trouble here. Now she understood why Linzel hadn't questioned…Leezel's?…assignment to Vinntag. Well, with Vinntag dead, that wouldn't be an issue anyway.

She and Maar walked out together. He would be going back to work. She could now concentrate on her search. They walked in silence. Zelmar left them with a huff. At the end of the road, Maar surprised her with a hug.

"I've missed you, 'Rima."

"I…I'll be…in Town…for a couple…of days, Maar," *if I live through this.* "We'll share some greets…before I leave."

"I'd like that." He strode off.

She watched him go, then made her way to a public bench, and sat.

Steef watched her weep. "Pill, do you know what this is about?" He casually brushed away some more Pulses. If they didn't quit soon, he'd have to do something about it.

"We'll have to check with the hive."

"Do so, please." Pop!

Pop! *"Here's what we know…"*

❧   ❧   ❧

SNAP!

Linzel found herself sitting in the middle of an amazing pile of garments and cloth. "What…?"

Pop! Pop! *"Bright day, Linzel!"*

"Peel! I…I'm confused! What am I doing here? What are you doing here? You shouldn't be…"

"We aren't Peel, Linzel. We are Pill. Peel knows we're here, though."

"You shouldn't be here, Pill, it's dang…"

"No, it's not."

"They *watch* me, Pill! Pool will tell the Blacks! They could Pulse in here any beat…"

"No…they can't. You need to listen for a few beats. There is news. Arima is in Town…"

"Arima?! Here?! Pill! You've got…!"

"Linzel, please! We know this is confusing. For now, please believe us, you are in NO danger! Try this…think you could glow yourself a bit?"

"Uh…I think so."

"Well, give just a little glow, please. Not too much."

In her dazed state, she didn't argue. A Black glow formed around her that, strangely, stopped in a bubble shape at half a staff away.

"*See that bubble?*"

"Yes, I see."

"*That bubble went up the beat after we arrived. Nothing will penetrate it. Nothing. Well…air. You've got to breathe. But you could dance in the center of Black GuildHall right now, and they couldn't touch you.*"

"I don't understand, Pill."

"*You will. Feel strong enough to take a little walk?*"

❧   ❧   ❧

"Arima? Is that you?" came a weak voice.

Arima lifted her puffy face from her hands. She was still sitting on the bench. She looked up to see…Linzel!

Her Linzel. No Locks. Arima sprang up, and they fell into each other, "So Maar changed his mind?! Bless him!"

"Maar?" queried Linzel. They separated, with the Black shaking her head, "No…I haven't seen Maar." Her brows furrowed, "Where *is* Maar, anyway?"

"But, if Maar didn't…" said Arima, "Pill!"

"*Yes?*"

"What have you done, Pill!?"

"*You're not pleased?*"

"Where is he, Pill?!"

"*Not far.*"

"You let him follow me…no…you *helped* him follow me?'

"*And if we hadn't, you'd already be dead. He's been blocking Pulses off of you since before you went into your brother's hut.*"

That sobered her. "Oh…tell him 'thank you' Pill."

"'Rima, who are you talking about?" asked Linzel.

"*Tell him yourself.*"

Steef emerged from his hiding place in the shadows. He hadn't moved. The Red Locks hadn't been an issue at this distance.

Arima nodded to her boy, and Linzel turned to look.

"Linzel, pumpkin, there's someone you just *have* to meet!"

❦   ❦   ❦

Pop! *"We're being followed. And watched."*

All three of them had gotten the message simultaneously. The two women looked around, apprehensive.

Not Steef, "Who's watching us, Pill?" Aggravating. So much to see, and a Black Master to talk to, and all of his beats were occupied! By nonsense!

"Pool. They are keeping their distance, but they're there. Do you want us to challenge?" Wings started buzzing in six ears at once.

"No. I have a better idea. How many families are in Town?"

"Buzzbie families?"

"Yes."

"All five main families have members here. Two sub-families loyal to Pool are here, as well."

"You're friendly with Peel and Paal?"

"Yes."

"How about Pull?"

"They've done us no harm."

"Can you warn them off, without warning Pool and their friends?"

"Yes. We can go to their hives. They will receive us. That won't get noticed."

"Tell them that when I give the signal, they will have exactly four beats to leave this valley. Will that be enough?"

"Yes." Pop!

They continued walking. Steef Pulsed a bit of White, to see where the human shadows were. Okay. There. There. And there.

Pop! *"We're ready."*

He mixed. Yellow and Black. "Pill...now," he said quietly. Pop!

Had they been listening, they could have heard 'Pop!'ing everywhere. Instead, they were watching him. Beat. Beat. Beat. Beat. Arima Saw the Pulse leave his stone.

Every Buzzbie still in the valley, died. Along with a few hives of tame bees, but that couldn't be helped. Shifting to White, another Pulse. Three bodies dropped in the shadows, sound asleep. Happily, the incoming Pulses also stopped. That was better. He began looking around, at the different huts, people, glows, Cores...etc.

They continued their walk to Cassa's. They hadn't even broken stride.

"What just happened?" asked a bewildered Linzel, as Pill returned. The commotion was just starting to be heard around Town. Masters who had Buzz-bies just a beat ago, didn't any more.

"Magic," said Arima. "I'll explain when we're safe."

"We're safe *now*, Aunt…Master Arima."

She just knuckled him in the arm. He grinned. Linzel looked confused.

※   ※   ※

Steef made sure they were safely tucked away at Cassa's, and that his Red Locks were still in place, then he left to go exploring. The others hadn't wanted him to expose himself further, after hearing of the morning's events, but Auntie had calmly informed them that she trusted he would be safe. She didn't explain 'why' to them, or 'from what' to Steef. She did caution her boy to try not to kill anyone.

After Steef left, earnest conversation began. Cassa was concerned for her parents, and began to talk to them about the idea of relocating to the Valley. Arima saw her Blue sister's concern, and had a thought that might do two pumps some good, with one striking. She turned to Linzel.

"Master Black," she began. That got everyone's attention. Linzel turned tired eyes to the Healer. Arima continued, "It appears that we may have to expect some trouble." She was carrying her old staff. Her newer one was in her trunk. Draining it, she handed the old staff to her friend, "We beg that you consider giving your Black services to our protection," she said formally.

A startled Linzel suddenly found herself in possesion of a Master's staff. It had been a long time. She ran her hands up and down the old wood, and over the stone that had served Arima so well. It flared bright Black. With her tears dripping to the ground, she bowed to the Healer, declaring, "I accept the charge, Master, and will defend you to the death until my services are released." It was the binding Black Guild's oath, long since neglected by the new Blacks.

Then Arima took her aside, and began explaining why it probably wouldn't be needed. There were a lot of 'that's not possible' s, followed constantly by many 'I oath you' s.

When at last Arima had convinced her, Linzel said, "Arima, did you know about this, the last time you visited my hut?"

Arima nodded.

"You wanted me to come train him in Black, didn't you?"

Another nod.

"And you knew I couldn't come…for the girls' sakes?"

"Yes."

Linzel gave that some thought. "Has he had any Black training since?"

A small shake of Arima's head.

Linzel smiled, "And you're here to kill Vinntag?"

"Ummm-Hmmmm."

"Which would eliminate my concern for Leezel, now wouldn't it?"

"Yep."

"And leave my daughter without training."

"Hadn't thought of that, but yes."

"Know any White Masters that could complete her training?" Linzel was grinning now. So was Arima.

"Might be able to find one."

"You train mine…I'll train yours?"

"Deal…*struck!!*" And they both laughed through their tears.

"Just one little problem, 'Rima," Linzel finally continued.

"What's that, sweetie?" She thought Linzel would mention resistance from Maar. Nope.

"*I*…want to kill Vinntag!"

CHAPTER 21

Steef had intended to observe as much Black and Red as he could, for no other reason than he'd had precious little experience in them, except the parches. But now, there was a Black Master back at the hut, and he could ask her questions all night tonight, if he wanted.

Time to look for Red.

It wasn't hard to find. Red was everywhere. Every shop had a Red glow. Every parch posted on public boards…had a Red glow. He was filtering it out, so the effect wouldn't reach him. Just the Sight. He would stand in one place for many beats, listening to conversations, watching people. Their Cores fell into two main categories. Either they were predominantly blue, which he thought must be fear, or they were black. He was surprised at how many of those there were. The black Cores weren't limited to any particular Power level, or Color, although there were more of them in the higher numbers than there were in the lower.

At exactly midday, he heard Town criers begin their daily messages. He ambled over to one.

"All of the Dust we took from you is gone," he heard. "You're going to have to find more. We're really enjoying…"

Steef set his staff to lower the filter for ten beats. He wanted to hear what the crowd was hearing.

SNAP!!

"…your benefit! We have wisely invested your contributions, and will be using the proceeds to improve the lives of everyone in GuildTown! We appreciate your generosity, and know you will continue…"

SNAP!!

"...so you'll just have to work longer into the night, and probably the seventh day, too, to make up for everything we've spent. We're not intending to stop, either, so you'll have to consider having your Mates..."

SNAP!!

"...the more of us that work together, the faster we can bring these exciting programs to completion! It's a bright day that brought us to the point where..."

SNAP!!

"...the few of us that control you can become wealthy off of your stupidity. Fortunately, none of you has the wit to do the numbering, or you'd realize that we can't take Dust from all of you, and give more Dust back to all of you. HaHaHaHa!!!...Now, get to work!"

Steef had alternately found himself reaching for his Dustpouch, and drawing his hand back. Fortunately, he'd already given his Dust away, anyway. This was a great puzzlement. More commotion over Dust! What more do these people need, than a good meal today, and opportunity to earn one tomorrow? Oh, and a good stick, too. Gotta have a stick. He moved on.

Mercantile row was about Dust too, in a different way. This time, there were products for sale. All of the products themselves had at least a trace of Dust in them, all with Red charges. Another round of snap'ing, and he understood why. The Red was misleading, making people think the products were better than they actually were, or 'prettier', whatever that was.

And there were floors in the merchant's huts! Wood and stone floors! They must have some sort of Cloaking in them too, because he felt the Power level drop when he entered one. It wasn't an issue, his stick had a 'seventh' Crystal in it, so he had all the Power he needed. Still, it was a puzzlement.

There were places that would prepare you a meal, and then charge you for it! One filtered look at the food was all he needed there. The Red made you like the taste, but there was little of value in it. Some of it even looked harmful.

His wanderings began taking him farther from the center of Town. The Red was disturbing, the lack of it refreshing. One last Red lesson remained to him, however. He was in a section of Town that was mostly dwellings, but one large hut stood out. It too, had a Red glow. Its front door was fashioned particularly wide and open. Almost inviting. He stopped just outside, to listen.

"...you have no business talking directly to the Creator! All of your dealings with the Creator should go through me! I will see to it that you feel loved, and looked after!"

SNAP!!

"…bring all of your friends to our meetings, and share with them the good news about our loving Creator! The more people we have here, the more love we sh…"

SNAP!!

"…the more Dust I can take in! This is really working out well for me. I like it! I'm good at it!…"

SNAP!!

"…your humble servant, I will continue to bring you messages from the Creator! You have been too generous…"

SNAP!!

"…you will need to come here first, before you pay your stipends to the Guilds!…"

"Really depressing, isn't it Son?" came a voice from behind him.

Turning, he saw an old wrinkled man, bracing himself on a stick, and slowly shaking his head. The old man had piercing eyes. Eyes that weren't clouded by Red.

"It's the table he's standing behind," continued the old man, "It's really a staff. He's really a Red Ten."

Steef looked. Flicking through his Sights, Green revealed that the odd, vertical table was fashioned from really good staffwood. Brown let him see the stone, buried inside the table so no one could know it was there. "He's not wearing a badge," observed the Master Clear, perplexed.

"Well, he couldn't, now could he? Then everyone would question what they'd heard."

"What is he doing?" asked Steef.

"He calls himself a Messenger. It means someone who has a message from the Creator."

"Well, the Creator seems to need a lot of Dust."

The old man coughed a laugh, "Odd, isn't it? Why would a Creator need Dust? A true Creator could just make his own." He laughed again.

"You don't seem to be affected," Steef pointed out.

"No," shaking his old head, "I'm not swayed by his deal striking."

"Why not?"

"I could ask you the same thing, young Five. In fact, from the road, I saw that you were taking turns being affected, then not. Very strange."

Oops.

His face gave him away. Another crude laugh, and a pat on the arm. "Never fear, young man. Your secret is safe, whatever it is! To answer your question, I really *am* a Messenger!"

"And so then, will you be asking me for Dust, Sir?"

"No," the old man replied, kindly, "The Creator I serve, the one true Creator, doesn't need me to do any Dust collecting. Just messages."

Steef liked this man. He reminded him of Papa, at least in attitude. "What's the message then, Sir?" The noise from inside the large hut had increased, and was forgotten.

"Love." He waited. They always asked more.

"That's a short message, Sir. What does the Creator want me to love?"

"He wants you to love *Him*! And…he wants you to love others."

"That still doesn't sound like a difficult message, Sir. He doesn't sound like a demanding Creator, this one you serve."

"It's harder to love than you might think, young Healer," the man said, tapping Steef on his badge. "Loving to the Creator's satisfaction means loving the way *He* decides, not the way *you* decide."

"And how might I do that?"

"Here's a glimmer…and then I'll have given you more than you need for one cycle. If there's someone you want to love to the Creator's satisfaction, your first thought must be to their well being, before your own."

"That still doesn't sound hard, good Sir," Steef said with a smile.

"Oh, but it is! It's not complicated, you mean! But it's very hard. Bright day to you, young man."

Steef watched him limp off. The stick in his hand was just that, a stick. The man was completely Inert.

The boat swung in over the village, and settled to ground. A crowd of villagers had gathered as the Masters were clambering down. They had no reason for concern, except that on closer inspection, three of the visitors wore Black Tens. Some of the villagers started to turn away. Wingor stopped that with a single Pulse.

He began questioning them, and discovered where the man with the supposed new leg was. They proceeded towards the indicated hut.

❦   ❦   ❦

"Smells good, doesn't it?"

Steef nodded. Sweetbreads. The little stall was at the edge of Town, and the man running it was also Inert. His sweetbreads weren't enhanced by Red. Just sweetbreads. And something else.

"It's a spice…the smell you're getting. An old, old spice that my family has had for over a hundred cycles." Reaching into one of his many pouches, he drew out some small seeds. "My great-great-gran had to work almost his whole life for a Green Master, just to get some of the old seeds sprouted. Now my family passes them down. My Son will get the next batch." He put them away.

"It's wonderful. What's it called?"

"Sinnmom. It's the brown streaks you see in the sweetener there. Want one? One Two cup, grade Three."

They'd taught him about the different cups, and he had an old set that Auntie had dug out of her trunks. Trouble was, he didn't have any Dust. Well, he had the 'seventh' Dust, but that wouldn't do. Especially if it went off, and hurt this nice man. Or the valley. He shook his head. "No Dust."

"Don't feel too bad, Healer. I've struck very few deals all day. No one has any Dust."

"I'd gladly perform a service for one, though," said the Master Clear.

The man laughed, "Do I look sick to you, Son?"

Actually, he looked like he could tickle one of the smaller Cats and make him like it, but Steef didn't say that. The baker was a really *big* man. "No Sir! But I'm really practiced at washing bowls and things."

The man was shocked, "Son, Power people don't do 'Nert work for 'Nerts," he said quietly. Someone might hear, and get this gentle boy in trouble.

"This one does. For a sweetbread."

Now, the baker was touched, "Tell you what, Son. It's getting late, and I haven't struck enough to pay for the day's work anyway. They won't be fresh enough to peddle tomorrow. You just take one." He pushed the tray towards the goodly little Five.

"Not without a deal struck…Sir," said the Master Clear.

"After dark, then. You come back when no one can see, so you don't get into trouble. I'll let you wash my things then." He would be gone by then.

"Deal struck!" And it sure tasted as good as it smelled!

❧   ❧   ❧

Well, it certainly *looked* like a new leg. There was a clear separation of skin color where the old leg stopped, and the new growth started.

"No, I can't explain it!" she snapped.

Wingor just smiled thinly, "Let's go check out this Yellow that the Healers were staying with."

"Yes, let's."

The man's limp body was carried to the boat, and loaded. They *could* have been careful. He *was* still alive. But they weren't, and now...he wasn't. Broken neck. Oh well, they could still show the leg. He didn't have to be alive for that.

Making their way up the hill, they noticed a group of low-ranking Yellows tending the beasts in the pens next to the hut. The Yellows were watching, but made no move to interfere. No point, with three Master Blacks in attendance. There were the Greens they'd been told about, waiting in front of the hut. Just...standing...there, together.

Someone should have told the idiot village boy about Blacks. He was standing in front of the Greens, throwing rocks at them and shouting. One of the Blacks idly sliced off both of his hands. Could have killed him with an easier Pulse, but she was showing off for her friends. They appreciated the gesture, and congratulated her on some fine Pulsing.

A quick Red Pulse, and the questions began.

Unnoticed, a couple of the bolder Yellows slipped over and tended to the wounded boy. They couldn't Heal him, of course...only the old White over there could have done that, and she wasn't moving. So they tied off his wrists, to keep him from bleeding to death. Hopefully.

Pop! Pop!"*Vinntag, we've lost more family! Every Pool that was in Town is dead! And Arima is in GuildTown! Word is, she means to challenge you!*"

"What?!" A skybolt of ice ran through the Healer. She shivered. Then, looking at the three Green bodies, her fear calmed as quick as it had started. "Maybe she will...and maybe she won't. Pool, tell Kuumit to leave her alone until we return. Watch her, but leave her to me."

"*Whatever you say, but this is getting serious. We're running out of family!*" Pop! Pop!

Well, this was about as perfect as it could get. Her old enemy didn't enjoy the protection of the Cats any more. She wanted a duel, eh? Vinntag had a surprise for her. Three surprises, really. She minded the others to load these more carefully, they'd be needed alive. They were Locked as thoroughly as three different Colors could Lock.

For Vinntag had finally heard the name 'Steef', and she had heard the word 'Clear'. She had also heard fantastic tales that she didn't believe, but she was taking no chances. These people meant something to Arima, so they'd be kept alive as long as it took. After that, she didn't care.

It was late. They couldn't leave before morning. She told the boat crew to expect haste when they did. She was in a hurry, now.

Almost dark, but Steef wasn't interested in going back yet. Too much to see, and he wouldn't be here long. He was truly at the edge of Town now, and there was a new puzzle. Power people. Had to be Power people. He could See their glows. Not a lot of them, but enough. The odd part was, they weren't carrying a stick! Or wearing their badges. And they were working! That nice baker man had said Power people didn't do Inert work, but here they were.

And they were almost all Masters.

Mostly Reds, but there were at least a few of every Color. A goodly assortment of Whites, too. And one bright Black. All of them had good Cores, though none of the people he saw looked overly joyful. Except the Black. Steef stood and watched as the puzzle worked around and past him, scurrying with a rush to get their work done.

He didn't know it, but he was at the border of where the Town stopped, and Nert Hollow began. All of the activities were preparations for tomorrow's Registry, and the attendant celebrations. If anyone felt like celebrating, which was in some doubt by what he overhead.

And there was this one Black. Steef was fascinated with the man. His only encounter with a Black had been this morning, and she had been too distressed at the time for any useful conversation. And he'd been busy himself. He wasn't busy now. He was watching the Black.

The man had his tunic off, loading sacks of what looked like whitefruit into a cart. They would be heading into Town before sunrise. The perspiration glistened on his smooth back, as clear cut muscles rippled under their familiar tasks. Finally, the man stopped what he was doing, and walked over.

"Can I help you Son?"

Steef bowed, like he'd been taught, "Your pardon, Master. I meant no offense. It's just...well, I've never really seen a Black before, and..."

"You have something against my skin color?" asked the Black. That was odd. No one cared about skin color, when there were other Color issues that mattered.

"No…Sir. In fact, my Uncle Seafer…"

"Steef, stop. He doesn't need to know that."

"…anyway, I meant your Power. Sir. Master…Sir." He bowed again, just in case.

The Master Black who wasn't…gave Steef a long, long, hard stare. "Come with me, Son." Pivoting, he strode away at a pace that made Steef pound to catch. He followed the Black Master around several tall piles of crates and produce, until they were out of sight of prying eyes, where the man whirled.

"I don't know what your secret is, Son, but you're not keeping it very well. No one could have known I'm a Master Black without Sight, and Fives don't have Sight." He flicked Steef's badge. "Second…you've got Buzzbies. They're being still, but not still enough."

"Pardon, Steef."

"Third, you're Cloaked so well, I can't See your life zones, and no one can Cloak that well. What *are* you Son?"

"I am Steef."

"What's a Steef?"

"I guess…me."

"Hmmm. Well, we've all got our secrets, I suppose, but around here, secrets can get you killed. Have a caution, Son."

Bow. "Yes, Master. Thank you, Master…Master, your pardon…may I ask…"

"They took my staff, Son…when I wouldn't kill on command. Nothing more useless than a Black who won't kill. I like this work better anyway."

"Your pardon, Master." Bow.

"Leemin. My name's Leemin, Son. You want to stare at a Master Black, you come stare at me all you want. Some others might not appreciate it much."

"Yes Sir. Thank you, Master." Steef had bowed at him continually, not really knowing when to stop. He felt like he'd been in Plivverr's presence.

"And be careful with your secrets!" came sailing over the Black's shoulders.

It got worse before it got better. He hadn't gone a hundred steps, when he felt a tap on his shoulder. Standing behind him was a Master Brown, also without a staff.

"Yes, Master?" bowed the Master Clear.

"May I see your staff, young man?" the old Brown asked politely.

"Certainly, Master." He handed over his stick.

The Brown looked long and close at the stone there. Steef had thoroughly Cloaked the Crystal itself, but there was no way to Cloak the blue glow of the 'seventh' coming from it. This Brown had Sight!

"Where did you get this stone, Son?"

"From a distant Valley, Master." Well, that was true.

"Who ground it for you, boy?"

Hmmm. Either lie outright, or…"Master Mokam, Master." Well, that was almost true. Uncle Mokam had shown him how, once.

"Mokam, eh! Well! How is the old stoneh…well, you wouldn't know, would you? If you ever see him again, boy, you tell him that Binder gives greets. Will you do that?"

"Certainly, Master." Never hurt to bow. Too many was better than too few.

"And you be careful with that. Mokam wouldn't have known better, but that's a dangerous Crystal. It'll burn the poor 'Nerts if you get it too close. But you're a Healer, you already knew that. Well, be careful, is all." He handed it back.

"Yes, Master. Thank you, Master."

This place was depressing for its own reasons. The farther he got, the more desperate the people looked. Hungrier, too. It wasn't long before he got to where there was less work, and more groaning. One of them called to him.

"Mercy, Healer. Have mercy, and help our family."

They didn't have to ask twice. And he didn't have to cry out that White service was available. They started to come. He stayed in White until well after full dark. Working his way through the Hollow, he'd gotten about halfway, though he didn't know it, when up ahead of him, he saw another White Pulse. Another Healer was down here, helping these people! Good. There was plenty of help a'needing. He went back to his work.

The White Pulses got closer, until he could make out a tall shape in the dark. He assumed whoever it was, wouldn't have the Sight to see his Pulses, so he glowed his stone briefly, minding the level. The figure glanced up, then bent back to the work, too.

They met a few beats later.

"I am Steef," said the Master Clear. He glowed a bit, to see. She was a tall girl, about his age. Dark hair. Blue eyes. Very blue eyes. Familiar looking features. She wore a Ten badge. A strange one, with markings he hadn't learned.

"Your pardon, Master," he bowed. "I didn't see…"

"I'm not a Master yet, young Five, but I thank you for the courtesy." Her voice sounded tired. "My name is Leezel…"

Pop! Pop! In the dark, Pill and Pill had left him, for unknown territory. They were in a nearby tree, but he didn't know that.

"*You tell him!*"

"*I'm not going to tell him! You tell him!*"

"*I'm not going…we'll just wait 'til he gets back to Town, and Arima can tell him!*"

"*Good enough.*" Pop! Pop!

"Did I just hear Buzzbies?" she asked in the dark.

"Oh, they're everywhere around here." That was the right thing, and the wrong thing to say.

"Oh my! Are they back!? And there is still so much work to do tonight!"

"Well, if it helps, I've already been Healing some of these people."

She smiled at him. A sad smile, "I'm sure you did your best, and I mean no offense, but I'd still better look at them."

"*As if she could Heal something you couldn't!*"

Steef couldn't speak to Pill, so he tapped him with his stick, which was still glowing. Of course, this looked completely silly to Leezel.

"Are you all right?"

"Just reminding myself of something, thank you, Master."

"I'm not…oh, never mind. Let's have a look at what you've done."

"Yes Mam."

They went back through some of the ground Steef had just covered. He politely listened to her instructions, even when she was wrong. It wasn't his place to correct her. And then something happened…

A woman's Mate had come back to their tent, late from work. He was late because he was lame. He was lame because some Black had sliced up his legs. And the woman was hysterical. "We gonna starve, you can' work! Wha' we gonna do? Oh, merciful Creator, help us! Wha' we gonna do?"

The Master Clear watched, as Leezel went scurrying over to the woman. She motioned for Steef to help the injured man, which he began absently doing, while watching…a new puzzle. Leezel put both her hands on the woman's face, and began to glow White. The woman's moanings lessened, and finally stopped. And Steef could See that Leezel had a smudgy looking…something…on her hands and feet. As Steef continued Pulsing into the man, Leezel walked to the sanitary ditch, and sloughed off as much of the sludge as she could.

Good puzzle! And no way to ask, without giving away his 'secrets'. He couldn't admit to Seeing her sludge, without admitting to Sight. Fortunately, she provided some of the answer herself, seeing the question in his face.

"I'm an Empath. I Heal hurtful emotions."

"I've never heard of that!"

"I'm not surprised. I'm the first one in thirty cycles. At least that's what I'm told." She looked like she was used to not believing everything she was told.

"How does that work?" asked an excited Master Clear.

"I can draw off those emotions, and people feel better about themselves."

"Your pardon, Master. That sounds a lot like what a Red does."

She didn't take offense. Her voice kept its tired smile in the dark, "I understand your confusion. I had it myself for a great while. Perhaps this will help. If you cut yourself, a White can Heal the wound, correct? Of course. A Red can convince you that you aren't wounded, but that doesn't help the wound. I can help you get past the distress of being wounded, without any lies, by drawing off the distress. The more severe the distress, the more Empathy I have to use. Sometimes, it can be very tiring." She sighed.

He wanted to ask…

"And then I have to slough off the emotion that I've drained from the wounded. Down here in the Hollow, there've been nights when I could barely walk, it gets so thick."

"The stuff you slough off, did you have some just now?" He knew she did, but it still wasn't actually a lie. He never said he didn't know.

"Yes, but not a lot. This wasn't a bad one."

"Could I touch it?"

"Why in the name of all that's healthy, would you want to do that?"

She couldn't see his shrug, "I like to learn new things." Well, that was completely true.

"I have to warn you, it's not pleasant!" She turned back the way they'd come, and directed him to where some of the sludge hadn't made it to the ditch. He could See it of course, but he let her guide him anyway. His outstretched finger…touched.

Despair! Fear! Anger! Despair!

He flicked his finger, trying to get it off. It wouldn't come off.

"Here, let me help. It won't come off unless I draw it." Before he could say anything, she had taken his hand. The Empath, the eater of emotion, had touched the man of pure joy. She wasn't prepared.

"Oh!…Oh, Merciful Creator!…It's too much!…Make it stop!"

Steef jerked his hand away. The sludge was gone. Leezel sat, with a plop. He glowed his stone into her face. She was wide eyed, glazed. Mouth open. Her tired countenance was gone, replaced by wonder. He knew the feeling.

"Are you all right?"

A little nod. "I've never been more all right in my life," she whispered. "Who *are* you? *What* are you?"

"I am Steef."

"What's a Steef?" She was still whispering.

"I am. Can I help you up?"

"Your pardon Steef," that was new, a Master asking pardon from a Five, "But I don't think I want to touch you again. I can manage."

They made their way together in silence, the long walk back to the center of Town. Each had their own thoughts.

"I have to go this way," he said, pointing right.

"I have to go this way," she pointed left.

"Bright days to you, Master apprentice Leezel," he bowed to her.

"And to you, Steef." She watched him turn away. "Steef?"

He turned back. "Yes Mam?"

"Are you here for the Registry tomorrow?"

Naturally, he didn't catch it. "Yes Mam. I have to Register. I've not been looking to Mate, but I have to Register. My Master says so." Oops.

"You're apprenticed to a Master? I'm impressed. Which one? I know the names of most of the White Masters."

Sigh. He just wasn't good at this 'secret' stuff. Oh well. "My Master is Arima." Auntie probably wouldn't mind. This young lady couldn't do any harm to her plans, anyway.

To Steef's amazement, Leezel stiffened, both hands taking a death-grip on her staff. Her face suddenly lost all of that wonder she'd had. "Oh, no!" she exclaimed, and burst into tears. Spinning around, she raced away.

"Very adept, Steef. The first girl you meet, and she runs from you crying."

Steef's head was shaking, "Well, I'm not too practiced at this, Pill. Shame, too. I kind of liked her."

"Of course…you would."

❊   ❊   ❊

Steef's Red Locks worked really well. There were two Black Nines and a Red Master watching the hut, and they were convinced it was empty. No one home. Nothing here. Nope.

Trouble was, that wasn't good enough. If no one was home, there was no reason *not* to go in and look around. The hut belonged to Blues. Blues can't Lock a wooden door, or stone. And who's afraid of Blues, anyway?

Well, they should have been, because an irate Blue Master was watching them through the window, and her staff was fully charged. Or, more accurately, one of Arima's two staffs was fully charged…with Blue. As was the other of Arima's staffs…fully charged…with Black. Oddly, the only female Master in the hut who didn't have one of Arima's staffs fully charged, was Arima. There was a mild dispute going on about who would get to meet their visitors at the door.

"It's my hut, Linzel. I thank you, but it's my stand to make."

Linzel didn't know what she meant by 'stand', but those Nines out there were a non-issue for her. If anything, she was more concerned about the Red Master. "But Cassa! I…"

"I know, Linzel. Your pardon, but my days of fearing Black are over. Step aside, please. If I leave any, you can have them." With that, she began to get up her wind, inside the hut. Her parents, Blues themselves, watched proudly as she controlled it so well. Nothing was disturbed.

"They're coming in, Cassa! Right…now!"

The door opened in. She let it. Three figures were framed in the lantern's glow. Three figures that found themselves flying backwards, staffs flung away, along with chunks of the front wall of the hut. They found themselves in the road, on their backs. One of the Blacks had gotten off an errant Pulse, and it singed her Papa's shoulder.

Out strode Cassa, Master of Blue and mistress of the Clan. Cassarr, tribe of Zallrr. There was fury on her brow, and Blue death in her stone. These three were destined for a night flight of their own, to the farthest reach of this valley. No one would find their bones for cyc…her staff went dead, and her wind was killed. It didn't die, it was killed.

The three intruders could get up, and they did, racing to retrieve their staffs.

"Ha!" cried the Red, "You had your Pulse! Now, you'll feel ours!"

"No, she won't," said a soft voice from the shadows.

The Red turned to his companions, "No, she won't."

"That's right," said one, "She won't." "Not gonna feel anything," said the other.

"There's no one here," said the voice.

"This place is empty!" "Waste of time!" "What are we doing here?'

"The ones you seek are at the other end of this valley," so soft, so reasonable.

"We've been looking in the wrong place!" "We've got to go!" And they did just that.

As they left, the chunks of wall Lifted, floating back to the hut. Fitting themselves together, there was a brief Brown flash, and the hut was whole again.

Cassa had dropped her lifeless staff, her fury replaced with glee, which was bubbling out in a joyclap. Behind her, her parents and Linzel were gaping, mouths open in disbelief. Arima, Antee, and Mokam had realized, when Cassa's staff went dead, that Steef was here. They had returned to their beverages before the wall had even been repaired. Old stuff.

Standing almost in the road, an exultant Cassa turned to her parents, "Papa! Mother! I'd like to re-introduce you to Steef, the Master Clear!"

"Sassy, you're being kind of loud now," Steef whispered.

"Tired of hiding, Shortstick," she said, grabbing his neck in a hug. He could breathe later.

❦   ❦   ❦

"Now let's see if I understand this, Cassa," her Papa said, very formally. He was in a bit of shock. "This young man has control of all seven Colors?"

"Yes, Papa."

"And, since that's not enough, he also has something that actually *is* Clear, which is stronger than the other seven?"

"Yes, Papa. That's about it." That wasn't even close to 'it', but it was enough for one night.

Mother was becoming airheaded, "What other wonders can he do, dear?" Talking about her Shortstick as if he wasn't sitting right here with them at the table. True, he was trying hard…not to be. He kept getting up to leave, but she'd grab his tunic, and drag him back.

He brightened at that, and reached into his pouch, "I can show you the seventh…" he had lifted his hand, when four voices rang out "No!" and Sassy tackled him to the dirt, sitting on his belly.

"Cassa Blue!"

Uh-oh. She knew that tone. "Yes, Mother?" She'd begun tickling him, hands under his tunic. It had turned into a good night. He was holding his breath, but it wasn't gonna work.

"Do I understand correctly, that your young man here is the strongest Master in the world?"

"Yes, Mother." *Right between the ribs. Yes!*

"And therefore, outranks all of us?"

"Yes, Mother." Any beat now. His face was getting red.

"You're sitting on his chest, girl. Shamefully disrespectful. Get off of him right now!"

The breath blew out, and he started to squirm. Good enough. "Yes, Mother."

Antee spoke up, "I know something remarkable that they could see, without blowing up anything," he said brightly.

"What's that, Uncle?"

"Steef, would you hand Casim your staff, please?"

The other three nodded. This was great. A bewildered Casim, whose shoulder was Healing now, took the strange piece of wood and looked at it skeptically.

"Now, Casim," continued Antee, "Walk away from Steef, slowly."

"Very slowly, Papa," added Cassa, still grinning.

Casim's face said 'my daughter's Mate is airheaded' but he complied. When he got to two staffs, the stick stopped. He bumped into it gently.

"Push on it," said Cassa, gleefully.

Casim pushed. Then he pushed a little harder. Then he put his back into it, but his back got bent backwards. Then he put some wind into it. He didn't have his own staff, but he was a Ten, and even unfocused, that could be a lot of wind.

Not enough. The wind reversed, with the help of the Blue Lock in Steef's stick. It just pushed Casim right over backwards, and leaped towards Steef, sending the table flying in the process. Family night was over.

After much discussion, Pill had been sent to Maar. He'd meant well, even if he was a 'stonehead' and a 'furhead' and an 'airhead', etc. No, Linzel wasn't coming home tonight. Perhaps tomorrow. Why were the girls crying? Both of them? Well, she'd talk to them tomorrow.

She didn't realize that for the girls, she'd been gone for cycles. To her, it was yesterday. She really didn't know what they looked like any more, but that hadn't occurred to her, either.

　　　🌿　　　　　　🌿　　　　　　🌿

"Shortstick, I've been thinking."

"What about, Sassy?"

Her parents were asleep, mercifully. The Masters were sitting and talking, too awake to retire yet. There was now a solid bubble over the hut that nothing would penetrate, save Pill.

"That demonstration tonight made me curious about your staff."

"Okay."

"The sticks that you gave us," she noticed him glancing at Linzel, "Arima says 'no secrets' from Linzel, Shortstick. That's good enough for me."

"Okay."

"Anyway, those sticks are a span long. And Master strength…yes?"

"Yes." *Where was she going with this?*

"And the one that killed Seafer…two spans?"

"Oh, no! Arima!" cried Linzel. "Seafer's dead? Oh, Arima!"

"It's all right, Linzel. Well, it's not, but it is. It's been a while."

"Anyway…" Cassa was typically relentless, "Two spans killed a Master?"

"Yes."

"So how strong *is* a fivespan?"

He mumbled, "You know I don't like to talk about that, Sassy."

"I know, pumpkin. But tomorrow, it just might be important. There are a bunch of Masters out there, and they may just all come for us. How many Masters, Arima?" As a Grader, she might have an idea.

"I've been away a long time, Cassa. There were rarely more than three hundred active at any one time, though."

"How many Blacks, Linzel?"

"When I left, Cassa, there were thirty eight that stayed. I don't know what the number is now."

She turned back to Steef. "So how strong is that stick, Shortstick? Five spans. Five times Master strength?"

Antee spoke up, "Your concept is accurate, Cassa, but your numbering is off. A Two is roughly equal to ten Ones, and a Three is roughly equal to ten Twos."

Cassa's eyes widened, and she whistled, "So Steef's fivespan is equal to fifty Masters?" She was impressed. And relieved. That evened the wager just a bit.

Antee chuckled, and Mokam smiled. It was Mokam that helped her this time, "Your numbering is still wrong, little Blue. If one span of Seafwood is equal to a Master, then two spans is equal to ten Masters. That's what killed Seafer."

"And five times ten is fifty!"

"No," said the Brown patiently, "Two spans is ten Masters. Three spans is ten times that. One hundred Masters. Four spans is ten times that. One thousand Masters. And five spans..."

"Ten *thousand* Masters!!!??? she exclaimed. "Oh, Merciful...and you can *charge* that thing?"

The Master Clear looked away, "You know I can, Sassy," his small voice said.

Antee pondered his sort-of Mate. Should he say it? She still didn't get it. Antee had known for cycles. Since Seafer had died, really. He knew Mokam understood, and Arima had seen the boy's flash, before she'd been blinded by it. But Cassa obviously still didn't get it, after all this time. *Guess she should. Hope she can handle it.* "Cassa, you might as well have it all. This staff is five spans. Steef, how tall is Seafwood?"

Her hands flew to her mouth. She'd forgotten about Seafwood.

He sighed. Maybe they wouldn't ask any more, if he did it this once. "Sixty two staffs, last I measured Uncle."

"How wide?"

"Don't really know. Fifty staffs, maybe."

"And...now we're not going to do it, mind...but if we were to carve up ol' Seafwood into fivespans, how many do you think we'd get?"

"Couple of thousand, at least, Uncle."

Antee turned back to Cassa, who was starting to shake. The question that had been burning them all for so long, had too much answer.

Arima was calm. She'd already figured it out. Linzel looked concerned, but she was too far behind in these things to really understand. Mokam was nodding, proudly.

Antee continued, "A couple of thousand fivespans, each of them equal to ten thousand Masters." He was looking his Mate in the eye when he asked, "And can you fully charge that whole tree right now?"

"Yes Sir. She's got a charge in her right now, though not a full one. She's always charged. Sometimes I change the tune, but I keep her charged."

"And Steef," Antee's voice lowered, almost a whisper now, but everyone heard just fine, "Can you *discharge* that tree?"

Beat. Beat. Beat.

"Yes Sir. But I'm not going to."

"What happens if you do?"

"Everyone...everything...on the maps as I know them...goes away," he said solemnly. "Except me," he added. Turning back to his beloved Blue Master, he said, "You see, Sassy, it's never been about how *much* Power I can use. It's always been about how *little* I can use at a time...safely. Those three hundred Masters you're worried about? Don't be."

"O...O...Okay...Shortstick." She'd spent cycles sleeping under that tree. Her hands were trembling, as she wobbled to her feet. "I'm gonna go be sick now."

As they watched her walk out, Steef was ready to change the subject, "You might be interested to know, Auntie...I met a nice girl tonight. I liked her Okay, but I don't think she liked me much."

"Oh really?" Arima was glad to have something less gloomy to end the evening on, "Was she a girl of Power?"

"Yes Mam."

"Well, tell us about her! What Color was she? What was her name? What did you talk about?"

"She's a White, just like you. In fact, she looked a little bit like you! Her name is Leezel, and..."

"Pill!!"

Pop! Pop! Pop! Pop! Pop! Pop! Pop! Pop! Pop! Pop!

CHAPTER 22

Pop! Pop! *"Steef! Wake up!"*

"What is it, Pill?" He'd had a long night.

"We can't find Kivverr! And..."

"What!?" He sat straight up.

"There's more! We followed the river down the Valley, thinking we'd misjudged his progress. We found bodies."

"W...what...you found Kiv..."

"No! Pardon! Pardon! Not Kivverr's body. Not Cat bodies. People bodies. Parts of them anyway."

"What were people doing in the Valley?"

"Good question. There's more! We went back to the cove, thinking, maybe Kivverr had made better speed than we expected. He's not there, but the rest of the Clan was, and they had a new toy to play with."

"Toy? Cat's don't have toys!"

"They did this morning! A hand. Well, it used to be a hand, and part of an arm. They were tossing it around."

"And no sign of Kivverr?" There was a strange feeling in his belly. He didn't like it much.

"No. None. We think that's good. There's also been no more sign of any of those snakes. Steef, we ask pardon for saying so, but if Kivverr had met one of those snakes,...uh...there'd...uh...be something...left."

For Steef, everything just stopped for a beat. *I should never have left. I should never have left. I should never have left. I should have gone back, and carried those females out one at a time. They'd have never gotten on the sled. Then I should have just walked them out with him.* You got all the snakes. *Maybe.* You know you did.

"*We think some people came to visit, and didn't enjoy themselves much. We also think Kivverr must have gone up into the woods, out of the flatlands, in case anyone else showed up.*"

That made sense. *Kivverr would want to protect the females. He's up in the woods. There's no sign of…bones. He's up in the woods. He's Okay.*

Time to go home.

He jumped up. Grabbing his tunic and stick, he headed for the closet where Auntie and Master Linzel were sleeping. She opened the door before he got there.

"I know what you're going to say, but we can't leave yet, pumpkin. Regrets for true, but our affair in Town isn't finished."

"Auntie, I've got to *go*! Kivverr might be in trouble! I don't care about a Mate! Never did!"

"I know, Son, and I won't make you stay for that. Not any more. But *my* affair isn't done, yet, and it must be finished, for the Clan to have peace. Pill, see if she's here this morning." Pop!

By now, everyone was up. Linzel, who was still carrying Pill right now, asked, "Who is Kivverr?"

Since Arima was trying to console Shortstick, Cassa answered, "He's a HornCat. Largest male HornCat…probably ever…right, Antee?" Antee nodded, obviously concerned himself.

"And this HornCat…is Steef's pet?" *What kind of boy is this? He's got a HornCat for a pet?*

No one spoke right away. Explaining…would take more beats, and more candor…than they were willing to give. Even to Linzel. Steef cut through the awkwardness.

"He's not my Pet! No one owns Kivverr!," he exclaimed. "He's my brother." With that, he turned and walked away, Arima and Cassa following.

Linzel turned to look at Mokam and Antee. Her face said that 'brother' was not an answer that solved her puzzlement or wonder. They just shrugged and nodded to her. If anything, 'brother' wasn't enough.

❦   ❦   ❦

Everyone of Power that could get away from work was there, though the mood of the crowd was subdued. It should have been a happy, happy event, the

Registry. For true, each Guild was trying to make it happy. There were seven stages set in intervals around the arena, and each Guild had set up its best musicians. They were all playing, though not the same tune. It was tradition that each Guild would normally try to outplay the others. Success was usually measured by the size of the crowd gathered before each stage. Not this cycle. People were staying in their seats, around the banks of the great bowl. They weren't missing much. Few of the musicians had celebration on their minds, or in their instruments. Even the tunes that were meant to have gusto…didn't. The only exceptions to this were the Red stage, and the Black. Those folks were having a grand time.

There was one separate stage in the center of the arena. It was built round, and there were seven seats and seven small tables in its center. Three separate sets of steps led up from the ground, for access and regress. Upon the stage sat representatives from each Guild. In cycles past, that glad duty had fallen to the respective GuildMasters, but no GuildMasters were here today. Only their assistants. Masters themselves, none of them looked happy to be there, either. Well, the Black wasn't a Master. He was a Nine, and looked *particularly* uncomfortable.

Gathered all around the center stage, were the young people that had come to Register. For now and hereafter, they would be available for Mating, their Guild sponsorship public, and their presence known.

"But you *have* to, Leezel!"

"No…I don't."

"But I want to see the new boys, Leezel! There's plenty here that have never been to Town before!"

"You don't want to see *them*, Zelmar. You want *them* to see you."

Zelmar flicked a side glance and a smirk at her sister, "And why not? We're the prettiest girls here. Shouldn't we get first choice?"

Leezel released another sigh. She sighed a lot around Zelmar, "You're the prettiest girl here, Zelmar. You know. I know it. They know it. It's one of the reasons I Registered privately on our birthday last cycle." *Among others.* Leezel knew that she wasn't hard to look at. She also knew that she wasn't even close to Zelmar.

"Well, it's not *my* fault that our birthday came after the last Registry! *I'm* not Registered yet!"

"So, go Register. I'll wait right here." They were standing at the inside edge of the bowl, where the flatland of the center met the banks of seats. Zelmar was alternately pulling on Leezel's tunic, and stomping with a pout.

"I can't go without you! Everyone knows we're doubleborn! They'll wonder where you are! How am I supposed to explain that, way up there on that stage by myself?"

"If I were up there with you, Zelmar, you'd still be by yourself," Leezel said tiredly, "And if you do ever accept a Mating offer out of all the boys that follow you around, am I going to have to come with you then, too?"

"But you're firstborn!" stomped Zelmar. None of her tricks were working. She would have dearly loved to use a bit of Red on her stubborn sister, but that old crone that Leezel was apprenticed to would See it. The last time GuildMaster Vinntag had Seen Red on Leezel, GuildMaster Wingor had spoken to Father! Nope. Can't do that again. *But she's just so stubborn!*

"Leezel...Zelmar," came a soft voice from the direction of the seats. They turned.

"Mother!"

※   ※   ※

There were over a hundred young men and women gathered to Register. It didn't make for a crowded situation in the open field of the arena, but it felt crowded to the Master Clear. He wanted to be elsewhere.

Auntie and Sassy had pounded on him, gently but firmly. Everything they said made sense, it just didn't *feel* sensible. And Auntie had someone she needed to see, and Pill was looking. Sassy said that, if nothing got resolved, he could take her boat tonight, when no one was looking and go back to find Kivverr. Meanwhile, he was here. Might as well do what he came for.

Any fleeting interest that he'd had in looking for a girl was gone, but he didn't *have* to look. They were all here. If he stood in one spot, with the movement of the crowd, every one of them would pass right by him. For they were moving. The boys that were there...and somehow, they all looked like boys, even though he knew that all of them were his age or slightly older...the boys moved in packs, like herd beasts. They were pushing and shoving each other continually, and issuing loud comments about the girls. The girls weren't as loud, but their behavior was just as strange. Sometimes they would roam in pairs, sometimes they had their own packs, but they moved more than the boys, often pretending not to notice them, and sometimes appearing irritated if they felt unnoticed. A puzzle.

He had a splendid view of all the prospects, which was the point of the Registry to begin with.

If he hadn't been preoccupied, this might have been fun, watching how these people interacted with each other. Their behavior surely was odd. For one thing, when he caught snippets of conversation, the words rarely matched the Cores. What was the point of saying things you didn't mean? Very puzzling.

But he *was* preoccupied, so what little attention he gave to the event was focused on his purpose. Looking for a suitable girl. It's what Sassy wanted, for true. Auntie too, though less true. Every girl that passed him by got examined much more thoroughly than she would have liked, had she known. He was switching Sights constantly. Power levels and Color were interesting. Judging by the badges they wore, none of these people had been Graded very well. The Color was always right, but the numbers they wore were seldom accurate. And the nicer their garments were, the more difference he saw between their badges and their glow. All of them were glowing. No one was Cloaked. A few even glowed visibly, if they came close to matching their badge. Finally, when there was a difference, the badge was always higher than the glow. Another puzzle.

The scrutiny didn't stop there. Tiny White Pulses would tell him the health of each girl. Surprisingly, some of them were infertile. He wondered if they knew? They must not be getting good Healing, if their eggs had been allowed to die. Shame, that. Yet another puzzle.

Then there was the matter of the Cores. Steef wasn't yet a Master on judging Cores, but few of these looked good to him. Cores of mixed colors, mainly red and green. A few blue, and several black. Very little white. From his experience, white Cores were the best. His Mama had a really white Core. All of his family, blood or no, had white Cores, though Sassy's would flutter sometimes when she got mad. So he was looking for white.

He hadn't Seen much white in anyone's Cores since arriving in this strange Town. That Messenger fellow…he had a good one. Most of the others he'd Seen were in that 'hollow' place, where all those poor people lived. The baker, he was a nice man, and those two Masters. All good Cores, if he was interpreting it correctly. He'd been too busy later, to check Leezel's Core. Especially when he saw her gift.

Auntie had tried to explain to him why Leezel ran away crying. Master Linzel had also tried to help. He just didn't get it. How could anyone believe things about someone they'd never met? More surprising to him was that Leezel was Auntie's niece.

"You never told me you had a brother!" he'd exclaimed in surprise last night.

Auntie had grinned then. A big grin. She'd looked around the hut, and Sassy started grinning, as did Uncle Antee, "You never asked," she'd said, and they'd all started laughing. That was Okay. He liked it when they laughed, though he didn't know what the jest was.

So Leezel was Auntie's niece. And she was apprenticed to someone named Vinntag, who didn't like Auntie much, and didn't like Cats, either. That explained why Leezel had run off. Oh well. She seemed nice enough. Who could dislike a Cat?

He noticed that some of the girls would look at him, too, as they walked by. Never anyone of high rank, but some of the Fives and lower gave him a good look. He smiled back at them if they did, but none ever stopped. Usually they just whispered to themselves and giggled. Very odd.

The Master Red on the center stage stood and announced through his stone that the Registry would begin at exactly quarterday. Everyone looked up to check the sun. Only a few hundred more beats. Sassy said that he would have his turn when the Whites went, and that he should go when 'S'es were called. It would be a while, and he was pretty sure he'd seen all the girls. Filling with Clear, which tuned off all Sight, he abandoned the search. Just get Registered, and get *out of here!*

He had a few spare beats to fret about Kivverr. Fretting was as new as girls. No practice. Now that he wasn't distracted with his search, he could fidget nervously, and began looking around, rather than straight ahead. And he'd been wrong. There were two girls he'd missed, off to his left. They were coming his way. No, they were coming straight for him. One was Leezel. The other was shorter, with red hair.

Sigh. Switching back to Sight, he gave them the same thorough examination that the other girls had received. The red-haired girl had Red Power, about Seven. Healthy enough. Strange Core, with strong reds and greens. Little bit of white. He Saw why Leezel was a Master's apprentice. Her White was as strong as Auntie's. That made sense now. Her health was good and bad. Better muscle tone than most of the girls here. Low nutritional values...she wasn't eating well. Best Core he'd Seen today. Almost completely white. Tinges of most of the other colors, but she'd been weary just last night from Healing. Perhaps she'd been weary in her Core as well, from her duties as an Empath. Both girls were fertile. Well, that was a plus. *Wonder why Leezel is carrying a flawed stone in her staff?*

They weren't chatting or giggling as they walked together. He expected them to stop and mingle with the boys. There were surely enough boys giving them attention as they passed. No, they were still coming. *Okay*. He bowed. *Leezel first, she's the higher Grade.*

"Bright day, Master apprentice Leezel. I hope you are well. Bright day, Lady Seven. I hope you are well."

There was suddenly a lot of interest on the part of many of the waiting Registrants. *All* of the boys in that vicinity were watching, which meant that all of the girls needed to see *what* the boys were watching.

The red-haired girl spoke first, which was out of the protocol he'd been taught, but this was a strange place. "Mother says we have to be nice to you. Would you care to explain why a Master Black cares at all about a White Five?" she asked.

Neither her words nor her tone suggested to Steef that she was being nice, but Steef assumed that it was just something else he hadn't had the beats to learn. He answered, which seemed to surprise Leezel, and interrupt whatever she would have said, "Thank you for your courtesy, Lady Seven. I can't answer your question with anything but a guess, and that would be her long and friendly association with my Master."

"Well, regardless of what she says, not everyone in the family is frien...ow!"

Leezel had gotten a good grip on her sister's right earflap, and twisted. When Zelmar looked up, she saw in her sister's face the look she dreaded most...the 'I've put up with enough from you. I'm firstborn, I outrank you, I'm bigger than you, and you're going to pay attention' look.

Leezel saw Zelmar's jaw set in the 'I don't like it, but I get it, and I'm indignant for being put in my place' look. It would do. Releasing Zelmar's ear, she returned Steef's bow before his back set in that position, "Bright day to you, Steef. This rude wench is my sister Zelmar." Zelmar knocked Leezel's hand away from her ear. "On occasion, I have known her to have a civil tongue. I ask pardon for her rudeness." Zelmar opened her mouth, prompting Leezel to give her another 'look'.

Steef bowed again...

He surely is a 'bowing' young man thought Leezel...

"No pardon is called for, Master apprentice. Your sister's rank entitles her to speak as she will to a Five, and she has done me no harm."

"Well, at least he knows his place, Leezel. I'll be going now. There are people to meet." Before Leezel could stop her, Zelmar was heading for the nearest clump of boys, who immediately perked up.

Leezel turned back to Steef and took a good look. She had cause. Last night's experience with their touch would have been enough, but now her

Mother had actually expressed approval, not only of Steef, but her Aunt Arima as well. Of course, Mother hadn't been well for many cycles. Leezel reserved judgement.

What she saw didn't improve her opinion much. In the light of day, without benefit of a long day's weariness, she cast a more observational eye on this young Healer. He was shorter than herself, by a good half-span. Garments were in decent repair, if worn. *Hmmm. Burn scars on his hands.* Her lips pursed. *He's been Healing himself, or this 'Master Arima' doesn't know her craft.* And he had a slight musky odor about him that she hadn't noticed last night in the Hollow, where strong odors tended to close the nose. He smelled a bit like...a stable. Mmm-hmmm. Beast musk. Not strong, but...*Arima...the Cats! Oh...oh, my.* Her quick assessment was distracted now. Wheat colored hair. *Sad, that he wore it like a Master. No doubt, trying to be like his own Master.* She got to his face.

That was an expressive face.

Steef wasn't the prettiest boy she'd seen, but his eyes were alight and after last night, she knew what that light was. And there was an innocence to that face...though it twitched with emotions that her training recognized as observation and gladness. This was not a stupid boy, though his awkwardness might lead to that conclusion.

"Mother tells me...us...that the stories we've heard about...your Master...might not be entirely true..."

He bowed again.

"...and that Zelmar and I will be meeting her later today...after the Registry...and that I...we...can decide for ourselves...look...that's plenty of bows." He'd done it again.

Steef righted himself, and smiled placidly, eyes wide. Waiting.

Beat. Beat. Beat.

"Mother says that I...we...should decide about you on merit, and not on rumor."

"Decide what?" asked a genuinely open Master Clear.

He couldn't be serious...could he? He surely didn't look...worldly...enough to be deceptive. They were standing in the middle of the Registry Festival. Was anyone *that* naïve?

Yep.

Beat. Beat. Beat.

"Look...Steef...you should know that I have no intention of declaring myself to a Mate before I take my Mastery...no!...don't bow again..."

"Okay." He'd already said much the same to her last night. They were in complete agreement. Though she *was* nice. Really good Core, too. He was confident that he was doing well, giving all the courtesy that Sassy had taught him. *Listen to them, Shortstick. Girls like boys who listen.* Master Linzel had said that all Healers these days were taught to hate the Cats. Shame, that. If he ever did decide he wanted a Mate, the girl was going to have to like Cats.

Beat. Beat. Beat.

"You were a bit chattier last night, you know."

"I was?"

Well, no, now that she thought about it, he wasn't. It was one of the things she'd liked about him. He hadn't tried to impress her. *Probably because his Power could never match mine.* But now, his reticence was a bit trying. Perhaps he just wasn't interested. That happened a lot.

"If you'd rather talk to my sister again…she *is* the pretty one…"

"Not to me." He hadn't Seen or seen anything about Zelmar that he found appealing.

Now, what does that mean? This was easily the strangest conversation she'd ever had. No one, not even grown men, had *ever* preferred her company over Zelmar's.

"Get away from my girl!!"

Both of them looked away from each other, into the direction of the noise. The gathered young people made a clear path for the young man marching towards them. As he was prone to do, Steef made a quick scan of the boy. Sure enough, his Power didn't match his badge. He wore a Ten, but his glow said Six. Black Power, black Core. Healthy enough, though his pressure was a little high right now. Steef bowed.

"Bright day, Master…"

"Step aside, country boy. That's *my* girl you're talking to!" The newcomer went to push Steef's shoulder, hit something solid, glanced aside, lost balance and dumped himself into the grass.

When he bounded up, his pressure hadn't improved. "You'll pay for that!" He began glowing visibly, for effect.

"Your pardon, Master. Pay for what?"

"Stop it, Nessel! Leave him alone!"

"Stay out of this, Leezel! This is between men!" Although the newcomer added a look to this comment, that he didn't think Steef was much of a man. They were starting to attract a goodly amount of attention.

"Now boy, this girl has been oathed to me!" Steef turned quizzical eyes to Leezel. "You're wasting your beats here…and risking your health!"

By now, the ruckus had drawn some other attention…in the seating area. The only true Master Black in the arena had been watching the exchange between daughter and young man. It had lasted a pleasantly long time. This new clod was an unwelcome arrival. Her natural instinct was to intervene, especially since she didn't know the young Black wasn't actually a Ten. Then she remembered who it was that her daughter was speaking to, and a relaxed smile crossed her face. The arena had grown still with tension, and she could hear some of the conversation, at least the parts issuing from the intruder.

"Speaking to Leezel is unhealthy?" Steef didn't think so. He'd already checked, and she was very healthy. Well…she could use an extra meal. *Maybe some of those sweetbr…*

"It is when I'm around!"

"Nessel, I've told you a hundred times, I'm not Mating with you!"

"Your Father arranged it cycles ago, Leezel. The decision's made."

"So it isn't Leezel that's unhealthy…speaking to *you* is unhealthy?" Had he missed something? Steef Pulsed again, an invasive White. No, this boy had nothing catching.

"Are you *thick*?! You must be thick. Country boy come to find a Town girl. You smell, too! Not surprising, with an old tunic like that! Say, how much Dust can a Five White make, anyway? There's not a girl here who'll even speak to you, did you know that!? And what kind of stupid staff is that? Looks like you cut it from an old vine!"

Steef had to admit, no one but Zelmar and Leezel had spoken, and they'd been told to. This boy was probably right. Didn't matter. All Steef wanted to do was get back to the Valley, and find Kivverr.

"Look at him, Leezel!" shouted Zelmar, making her Mother frown, "He can't even speak, he's so afraid!"

Many of the young people began laughing. But Leezel was just furious. At Nessel. Then she glanced at Steef. She had a closer view than the others, and Steef's face hadn't changed. Same wide eyes. Same placid smile. She didn't see any fear. *Either he's too stupid to be afraid, or…*there was no 'or'. But she didn't think Steef was stupid. This boy was getting odder with each beat.

"Steef, even with his rank, Nessel can't speak to you like that! Nessel, move away! I'm a Ten too, and I say move on!"

"Now you've got a girl fighting for you, country boy!" More laughter.

Ignoring the Black, Steef said, "I thank you, Master apprentice," another bow to Leezel, "But this boy has done me no harm. He doesn't know me, so his opinions are guesses at best. He is just wasting his air, and it's his to waste." Steef was hoping this would give the Black an opportunity to exit gracefully. He didn't want to be challenged. Auntie had said that killing people was bad form. This 'Nessel' hadn't hurt anything, and Leezel might be squeamish.

Leezel's mouth dropped.

There was a gasp from the assembly around them, who'd nudged themselves closer to hear. They started backing up now, though some of them were snickering…at Nessel.

If Steef had worried about Nessel's pressure before, now he could be completely concerned. The young Black's face clouded over with fury, and turned bright red. He Pulsed without warning.

But Nessel's target had spent cycles trying to catch 'seventh' blue, which was really fast. The Black Pulse was slow by comparison. It also helped to See it coming. Steef released his own bubble, thinking the Black might glance off and hit someone, like Leezel. He put the bubble around Nessel, instead.

It was fortunate for Nessel that he was only a Six. A stronger Pulse would surely have killed him. Instead, it just bounced around inside that bubble, slicing off bits of Nessel here and there. Since the Pulse was visible, it made for quite a show. His dancing helped, too. The crowd began laughing outright, at Nessel's obvious inability to make an effective Pulse.

When it was over, Steef released the bubble and reached in, "I can Heal that for you, if you like," he said sincerely. In fact, he'd already started, Pulsing some White to relieve the boy's pressure, which was surely about to blow his head off.

Leezel popped her mouth closed, bemused. *A Five can't Heal a Ten! What kind of training has Steef gotten?*

Nessel was crouched in pain, but had plenty enough fury left to look up and glower at Steef. Unexpectedly, he snatched Steef's staff from his hand, and spun away!

Several things happened at once. In the seats, Linzel charged her staff. The crowd, seeing Nessel was leaving, made a new path. Leezel tried to grab his tunic, and missed. Then she turned to Steef, to ask pardon for his loss. She fully intended, on the spot, to get him a new staff. Fivespans weren't particularly expensive.

Wide eyes. Placid smile. Steef straightened the little bit he'd been leaning. And waited. There were just enough beats for Leezel to add one more puzzle to this mysterious boy when…

Nessel got to two staffs distance and the staff stopped. Of course, Nessel didn't. His nose was softer than Steef's stone, so the stone reshaped it for him. And Nessel found himself once more on the ground. It hadn't been a good day for him, and the Registry hadn't even started. He was able to crawl off unnoticed, however. The crowd's attention was elsewhere.

Amidst a stunned silence, Steef's staff floated back to his outstretched hand. Leezel hadn't seen Nessel's abrupt stop, but she saw the floating staff. Her mouth dropped open again.

"Steef…"

"Yes Mam?"

"I've got to go now."

One last bow, "Bright day, Master apprentice Leezel," said the Master Clear, amiably. He turned back to the Registry stage.

"Bright day…Steef," She numbly offered to his back, as she turned away. The very silent crowd made a fresh path for her, and all of them hoped that by not looking at him, the strange Five White wouldn't notice them.

Leezel made a straight path back to where her Mother was sitting. She wanted answers.

Linzel wasn't giving any.

❧   ❧   ❧

It took a while. Black went first. Then Red. He'd listened to a lot of…'My name is!…I wield Black!…My sponsor is Master!…I work at!…' Some glowed, some didn't. Popularity and acquaintance could be judged by the reception each youth sparked. Some got rousing applause. Some only scattered.

When the Reds went through, some of them had actually Pulsed, trying to sway the assembled. Steef assumed they really must want to find a Mate. Zelmar had taken her turn without using her Red. She used her hips. Well, she used everything…but Red. She was well received.

White went next. Steef started moving forward, which he found easy to do, since he was given ample room. Leezel should have been ahead of him, but he didn't see her. He supposed she just wasn't going to Register. Perhaps he'd misjudged her age. Oh well.

Finally, it was his turn. He'd watched the others. It was a simple process, really. Stand in front of the table of your own Color, and proclaim yourself. They were recording names. Then sign the Register and move on. He hoped Auntie had found that Vinntag woman, so they could go. Auntie had a bubble around her, so she was safe. All of his family did, even Master Linzel. Pill hadn't said much all morning. They still couldn't find Kivverr, but the Valley was a big place.

"I am Steef!" He didn't know how long he should wait. Give it a few beats.

A couple of the girls giggled, but someone hushed them.

"I wield White!" Well, he *did*...amongst others.

Silence.

The White Master sitting behind him cleared his throat, "You have to have a sponsor, young man."

Sassy hadn't told him that. Bow, now, "Your pardon, Master. I was unaware..."

"You have to have a Master to sponsor you. Master's Law, young fellow. We posted parches in all the outlying villages."

"Okay," he shrugged. The giggles started again. Steef turned to walk off the stage.

"I'll sponsor him!" came a familiar female voice. Sassy was striding purposefully across the grass. "If he needs a Master, he's got one!" She took the steps two at a time, and planted herself in front of the White Master.

"And you are?..."

"Cassa, Master Blue. Certified Steerman, Controller, and Heavy Water. Will that do?" She tamped her staff on the wooden floor. Arima's staff, actually.

"Blue Masters have masts, Cassa. They don't carry staffs."

"This one does. Need a demonstration? My Master's rank can be verified by *him*!" She pointed to the Master Blue sitting behind his own table, who looked like he wanted to be elsewhere.

The White looked across at the Blue, who nodded. "I'm afraid that's still not good enough, Master Blue. You see, this young man is a White. He must be sponsored by a White Master."

Steef tugged on Sassy's sleeve and whispered, "It's Okay, Sassy. Let's just go." He didn't care if they laughed at *him*, but he wouldn't have them laughing at Sassy...for her sake, or theirs. Enough of it, and it would have to be challenge. He didn't like this Town much.

"We're not going anywhere, Shortstick," she whispered back. Then to the White, "Am I to understand that your Master's Law prevents me from sponsoring him?"

"Yes. Your pardon, Master…"

"Well, since I am a Master also, how about I just set aside the old Master Law and make up a new one! One that says…"

"Steef *has* a White Master to sponsor him," came another familiar voice.

Heads had been turning from Cassa, to the White Registrar, to Steef, back to Cassa, and now to the steps, where Arima was stepping up.

Guess her search is over thought Steef. *Good. Maybe we can go home now. This is more trouble than it's worth, and the only girl worth talking to keeps running away.*

Arima took her time. She stepped up to the White Master, who had gone from official-looking, to stricken-looking. Squinting, she was thumbing through the parches of her memories. "Mmmmeeb…yes, that's it. Meeben. Bright day, Meeben. Are you making difficulties for my apprentice?"

Steef was startled to see an abrupt change in the man's Core. It had been an odd mix of colors, though not dark. Now, however, it flared white, with just a hint of blue.

"Ma…Master Arima! I had heard…but you can't believe rumors…you're here!"

"Is that a problem, Meeben?" She gave him a stern look.

Steef knew that look. He'd seen it often enough. Now he tugged on Auntie's sleeve.

"What is it, Son?"

Tilting up to her ear, he whispered, "He's *glad* to see you, Auntie."

Her eyes narrowed further, "Are you certain?" She really wanted to be angry at someone, and this 'Meeben' looked promising for that.

The Master Clear nodded.

Sigh. She still needed someone to be mad at. "Well, Meeben, I suppose you'll do! Put the boy's name down, and I'll oath to his sponsorship." The two Masters bent to the parch.

Steef looked up to see sixteen Black Pulses coming in. Sigh. He put a bubble over the stage.

"Pill, there's obviously some Pools here," he said quietly.

"*They haven't moved since we got here, Steef. They're being careful.*"

"Well, so are you. Any reason why we shouldn't get their attention like we did yesterday?"

"None that we can think of."

"How many beats do you need, once you leave?"

"To tell the other families, and then clear out? Ten…no, make it twelve."

"Start now." Pop! Pop!

Auntie and Sassy flinched briefly as their Pills left them.

…Nine. Ten. Eleven. Twelve.

Dead Pools fell from the heads of five of the Registrars. The Black, a Nine, didn't have Buzzbies. Meeben, a Master, strangely didn't have any either. Steef liked him better with each beat.

Coincidentally, Yellow HiveMasters around that valley, who'd brought in new hives after yesterday's debacle, got really frustrated about then.

The Black Pulses had hit his bubble, and some of them had deflected into the crowd. Several people were hurt. Most started screaming. All of them started running. And another round of Black was coming in.

That was *enough*, now! Green for aim. Brown and Black for affect. He Pulsed again.

Scattered all around Town, sixteen separate Nines suddenly found themselves in possession of burning staffs. The flames roared up faster than they could let go, and all got their hands burned. In their pain, they failed to notice that their stones had burst, as well.

The crowd was rapidly leaving. The Registry was over.

From the side of the field, Leezel had watched Steef's declaration. She watched as he endured what would have mortified anyone else, and his face hadn't changed…still. Still smiling, still looking around with those expressive eyes. Her feet started moving on their own. Then Master Arima had arrived. Even from here, Leezel could see the resemblance. She moved closer still, wanting to catch their conversation. Her Aunt's bearing, her gestures, her voice…they were Leezel's own. Master Arima was bending to the table, and Steef had lost interest. Completely. He'd *meant* it…when he said he wasn't seriously looking for a Mate. She wasn't used to the truth from boys. Everything about this boy was true. Whatever it was.

His lips were moving. Her feet were moving.

Then people started getting hit with Black Pulses. Had to be Black. There was panic, and she was jostled. Still, she moved forward. She'd lived in the shadow of Black fear most of her life, and she wanted to see. Her Aunt, and this strange boy. She couldn't get any closer for the crowd, stopping to let them flow around her. Looking up at the stage, from her Aunt…to Steef. Arima. Steef.

Steef was Looking, watching for any more Pulses. Pulsing White himself, at any who'd gotten hurt. The Red Master on the stage had jumped up, Pulsing in the general direction of Auntie and Sassy. His staff also went up in flames. That's when the stage got cleared out. Everyone left but his family, and that Meeben fellow.

So Steef was Looking and looking, and his eyes fell on Leezel. While everyone else in Town was fleeing, she was standing still. Looking up at the stage.

Standing.

This was serious. He'd liked her Okay before, without serious thought. Cared about Healing people. Good Core. Good Power. Good eggs. Nice smile. Really blue eyes.

But in the midst of all the mayhem, she had stood. No steps back. That was something to respect. Amongst all the girls here, she'd been the only one of interest. And she was a Healer. That would be handy. Master strength, so she *could* Heal him…some. And she was Auntie's niece, and Master Linzel's daughter. More good things.

And she was an Empath. She could teach him about emotions. He could even experience them. The unpleasant ones, at least. He couldn't truly appreciate the sweet ones, if he never tasted the sour.

And she was standing.

Leezel was what Uncle Antee called 'the best of the birthing'. Out of all the girls here, she was the only one that had done him courtesy. It would be Leezel, or no one.

Their eyes met, and this time he held her gaze. Behind him, Cassa nudged Arima, who turned from Meeben's prostrations, and the two women exchanged a look. Their boy had chosen himself a girl. Arima recognized instantly who she was, but the kinship wasn't really an issue for her either way. This girl was a stranger to her.

Now, if she would just choose him back.

Cassa shared a bright grin with Arima, and the two of them gave Steef a shove in the back, forcing him off the edge of the stage. He dropped to the ground, and started walking towards the young Healer.

Neither youngster noticed, but there were people converging on them from several directions of the almost-empty arena. Cassa and Arima made their way to the steps, intending to witness the oathing, if there was one. Linzel was coming in from her spot. Antee and Mokam had arrived with Cassa, and they were stepping out. And Zelmar had done the only thing she was good at. She had gone to get her Father.

Steef noticed none of this as he got close enough to speak. For the first time, he didn't bow to her, on this occasion when he actually should have, "Leezel, I offer myself as Mate," he said simply. Typical Steef.

Her eyes never left his. "I knew you would," she replied, observing him closely. He still had that...

Steef put on his 'concentration' face. Thankfully, he didn't stick out his tongue. "You did? When?"

"Last night." She'd thought he had been playing with her, like her sister's suitors always did. He hadn't, and she knew she'd been wrong. Yet, she'd been right, too, for here he was, offering himself. This was a strange boy. "Mother," she said, nodding to the arriving Linzel. "Master Arima."

Arima would have loved nothing better than to hug the girl, and have a long reunion. But there was a more important issue going on. She bowed to her new/old niece, and remained silent.

"Steef, I..."

"No, Leezel," she heard her Father's voice behind her, solemn, but not unkind. She didn't turn, keeping her gaze on Steef, trying to figure him out. Her Mother had been no help, saying she should 'come to her own conclusions' about something so serious.

"I won't be Mating with Nessel, Father, and I don't ask pardon. That was your idea, not mine."

"I know, daughter. I was wrong, and I intend to return his Father's Dust. But you don't know this boy, and Leezel...he's a Five!" Maar's old values had been dashed over the last few cycles, but good sense said that a future Master could do better than a Five. He'd had no help finding new values, with Linzel Locked up in Red. "What can he offer you?"

Steef replied, surprising everyone, "I can offer great joy..." he reached out his hand, but she pointedly pulled hers back. This was not the time or place for that. "...and it seems to me that would be something she's missed." He pulled his hand back. "And, I offer to share the great adventure that is my life."

It struck Arima that her boy had found eloquence, without knowing it. Shame this young girl could have no way of knowing what was offered in that simple statement. Good, too, that Leezel's decision wouldn't be swayed by outside considerations. She would decide on Steef the man, not Steef the Master Clear.

"It's my decision to make, Father. It always was. And I will make it." She still hadn't turned from Steef's face. "Steef...I like you...I think. And I know the joy you offer is real...and special...but...I really do want to complete my Mastery. We are too young for this yet. I…must…refuse." She wanted to add that there were cycles left for the two of them to get better acquainted. No final decision need be made now. She assumed he knew this. She'd watched for cycles as Zelmar's suitors had refused to take the first, or even tenth, 'no' for an answer.

But Steef wasn't any of those boys. He'd asked. She'd answered. It would be no one.

Serene, placid smile again. Quick nod. "Okay."

Something about the finality of his response struck Leezel, and she knew. In fairness, she hadn't known him long. Also in fairness, she'd had enough clues to know one thing about this boy. He didn't Play The Game. He'd offered. Been answered. She felt the urge to shout 'Wait! Let's talk about this!'.

Four Masters were saddened beyond words. Each of them understood everything that had transpired in a few simple words, and everything that had been missed. It was too important to interfere, and too important not to. Arima glanced at Linzel, and saw that she, too, had an idea of what had been missed here.

"There he is, GuildMaster!"

With the intensity of what they were immersed in, the shout jolted everyone. As one, they turned in that direction. Nessel had retrieved someone, too. Kuumit.

GuildMaster of Black, striding towards them, with an entourage of sixteen Black Nines, and Nessel. The Nines had staffs in their unburned hands. Staffs that had been jerked out of the hands of other Colors. They began encircling the group, as Kuumit continued to approach. Steef and Arima could See that his staff was charged.

But Kuumit wasn't the only Black Master there with a charged staff. "Challenge, Kuumit!" shouted Linzel, suddenly shifting from Mother to Master. "I give Challenge!" She stepped out of the family group, where Kuumit could see exactly who would be killing him today. "You don't have a Guild full of Masters at my back today, Kuumit!" She planted her feet, and staff, in 'ready' stance.

So did Kuumit, "I have sixteen Nines though, Linzel! Even *you* can't match all of us!"

"The Nines won't be much help to you, Kuumit…will they Steef!?"

The Master Clear shrugged, "Do you ask aid in this challenge, Master Linzel?"

"I do."

"Okay." Sixteen more burned hands. In general, Black Guild was having a bad day. The staff crafters were going to be happy, though.

Linzel smiled, "Now, Kuumit. Just you and me."

"Uh…Linzel…"

Arima grabbed Steef's arm, "You See it, don't you?" she whispered hoarsely.

Of course he Saw it. Linzel and Kuumit's Power were very closely matched. Neither had an advantage. When they engaged, both would die. He nodded.

"Well…*do something!*"

"It's not my challenge, Auntie," he said quietly. The issue with Leezel was over. He liked Master Linzel, but this was her challenge to make. He'd given the aid she'd requested. This was a brief interruption, and then he was heading home.

Sometimes, she wanted to…no, "He might know where Vinntag is! I could finish my affairs, and we can *all* go home!"

That was different. Two Black Masters suddenly found themselves in possession of dead staffs. Steef wasted no beats. Marching across the distance that separated them, heedless of Master Linzel's distress at not getting to kill her old enemy, Steef faced the GuildMaster of Black. He Saw that Kuumit had some small Red Locks. Not large, but fairly strong. Wiping those away, he said pleasantly, "GuildMaster, I am in need of some information."

SNAP!! Kuumit had been aware of his surroundings, and their events. He was just no longer waiting with anticipation for his devoted friend Wingor to return. No longer feeling the urge to lay any eggs, he instead felt an urge to kill Wingor. After he killed this little White in front of him. No, Vinntag had said be careful if he ran into a 'Steef'. He couldn't contact Vinntag. Everyone's Pools had died again. Aggravating, that. There was still Linzel to deal with. He needed help, and none of his Masters were back yet. Oh, yes, Vinntag wanted to talk to this 'Steef'.

"You'll be coming with me, boy!" Kuumit reached to take Steef's arm.

Sigh.

The Black Nines were gone. Nessel was gone. Steef could hear that his family had followed behind him.

"GuildMaster, I have a question for you." Soft. Gentle. Such a *good* friend.

"I would be honored to help," replied the GuildMaster. His brief respite from Red was over.

"Would you know where someone named Vinntag might be?"

"She's travelling back here as we speak, dear friend. She should arrive tomorrow morning."

Steef turned to Auntie, they nodded at each other. Then another question came to him, "Has she been to the Valley of the Cats?'

"No, young Master. She would never go there."

Had Steef had any real Red training, other questions might have presented themselves. But he was not a skilled interrogator, and for once, his single-mindedness worked against him. It was a profound mistake.

"Auntie, it appears that we need to wait until morning." She nodded, the others listened.

"I think I'm going to let the GuildMaster here…detain me." They drew back. "He won't remember that you're here. If he has me, then you can give your challenge undisturbed, and then…we can go home."

She nodded again, wordlessly. They couldn't hurt him. This might be best.

He addressed all four of his family, "You need to keep everyone right here for a few beats, until we're out of sight. Auntie, you'll know when."

"All right, Son."

"GuildMaster, would you care to lead me to…"

"The holding hut," interjected Arima.

"…your holding hut, pleasing?"

"I'd be delighted! Shall we go?" The two of them walked off, with Kuumit's arm around Steef's shoulders.

The four Masters knew that Steef would be putting a bubble up. Arima watched them out of sight, when she Saw a large Red flash. They were now no longer even a memory to anyone near.

Meanwhile, Leezel hadn't moved. She'd been on the verge of a really thorough cry, when the world of Black had exploded around them. It had been a trying day.

"Mother?"

"Leezel, we can talk later. For now, I have to go with these good people. I gave my oath…"

"Linzel," asked Maar, politely, "Will you be coming home, after?"

"Yes, Maar. I'll be coming home. For a while, at least." She swung her staff around, fully charged again, putting the stone near his chest. "But no more Red, Maar. For me…or the girls."

Maar knew that staff. He'd helped his parents earn the Dust that bought it for Arima…so many cycles ago. He remembered the celebration they'd given her, presenting the staff, preparing to send her to her apprenticeship. His envy had found itself that day, changing his life. The result was a sister he no longer knew, a Mate that distrusted him, one daughter that was just like him, and thankfully, one daughter that was like her Mother. And her Aunt. He wrapped both hands around the stone, feeling the Power there. More Power than he'd ever known, or could handle. It crackled in his palms. Pulling the stone in, he held it to his breast. A breath away.

"No more Red, Linzel. I oath you."

Maar had changed, while she'd been in her Red fog. She could see it. Her staff drained. "Take the girls home, Maar. I'll come when I can."

Maar gestured to the sisters, and Zelmar turned to go, triumphant, oblivious.

Not Leezel. She needed answers...still. "Mmmooothhherrrrrr..." came a low growl, "What just happened here!?"

Her four friends were starting to leave, and Linzel needed to catch up. But, this *was* Leezel, "Let's see. Some people got hurt. You met your Aunt, sort of. Your Father seems to have found his humanity again. The Black Guild is in shambles, though I missed my last chance to kill Kuumit...because I think someone else is going to do that for me...and, somewhere in there, you managed to talk your way out of an amazing opportunity...the real tragedy of *that* being...the apprenticeship you're valuing so much...is coming to an end tomorrow." She patted her daughter on the arm, and followed her friends, leaving Leezel to her own thoughts.

❦　　　❦　　　❦

"*They've Locked you in here, you know.*"

"No they haven't."

The closet they'd put him in was dark, of course. The walls and floor were Cloaked, to block anyone from drawing any Power, lest someone have illusions about breaking out.

Pop! "*Arima and the others are safely back at Cassa's hut.*" Pop!

Good. He put up a new bubble, one that let in only air, and Pill. Stretching out, he tried to rest. There hadn't been much sleep last night, and tomorrow, they would be starting their non-stop flight back to the Valley.

The Sevens and Sixes in charge of the holding hut had watched in wonder as Kuumit had led Steef to this closet without removing the Five's staff. A Brown Master on duty here had sealed the wall, and Locked it. Steef had watched in silence. Uncle Mokam could have done a better one.

Kuumit went back to his closet, and sat there humming. The personnel, while amazed, held their opinions. It was an improvement.

Meanwhile, the boy who'd had his Mating offer rejected, was fretting about a Cat.

✳   ✳   ✳

"Leezel, are you still crying?"

"Go away, Zelmar."

"He was a scruffy little Five, Leezel. You can do much better."

"Go *away*, Zelmar!"

Father had said 'No Red, Zelmar' and he meant it, but Leezel sure did need some. What *was* her problem? Zelmar said 'no' twenty times a day, to far better offers. Well, *some* of them were better. Some of them were…well, some of them were better. That boy hadn't even been particularly good looking. And he was *strange*. Had to be. He hadn't noticed her at all.

"Father says we have to go to the final Festival at dark, Leezel. He says…"

"I'm not going."

"Father says…" Zelmar ducked under the flying parch. "I'll tell him, but he won't like it." What was it to her, anyway? She had her own problems. Mother hadn't finished that new tunic she'd planned to wear. She left.

"Leezel?"

"Not now, Father."

"I ask true pardon, Leezel. For everything." He pulled up her chair, and sat next to her pad. "But my Guild has required all of us to attend tonight. They have some special event planned. They're actually closing the Vault early."

"I'm not Red, Father."

"Of course you're not, daughter. But it would be noticed if you weren't there. As the daughter of a prominent Red, it would be noticed. Could you make the effort…for me?"

Leezel had never heard those tones from her Father. She opened her eyes, to see the strain on his face. She knew that things had changed for him, these last few cycles, but he'd always been too stuffy to share those worries with her. Not now.

"All right, Father. I'll try."

"Many thanks, Leezel."

✳   ✳   ✳

Pop! *"They're dead again, Vinntag!"*

"Who's dead, Pool?" She'd had all the boat she wanted, and her thoughts were troubled. There'd been beats a'plenty to contemplate this 'Clear' nonsense. Added to that, her snakes were dead. Something Powerful had done that. And she hadn't heard from Kuumit.

"All of our family that was in Town. They're dead. We're not going back."

"You aren't going to be much use to us Pool, if you won't go into Town."

"If you and Wingor and Kuumit don't find and deal with whatever's doing this, we don't plan on being any further use to you, anyway. Ever."

"Did you see Kuumit?"

"Oh, yes. Kuumit's fine. Better than fine. He's happy as he can be, sitting at his worktable, humming to himself. Gave greets to us. Asked how we were. Then he went back to his humming."

Wingor looked up at that. He was getting the same report. Trouble was, he knew right away what that meant. Someone had broken his Locks. Vinntag wouldn't know. She was enjoying her own Red Locks. This was serious.

Both Masters turned to look at the three bundles at the bottom of the boat. They might really be needed now. The two largest ones were still squirming a bit. The small one wasn't.

They looked back at each other. Two would have to be enough.

CHAPTER 23

Pop! *"Steef! Wake up!"*

He opened his eyes, "What is it, Pill?" *Where AM I? Oh...the holding hut.*

"We've found Kivverr..." Pop! Pop! Pop!

"Good, where was he?" Whew!

Pop! Pop! Pop! *"...No! It's not good! He's in trouble! You've got to come! Right now!"*

"Trouble?!" Steef was vertical, his staff springing into an open palm. "Tell the others! I'll meet them at the boat!"

"You don't need the boat! Kivverr's HERE!! You've got to HURRY!!" Pop! Pop! Pop! Pop!

"Here?" The four walls between him and the road suddenly melted. He was already jumping through the first one before the fourth was down. "Where, here?"

Pop! Pop! *"At the arena! You're not hurrying fast enough!"* Pop! Pop! Pop! Pop!

"How'd he get *here*?" Sprinting down the road. Pills covered his back, wings beating, trying to push.

Pop! Pop! *"Faster! You've got to HURRY FASTER!"* Pop! Pop! Pop! Pop!

In the twilight, Steef could see light coming up in the distance from the direction of the arena. Faint swells of crowd noise reached him. He put Lift on his trous and tunic. His bounds were carrying him three staffs at a time.

Pop! Pop! Pop! Pop! Pop! Pop! Pop! Pop! Pop! *"We're running out of beats! Get there NOW!"* Pop! Pop! Pop! Pop! Pop! Pop! Pop! Pop! Pop! Pop! Pop! Pop! Pop! Pop! Pop! Pop! Pop! Pop! Pop! Pop!

Pill covered him now, from the knees up, just leaving enough space to see and breathe. Putting Lift on himself, he felt his pump accelerate. A brutal tail wind came in, giving him twenty staffs at each bound. If Pill was speaking now, Steef couldn't hear for the wind, and the loud drone of wings.

There was the arena, with two boats hovering above it. Crowded with people, and he could hear cheers. No way through the crowd. He leapt, bounding over the fringe of people, his path following the downward slope of the arena's bowl.

And he saw Kivverr.

His brother was tangled in nets. The Cat could barely move, but he was trying. There were people all around him, taunting him. They were all carrying some kind of sticks. Three people lay on the ground, cut almost in half by claws.

But Kivverr had some of those sticks…sticking out of him. He was snarling and roaring, swiping at sticks and throwers, best he could. As Steef's bound brought him closer, another stick was flung, catching Kivverr in the chest. The great Cat fell to his knees.

"NNNNNNNNOOOOOOOOOOOOOOOOOOO!!!!!!!!!!!!!!!!!"

For cycles to come, there would be parches written of that very beat, and the fact that the Master Clear thought of White first, and not Black. People would speak in whispers, of the goodness of the Master Clear, that White was always his first choice. The Master Clear himself would never say, preferring not to relive it. Those close to him would say that, more likely it was the fact that he'd used White so often to deal with people that were troubling him, it was habit.

Whatever the reason, a savage White Pulse went out, and every soul on the floor of the arena dropped. Pill Pop!'d out, all but his two regulars, who wouldn't leave him. He landed lightly on his own, releasing the Lift, and sprinted the remaining distance to his brother. A bubble went up, as Steef threw himself to his knees, his staff Pulsing Yellow before they touched.

Pop! Pop! Pop! Pop! Pop! "Arima!" "Antee!" "Cassa!" "Mokam!" "Linzel!" Pop! Pop! Pop! Pop! Pop!

Once again, there was a hole in the front of Casim and Liksa's hut. The two Blue Tens watched in bewilderment, at the swiftly retreating backs of the five Masters.

✤   ✤   ✤

It was a disgusting thing they were doing. Whatever she might think of Cats, and her opinions had been questioned somewhat in the last two days, this was primitive, and beneath human. She watched as a Red Master shouted through his stone to the crowds, stirring them up. If she'd been sitting anywhere but with the Reds, his Pulses would have gotten her too. Untouched by his persuasion, she chose not to watch. In fact, she tried to leave twice, but Father pulled her back down. She could see that he was as repulsed as she was, but if he left, his work might be forfeit. Even her sister was affected, her skin pale, and her eyes wide in horror. Perhaps there was hope for her yet.

And so it was, that Leezel, Master apprentice Healer, her eyes averted from the savagery below, was gazing up and away instead of down to the field. In that beat, her mood turned from horror to wonder, for she saw a swarm of Buzzbies come gliding over the crowd, which was strange enough on its own. But as it got closer, she saw that the swarm of Buzzbies had legs...and arms...and a staff!...and *she knew that staff!!!*

Before the Buzzbies had cleared. Before Steef's feet had touched down. Before, even, his crying out...her feet were moving on her again. Father had once more reached to grab her, but she jerked her sleeve from his grasp, pulling her staff out of the dirt with her free hand, and began running down the open lane of the seating area, towards the arena floor.

That was her Mate out there. She'd known it from the beat his hand had touched hers. She'd known it with all three of their parting greets, each parting having its own share of turmoil. And she'd known it for true when his simple 'Okay' told her that she'd missed. Whatever his secrets were, they would be hers, for she was headed to his side, plunging unthinking into the carnage before her.

Perhaps the Creator himself was smiling on them in the horror, for she had far enough to go, and Steef's Pulse was precise enough, that she was still in the seating area when his White leveled the field.

✤   ✤   ✤

Whew! He could Heal this! Kivverr was grievously wounded, but it was still Healable. Just barely. He was bleeding inside, though. Got to do it now.

"I am glad you are here. I was not enjoying this much."

"Well, we're gonna Heal you right up! You'll need to close your eyes." Steef reached into his pouch to retrieve his 'seventh' Dust. This would take a lot of it.

"No."

"What, no?" Steef's staff was already pouring out Yellow, and the Master Clear was filling the arena with his Yellow glow, though no one was there to See it. It would be a massive discharge.

"You cannot blast me with your stick."

"What? Sure I can!...I will!...now, close your..."

"You will go to sleep, and those killers will have us both."

"Huh?...No...that's Okay. The blast'll kill them anyway. Now..."

"No."

"WHAT!? NO!...Kivverr, we don't have many beats..."

"You will kill everyone that way. That is not good."

"OKAY! OKAY! I'll just go kill these..."

"No."

"Kivverr...please...we're running out..."

"Are you going to eat them?"

"Huh? Of course I'm not gonna eat..."

"You are Clan. We eat our kill."

"Just this once..."

"I have not spent my life on you to see you become a killer. You are the Mix-Master. You are gladness and good things. Why do you think I stayed? If you become a killer now, because of me...I will have no Rest."

"But..."

"These are miserable two-legs, not worthy of the MixMaster."

He could fix this. He could Heal Kivverr. He could discharge White, putting everyone to sleep, giving him the beats he needed. No...Kivver was weak, the White blast would kill him. He could do this...he just needed beats...he was running out of beats...just a few beats.

Then, there weren't enough beats. He could feel it. Kivverr had lost too much blood inside. No amount of Yellow could put back all the blood. He was out of beats.

Kivverr was going to die.

"AAAAAAAAAAAAAAAAAAAAAAAAAAAAAAAAAAAAAAAAAAAAAAHHH HHHHHHHHHHHHHHHHHHHHHHHHHHHH**HHHHHHHHHHHHHHH-HHHH!!!**"

※   ※   ※

They heard it across Town. Into the Hollow. All through the valley. A cry of anguish, amplified by the Power of Clear. Rending the spirits of glad people. Emboldening the wicked.

Their passage slower than Steef's had been, the family of five Masters hadn't covered half the distance they needed, when it struck them.

It broke Arima. All her fears realized. All her cautions failed. She stumbled. "My boy. My boy. I knew it. I knew..."

Cassa and Linzel caught her as her knees touched, lifting her, half-carrying her. Hastening as they could, for their own grief was kindled. But they couldn't stop. They *had* to *get* there!

※   ※   ※

Leezel was just over half way herself, across the open field of the arena, when the cry hit her. Empath, glad and open spirit racing to her Mate, she caught the full force of his torment, as if stepping out of a sheltered wall into a swirlfury wind. With a simple "OOHHMMPH" she was knocked flat back, instantly covered with her own shedding sludge, dazed from the impact.

※   ※   ※

Most of the Black Guild's Masters had returned with the boats bringing the Cats. The three female Cats had died in the journey, too weak to handle the stress. They hadn't required any attention upon arrival. A few of the Masters had gone to the Black GuildHall to report in, since none of their Pools would come into Town. They found their GuildMaster remarkably friendly, and remarkably unconcerned about any impending events.

The remaining Master Blacks had stayed at the arena. Some of them on the field, to assist in the killing. Some in the seating, to maintain the crowds.

When the Masters in the seating saw their brethren fall, they had all started down to the field. Then, they caught sight of Steef, apparently flying through the air. Landing near the Cat. Tending to the Cat. Their puzzlement, and fear of the unknown, had stopped their progress. Steef's cry brought new life to their purpose, and as one, they began entering the field. All twenty of them.

❧   ❧   ❧

"You are being very loud now."

"……O…kay." Steef's response was no more than a whisper. He couldn't see for the tears. That was Okay, he didn't need to see.

"You must tell my brother that I stood."

"……O…kay."

"You must Rest me in the paws of our tree…"

❧   ❧   ❧

She just…had…to…PULL…her…other foot…OUT! She was free, staggering, still making her way to where Steef was…slumped over that Cat.

The Blacks are coming! Taking a breath, she doubled her pace, only to slam face-first into something hard. Something she couldn't see.

❧   ❧   ❧

There were too many people in the way, all crowding to see. The five Masters were sobbing now, even Linzel. She'd never met a Cat, but she'd met Steef. She'd felt his cry. She'd listened to the constant account that Pill was giving each of them. It tore them more with each step, though the steps were fewer here, for the crowd was in their way.

Cassa was not interested in waiting. She still had one of Arima's staffs, and its stone flared now, violent Blue. Her wind preceded them then, pushing people aside whether they wanted to move or not.

❧   ❧   ❧

"When I am Rested, you will show these crooked two-legs that you are the MixMaster. You will show them your gladness."

"…I'm…not…feeling…too…glad…"

"That is crooked. I am only Resting. I have lived well, and you can moan me when it is proper. They must know that I am Kivverr…HornCat to the Mix…"

"Steef!…Let me in!…Can you hear me in there!?"

Who was that? He lifted his head, trying to clear his eyes. Blinking. Wiping. There were people running down onto the field. A few Black Pulses coming his way...*Leezel!...what was she doing here?...she'll get hurt!*

He released his bubble for just a beat, and Leezel fell flat forward. The bubble went back up.

Nose bleeding, she scrambled on hands and knees to his side...where she was supposed to be. He had slumped back onto the Cat. She was afraid to touch him, but she *needed* to touch him, hold him, comfort him. It's who she was...Empath and Mate. But if he overwhelmed her again, she wouldn't be able to function. Now that she was here, she was helpless.

"Is this...your beast?" she asked as softly as she could. Her tears had begun. For him.

"No," came the muffled reply, "He...he's...my friend. My...only...friend."

She didn't understand *that*, but she understood his pain. That was real. Her hand went out, drew back, and laid itself on Kivverr's side.

"...*this your female?*"

"No...she...refused me."

"*Then you must ask again. I can feel her. She tastes good. She will make good cubs for you.*"

And Leezel the Empath could taste Kivverr. Tribe of Rivverr, line of Kings. Everything that was the majesty of a HornCat. Their honor. Pride. Discipline. Courage. She could taste something else, too. This Cat loved Steef. Complete, unconditional love...for Steef. The Cat was at peace, with Steef at his side.

"*Do not be sad. My time would have come soon, for I am not young. I am content. There is truly only one thing I regret.*"

"Wh...what...what's that?" Kivverr was almost gone, in spite of all the Yellow. At least he wasn't in pain.

Steef should FEEL this. He should KNOW. Had Leezel known the phrase, what she did then was 'no steps back'...for reaching out, she put her other hand on Steef.

Steef's body jerked upright with the contact. All those cycles, he'd been able to hear his friend, his brother. When he would ride in his mouth. Or on his back. Lying against his side. He could hear him, but he couldn't feel him. He knew the love was there, though HornCats never said such things. But Kivverr had been 'tasting' him, their whole lives, and the gladness that was Steef, had become the gladness of Kivverr. They truly were brothers. And Kivverr *would* Rest well, waiting for his brother to join him.

"*I regret that I never did eat you when I had the chance.*"

Beat. Beat. Be…

"ha……ha…Ha…Ha…HA…HA!…HA! HA! HA! HA! HA! HA! HA! HA!
HA! HA! HA! HA! HA! HA! HA! HA! HA! HA! HA! HA! HA! HA! HA! HA!
HA! HA! HA! HA! HA! HA! HA! HA! HA! HA! HA! HA! HA!

There was a note of hysteria in the Master Clear's laughter. Steef's own joy
had left him, replaced by unimaginable grief…leaving a void. Through Leezel,
Kivverr was filling that void with his own gladness. With his last beats, his big
brother was still teaching, still giving. When the two forces clashed inside him,
it just had to burst out. In its wake, it left a kernel of wisdom. A piece of understanding. The Master Clear's adulthood had begun.

*"Play me the simple song. Then show these crooked two-legs who we REALLY
are."*

Catching his breath, Steef kissed his brother's brow, and whispered into his
ear, "I'll do both." The beat had come for Steef to stand. He had to hurry.

"Leezel."

"Yes?" She turned wondering eyes up to her Mate.

"You'll need to lie on the other side of Kivverr. His body should shield you
from the blast. And cover your staff…and your ears."

"Blast?" She didn't understand

"Leezel…pleeeaasssse."

"All…all right." *Blast?* She hurriedly complied. She could ask later.

He still had the Dust in his clenched fist. That fist opened now, and the Dust
flared. It was a lot of Dust. He lifted it to arm's length, leaving it in his palm.

"Pill, discharge warning. Tell your friends," he said quietly, still looking
down at *his* friend.

"How far?"

"Yonder peak…end of the valley. Any closer won't do. You need to hurry."
The 'Pop!'ing began, and became a torrent.

"Goodbye, old friend."

Kivverr blinked.

The Master Clear turned to the onrushing crowd of Blacks. There would be
no flaming staffs this time. He wanted them to hear. Twenty staffs got Lifted
into the sky, shooting up until they were out of sight. Switching briefly to Red
for amplification, the Master Clear spoke.

"I AM STEEFRR!…THIS IS KIVVERR!…HE IS HORNCAT TO THE
MIXMASTER!…WE ARE CLAN!…MY BROTHER WANTS A
TUNE!…HEAR, THEN!…KIVVERR'S SONG!!!!"

With that, the Master Clear pursed his lips, and put them to his staff to blow. At the same beat, his other hand came down on the stone.

※   ※   ※

Through blurred eyes, Arima had Seen the Yellow glow building, even from outside the arena. A discharge was coming, and they were running *into* it. Not that it mattered. She didn't warn the others. No point. There was nowhere to run. The blast would lay waste to the Town. Probably the valley, too. *Time to die.*

She didn't mind. One hurt too many. Weary in body and spirit, her only regret was that Vinntag couldn't be here to share it with her. Seafer and Rivverr were waiting.

Then Cassa burst them through the crowd, and all of them beheld the awful sight. Three dead female HornCats, in a tangled heap of nets at the far end of the arena. A ring of Master Blacks, encircling the center, where Kivverr's unmistakable form was lying motionless, with deathsticks protruding from him grotesquely. Steef was rising to his feet at the Cat's head, and Leezel...*what was Leezel doing there?!*

All of them saw the staffs fly up. All of them saw Steef raise his hand, and the sharp needle of light that sprang suddenly from it. *My Son. My Son.* In his wrath, he was going to throw Tommik bubbles at them. A fitting end to this Town.

Then the Yellow turned to...Pink.

"Get down!" screamed Cassa, dragging on Arima's arm. "Down and drain!" She couldn't See the glow, but she could surely see the 'seventh' in Steef's hand. Arima let herself be dragged down.

※   ※   ※

He'd meant to play the entire tune, but it was too much Dust. Too much 'seventh' for his fivespan. The sixspan might have carried it. He needed a bigger stick. Only one huge, Pink bubble burst out. 'Burst' is what it did, blowing off the bottom third of his stick.

And then, the bubble popped.

It was as if the Creator himself had swung a mighty hammer, striking a great bell. The note rang out true and pure, for the MixMaster had put his brother's gladness into it. Every ear in the valley got to hear it, and none were unaffected, for Steef had tuned it well.

Only the MixMaster could have fashioned such a note. Red for aim, targeting any black Core. White for Healing, and the carrying of joy. For Steef had Seen that Cores could change, and though it might not last, for tonight, everyone would know the gladness that was Kivverr. Those fortunate people that had less-than-black Cores, would hear a glad sound, and be lightened. Those that Kivverr saw as 'crooked', would just have to endure it as sweet pain.

The Buzzbies had an amazing view from their spot at the valley's heights. Four entire hives were there, to witness the grandest story a Buzzbie had ever seen. The force of Steef's note expanded in a wave that swept out in every direction, speeding through the Town and into the outlying regions.

It washed away all of the Red that had saturated the Town, leaving everything cleansed. The Buzzbies watched as the wave swept over Red GuildHall, which also served as the Vault. In that building was stored most of the Dust of the nine Territories, much of which had been made 'safe' in recent cycles. The Power of the note set off the Power of the Crystal held there, the purest of which was deep underground. There fountained then, an enormous Pink blast, straight up, that could be seen by everyone. No Sight needed. The Dust absorbed Steef's 'seventh' charge, becoming permanently Pink, as it spread into every small crevice of the valley. For cycles to come, this valley would be a place of gladness, a place where people of misery were loathe to dwell.

Steef was surrounded by prone, unmoving bodies. All of the Master Blacks were unconscious. Unable to tolerate the note and its joy, they were overwhelmed into a deep sleep. Anyone not knocked unconscious, had fled.

Clouds of Buzzbies blew into the arena area, buzzing loudly in a swirling mass above the littered field. Steef's face took on a stern, almost fierce expression, and a bubble formed in the air, capturing the nearest swirl. A few of the insects instantly tried to Pop! out, only to smash themselves on the inside surface of the bubble, for this bubble was allowing no passage. Steef approached, as some of the trapped insects began buzzing with agitation. Others of them calmly came to rest on the bubble's bottom.

He switched to Yellow again, and gave the large bees a closer Look. There were five distinct colors of bee in there. He began separating them, moving bee by bee, sorting them into their own bubbles.

It surely must have been an interesting sight to a recovering Leezel, who dazedly rose from her shelter to see the back of Steef standing before a mass of Buzzbies, waving his arms wildly as the new groups formed. Shaking her head, hoping to get the ringing out of her ears, she stood mute and watched, her bleeding nose unnoticed.

When he had the separating done, he called out, "Pill!" There were now five bubbles floating before him, though one held only a few Buzzbies.

Pop! Pop! *"Yes SIR!"*

"First, tell me what Cassa calls me."

"What?"

"Pill!!"

"Uh…she calls you Shortstick…why?"

"And what do I call my sister?"

"Sissy."

"Good enough. Now, Pill. Which of these are your family?"

"Far right."

Steef released that bubble, and the captured Pills, who'd been the calmest, were free. Steef thought he knew, but he asked anyway, "Which are Pools?"

"Second from the left."

He'd been right, the angriest group, and the smallest.

"Peels?" Paals?" "Pulls?" They all got released, after he'd made sure to note which was which. That left the Pools. He walked up, and put his nose against the bubble holding them.

"I need one Boss Pool," he said. They were bashing themselves against the bubble, trying to get to him. "I can wait here all night. It's your air," he continued calmly. Finally, one of them stopped buzzing long enough to hover. He separated the Boss into its own tinier bubble, and addressed it.

"I am Steef," he said, his voice strangely soft, "I am Clan. Your family has worked to help attack my Clan, and my family. Now, you have helped kill my brother." The Master Clear leaned in, and breathed, "I accept your challenge."

"Take this message," he said, raising his voice as he straightened back up, "Back to your hive. I can catch you. I can tell you apart. I've shown you this. I know you now, Pool. Any Pool I see…anywhere…anytime, will die. If I find you actively working against me again, I will seek out your hive, and extinguish your queen and your family, forever."

"If you understand this message, spin around once."

The Buzzbie spun.

"One more thing, Pool. An example…that you will know…I mean what I say." Turning, he squeezed the remaining bubble tight. The captured Pools became goo, and plopped to the ground.

"Do we understand each other?"

The Buzzbie spun again.

"Go." He released the Boss Pool. It Pop!'d away.

Stepping to the goo that had been Pool, he knelt and stuck a finger in it, proclaiming to the air, "I am Steefrr! I am Clan! We eat our kill!" The bit of goo went into his mouth, and was spit right back out.

His family had finally reached him. As Linzel and Leezel watched in amazement, the four Masters repeated the ritual. Then Arima came to him, and with wavering voice, said, "You've made a serious enemy here tonight, Son."

He turned a face to her then, that she'd never seen before, and would pray she never saw again. Grim. "No I haven't, Auntie. They were already enemies. I just accepted."

Cassa, Antee, and Mokam took the dreaded steps to view Kivverr's body. Cassa's sobs began afresh. She left Kivverr then, and methodically went to each body on the arena floor. Still sobbing, she stopped at each only long enough to deliver a single vicious kick to the ribs. Mokam went to retrieve the floating boats, whose crews were unconscious in their bottoms. And Antee knelt, and began to delicately pull the sticks from his friend.

Steef's left hand was badly burned. Arima noticed, and absently took it to begin her White. A routine act that neither of them had to think about. But the small gesture brought Leezel partly out of her shock. Healing was something familiar, in a tragic and bizarre evening. "Master Arima?" she queried.

Arima didn't look up, "What is it, child?"

"Your pardon, Master, but I think…Healing Steef…will be my duty now…" she turned to him, "…if the offer is still available."

Steef didn't answer. He was watching Uncle Antee, wincing with each stick removed. The tears had started again.

Arima glanced at Linzel. Both of them were bleak from too much strain. But Linzel didn't object, and Arima took Steef's silence for acceptance. "Come here, child. I'll show you. It will take a full charge, now. Just short of discharge. Nothing less will affect him."

Leezel stepped up, and began to charge her staff, reaching for his hand. She had closed herself off, Cloaking her Empathy. Strictly Healing.

Steef finally noticed. "Stop!" he exclaimed.

Leezel flinched. She'd been right the first time, her chance had passed. Head dropping, she whispered, "Then...the offer...is...withdrawn?" He certainly had the right to do that, after her refusal.

"No...you misunderstand me," replied the Master Clear. Taking a deep breath, forcing himself to the here-and-now, he softened himself for her. "You mustn't fully charge that stone. It's flawed. The backcharge would kill you." Without thinking about it, he Healed her bleeding nose.

The staff didn't interest her at all just now, "So...your offer...is...?" She lifted her chin...just a fraction to meet his eyes. Noticing her bleeding had stopped, she wiped her nose on her sleeve.

Two female Masters held their breath. Arima wished that Cassa could hear this, but it was happening unexpectedly, and fast. And Cassa was busy.

Steef regarded the girl before him. Though his thoughts were elsewhere, Leezel had earned his attention with courage, and a rare gift. She deserved her answer, and she deserved the truth, "It occurs to me Leezel...that the offer I made before...has changed."

Her body tensed, as her face questioned.

"I offered you great joy. That joy is gone right now. I...I don't know...if I can get it back."

Beat. Beat. Beat.

"We could find some together...maybe," she whispered

Beat. Beat. Beat.

"Maybe," he replied, with a jerky nod. "If so...that would be a good thing to share. But...I also offered...to share the adventure of my life. That adventure," he paused to gesture around them, "Seemingly...is now changed as well. I believe it may now include...peril. It's only fair...to you...that the offer be...redefined."

Her chin went back down. Eyes averted, in apprehension she wouldn't have believed yesterday. Tiny voice. "And is this new offer being made?"

His brother had told him to. In days to come, it could become a pleasant thing, if the pain subsided. "It is."

Arima and Linzel saw the building tension in the girl's body snap, as the stress released.

"Then I say to you," as she cleared her throat, and found a bit of her voice, "That the only peril I fear from this adventure...is our children."

He couldn't muster a real smile just then, but he gave as much as was in him. He replied, "And I...I sure hope...you like trees."

She returned his smile, the first one she'd truly felt like giving in many cycles. Putting her hand on his badge she said, "May I ask you something?"

"Anything."

She knew now, how deeply he meant that, "You're not *really* a Five, *are* you?" Before he could reply, she'd ripped the badge from his tunic.

❧   ❧   ❧

Steef was bent at the knees, crouching over one of the prone bodies. He held what was left of his stick in his right hand, while Auntie and Leezel held his other hand in the air. Auntie was showing his Mate what to do with her repaired staff.

He Pulsed, and stood back up, moving to the next body, with both women following, attached at his hand. Crouching again, he Pulsed. Moved.

"Steef?"

"Leezel?"

"What exactly are you doing?"

"Well, there is a gland in the neck…"

"Yes?"

"It's our Power gland."

Two Healers, young and old, stopped what they were doing and looked at each other. Neither had ever heard such a thing.

The Master Clear continued, "All of our Power is controlled through that gland."

"Are you sure?" Both women asked as one.

"Yes."

"And you are doing…what…exactly?" persisted his Mate, sounding *just* like her Aunt.

He Pulsed on the third one. A permanent Clear bubble around the gland. "Rendering them Inert." They would never hurt anyone again, and no one had to die. Kivverr would have been pleased.

Next.

"But you can't do that!" exclaimed Leezel, as they followed him. She started her own White again, amazed at how much it took.

Stoop. Pulse. "Why not? This Town is ruled by this 'Master's Law' thing, and I'm the ranking Master here." He didn't add that he was the ranking Master anywhere. It would have sounded vain.

Leezel was still trying to digest that concept. She'd only known for a couple of hundred beats, and the explanations had been understandably brief. But that hadn't been what she meant. "I didn't mean you *shouldn't!* I meant…it's just…not possible!"

Arima's eyes rolled. Cassa coughed. Her foot would need some White, but that could wait.

Steef stopped, lifting his head without turning. Looking off into the past, he said, "You know, I used to hear that a lot." Pulse. Next.

"Steef?"

"Yes Auntie?"

"How long have you known about this?"

"About what, Auntie?"

"This 'gland' thing."

"Since my studies with the groundcrawlers, and our first Healing trip." Pulse. Next.

"But that was…cycles…ago!"

"Yes Mam." A glimmer came to him. "Auntie…I'll try to remember from now on."

"Remember what, Son?"

"The things you don't ask. I'll try to remember to tell you."

And it occurred to her, what a gift that really was. "I thank you, Master Clear," she said with a bow.

From his position, he couldn't bow, "You're welcome, Master White." Pulse. Next.

"Pill."

"*Yes Sir?*"

"I need to know how many people are asleep in this valley as a result of my discharge. Soon as you can."

"*Right away, Steef!*" Pop!

"Pill."

"*Yes Sir?*" There were an abundance of Pills on him. They covered his shoulders, buzz-fighting for earspace.

"Leezel needs Buzzbies. I would prefer they be Clan." Pulse. Next. It was going faster.

"*Uh…Steef…actually…well…she's still not a Master.*"

"Now, Pill." Pulse. Next.

"*Yes Sir.*" Pop! Pop!

Leezel's face brightened further, with their arrival. Linzel reached up, one hand cupping Leezel's cheek, while with the other, she untied her daughter's hair.

Pop! *"Four hundred eighty six."*

"Any of them *just* sleeping?"

"We thought of that. We gave each just a bit of sting. Four hundred eighty six didn't wake up."

"How many did?" He hated to disturb decent folk, and waking to a Buzzbie sting was probably disturbing.

"It's not late, Steef. Only twelve."

"Auntie, we're gonna need some help."

"What do you have in mind, Son?"

They discussed it at length, before Arima sent Pill to find the Town's Labor-Master. He was only too happy to oblige, once he understood the problem. So were his laborers, who refused to discuss payment.

❋   ❋   ❋

There were bodies everywhere on the arena field. They'd tried spreading them out at first, but walking became difficult as the ground got cluttered, so they had to stack them some. When word had gotten out what was happening, the common laborers found themselves aided by Powered people who'd enjoyed the strange musical note, but hadn't enjoyed the last few cycles in Town. At first, some of the incoming bodies arrived…well…abused. Steef had issued a stern message then. No harm was to be done. The disappointed army of workers then found a new method of displaying their long-stored frustrations. When these new 'Nerts awoke, they would surely need to bathe.

Five of the arriving bodies bore GuildMaster markings. One of them, of course, was Kuumit. That gave Linzel no small pleasure. It was better than killing him.

One hundred fourteen Masters, in all. Mostly Blacks and Reds. Various other Colors, and various other Grades. Surprisingly, a few 'Nerts, too. Since it wasn't possible to make them 'Nert'ier, even for Steef, their names were recorded by the LaborMaster for close scrutiny in the future.

One of the Black Masters, found in one of the hovering boats, was missing a hand. He was still alive, only just. Steef asked Auntie to do what she could.

A more vindictive man than Steef might have also enjoyed Nessel's unconscious arrival. Leezel saw him too, of course, since she spent every beat of that long night at the side of her Mate. Neither of them spoke about it. Just a raised eyebrow shared.

Once Leezel understood how the bodies came to be unconscious to begin with, she worried some that Zelmar might ultimately arrive. Thankfully, that never happened. She hadn't seen her Father or her sister since running onto the field. Apparently, there really *was* hope for Zelmar.

🦋   🦋   🦋

Pop! *"Steef?"*

"Yes Pill?"

"Can we tell now?"

"Tell what, Pill?"

"Tell...everything. About you. About the Master Clear. We've waited for seventeen cycles."

Hmmm. True enough. That was loyalty, for true. "I don't mind Pill. But there are some things that probably shouldn't be told, ever."

"Like what?"

"Well, like Clan things. And other...you know, Pill, I'm not real good at secrets. Why don't you ask Auntie, Sassy, and the Uncles? They'll know best. You can say that I'm agreeable...to whatever you decide together."

"THANKS!!!" Pop!

Shortly, the details had been worked out, and an excited Pill family sent Bosses to three other Hives. It would have been impossible to recount everything in only a few beats, but the major points were announced. There was much buzzing everywhere, in spite of the fact that it was past midnight. Peel and Paal decided they couldn't wait, and sent their families to the few remaining Masters they were serving, and all of the unstaffed Masters that had previously been served. When the Buzzbies found their Masters asleep, they woke them.

Lanterns came on across the nine Territories that night, and word went out...about the Master Clear.

Ironically, Leezel was the last to get completely informed. There had been scant beats to tell her much earlier, and then busy had set in for the remainder of the night. It wasn't until late the next day, after all events had unfolded, that Arima, Linzel and Cassa sat her down to share the entire story of what her future held. Once again, there was a dance of 'that's not possible' and 'I oath you'. Had her Mother not been there, she might not have believed it then.

❦   ❦   ❦

"Steef, I think these people want to speak with you," Leezel said. She was delightedly still Pulsing White into his hand. The repaired stone flowed more Power than she could remember. It was a good feeling. Master Arima had left her to the task of Steef, while other Healing needs were met. There'd been more than a few sets of damaged ears.

Steef looked up from the work. Four very dirty people, three men and a woman, stood before him. All of them looked to be about Uncle Mokam's age, or older. All of them with Master Yellow glows. No badges. No staffs.

"Your pardon, Master," began one of them with a bow, "We were wondering, if you don't mind…what we're hoping…that is…"

The Master Clear rose to return the man's bow, "Your pardon also Master Yellow…" they all started at that. The stories were true! He *was* a Master Clear! He had the Sight! "…As you can see, there is much work here…" which they really couldn't see, for they had no idea what he was doing, "…could I ask you to speak your purpose…soon?"

"Of course, Master!" all four of them bowed, "We were wondering if we could…with great respect, of course…stand watch over your fallen friends," he bowed towards Kivverr, and the three females, who'd been moved carefully to the great male's side. Antee was directing the removal of the nets. "We would see to it that they remain undisturbed while you conduct yourself." Throwing out his hands, he added, "We would be very reverent, Master."

The Master Clear exchanged a look with his Mate. She gave a quick nod.

"Pill, hunt through these piles of people, and see if you can find the Yellow Masters here some clean tunics with proper badges, please." Pop!

"Masters, my Mate and I are honored to accept. Please see Master Antee over there first. He's the one with his back…"

"We know Antee well, Master. And he knows us. Thank you, Master."

CHAPTER 24

✿

It had been a long night. Though it didn't take long for each person 'Nerted, as it came to be called, there were just so *many* of them. Just before sunrise, the work was complete. Cassa's foot was better. She, Antee and Mokam made for her hut, to repair the wall and get some rest.

Linzel had sent Pill to Maar several times, keeping him informed of their activities, and in fairness to the man, Leezel's new situation. He had a right to know. When he received the news, he was apparently still under the influence of Steef's discharge, for his reply was courteous.

Now the four of them were making their way back to the hut of Maar, Nine of Red. Leezel had to give parting greets to her Father and sister, for after a short rest, she and her Mate would be departing for the Valley of the Cats. Linzel had conversation to make with Maar, herself, but it could wait until Leezel's duty was done.

With a spirit laden with sorrow and weariness, they entered the hut to find Maar and Zelmar still awake, waiting for them. Waiting with them was Linzel's brother, Zellin. Maar's good cheer had worn some with the passing beats, and he'd sent his remaining daughter to fetch her Uncle, expecting him to lend support for the upcoming contest of wills. The last time Arima had seen Zellin was at the Festival where she'd met Steef. She hadn't trusted him then, owing to his close friendship with Maar. They both liked their Dust too much. But Zellin didn't appear to have enjoyed the last few cycles, which Arima accounted to his credit.

Maar made the expected arguments. To be fair, he was courteous. Being a Nine, no Buzzbies had come to him in the night with any stories yet. Zellin had gotten the news, but was holding his peace.

Linzel held herself back also, for Leezel determined to confront the issue.

"Father, Steef's rank is not the issue here!"

"What future will you have, Leezel? No...Arima, wait a beat. This is between Leezel and myself."

"Whatever future we have together, will be brighter than any I could have looked forward to here, Father."

"How will you live, daughter? Your Mastery isn't complete, and you know that a Five...?" Maar had finally looked at Steef, seeing that the badge was missing.

"That's what we've been wanting to tell you, Maar!" exclaimed Arima. She wanted to get into this. She needed to get into...something!

But Leezel wasn't through, "Master Arima..." she held up her hand to her Aunt, "Wait, please. Father, Steef's rank is not an issue for *me*! And I hate to point out...caring about rank has never served you well, either."

Whew! thought Arima. *That had to hurt!*

"I have oathed my life and my love to Steef. He has done the same. It's done." Leezel's arms crossed her chest, and her foot began a little 'pat' on the dirt.

Arima looked at her niece, but Leezel shook her head.

Maar looked around the hut at the faces there. The only one surprised was Zelmar, who really had no glimmer of what was happening. Maar's gaze settled on his sister.

"She's just like you 'Rima, when she acts like that. You remember?"

"I do, Maar. I remember there were beats you deserved it, and beats you didn't."

"Do I deserve it now, 'Rima? You know this boy well, I assume?"

"Every day for seventeen cycles."

Steef spoke for the first time, "Aunt Arima raised me, along with my own Mama and Papa."

Zelmar snorted, "She's not your..."

"I am Steef's Aunt by his kind indulgence," interrupted Arima, "And by my own disposition...and great good fortune. Now hush child, until you can speak of things you understand."

"Maar," she went on, "Since Leezel has made it clear that her mind is set, and her oath made, there are some things you ought to know. They might ease your mind a bit." For the next several beats, Arima and Linzel took turns bringing some of the news to the ears of the three uninformed people there.

When they were through with the first wind, Maar was silent, but Zellin spoke.

"Paal told me this 'Master Clear' nonsense. Fables! Dreams! And now you present us with a young country boy who can't even carry a decent staff!"

Leave it to a Green to look first at someone's staff sighed Arima to herself. Of course, everyone then turned to look at Steef's stick, broken as it was at the narrow end. No more than three spans of it were left. The stone, which Steef had Cloaked before they left the Valley, looked clouded, much like a minor gem. It gave no evidence that it was a Crystal.

"That staff, Zellin, just had a simultaneous duel with...how many Masters, Steef?" inquired Linzel, sweetly. She was looking forward to the look on her brother's face.

"One hundred fourteen, Master Linzel," replied the Master Clear, puzzlement obvious in his voice. What was the fuss about? He'd just get his old sixspan back out when he...they...got home.

"A hundred and fourteen Masters, Zellin. At one time. I saw them." She waited a beat for it to show on his face. "There can be no doubt."

It wouldn't have taken much of Cassa's wind to knock Zellin over right then. When he spoke, it was no more than a fashioned breath, "That's not possible."

Shaking her head, Arima said, "Steef, would you drain your staff for me, please? Thank you." She took it from his hand, and thrust it at Zellin. "Make it glow," she challenged.

Judging by his own stone, Zellin tried. His stone glowed bright Green, but Steef's stick remained dark. "It's dead. Just dead. This wood's not good for anything but a fire," he said, puzzlement clear on his face.

Arima almost jerked it back, giving it to its owner, "Steef, if you would please? Just a small one. We don't have the beats for Healing any eyes this morning."

The stone flared, about double the Green that Zellin's had given off.

"Zellin," she went on, "Pick a Color. Any other Color."

More puzzled still, he blurted out, "Brown!"

"Steef? One more glow, please?"

"Auntie...?"

"I know you don't like boasting, Son, but this is Leezel's family. It's important to her...and them, that they believe."

"Okay." His stone was still glowing Green. Without a beat between, it switched to Brown. To settle the question and save beats, he then flashed through all of the Colors, finishing with White.

"Now, Zellin," said Arima, "I trust that concludes your skepticism?"

Zellin was nodding, numbly, "What's his rank, 'Rima? A hundred and four-teen…?"

"We really have no way to measure, Zellin. All we know for sure…"

"How can one staff carry all that Power?" he continued, now unaware of Arima. "You say it was five spans before it was damaged?"

Before Arima could catch him, Steef said, "It's the tree Uncle Seafer grew for me. All of my staffs…"

"*Seafer*?!" exclaimed Zellin. "*Seafer*?! I haven't seen Seafer in…twenty cycles! This is *Seafer's* doing?" He stopped, and his eyes started dancing. "Seafer's *acorns*! You mean…they *worked*?!"

"Steef," Arima tried to stop this, knowing it was too late, "I'm not sure we should…"

"He always intended to share it, Auntie," said the Master Clear softly to his Aunt.

He's right she thought. She just didn't want to share it with Zellin. Or anyone. But Seafer wouldn't have cared. Any Master Green would have suited him. Every Master Green. She also reminded herself that Zellin was still standing. Still *could* charge a staff, even after last night. It helped.

"How *is* Seafer, then, 'Rima?"

"Dead," she said flatly, "Backcharge from a twospan of this same wood."

Beat. Beat. Beat.

"Young man," Zellin's eyes went wide, his tone a good bit more respectful now, "Could I see that staff, again…please?"

Steef drained it and handed it back. Zellin's eyes took on a light of their own. Now he examined it thoroughly, almost lovingly. And he noticed that it was laced throughout, with Dust. Then he came to the stone. His eyes gave the question to the Master Clear.

"Crystal. Cloaked. Laced with the seventh primary."

Zellin hastily handed it back. "*Here* is Leezel's future, Maar!" he proclaimed. "Do you have any idea what a staff like that is *worth*?!"

Thought so. "It's not worth anything to Leezel, Zellin. Or Maar. Or you. It's tuned specifically to Steef. All the staffs in that tree. Tuned to Steef."

"I meant no disrespect, 'Rima. Truly." replied the Green. "But Maar *is* concerned for his daughter's future."

"My future is Steef, Uncle Zellin! Not his staff."

"Of course, child. Of course. But you have to eat, at least. Young man…your pardon…Master Clear…with respect…with great respect to you, your tree, and your…uh…Uncle Seafer…did this tree ever produce…acorns?"

Don't tell him. Don't tell him. Don't…

"Yes Sir."

"Would you happen to have any of them…stored?"

"Yes Sir." Then, to Arima's everlasting relief, Steef added, "But I will strike no deals with them." He had finally caught on to what was happening here. It was about Dust again. More fuss about Dust. Wasn't an issue. He had Dust. Leezel would know that soon enough, but Steef didn't think he would be telling anyone else. Ever.

Zellin considered that for a beat, sharing a glance with Maar, first of concern, then resignation.

"How many? How many live acorns do you have…Master?" Zellin drew in a deep breath, and held it. That was probably a mistake.

Steef's eyes questioned his Aunt. She had always trusted his motives. Now she trusted his judgement. *It's not like anyone can force them from him.* She nodded.

"One hundred twenty two thousand, six hundred and twelve…Sir."

❋   ❋   ❋

The sun was thoroughly up. Zellin was roused from his swoon. Maar was accepting Leezel's reality, for in truth, there was nothing he could do about it, and it wasn't as bleak as he'd anticipated. Linzel was comforting Zelmar, who was stuck on 'But I saw him first!'

Pop! Pop! Pop! Pop! Pills came in to Steef, Arima, Linzel, and Leezel.

"Steef, Vinntag's boat has landed at the Field, and they're heading for the Black GuildHall!"

"Good. Now Auntie can finish her challenge."

"There's more, Steef. There are no Pools around now, so we went into the boat, to see what's what. There are three Black Masters with them. The Red GuildMaster is there, too. One of the Blacks started Pulsing at us, and several of our family were burned dead."

"They killed more Clan!?" More challenge to accept, and he was already tired. Not that three Blacks concerned him, but he'd oathed Kivverr, and he didn't want his fatigue to cause a mistake.

"Steef, there's more. They…uh…they…"

"What is it, Pill?"

"They have your family, Steef. We're sure it's them. All three."

The Master Clear's jaw set. His oath to Kivverr hadn't lasted long. He looked at Auntie, who was getting the same report. So were Linzel and Leezel, whose stun was showing in their faces.

"Do they ever stop, Auntie?"

"No, Son. They never stop."

"Leezel, could you lead to me to the Black GuildHall from here?"

Her reply was to take his arm and lead him out.

Arima moved to follow, but Linzel took her sleeve. "There is still a dispute between us, my sister," she said grimly. She held up a fist with two sticks protruding. "Choose."

"Arima, there's something we didn't tell Steef."

She drew a stick. "What is it, Pill?"

"Malem wasn't moving."

Merciful Creator!!

❦   ❦   ❦

Steef would have liked nothing better than to Lift himself again, for his haste tormented, but Leezel was with him. Also, he didn't know if his pump could take a second strain so soon. He'd have to have Auntie…no…Leezel…well, someone…look at it soon. They made the best pace they could, winding through the roads and rows. Leezel knew the Town well.

He sent out a White Pulse, searching for the three tunes he knew so well. Nothing. Fear constricting his throat, a second White went out…with furious intensity.

At the Black GuildHall, the three bundles, still wrapped in Cloaking blankets, had been laid in a Cloaked closet. The Master Clear's first White struck the closet, and it rocked. The second Pulse blew away all the Cloaking properties found there, and the White Locks that had been placed on the captives.

That was better. Three separate returns, two erratic, one weak but steady.

Someone was coming into view.

❁   ❁   ❁

Vinntag, GuildMaster of White, was having her very last bad day. She had been under constant scrutiny since their boat had approached the Landing Field. From the air, the boat's occupants had seen the stacks of bodies in the arena. Some of the people working there had stopped to point up at their boat. There weren't any traffic sleds in the air.

And the Buzzbies! They were everywhere. One of the Blacks with them had managed to kill a few, but it hadn't made an impact, except to keep the Buzzbies out of accuracy range. They were overhead now, so many that they looked like flocks of birds. And she knew without being told that none of them were Pool.

Wingor had insisted on keeping the three Black Masters with him. Upon arrival at Black GuildHall, instead of finding Kuumit and his squad of killers, they'd found no one above an Eight, and none of them wanted anything to do with Vinntag. The three Black Masters had been forced to 'encourage' two of the Eights to stand guard on Vinntag as she made her way through Town.

Arima was here, she knew. There was only one place she'd be…at Maar and Linzel's hut. Linzel didn't have a staff, and Vinntag had her hostages and her Eights. This could still be salvaged.

But where was Kuumit?

All manner of questions and doubts were blazing through her. She needed information, and Pool was gone.

And then her answers came racing around the end of a building. All of them. Vinntag the Sighted Grader, beheld the Master Clear unCloaked. Even at this distance, she could See the waves of Clear Power pounding off of him. As she watched, two separate stabs of White left his stone, the second one so severe, it made her eyes hurt.

All of her answers. This was the Power that had defeated the snakes. This was the cause of those bodies in the arena. This explained why Kuumit couldn't be found. This was the reason all of her plans would fail.

And it was this young man's family that she had helped abuse and take captive.

As the two young people raced by her and her guard, she finally noticed that Leezel companied the Master Clear. Leezel was glaring at her, holding her staff up…the staff that Vinntag had such great hopes for…and glowed the stone! A full charge glow! Somehow, the stone had been detected and repaired, though she knew that wasn't possible.

They sped on by, leaving Vinntag relieved, and unfulfilled, "Stop him! Kill him! Why are you standing there!?"

Steef listened as they continued on their way.

"No, GuildMaster," replied the older of the two.

"No!?…Don't you tell me no!…I *paid* you!"

"Yes you did, GuildMaster. You paid us to defend you, and we will if you are attacked. We were not paid to hurt people on your whim."

Steef and Leezel passed out of hearing. *So that was the 'Vinntag' that Auntie intended to challenge?* Auntie was right, she would win this. Master Linzel could handle the Eights if need be, but they had good Cores. He put his mind back to his task.

❀   ❀   ❀

Pop! *"Boss, you're getting close! You should know, those three Black Masters are waiting for you, with the Red GuildMaster behind them."*

Pop! *"Boss, a message from Paal. Maar says the Red Master is probably Wingor, the GuildMaster. He says to be careful, he's a Powerful man, and hateful."*

"Do you know which one was Pulsing at you Pill?"

"Yes. She was glowing. Showing off. It's the woman in the center."

"Okay." They were coming into view, and he could see that the one in the middle wasn't as tall as her companions. It was a little far for him to perfect such a delicate Pulse, but he wasn't in the mood to care. The woman suddenly had trouble swallowing, and her staff went dead. As she clutched her throat, she noticed that her feet got cold…

"She's yours, Pill."

"Do you want us to kill her?"

"That's up to you, it's your challenge. Wait!…I have an idea…"

❀   ❀   ❀

It was hard to swallow, she couldn't draw up any Power, she was getting chilled all over…and her head, neck, and shoulders were covered in Buzzbies. And they weren't Pool! She had just enough beats to wonder 'What's a Pillrr?' when the first stinger went in. There were several to follow. She took off running, having nowhere to go.

That left two, with the Red behind them. Steef could See that the Red's glow was as strong as any he'd Seen. Just not strong enough. He was still getting White Pulses back from the GuildHall, but they were weak. His pace quickened, leaving Leezel behind in a bubble. She'd be safe enough there. *What to do about the Blacks...?* They'd started Pulsing as soon as they'd seen their targets.

Someone decided for him. Both Blacks were cut down from behind. Someone had gotten to them first. As they fell, he saw Leemin, Master of Black, standing behind them, one charged staff in his right hand, a bundle of staffs under his left.

Wingor didn't like puzzles, and he'd had a morning full of them. All those bodies in the arena. The missing Blacks. Those two puzzles probably explained each other...but how?

Two figures came running into view. Both of them had those disgusting white Cores, the ones simple-minded people carried. Both Cores were tinged with fear, however. Now *there* was something he could work with. One of the Cores was intense. He'd never Seen such passion! Oh, what he could have done with *that* spirit to work with...if he had the beats!

Instead, he instructed his three guards to dispatch the two intruders. He assumed they were waiting for something...he couldn't see any Black Pulses. Should have told them to make them visible. *Why was she running away? She drove those Buzzbies off before, why not now?*

His other two guards fell dead. Fear gripped him. In panic, he Pulsed, hoping to slow things down. He sent out fear himself. No affect.

That left the Red. Steef was running now.

"Pill, tell Leezel and Master Leemin to close their eyes tight. Two beats." Pop! Pop!

Five staffs away. The Red was Pulsing, but it washed off of Steef's bubble. Steef was full of Red himself. *He wants a Red duel...he'll have one.* Tuning it to be visible, he released it. It wasn't necessary to discharge, which would almost certainly have killed someone. The flash alone would blind the man.

The last thing Wingor ever saw was blazing Red, so much that…

As he passed the slumped figure, who was already starting to drool, Steef plunged into the doorway of the Black GuildHall.

"I'll deal with you later."

❧   ❧   ❧

"So, Arima, you've been keeping some secrets down in that Valley of yours." The two groups had met, Arima and Linzel having the advantage of Pill's directions. Vinntag had turned away, but her legs were too short to outdistance her pursuers, so she'd stopped and waited.

Vinntag's own fear was in full bloom. Arima and Linzel both carried staffs.

"Clever of you, Vinntag, to disable Leezel's staff. Two stones, so perfectly cut and matched…that they appeared as one. Until they got fully charged with a Master's charge…say…in a duel, perhaps?"

Vinntag thought Arima was being awfully polite. *Probably knows I've got those savages in custody. She can't hurt me as long as they might survive!*

"She had your glow, Arima," spat Vinntag. "She has your blood in her. The day would come that she'd challenge me, and I'd finally get to defeat you. Through her!"

"That alone is enough for me to kill you, Vinntag!" growled Linzel. "We drew shortstick, Vinntag, my sister and me. To see who got to kill you."

"I lost," Arima's voice held an abundance of disappointment. At least she'd get to watch. "So I'll give you something to think about…for a beat or two, anyway. If you'd just left everything alone, you would have lived past today."

"I'm not simple, Arima! You came here to challenge me!"

"Yes…yes, I did," agreed Arima, nodding. "After you sent those snakes. If not for that, our only purpose here would have been to Register our young man for Mating. Nothing more. But your own schemes were the sparks that have kindled your undoing."

"Look close, Vinntag," said Linzel, unable to wait any longer, "I'm told that you should remember this staff."

The old White squinted, then went rigid. "But I've got a guard, Linzel," said Vinntag, trying to gather herself. "You can't kill your own Guild members, can you?"

Linzel addressed the Eights. "Skirran, you and your young companion had best stand down." She flared her stone to make her point.

The Black Eights stepped forward, and Skirran said, "Ma...Master Linzel...it's a glad thing to see you with a staff again. Truly. I...we...offer pardon Master. But...we took this daycharge...to protect the GuildMaster today. We didn't know...Master...we didn't know...that you had challenge on her."

Pop! A Pill left Linzel.

"Then stand down, Skirran! You can't possibly stand against me! I don't want to kill you, too!"

"Y...you...your...pardon...M...M...M...Master Linzel, but we... we... we... oathed... the... Bl... Black."

"They gave that stupid oath, Linzel," gloated Vinntag, showing more bravado than she felt, "Old Guild. You're old Guild, too. You're going to have to go *through* them! Ha! Ha! Ha! Ha!" Linzel was too softheaded to do it!

Two Eight grade stones began to vibrate violently. Then, with a muffled 'Crack!', they exploded into Black spheres that floated gently away, until caught by a breeze.

"It appears Skirran, that you are now both unstaffed. I believe that releases you from your oath. Now, *stand down!*"

The Black Eights were happy to do just that. Linzel watched them move aside, clearing the way to Vinntag. "Now...Vinntag," Linzel said lightly, turning back. Finally.

But Vinntag wasn't there. Her small frame was moving before her staff could hit the ground.

Linzel turned a quizzical look to Arima, as if to say, 'Where does she think she can go?' The Master Black let her get a good three staffs before Pulsing.

Arima Saw the Pulse leave. Saw a really *large* hole open, center of Vinntag's back. Saw her enemy fall. Just that quick, it was over. *Somehow, it should have been more dramatic* she thought.

"Skirran, you and your friend there can arrange to have *that*...cleaned up." Linzel stepped to Vinntag's fallen staff and picked it up. *It's useless with all that inlay on it* she thought, so she charged the staff until the soft yellowmetal had all melted off. Arima had come up behind her, and Linzel held out her friend's staff.

"I thank you, Master Healer," she said, "For the loan of your staff. It appears that I will no longer have need of it."

Arima nodded, taking the staff, "You know, Linzel. After all these cycles," she was gazing at Vinntag's unmoving form, "You'd think this would bring more pleasure."

"There's never any pleasure in a killing, 'Rima. Even one this necessary."

❧   ❧   ❧

They had Locks on them. Black and Red. The Black Locks were set to erupt if tampered. The Red Locks were strong and invasive. Care would be required to protect their minds. All three of his loved ones were filthy and soiled. They'd been wrapped in Cloaking blankets that subdued their Power, keeping them weaker still.

But they were alive. Mama and Papa were in distress, straining against their Red Locks. Sissy's pump was beating slow and steady, but she was still. Unmoving. Steef slowed himself, despite the fear.

sssssssSSSNAP!!

"Sissy…"

"Huh?"

"Sissy, wake up." Gentle White now. Too much would overwhelm her.

"Bubba?" her weak voice trembled, and he almost dropped his stick, in his relief.

"It's me, Sissy. I'm here."

"Oh Bubba!" she started to cry. "I knew you'd come! I told them, too."

"Told who, Sissy?" The Master Clear softly stroked his sister's face, while for the second time in less than a day, he experienced tears. Only…these were good ones.

"The dream people," she whispered, "They tried to make me afraid. They said you were dead, and they were gonna hurt me."

"They can't hurt you now, Sissy. I'm here."

"I told them, Bubba. I said my Bubba would come. I knew you would. I wasn't afraid."

"You're gonna be fine, Sissy. I've got to help Mama and Papa now."

She suddenly siezed his arm, "Oh! Bubba! They cut off his hands!"

Steef jerked around but, no…his Papa's hands were Okay. "Who's hands, Sissy?"

"Cirlok! They cut off his hands! He tried to protect us Bubba, but they were too strong!"

"I'll take care of it, Sissy…Pill, please send someone to see about Cirlok. You know where…?"

"We'll find him, Boss." Pop!

"I'm cold, Bubba."

He'd gotten the blanket off of her, but she needed out of this closet and he didn't have the beats for that yet. The roof of the GuildHall began to crack, with rubble sliding down away from them in an arc. Sunlight came flooding in.

"I'll be right back, Sissy." Mama and Papa were still being troubled by their own Red Locks. He had to go slow. Be careful. "There's someone here to help you. I'll be right back." She let go of his arm. He said he'd be back.

Bubba moved away, and another figure loomed over her. The light hurt her eyes, and the face over her was shadowed.

"Who…who are you?'

"I'm here to help you, Malem. My name is Leezel, pumpkin. I'm your new sister."

❋   ❋   ❋

Arima and Linzel arrived at the Black GuildHall to find Leemin standing over two corpses, and one blithering Red GuildMaster. The two Blacks gave each other deep, glowing bows.

Leemin gestured to his victims, "They didn't stand back-to-back Linzel. Oldest mistake they could make."

Linzel laid a gentle hand on her old friend, "I can remember a time when we made that same mistake, Leemin," she said with a soft smile.

"More than once," he agreed.

"Wait just a beat!" exclaimed Arima, "Leemin? LEE-min?"

"Do I know you, Healer?" he inquired.

"Leemin, this is Arima."

Master Leemin turned and gave an equal bow to Arima. "Linzel spoke of you often and well, Master Healer. I am honored to meet you. Indeed, I should have seen your resemblance to Maar."

"Never mind that!" she tugged on Linzel's sleeve. "LEE-min?!"

"Yes, Arima," laughed Linzel, "Leezel's namesake." Leemin started to chuckle.

"You've got to tell me! Tell me now, before she comes back out!"

"That was Leezel? The girl that just went in there?"

Linzel laughed for true, then, "You should see your faces!...oh!...that's too good!" They just had to wait. "Yes Leemin, that was Leezel, if she was companied by a young man with light hair. She's grown, hasn't she? And yes Arima, Leezel is named for Leemin."

Arima just waited. Linzel already knew the question.

"Leemin and I apprenticed together, since we were in our early teens, really. He's the finest man I've ever known. Always was. Always will be. He earned my love, and my oath...long before we were old enough to Register." She had to catch some air.

"But then your brother came along. Did you know, Arima, that you were the only family member to ask...no, beg...pardon for your brother's behavior? No, I didn't think you did. You spared Maar's life that day, for Leemin was prepared to kill him on the spot. But I hesitated, just long enough to get home...and see the look on my Mother's face. Maar had bought them a new hut. I couldn't bear it, thinking of taking that away from her. So your brother...bought me. My oath to Leemin was forfeit."

"But Maar didn't really want a Mate, not really. He wanted a Master on his arm. A pretty one. And that's all he got, for cycles. As he got older...your pardon Arima, but it's true...anyway, he knew that his age was catching up to him, and he wanted more. He wanted children, while he still could. Specifically, he hoped for a Master child. So we struck a deal, your brother and I."

Arima nodded, "You'd give him his children, but his firstborn would be named for your love, and the secondborn would have his name...last."

Leemin chuckled again, causing Linzel to gently thump his chest, "That's half of it. Doubleborns are common in my family. You know that Zellin and I are doubleborn...?"

"Yes."

"I went to the White GuildHall. You'd been assigned away, but a nice Ten there checked me every fourth sevenday. When he finally felt two eggs come down...I finally...gave myself to Maar."

This took a few more beats. The Blacks waited, while Arima's thoughts caught up. "You finally gave yourse...you mean, in all those cycles...?"

Linzel smiled a wicked little smile, and held up one finger. The three of them held themselves for beats, but it was just...too...sweet. In spite of all the mayhem and despair of the last few days, they...couldn't...stand...it...and *exploded* in laughter.

"...Ooohh!...Poor Maar," Arima finally got out, wiping her eyes. "He got his Master Grade child, and she's nothing like him!"

"No…she's you!" Linzel agreed, "Don't give him many regrets, 'Rima. At least he's alive. Leemin could have killed him any time, and no one would have questioned a Black Master. I'd have gone with him, too. Willingly. Right up to the beat the girls were conceived. Maar has spent his life on given beats. Leemin was just too fine a man to do such a thing. Did I mention that he's the finest man I've ever known?"

"Does Leezel know?"

Leemin shook his head, "We've never met, by purpose. I'm not her Father. She needed to know her Father, not me."

"Did I mention…?"

"Yes, you did," Arima just shook her head. "Linzel, Leezel really should meet him, you know."

"Meet who, Master Arima? Mother, you simply *have* to meet Steef's family! Mama Maleef is so *sweet*! Steef sent Pill to the LaborMaster, to get help carrying them. I've invited them to our hut, Mother. They need food and rest, and more White…meet who?"

Arima would long remember the look on Linzel's face as she left them to go visit her friends inside.

"Uh…Leezel…pumpkin…"

❀   ❀   ❀

"Master Leemin…"

"Just Leemin, child."

He got a smile for his comfort, "Leemin, I think I would like to know you better, when days permit. But there are other obligations right now, demanding my beats. Perhaps later?"

Leemin bowed to the only child he would never have, "I have waited eighteen cycles to make conversation with you, child. I can wait a little longer."

"No longer than necessary, then…Leemin," and Leezel gave him his due, bowing gracefully.

Steef came out then, leading the bearers, and Linzel got to meet his parents, briefly. They were hustled off to find well-deserved comfort, but not before Steef had a word with Leemin.

"I was given to understand that you disliked killing, Master," the Master Clear said with courtesy.

Leemin bowed low, with glow. "And I was given to understand that you were a Five White…Master Clear," he said with a twinkle, "But I will answer your question. I detest killing, and detest that killing is the only Power I have. But if someone *must* die, I prefer it be the killers of innocent, rather than the innocent themselves."

The Master Clear absorbed that. A good lesson to go with Kivverr's last, and a deeper puzzle than he'd wrestled with before. Directing the laborers to collect Wingor, they left, leaving Leemin and Linzel alone.

"Where did you get so many staffs, Leemin?"

"Why, Linzel…there was a beat last night when it was *raining* Master Grade staffs. I happened to be in need of one at the time, so…" He shrugged. "That's why I was coming here."

"And why so many?" He had four under his free arm, but he dropped one now.

"Well, I see you have one for yourself. Including you and I, Linzel, there are five of us left."

She knew what he meant. Five left of the original nine unstaffed Blacks.

"Only five? Oh…Leemin!"

He nodded solemnly, "Mosim passed from age. Then we lost Pinbil, Cappmas, and Imon. All died in the Hollow, trying…without a staff…to defend someone from being wronged. We need to change our training, Linzel. We've leaned too much on our staffs, no jest intended. If we're going to be the guardians of the Guilds, we'll have to learn to guard better."

"Does this mean you'll finally challenge for GuildMaster, Leemin? You've never wanted it before."

"I didn't want to lead the kind of Guild we had, Linzel. You know that. But I don't think a challenge will be needed now…unless you're…?"

"You know better."

Beat. Beat. Beat.

"You'd better go, Linzel. We'll speak again."

Beat. Beat. Beat.

"Bright day, Leemin."

"Much brighter now, Linzel. Much brighter."

❊   ❊   ❊

The solemn entourage was making its way through Town, heading for Maar's hut. There were a few people out now, mostly looking bewildered. Their thoughts had so long been influenced by the constant Red, they were having difficulty thinking for themselves.

Pop! *"Boss, Cirlok is alive, but he's in bad conditon. Some of Antee's apprentices are tending to him, but his arms don't look good."*

"Well, we'll send him some help…and Pill?"

"Yes Sir?"

"What's this 'Boss' nonsense?"

"That's not for us to say. You'll need to go back to the arena for that. The LaborMaster wants to talk to you anyway."

"Okay. I want you to go to the White Guild. Tell them I need one Master to make a Healing trip. They will be gone several days. Tell them to bring all of their cutting tools."

"Right away, Boss!" Pop!

"Auntie, Leezel and I have to go see the LaborMaster. Can you…?"

"I'll tend them, Son. Never worry," she said. "But what about that?" She nodded to the laborers carrying Wingor.

"He won't be any trouble, Auntie. I have a few questions for him, later. Just keep him outside of the hut, so he doesn't make the place smell."

❦   ❦   ❦

"Master Clear," the LaborMaster and his workforce had stopped their activity, and jointly given a deep bow.

"LaborMaster," replied the Master Clear. He liked this man. Good Core. Good laugh. Someone had gotten large bolts of unsewn sail material, and covered the Cats' bodies. He noticed that there were a lot of Yellows there now, standing all around the bodies, facing out.

"Your pardon, Master," the LaborMaster went on, "But can you tell me when these…" he jerked a thumb over his shoulder at the piles of people, "…will be waking? And what do you want us to do with them?"

"They won't stir until I wake them, good Sir," replied the Master Clear, "Which I will do when you are ready. As to their future, why…that will be in your hands. Their only usefulness now will be their backs, and what service you can put them to."

The LaborMaster studied on that a few beats. "It's true, then…they've lost their Power? They're 'Nerts like us?"

The Master Clear shook his head, "No Sir, not like you. They're Powerless like you…your pardon…but they will need cycles to prove their worth, as you and your people have already done."

The words of the Master Clear rang out across the open arena, which had gone silent to listen. His first public pronouncement would begin a devotion amongst the Powerless that grew for all of his days.

Before the LaborMaster could turn to bark his orders and prepare to receive a new workforce, the air became stirred. There had been Buzzbie activity all over Town that morning. They were everywhere, Pop!'ing and buzzing excitedly. Now with a WHOOSH! and a BANG!, the sky was once more blotted out with a cloud. All hovering. All buzzing.

"We've got to make room, Boss!" Pop! Pop!

Pop! *"Steef, I am the Boss Pill."*

"The Boss? I thought there were many Bosses?" He watched as Leezel began spinning slowly around, hands up, Buzzbies swirling in and around her, too. All of the assembled laborers were spellbound. Some of them had never heard of Buzzbies, much less seen one.

"There are currently seventy six Boss Pills. I am the Boss of the Bosses."

"What can I do for you, Pill?"

"I am here to tell you what WE will be doing for YOU. We have been having a Hivemeet. All four families. Such a thing has never occurred. We want to offer service to you."

"You already serve me, Pill. Very well, too. We are Clan. That is enough."

"We don't think so. We have been discussing this. If we…Buzzbies…all Buzzbies, had been watching closer, these things might not have happened to you."

Steef didn't have to ask what 'these things' he meant. Pill went on.

"If we didn't insist on only riding Masters, someone would have been with your family. It didn't occur to us to watch them. One of us should have been with Kivverr, and every HornCat for that matter. We failed you. Our own vanity…failed you. We will not fail again."

"The Pill family is your Clan. To that, we add this oath. We will watch whatever you need watched. We will ride whomever you say ride. We will be wherever you need us. Your word will be command to us before any other, for all of your days, and the days of your new Mate. No longer will we live for the story. We will be part of the story. We oath this. Pill has spoken." Pop!

"Pill, this isn't…"

Pop! *"Master Clear, I am the Boss Peel."*

"I am glad to meet you, Peel. Master Linzel has told me of your courage and devotion to her. And Pill speaks well of you, too."

"The Peel family is honored to know you, Master Clear. We thank you…for three times, you sent Pill to warn us of your Pulses. The stories that Pill has been

sharing, they tell us that our family has made the same mistakes as theirs. We offer the same service and oath that Pill gives." Pop!

"Peel..."

Pop! *"Master Clear, I am the Boss Paal......."* Pop!

Pop! *"Master Clear, I am the Boss Pull. The Pull family has long been neutral in disputes. We like our neutrality. But we have a debt to you. You spared us too, when you didn't have to. We do not offer service as the other three families, but we offer this. We will cooperate with the other three families, and we will watch. If we see that the service you require from them satisfies us, we will reconsider later. Further, we will no longer offer neutrality to Pool. They are your oathed enemies. They will be ours. Is this satisfactory?"*

"Yes."

"Bright days to you, Master Clear." Pop!

Pop! Pop! Pop! Pop! The four Boss Buzzbies were in a hover, directly in front of him, awaiting a reply.

"I accept your oaths, my friends, with one condition. The Pill family has earned my special devotion, through long service and great sacrifice. I will receive direct messages only from them, excepting emergencies. They are family. If this is satisfactory to you, would you please show me?"

All four Bosses spun around once. The Master Clear bowed to them, glowing White.

"Pill, my two regulars will do."

Pop! Pop! *"What are your instructions, Boss?"*

"First, go to the ClanCat. Tell him what has happened. Tell him that Leezel and I will be returning shortly, to Rest...to Rest...Kivverr. Tell him to prepare. The danger is over." *For now.*

Pop!

      ❦   ❦   ❦

The long beats were catching up to the new Mates, as they made slow progress back to Maar's hut. Stories were being told now, and people watched them pass in awed silence. Leezel had taken Steef's left arm as they walked, setting her staff to continue Healing his hand. They hardly looked up as they passed the huts and faces, until a voice broke their reverie.

"Your pardon, Master. You sent for a White?"

Looking up, they saw...Meeben. The man was shaking, from the ground up.

Leezel spoke, "Master Meeben, what are you…?"

"I asked to come, young miss. Begged…" he fell to knees. "Oh…please, Master! Just kill me! Please!" He gripped one of Steef's trous legs.

"I don't kill people, Master White."

Meeben looked up into the eyes of the Master Clear, "But…" And he waved a sweeping gesture, that encompassed all the events of the past days.

"I have killed no one, Sir," replied the Master Clear, "And I'm not going to start now. Why would you be asking such a thing?"

"But I told her! *I*…told her! I sent her down there! They say she found your family. You *must* kill me!"

"Sent who?"

"That…that…Vinntag!" and Meeben literally spat into the ground, trying to cleanse his mouth.

"I understand."

"You don't! No!…I knew it had to be Arima doing that Healing! A new leg! So much possibility. Only Arima could have had the Power for such a thing! Even Vinntag…," he spat again, "would want White Guild to have such a Power! I didn't know! I didn't…that's no excuse! Please! Just kill me!"

But Steef did understand. He could See the man's Core, the torment there. "There will be no killing here, Master," replied the Master Clear. He bent, and helped the pitiful man to his feet. "We are in desperate need of a Healing in that same village. Would you be willing to go there on an errand for us?"

The two young people waited quietly, as the old Master struggled with his now-non-ending life. "You would let me do that?"

"I must tell you, the Healing will be for a Powerless person. Does that bother you?"

"No! Good Master! No!…Healing is Healing, Sir! Healing is all I ever wanted to do!"

"Then here are my instructions, and you must follow them exactly. You will find a young man there whose hands have been cut. You will remove whatever you have to…to save him. You will Heal what's left of his arms without Locks. When you are done, you will take this into his hut." With that, the Master Clear fashioned a bubble, about the size of a man's head. Filling it with a specially tuned and mixed White, visible so that Meeben could see it, he handed it to the Healer. "This bubble must *not* enter the hut until your work is done. Just leave it in the boat until then."

It was clear that Meeben had no glimmer of what he was holding, but he said, "It will be exactly as you have instructed, Master." He held it as if it would break with a touch.

"You can't hurt it, Master Meeben. Just don't lose it. Secure it in the boat tightly, and take it into the hut when you are done…Pill."

"*Boss?*"

"What family serves Master Meeben?"

"*None of us, Boss. Peel used to, but Pool drove them off. Then, Pool stopped serving him, too.*"

"Ask Peel if they would come back, please. Instruct them how to find Cirlok."

"*Right away, Boss!*" Pop!

Pop! Pop! Meeben's head went down, with the arrival of his old friends. "You are too kind to me, Master."

Pop! "*Boss, we're going to go along too, and make sure Peel finds Cirlok.*"

"Thank you, Pill."

Steef thought he was finished with Meeben, but two days later Pill came to him saying that Meeben was crying inconsolably. He had tended to Cirlok, but when he brought the bubble into the closet where the boy was resting, it had popped! He just knew he'd failed the Master Clear. Steef had to send several Pills and Peels to assure him that, no, he hadn't failed. The bubble was supposed to pop.

Meeben would never leave that village. When it became clear that Meeben wasn't returning, Antee urged the old Healer to take up residence in his own hut, and there he lived out the remainder of his days, Healing any who asked. He never accepted payment, but the villagers brought him food and supplies as needed, often staying to cook for him. When his cycles came to an end, the entire village and its surrounding valley mourned. Peel took the message of that mourning to all Whites, everywhere.

❦   ❦   ❦

"There's another whole Territory?"

"Yes, Uncle," Steef just thought he was tired before. Now he'd spent many beats questioning Wingor, and he felt a need to bathe. "East of here. Apparently eleven hard days of flying."

"And this Wingor fellow helped arrange all of…" his wave said 'this'.

"It would seem so. The idea to kill the Cats was Vinntag's. Kuumit's Guild was used to enforce whatever Laws they wanted. But Wingor controlled them both."

This was Steef's strangest puzzle. He understood Vinntag's hatred. Understood the concept, at least. And he thought he understood Kuumit's vanity. But Wingor was just cold. His Core was the blackest Steef had Seen. He wondered if he would ever understand enough about people to know what would compel a man to want that much control of people's lives?

"It doesn't look like they knew how deeply they'd been betrayed by their friends in the east."

"What do you mean, Son?"

"Those snakes they brought, they wouldn't have ever stopped, if we hadn't stopped them."

"You mean…?"

Steef looked at his beloved Uncle's face, seeing the puzzlement there. It wasn't like Uncle Antee to not 'get' something. "Uh-huh. Those beasts were bred and altered to do two things. Eat and grow. They would have eaten every Cat and every cow and every sheep in the Valley. When that ran out, they'd have come out of the Valley…hungry. Looking for something else to eat."

Antee's face went white, "They'd have eaten everything," he whispered

Steef nodded, "Uh-huh. And everyone."

"What do you intend to do with *him*, Son?" Antee gestured to the mess that was Wingor.

"Nothing."

"Nothing!? But…"

"Seems to me, Uncle, that there is one party left who still has grievance. I've had my say about the injuries done to me. Kuumit will answer for that…for many cycles. Auntie and Master Linzel had their say, and Vinntag has been punished. Now…" the Master Clear shrugged.

Antee got this one. He gasped. "You know what He'll do, don't you?"

Steef turned a resolute face away towards the hut. Auntie, Sassy, and Master Linzel were in there, talking to his Mate. He could see her face through the window. Her eyes held disbelief.

"That won't be my decision, Uncle."

❧   ❧   ❧

"What are your plans, Son?" Arima knew without asking, that her days of making plans for him were at an end.

"We're going to Rest Kivver…and then I have to introduce Leezel to Seafwood."

"And then?"

"Then…I think…I think I owe Uncle Seafer a few tears." He hung his head.

She took his chin, and lifted until their eyes met, "If you can wait just a while…I'd be honored to join you."

"I'd like that, Auntie."

The Master Clear and his Mate entered the boat. It was one of the two boats that were still at the arena, the ones that had brought the Cats in from the Valley to begin with. Their previous owners wouldn't be needing them any more.

The second boat held the bodies of the Cats. Steef had Lifted them gently into it, and they'd been covered back up by the devoted Yellows, who afterwards followed Antee everywhere he went.

All of the newly 'Nerted' were gone, already hard at work on assigned tasks. And though it wasn't much past sunrise, the arena was filled with onlookers, who maintained a respectful silence. Everyone in Town now knew the story of the Master Clear and his fallen brother.

The boats Lifted. The second one had a furled sail, and was attached by tether to the first. The crowd watched, seeing the Master Clear at the mast, his Mate beside him. There was no traffic in the air. None was allowed. All necks felt the wind come up, as the Master Clear filled his sail. Had there been any doubt before, it was gone now. He was Lifting and Steering his boat, alone. Only a Clear could do that.

The two boats climbed swiftly and moved out of sight.

❧   ❧   ❧

It was a peculiar day for the Red woman. She had come to her workcloset in the Registry, as she always did, for no other reason than…she always did. The days following a Registry Festival were always filled with young people coming to oath their Matings. It was usually a busy sevenday. Not now. No one had come. This was the third day after, and she hadn't seen a single pair. She had to admit, it had been an unusual Festival, but *someone* should have come.

Someone did.

Looking up at the first sound of footsteps, she watched as an amazing assemblage of Masters began filling her small closet. Seemingly, at least one Master of every Color. Well, no Red Masters, now that she noticed, but she recognized Maar and Zelmar from the times she would see them at the GuildHall. But every other Color had a Master here. One White, an elderly lady, whose face looked familiar. She was good with faces, one reason she had this work. A small Blue. Now, she knew that Blue! The woman had been in here a few cycles earlier to Mate with a Yellow. There he was! An old Brown. And Blacks! Blacks everywhere! The new Black GuildMaster was there, along with four other Black Masters. Three of them looked like they could use some fresh garments. The one Green Master had red hair, and surely was kin to Maar's Mate.

And three low-ranking Greens, who were each being physically helped by one of the Masters. This was surely a strange assemblage.

It got stranger. Amongst all of those high-ranking people, the first to speak…was a Green Two!

"Your pardon, Mum, bu' we're here to Reg…" he looked up at the Yellow Master that was helping him.

"Register," said the Yellow.

"Tha's righ', Mum. Register our babes to be Mated. They had t' leave, y'see, so we'll be oathin' for 'em," he finished, with what looked to her like a strain. But he was trying to smile.

She watched as Maar stepped up to her table as well, and nodded to her. He looked almost pleasant about it.

"All right, Sir," she said, perplexed. She noticed that the little Blue was starting to grin. "What is your child's name?" She had her inkstick poised over the Registry, ready to mark next to any of the new names listed there.

"Steef, Mum, and thank'ye," he said. "I'm Stem, and tha's my Mate there. Her name's Maleef."

The woman looked up to see the other Green Two nod. She was being held around the waist by the Master White, and Maar's Mate. *Hadn't Linzel been unstaffed?* This just got stranger and…"What is his Rank, Sir?" She couldn't find a 'Steef'. Lots of names hadn't gotten entered, since the Festival had been interrupted.

"His Rank, Mum?" the Green Two looked up again at the Yellow, who mouthed the answer. "He's Master rank, Mum. Thank y', Mum."

She was a bit skeptical. A Master in the family of Green Two's? What was that Blue laughing at? Well, there were a lot of Masters here. It must be true. "What Guild then, Sir?"

The man got another puzzled look. The Yellow gave him another answer, "No Guild, Mum. Our Steef, he would be a Clear."

She dropped her inkstick, as Cassa's laughter came bubbling out. Indeed, there were a lot of laughing Masters in her closet right then. Even Maar was smiling, which would close out many a wager at the Red GuildHall...if there were a Red GuildHall...which there wasn't.

Before she could respond, the little Green Three had pulled out of the Blue Master's arms, retrieving the inkstick from the dirt and handing it back.

"Your Son...is the *Master Clear*?!" She'd heard of course. She just hadn't heard his name, which wasn't particularly odd, since most people didn't actually know Steef's name. Just his title.

"Yes'm. Tha's our boy," said the Green Two simply.

She turned to Maar, "You could have told me, Maar!"

"Well, Elin," said Maar, actually chuckling a bit. She didn't know he *could* chuckle. "It's proper for the boy's Father to speak first. Form, you know."

"And what part do you have in this?"

"The boy is Mating to my...our...daughter."

Elin glanced at Zelmar, whose eyes were puffy from crying. That was the only unsurprising thing about this. Zelmar cried whenever she needed to.

"You mean, Leezel...?" Elin turned her glance to Linzel, who was grinning and nodding.

"That's right," agreed Maar. Zelmar started crying again.

The entire group exited the Registry hut to find two Black Eights waiting for them. Linzel glanced at Leemin, who gestured her forward. "Skirran, do you have duty here?" she asked.

Skirran and his companion had found themselves new staffs. Those staffs now glowed Black as they bowed.

"Your pardon, Master. We have come to offer our services."

"What services?' inquired a puzzled Master Black.

"It seems to us, Master, that we are in your debt. Yours, and the Master Clear's. Either of you could have taken us that day, and you didn't."

"There was no need, Skirran, and you were just honoring your oath. I happen to believe in that oath."

"As do we, Master. We want to offer you another oath of service. There are some 'Nerted people around that might not like you right now. You, or any of your family."

"And you think that I can't handle them, Skirran?"

"Of course you can, Master. But you can't be everywhere, and even 'Nerts can use knives. We offer our services for you and yours, Master. We oath you." The young man Skirran partnered with still hadn't spoken. Too many Masters, probably. But he nodded vigorously. "GuildMaster Leemin has already approved our request," Skirran added.

"We made a lot of enemies, Skirran. This oath of yours could cost you a lot of days."

"Whatever it takes, Master."

❦   ❦   ❦

Pop! *"Boss, you should know, Pool has swarmed."*

In the twilight of the setting sun, he was watching Leezel's face. Her eyes were closed to the wind, hair blowing back to reveal her Pills. They'd be at the Valley tomorrow, but for now, he was letting his Mate enjoy her first boat ride in peace. They'd made some conversation earlier, mostly about Seafwood, but there would be cycles to get completely acquainted.

"Did they take everything, Pill?" He meant their queen. Pill knew that.

"Yes. All four families watched them leave. They can't 'Pop!' with the queen. Queens don't travel that way. So they have to swarm, helping her along."

"Where'd they go?" He already knew the answer.

"East. We followed to the edge of the blue valley. They just kept on going through. You should also know…that's dangerous for a Buzzbie. The heat of the place can kill us."

"How many were left?"

"It looked like less than a thousand. It will take cycles for them to become a true hive again. If ever."

"Thank you, Pill." Pop!

❦   ❦   ❦

Seafwood was ready. After Steef's explanation, she had opened her great roots, exposing a giant hole. All of her leaves were drooping. One task remained to be done before the Resting. It couldn't be allowed to distract from the Moaning.

SNAP!!

Wingor came back to the here-and-now to find himself unable to see, which was disorienting enough, but his nose worked fine and it was being assaulted. The smell of stable was all around him, as was the strong odor of someone who'd been soiling themselves a lot. It was a foul mixture.

Added to that, was the constant bumping and rubbing. Wingor was sitting…on grass, it felt like, and something large kept bumping him. Hard. It was difficult to stay upright.

Every beat brought more sensations. He could hear rustling now, as if something were pacing around him. All around him. Other than that, there were no sounds. It was eerily quiet.

"He is aware of us now?"

"Yes, your Majesty. He is aware." Steef was standing on one side of Plivverr, Leezel on the other. She had been accepted into the Clan the very beat her foot touched the soil. As female to Steefrr, she was Clan. As Mate to the MixMaster, she was granted immediate access to the ClanCat. Her pump was filled with strong 'tastes' just now. The ClanCat was as magnificent as her Mate's brother had been, but the work at hand was foul. Necessary, but foul. Steef had explained this morning while they were still in the boat.

"You understand, Majesty, that this is one victory meal we cannot share," said the MixMaster.

"We understand, Steefrr. It is not a problem. He is not very big, though we do not look forward to this ourselves."

"Oh?"

"It is true, though we would not want other two-legs to know it. It serves us better that they always doubt."

"Doubt what, your Majesty."

"We do not actually like to eat two-legs. We think it is the Power you have. You do not taste very good." With that, Plivverr stepped forward to take his place in the circle, giving a low growl that set off the Clan.

Steef and Leezel looked at each other in amazement. Their laughter was drowned out by the Clan's sudden screeching and roaring. And one short scream.

❧   ❧   ❧

Kivverr was given a Moaning of only a sevenday. There was much to be done, and many things needed Healing. Apparently, Pill felt it should have been more, because, every cycle, on the day before Kivverr's Resting day, Pill would buzz into the ClanCat's ear. The next day would find Clan at Seafwood's paws, moaning from sunrise to sunset. This ritual would last for Steef's entire life.

Steef and Leezel had eight sevendays of privacy, before anyone else returned to the cove. They had to get acquainted, and do some Healing of their own. Steef's wounds were Leezel's wounds. They decided together that she should not use her gifts to Heal them, letting the days do it for them. But she shared them, as a Mate should share grief. The young couple would have to wait, to begin 'finding the joy' together.

Seafwood accepted Leezel immediately. The young Healer never felt one shock. Well, one shock. That occurred when her Mate informed her that the entire tree was actually a staff, and yes...he could charge it. He showed her, bringing Seafwood to almost full charge, while Leezel looked out at the cloud of Power that surrounded them.

The next few sevendays would be filled with surprises for her.

CHAPTER 25

The Buzzbies had a genuine problem. All of them. Whatever it was that they used to form words for speaking, just couldn't get itself around the name 'Leezel'. Oh, they could hit the 'ee' sound. They did it often enough with 'Steef' and 'Maleef'. They could handle the 'zz' sound, too, as they proved with 'Linzel' and 'Zelmar'. But when the two sounds came together, what came out was 'Leeeeezzzzzzzzzl'. They took to calling her 'the Lady'.

This actually became significant. Messages began pouring into the cove. Steef had instructed at first, that only messages from family members get through. Soon enough, though, he relaxed his restrictions. Several days were filled with questions and requests, until finally, in self-defense, he limited outside queries to the first eighthday after firstmeal.

He sent replies to many of these messages. Each time, he instructed Pill to deliver his reply as being from 'Steef and Leezel'. Every time.

However, the messages always arrived at their destination with the signatory of 'from the Master Clear and his Lady'. Every time.

Steef might not want any status, but his Buzzbies wanted their Boss to get his due.

The result of this was that very soon after leaving GuildTown, most everyone in the nine Territories was referring to them as 'the Master Clear and his Lady'. Or just 'the Lady'. Or 'the Master'. Their actual names became irrelevant.

Every Guild begged Steef to take their GuildMaster position, with the exception of Black. He declined. When they insisted, his reply was sent to all Guilds simultaneously. It was typical Steef. "I have no inclination to lead a Guild. I have no training for it, and I do not have the cycles for such responsibilities. You must find your own ways. I give only this bit of advice. You have chosen in the past, to have leaders who displayed the greatest Power, and you are doing so again with these requests. I would remind you of the recent results of that policy, and urge you to look for wisdom over Power, and value compassion as a strength."

Neither of them would ever rule anything, though they would exert sway and influence that grew over the cycles. It would only take them a few quarters to realize that their smallest gestures were scrutinized, their tiniest whims able to launch massive efforts. They would learn to be cautious with each word, lest someone make life-changing decisions based on a casual remark.

Leezel would grow into her title of 'the Lady', for she would spend many days in the company of Plivverr and Arivverr, and their majesty would infect her. It would be tempered with Steef's own humble spirit, and often that of his Mama's. Leezel would become the beloved Lady that people ascribed her to be.

❦   ❦   ❦

The Guilds had a problem. After the Master Clear's message, no one wanted to go back to any of the old ways of doing things. The Master's Law had been abolished, of course. The so-called 'alliance' was abolished, too. Brown found itself in prominence almost at once, for the Territories needed Dust, and in a hurry. Every effort was made to help facilitate that effort.

It was decided to abolish the Guild system entirely. All of the Guilds merged into one. Each Color had its own HeadMaster, who was selected by voice count, and every person got a single voice, regardless of rank. One GuildMaster was selected, also by voice count. Ironically, he happened to also be Black, but that was coincidence, not influence. It's just that, when he led, people followed. Since they agreed to follow in the directions he wanted to lead, he agreed to lead.

All of the GuildHalls were torn down, most of the work being done by the new 'Nerts, since the Browns were busy digging. A new GuildHall was begun, that would house schools, and one great meeting Hall.

Under the guidance of the new White HeadMaster, Healing was given for free to any in need. All fees were abolished. Healers would live off the kindness of the people, with a bit of help from the Guild. Every Healer was given a Buzzbie, and Paal volunteered for the service, the family wanting to prove itself. They rode any Grade of White, bringing news of emergencies from lower Grades to the ears of Masters, when needed.

❦   ❦   ❦

Kuumit finally got to see his name in the history parches, just as he'd pre-dicted. The LaborMaster made sure the man had ample beats to read each new parch that was posted. Of course, the accounts of his deeds were probably not what Kuumit had hoped for.

❦   ❦   ❦

She used to be one of the deadliest of Black Masters, her Pulsing accuracy a source of pride and conversation. Now she could hardly swallow. She could barely breathe. She certainly couldn't eat much without stopping for breath, and even then, she had to take very small bites. She couldn't know it, but the bubble in her neck was larger than it really needed to be. There had been haste that day, at distance.

And that wasn't the worst of her problems. She was watched, everywhere the LaborMaster sent her. Buzzbies. They called themselves 'Pillrr'. She knew this, because every morning at the first hint of light, that name would be buzzed into her ear, while somewhere on her body, a stinger would sink in. Just one. Never in the same place.

Every morning.

She'd tried staying awake, but they came anyway. It was a terrible way to start each day. She was coping, best she could. At first, it was just a painful aggravation. But over the days, then the Quarters, she was losing sleep, antici-pating her wake-up sting.

She was losing weight, too. From hard work, lack of sleep, and tiny meals. And she was slowly getting 'crooked'. Very 'crooked'.

After almost a full cycle, she got completely 'crooked', and flung herself from a rockface. Pillrr watched her fall, watched the impact, and reported it to the Boss.

The Master Clear had forgotten about her. He had forgotten his hasty sug-gestion that Pill remind her every so often of the wrong she'd done them. He regretted now that he hadn't given it more thought. His Lady reminded him that the decision had been made in haste, and it wasn't a haste of his making. It helped.

❧   ❧   ❧

Zelmar had her own problems. Their names were Skirran and his partner, Woonik. One or both of them followed her everywhere. It had been exciting at first, having an escort of Blacks. She flaunted them to her friends and suitors. She soon discovered, though, that the friends thought it was stupid, and the suitors, well, there soon weren't any suitors. No one wanted to call on someone who had Black Eights watching everything, no matter how pretty she was.

So, being a Red, she naturally tried to…well, fix the problem.

New problem. There was a Grader living in her hut. That Grader spoke to her Mother, and/or Father, and her Locks would be removed from Skirran and Woonik. She tried Locks on the Grader, at night of course, so she wouldn't See them coming. The Grader awoke so pleasant and docile, that Father had immediately noticed, and removed the Locks. Sigh. When Mother heard, she scorched Zelmar's bottom. Literally. Zelmar couldn't sit for a sevenday. This just wasn't working out.

Finally, in desperation, she used her last remaining weapon. She began flirting with Skirran and Woonik. Especially Woonik, who was only a few cycles older than she, and unMated. They were immune, cleaving to their oaths. She had to give up.

A strange thing happened, when she gave up. She had beats on her hands, with nothing to do but think. It began to occur to her that maybe, just maybe, it might be nice to spend beats with a young man who wasn't affected by her Red or her flirting. But, what else was she? She didn't know what else to be, besides a Red or a flirt. She asked. She asked the one young man available. Woonik.

What a concept! Actual conversation with a man! Five sevendays later, they had pledged themselves.

Now there would be a Mating ceremony. Mother insisted, and Father didn't mind. Their other daughter had missed out on any ceremony, so both parents were pleased as they could be to make this one spectacular.

Then word was received that the Master Clear and his Lady would be attending. Now the entire Town wanted this ceremony to be spectacular! Zelmar had *another* new problem. She looked forward to seeing her sister. She loved the attention, and she surely loved all the plans being made by…well…everyone for *her* Mating ceremony! That was splendid!

She also knew that it had *nothing* to do with her. A real conflict was tearing through her.

The Master Clear and his Lady arrived a few days prior to the ceremony. Their family would arrive later, in Master Cassa's boat, for the Master Clear was Steering a sled! As it drew near, the assembled crowd gasped! There was a HornCat on that sled! They drew back in fear.

Steef, Leezel, and the ClanCat stepped lightly onto the Landing Field, and waited. Auntie came up at once of course, bringing an apprehensive Linzel with her. As was proper, the Grader paid homage to the ClanCat, before the entire gathered crowd. Then, she bowed brightly to the Master Clear. Then, hugs were exchanged. When Master Arima hugged Plivverr's leg, the crowd gave a second gasp.

Arima then introduced Linzel to Plivverr, though conversation was withheld. That could come in the privacy of the cove, as appearances must be maintained. A great procession followed them through Town, to Maar's hut, where the ClanCat found himself a nice resting spot in the shade of the hut itself. The shade covered most of him. The entire Yellow Guild took station on the road of Maar's hut, in silent respect. It wouldn't be until Antee arrived, that they would make any gestures. Antee's reputation, already inflated, went beyond reason after that.

The morning after their arrival found the Master Clear back at the arena, doing delicate Brown work. As the sun got up, the crowds watched him form a giant figure, in the shape of a HornCat. They couldn't know, but it was the exact image of his brother. The exact size. The exact color. He knew every hair, every muscle. The only difficulty was getting the stone shaped and colored...just so. Well...it was often difficult to see, too, through the tears. The crowd gave him respect. As he neared completion, Pill left him to tell the Lady that the project was done. She appeared soon after, in the company of Plivverr, and the crowd parted gladly for them. Plivverr approached, stopping with his shoulder against Steef's. This was what He'd come for.

"*This is the spot where my brother Rested?*"

"Yes, your Majesty. As close as I can remember." Leezel was nodding, too.

"*He stood well?*"

"He stood well. So did Leezel."

"*I believe that. Leezelrr tastes strong. She is a fit female for my brother's brother.*"

They stood in silence for many beats, Leezel sharing tears with her Mate.

"*We learned from him. You should know this.*"

"Oh? What is that, your Majesty?" asked the Master Clear.

"We learned that not all crooked thinking is wrong. This is important. It was crooked to stand behind your hard air when the two-legs came. But it was not cowardly. It was wise. Crooked, but wise. If we had come out, all HornCats would have Rested. There would be no more Clan, now."

Steef digested this. "Then every new cub will be his legacy."

"That is true. It is also true that every new cub will hear his name. For as long as the line of Rivverr shall last, every remembrance circle will include the name of Kivverr. I oath you this."

It wasn't enough, but it was something. Auntie had once told him that he always 'looked for the joy' in every hurtful thing, to balance out. This was a joyful thing from Kivverr's death. It wasn't enough for balance, but it was something. It would have to do.

Steef rose up one last piece of rock, and carved:

KIVVERR

HORNCAT TO THE MIXMASTER

Then he put the strongest Locks he had on the statue. Brown Locks went out in every direction, stabilizing this valley. Not even a groundshake would disturb this monument, lasting for as long as the Master Clear could make it.

He wanted people to know. They were already writing parches about him, and he didn't like it. Saying that 'the Master Clear had saved the Town and the valley'. He hadn't saved anything. He'd been completely willing to discharge himself to save Kivverr. That wouldn't have saved anything but himself and Kivverr. Then he'd been willing to discharge a killing Pulse, and *then* Heal Kivverr.

No. Kivverr had saved this valley, with Leezel's help. While they were killing him, he'd saved them. He'd saved Steef, too. With his last beat, still loving, still teaching. The Master Clear was determined that people should know. They *would* know. And they could come here to remember.

The statue was right in the middle of the arena. Right in the way of any future function, including the upcoming Mating ceremony. Oh, well.

❧   ❧   ❧

Antee had a problem, and its name was Cassa. There was revelry all around Town, the night of the ceremony. All of the Master Clear's family had arrived from the cove, both natural family and chosen. They had all watched as the Townspeople had tried to make the ceremony itself and the attendant celebration, about the Master Clear and his Lady. They had watched as both young people constantly turned that attention aside, gladly sending it to Zelmar and her new Mate.

Zelmar was a new person, herself. Two days before the ceremony, her sister had quietly taken her aside, out of anyone's view, and talked her into touching the ClanCat. After a stunning few beats, the red-haired beauty had gone sobbing into the hut, in search of her Aunt, flinging herself onto the dirt at Arima's feet, clasping the old Healer's knees. On the day of her ceremony, the girl had been radiant with newfound light in her eyes, making everyone glad.

That gladness had affected someone else. Cassa searched him out, hiding as he was from the persistent Yellows. He couldn't hide from Pill, though, which meant that he couldn't hide from Cassa.

As she arrived, she said, "Pill, this will be a private conversation, please."

That got Antee instantly on guard.

Not Pill. *"Your pardon, Cassa, but we're watching for the Boss."*

"And do you know what he will say when I tell him you've been stubborn?" Pop! Pop! Pop! Pop!

"That's better." She smiled at Antee, making him think *Uh-Oh.*

Turning back to the festivities, she said, "Antee, I've been thinking. This place is beginning to look much brighter." A peaceful smile remained fixed on her face, though she would occasionally rub her chin. Almost thoughtfully.

Still not knowing what was coming, he said cautiously, "Yyeessss, I think...you're right."

She swatted him lovingly in the shoulder. A sideways blow, it didn't sting. Much. "Get a little 'crooked' old man. I don't bite."

"No, you hit."

She grinned up at him, "I do hit, don't I? Anyway, the future is looking brighter than it has in many long cycles, and I'm thinking about something that I wouldn't have believed possible."

Sigh. No way around it. Just ask. "Okay...what?"

"I want to have a baby," she said lightly, still watching the crowd.

Relief. He thought it would be something important, like taking over the entire Guild. "Well, there's a field full of men right out there. Any of them would fight for the chance to Mate with the Master Clear's Blue teacher. While we're here, we'll just go to the Registry, and dissolve our oath." This was easy. They'd never lived together as Mates, ample grounds to separate a Mating. There weren't many acceptable reasons, but that was one of them.

To his everlasting surprise, she didn't agree. "I already have a Mate," she said simply. She was rocking a little, back and forth, heel to toe, still smiling. Still rubbing.

"Now wait, Cassa! You can't be serious…"

She nodded to the open field.

"…That was never a part of our arrangement! Why, do you know…"

"Yes, I do."

"…But I'm…"

"Yes, you are." She turned to him, took his head and turned it back towards the field. Pointing at her Shortstick, she whispered, "But you don't have to be, now do you?"

Since he obviously wouldn't be speaking for a while, she went on, "Shortstick tells me you've got as good a Core as any man he's ever Seen. I believe that, because I know you. You also have as good a mind as any I've known, which isn't as important, but it's nice. To be fair, you don't look all that great…"

"But my Power, Cassa! I'm as weak as I can be, and still be a Master!"

"And you of all people, should know how little that means to me!" She began pacing in front of him.

He tried to argue. He was certain that, given enough beats, he could get her to be sensible. What he hadn't counted on was that Cassa was a Master of Blue. She was skilled and experienced in wind, water and weather. She understood better than most, the meaning of 'relentless'.

Half a cycle later, he would find himself back at the cove, feeling better than he had any right to, while Leezel and Arima took turns showing him how to make tiny Pulses with his little White stick into Cassa's swollen belly, where she was growing him a Son. Merciful Creator!

He would often hesitate, not wanting to Pulse at all, for fear of harming the baby. Then Cassa would reach across her belly, swatting him on the shoulder, telling him to 'get on with it, she needed to eat'. Leezel would kindly Heal his bruised shoulder every few days. He didn't mind. His Mate would soften the blow with her sweet smile, putting his hands on the baby when it kicked.

And that would cause another problem. Cassa had insisted that Shortstick get to feel the baby kick. He hesitated at first, surprising everyone. He *was* a Healer, after all. But this was Sassy, and it was…personal. He finally relented, laying his hands on either side of her belly. Little Antsa was kicking away. Then, as Cassa watched, her Shortstick got his 'puzzled' look for a beat or two and fear blew through her. Arima had assured her…but Arima wasn't Steef.

He saw her face. "No, Sassy. There's nothing wrong. He's a fine baby boy…"

Later that night, around the fire, Antee addressed Arima. He and Cassa had been talking together most of the day. "Arima, we'd like to ask…well, you see…Steef felt of the baby…and…"

Everyone was watching. Leezel even giggled a bit. This was fun. Uncle Antee never got his tongue tied up. Of course, *she* knew what his problem was. Steef didn't keep anything from his Mate.

"Yes, Antee?" queried the Master Healer. Mokam looked puzzled. Linzel just watched.

Cassa swatted him again. Her swats *were* getting gentler. She thought so, anyway. "Merciful Creator, Antee! She won't even hit you!…'Rima, you know we've been planning to call our boy 'Antsa'?"

"Of course, Cassa, why wouldn't you?" Their next one would be Cassee. Natural as breathing.

"Well, the Master Shortstick here felt of my belly today. First time." She pointed her little Brown stick at him.

"All right."

"Seems he can do something no one else can do. Now…'Rima…there's no point in saying it's not possible…"

Everyone laughed.

"…He Graded our baby. Right in my belly. You want to tell him that's not possible?"

Arima looked over at her beloved Son/Nephew. He shrugged. She shook her head. "That's wonderful, Cassa! Was the news good?"

"We think so. You'll have to decide for yourself. Our Son will be a Master Green."

Beat. Beat. Beat.

"He's gonna have my strength, 'Rima. Shortstick says he hasn't Seen any Greens that strong."

Beat. Beat. Beat.

"If you don't mind, 'Rima," Cassa voice softened, "We think now, that maybe we'd like to name him Seafer."

❀   ❀   ❀

The big man looked out of place in the new, polished Vault. He'd been traveling for days at the urgent summons he'd received. Been told by some strange talking insect that they'd been looking for him for almost half a cycle. He'd tried to be hard to find, after all the turmoil in Town.

He had the grime of his journey still on him, and some flour, though he didn't notice. He never noticed the flour.

The beat he arrived, several Reds had pounced upon him, ushering him swiftly into the workcloset of a tall, elderly Nine. The Nine had actually risen from his seat and bowed to him! This was getting strange.

"My name is Maar, good Sir. Welcome back."

The baker said nothing, but he returned the bow.

"With your indulgence, I'll get right to the deal I hope to strike. I have secured a workhut for you in the center of Mercantile Row. All of the equipment and ovens you need are already waiting. You may take up your work there the beat you leave here, if you choose."

Now it was *really* strange. But the Nine wasn't finished.

"You may work there, and peddle your goods, free of charge, for as long as you like. For as long as your children like, if they're a mind to. There is only one condition."

Here it comes.

"Every workday, you must offer one free sweetbread…with your special spice…to anyone that asks. One per person, per day. You will keep a tab of your expenses for this service, and present that tab to me each Quarter. The tab will be paid. Do you have any questions?…no?…excellent. This…" and the Nine pushed a pouch of Dust across the table. It had been sitting there for over a Quarter…"Should cover your first cycle for starting up. When can you begin?"

It would be almost another full cycle before the baker's benefactor entered the shop for his own sweetbread. With the badge he wore, and the crowds that followed, the baker finally understood. The Lady had asked if she might have just a small sample of the strange spice, to prepare her Mate some sweetbreads at home. He had gladly obliged, and added some seeds.

By then, he'd already quit keeping a tab on the free pastries. They served as samples and brought in more work than they cost.

The Master Clear had a problem. Something GuildMaster Leemin had said kept chewing on him, making a puzzle that he couldn't define. He'd said he 'detested that killing was the only Power he had'. Mama Linzel had been training Steef in Black, and he was amazed at how little he'd known. Good thing he'd never used it much! Each journey to GuildTown now included some beats spent with GuildMaster Leemin, talking about Black Sight. Dangerous stuff.

Then, he finally had his glimmer. A remembrance, of the one occasion when he himself had used Black for something other than killing. There'd been a man with a bad leg. He sent a hurried message to Leemin.

Now there were volunteers from Black, working with volunteers from White. A new alliance, of Healing. Careful experiments were made, cutting into sick people without a knife. Black had new purpose, and Leemin sent grateful greets daily for a Quarter.

Life settled into a pleasant routine in the cove, if intense. The intensity was the training. All of them lived there now. Stem, Maleef and Malem had returned. Malem was no longer distressed at the solitude, for there wasn't any. She had her pick of willing HornCats for conversation, though Timmerr, Antimmerr and Teemmerr were her favorites, which was fine with Uncle Antee. Malem also had duties. Her Bubba had brought Cirlok to the cove, and he had his own small cave near her family's. She spent many beats helping him do the simplest tasks, as his new arms and hands grew in. He was perfectly willing to show them to any that cared to look.

The training was like one of Cassa's swirlfuries. Linzel's arrival gave the Steef Guild five Master members again…the number they'd begun with. The Lady would be the sixth, when she achieved her Mastery. The five of them ultimately came to wear identical leather sashes across their shoulders, tied at the waste. Attached to each of the sashes were six loops, each loop holding one small onespan stick. Each stick had two stones and was stained a different Color.

When they went into public, the Master members of the Steef Guild wouldn't answer any questions about the sticks, just giving a mute smile. There was a brief fashion, when people copied the sash and sticks, though no one ever knew what they were for. But privately, the training was non-stop. The

Steef Guild had its own share of secrets, which was especially ironic, since the other Guilds had divulged all of theirs to one another.

The training would often include the Master Clear. But sometimes, he and the Lady would slip away on their sled, disappearing into the sky, Lifting to unheard-of heights. These trips were always accompanied with high-level sky-bolt storms. On the ground, there would be accompanying smiles. Their children were finding some joy together, the Empath and the man of joy.

That was always true, though not always in the manner expected. Sometimes the Mates would just Lift above the storms, and hover their sled. Climbing down a steprope, they'd lie on the inside of the bubble, nothing separating them from the clouds and fury but hard air, and just…watch. Steef never, ever, *ever*…climbed down there without a small stick.

❧   ❧   ❧

"Steef?"

"Lady?"

She was playing with the hairs on his chest. He had five. Judging by his Papa, he would never have many. *Oh! That was a big one!* she thought, as the sky lit up. She'd thought the storm was almost done.

Touching him was the best training she could get for her Empathy. She would start Cloaked, and let just a little of him seep in, a few beats at a time, increasing the exposure gradually. UnCloaking suddenly and completely was…incapacitating.

He'd told her it was similar to when he'd practiced his different discharges. There'd been no one to teach him how, either.

"Have you ever noticed that you have a *lot* of names?"

She loved to watch his face. His jaw was twisting up now, chewing on her puzzle.

"I am Steef," he concluded. *A little more Blue.* He added one more Pulse. There was still daylight left, and his Lady liked the big skybolts. He liked the way they lit her face.

"Yesss…but you're also 'the Master Clear'" she said in a stern, gruff voice. Then she giggled. "And you're 'Steefrr,'" she purred, her finger now tracing the round little scar at his side. He'd said that only she knew how it got there. "And you're 'the MixMaster'…and 'Shortstick'…and 'Boss'…"

"I suppose so…but I'm still just Steef."

"Mm-hmm. You are, my love. And that's what I like best about you…but I want more."

His face just couldn't twist up any more…so…she knew it would come…*yes!*…there was his tongue!

"More what?"

"I want another name. One that I can call you. A name no one else uses."

"Okay." He didn't care. He'd answer to any name she called out.

"So choose," she said lightly.

"You want *me* to choose? Shouldn't *you* choose?"

"Something that you'd really enjoy. Something that's just between us."

"Anything with your voice will do."

"Oooohhhh!!!!" She started to tickle him, between the ribs like Sassy had shown her. He drew in a breath, but it wouldn't last. It never did.

Whoosh! "Okay! Okay!" he squirmed, smiling, and caught her hands.

When they finished laughing, he said thoughtfully, "How about 'Sprout'?" Then he told her why.

The Town had a problem. Well, the entire nine Territories had a problem. It had been over a cycle now, and there hadn't been a Grading.

There were infants to Grade, and, in truth, the Guild was realizing that many of its younger members weren't displaying the strengths they'd been assigned. All of the rankings were suspect.

Trouble was, there weren't any Graders any more. Vinntag had completed her plan too well. The two youngsters in White weren't ready. Far from it, what little training they'd had was also suspect.

So, with serious trepidation, the White HeadMaster sent a Buzzbie to the only Grader they knew, asking her advice. Knowing what it would be.

Though his army of Buzzbies searched for cycles, the Master Clear would never find the old Messenger he'd spoken to. When he finally stopped the search, he'd decided it didn't matter any more. He'd gotten the Message. Indeed, looking over his young life, he could cite so many places where someone had practiced that Message on him, why…they were beyond counting.

Now there was ample opportunity for him to spread that Message himself. By example.

❧   ❧   ❧

Middle of the night, and Leezel was giggling again. He loved to hear her giggle, and he would do much to make it happen. They were standing outside of Cirlok's cave. The cove was quiet enough that some of the Cats sleeping around the different cave entrances looked up at Leezel's giggle.

Steef was fashioning a small little bubble. It had been his Lady's idea, but it was a good one, and he'd puzzled over it for a few sevendays. Cirlok's hands were almost grown. He was even starting to show a bit of nail. A good day to start.

Sissy would be so pleased. It would be an early Mating gift.

The tiny, tiny speck of Dust flared into its 'seventh' spark, and the Master Clear lightly blew the bubble off of his palm. It floated into Cirlok's cave, drawn to the tune it picked up there. It had a fine tune of its own, and reaching Cirlok, it still wasn't satisfied, floating up the sleeping boy's body until it reached his neck. There it settled, just above his skin, and with a brief flash, it popped. He never roused.

Leezel laid the other half of the gift on the ground next to the cave entrance. Next morning, Cirlok almost stepped on it. A threespan stick, and a Green badge.

Another secret for the Steef Guild to keep.

❧   ❧   ❧

Arima had a problem.

They were coming! All of them! The entire Town practically, and a goodly portion from each of the nine Territories. For Grading.

All of the infants, of course. But others, too. Anyone under the age of eighteen would be getting a new Grading, or remove their badges permanently. It was a lot of people. Fortunately, they wouldn't all come at once. But the waves that were coming each sevenday would still take half a Quarter.

She already had duties training her niece, who, admittedly was an excellent student. The Lady took her studies seriously, much like her Mate had always done. And also, Arima had to admit, like her Aunt before her.

To add to her burden, two young apprentice Graders would be coming to learn.

There was help, of course. All of the Steef Guild was helping organize, and an army of workers from each Color had arrived early, setting up semi-permanent tents. The Master Clear would be helping with the Grading, and possibly even the new apprentices.

The Greens hadn't been much help. They were distracted, constantly pestering anyone in the Steef Guild about 'The Tree'. So, after much wrangling, the Master Clear had taken some of them to see Seafwood, though none was allowed up into her. They also weren't allowed into Seafer's cave. That would remain a secret sanctuary for the Steef Guild only. Linzel spent many beats there.

The Master Clear also granted them permission to remove some of the saplings and use them as they saw fit. Finally, the Greens were given one thousand acorns. The Master Clear said he would see how they used all of these gifts before dispensing more. He had one condition for all of this. Every staff that came from a sapling or an acorn must be called a 'Seafer'. They had agreed at once.

None of that was really Arima's problem. She had created her own problem, really. In her excitement, she had frivolously asked the Master Clear for a Freshening. Not just any Freshening. She had specifically asked that he give her his 'best'. It was a careless remark, and he had questioned it immediately. So had the Lady.

"Auntie," she asked, "Are you *certain* you want…Steef's *best* Freshening?"

"Absolutely!" she'd replied. Odd, what a little good news can do to one's judgement.

The two youngsters had exchanged a look, shrugged, and said, "Oook-kaayyy!"

There was a brief flash of White…

She awoke three days later, and seventy five cycles younger.

Sigh.

Now, excepting an accident, Seafer and Rivverr would have to wait a lot longer than expected. In truth, she felt wonderful! And her hair started getting its color back. In four sevendays, it was as dark as the Lady's again.

That was the twenty eighth day after her Freshening. On that day, she received another reminder of her folly. She would get that reminder every twenty eight days, for many cycles to come.

Sigh.

The worst part was, her appearance would probably give away one of the Steef Guild's most closely guarded secrets, and it couldn't be undone. Anyone who knew her well, would know.

❀   ❀   ❀

Mama Linzel presented it to him the day before the Festivities were to begin. A new tunic, with a new badge. She'd designed it herself, though she'd had the embroidery done in Town. She had a strong distaste for sewing now.

The badge was a circle, of course, empty of any Color. Instead, there was a "C" embroidered inside. Seven different Master's marks adorned the outside bottom edge of the circle. In nice, neat rows beneath the circle, were all the various marks of Crafts that he'd Mastered, in their respective Colors. Through it all, protruded two twisted horns.

His Lady had her own new tunic. The Whites had insisted that she be given Master's status. She preferred to wait until Auntie bestowed an earned accord, but for public functions, she'd wear it. The Steef Guild understood.

❀   ❀   ❀

Would you look at all the boats!

Everyone was at the Landing Field, except the Master Clear and the Lady. They'd be arriving later, for some reason.

Arima saw that Cassa was feeding little Seafer. She was sitting twenty or so staffs back from any Landing hole, propped against one of her many females, surrounded by even more females. The only thing of Cassa that could be seen was her head, sticking up out of a group of Cats.

He'd apparently finished, for Arima watched her Blue sister rise. Laying the baby down inside that circle, the little Blue was making her way over. Arima knew that the boy was safer there than any other place in their world, save the Master Clear's arms. Not even Arima could approach Seafer through those females. Perhaps the Master Clear could…maybe.

All of the Clan was here. Even every female, though they weren't needed for the Grading itself. But the ClanCat wanted the two-legs to see that his was still a proper Clan. Their numbers had been depleted, and Plivverr had instructed his Clan. Now, every female that was able, was heavy with cubs, and some that Arima wouldn't have believed were able. She wondered if Steef had…no…none of her concern. The males were full of themselves, strutting around with their tails and horns held high, ready and eager for the Grading to commence.

Plivverr and Arivverr stood on either side of her. None of the other Steef Guild would be touching the males during these days, at least not in public. Some decorum had to be maintained in front of the two-legs.

The first boat landed, and the HeadMaster of White stepped out, with two youngsters following. The three of them proceeded to where she was waiting, her hands actually shaking a bit. The HeadMaster made the correct homage to the ClanCat, as Arima had instructed him through Pill and Paal. Then he turned, and received Arima's bow, returning it with glow.

"Welcome HeadMaster, to the Valley of the Cats!" She couldn't believe she was saying that!

"On behalf of all Whites, and the Guild itself, I thank you for receiving us Master Arima," he replied genuinely. He had to have noticed her appearance, but he made no sign of it. His discretion was something she'd always liked about him.

"In truth Master," he went on, now that the formalities were accomplished, "It feels...unseemly...to have you bowing to me."

"I gladly give respect to the office, Ormis, and its current holder. You will do well." He was the first non-Master 'head' anything. Ever. And deservedly so. "Are these my new apprentices?" she asked, giving the boy and girl a smile. They were terrified, of course.

"Yes, Master. Will you receive them?"

"I will, Ormis. As will the Clan. They will be introduced to Arivverr, before the day ends." As Arima had done at that age, these youngsters would meet the male that would be ClanCat when they reached their Mastery. That would be Arivverr.

Her formal duties done, she waited for another boat to land. Maar was there. In all their cycles, she'd never gotten him to come to the Valley. To *know*. That would change now, though she still hadn't been the reason. There had been another inducement to his visit, one that he just couldn't ignore. Well...two, really.

Steef was edgy. He was preparing music bubbles, in groups. Giving them some visible Color, so people could see them. Bundling them in nets to be tethered behind their sled for the short trip up the Valley. His Lady was reclining against Seafwood. Their tree had grown some soft leaves at ground level for her comfort.

She was unable to climb right now. She would be birthing in twenty six more days.

He was edgy because the ClanCat had commanded him to stay here in the cove, until it was absolutely necessary to leave. The last occasion of a direct command from Plivverr had included some snake killing. As a dutiful member of the Clan, he was obeying, but he was edgy.

So when his Lady called out "Sprout" he jumped a bit. Turning, he saw her pointing. "Look," she said.

A lone female Cat had come into view around the edge of the cove. He recognized her at once.

It was Mepprr.

She made a straight path to Steef, and lowered her head to bump his belly.

"Greets, Steefrr. You are well?"

"Yes, Mepprr. Thank you, I am well."

The Lady's head tilted. 'Mepprr' was a name she'd heard, as her Sprout had recounted his days with his brother.

"Is this your female?"

"Yes, this is my Mate. She is Leezelrr…" Mepprr abruptly walked away, stepping to his Lady, sniffing her all over while Leezel held her arms up, a delighted smile on her face. Females usually paid her scant attention.

Mepprr returned. *"She carries your cubs…yes?"*

"Yes…uh…she carries my cubs." *How could she know that Leezel was growing two babies?*

"That is proper. Your cubs will run with Kivverr's cubs."

"What?!"

But she'd turned away again, giving a series of 'yips'.

As the Master Clear and his Lady watched and listened in stunned amazement, those 'yips' were returned, and followed by two floppy-pawed male HornCats. The two youngsters went romping across the cove, tussling and tumbling, jumping and swatting. They were behaving altogether…'crooked'.

Mepprr gave a roar, which brought up two heads, pointed their way. With obvious resignation, the males came over, padding an unwavering path for Leezel, and her belly.

They sniffed carefully there, keeping their little horns out of the way. Very carefully, for they'd been told.

Their Mother had told them, when they were hiding in a small cave at the southern end of the Valley. They'd watched from behind her, as the big slithertooth had passed back and forth, unable to enter. After the slithertooth left, big males had come to get them, saying the way was clear. The males had told them, too.

And finally, the ClanCat himself had come to them, with his cub Arivverr. Each giant male had held one of the cubs to the ground, giant paw to small neck, making clear the message. The message was always the same.

"You may be as 'crooked' as you like. You may grow to be as 'crooked' as you like. You will have one duty only to the Clan. When the MixMaster has cubs, you will company them, for all your days. You will watch them. You will protect them. You will teach them...even to be 'crooked' if you like. But you will not hurt them. If you do, you will answer to the Clan."

So the two 'crooked' males were very careful as they sniffed at Leezel's belly. Their future was in there.

Curiosity satisfied, they bounded to a transfixed Steef. The Lady watched with glee for her Mate, as he was knocked over, his eightspan sent flying and the tussling began anew. One of them had an arm, the other a foot.

"I am Keefrr!"

"I am Stivverr!"

"Play with us...or we will eat you!"

0-595-28931-2

Printed in the United States
1506500003B/34